The Rivergrass Legacy

A Novel

John Chaplick

Cricket Cottage Publishing

For information about group sales and permission, contact Cricket Cottage Publishing, LLC, 1889 South Kirkman Road, Suite 614, Orlando, Florida 32811 or call 407-255-7785.

This book is a work of fiction. Names, characters, places, incidents, organizations, and dialogue in this novel are products of the author's imagination or are used fictitiously. Any resemblance to actual events or locales or persons living or dead is entirely coincidental.

The South Florida swamp scene cover, which captures the essence of the geographic background of *The Rivergrass Legacy*, is a photograph of a painting done by Marie Schadt, a local artist whose work is on display at several Tampa locations.

ISBN: 978-0692343838
ISBN-10: 0692343830

Acknowledgements

No book, including this one, was ever written by its author alone. I wish to express my deepest gratitude to those special people whose help and patience made *The Rivergrass Legacy* possible:

My wife, Avis Anne, who took the time to edit each draft of my manuscript, and who managed to maintain a calm understanding while I sequestered myself away for far too long.

My two sons, Trevor and Kyle and their wonderful families who have always encouraged me no matter what I was doing.

My editor and critic Paula Stahel who, gently and firmly, helped turn a raw manuscript into an engaging novel.

My friend, beta reader, and critic, Ginger King, whose experience as an accomplished actress on stage provided a new dimension to the dialogue in the book.

My critique group members whose combination of objective assessment and warm encouragement helped me to develop my craft:

> Tracy Bird, Golda Brunhild, Gene Cropsey, Kathryn Dorn, Shaun Darragh, Elizabeth Griffith, Michael Hanson, Bob Hart, Vaughn Jones, Jeff Stark, Shaunte Westraye

My publisher, Jo Ann Robinson, and her dedicated staff at *Cricket Cottage Publishing*

I wish to offer a special thanks to Marie Schadt whose cover painting represents an enticing invitation to the book's contents. Marie is a Tampa artist who has presented her work throughout Florida and parts of the southeast.

Chapter 1

Grant Abbot Lonsdale III never suspected that someone planned to kill him in an act of revenge for what his father had done. From his apartment on Boston's Beacon Hill, the sole heir to the Lonsdale dynasty watched the morning come into its infancy wrapped in the cool, pale, dawn of an early New England summer. Before he rehearsed an articulate objection to his new assignment he allowed himself a ten minute window to relax with a black coffee in one hand and the *Wall Street Journal* in the other.

Grant downed the coffee, pushed the paper aside, and spent the next half-hour polishing up his arguments for being assigned to a more prestigious client. Shower, shave, a splash of his forty-dollar-an-ounce Sandalwood aftershave lotion, and he was ready to present his case — something akin to attempting to beard the lion in its den.

Grant knew Angus MacIver hadn't become managing partner of Warren, MacIver & Patterson by allowing the firm's professional staff to choose the clients with whom they worked. Still, it was worth a try. Anything to avoid being sent to Okeechobee — a seedy little South Florida town where old men probably sat in rocking chairs outside the general store and spit tobacco juice on the ground.

More to the point, he didn't see the need to commit a Harvard MBA to the routine acquisition assessment of a nondescript fish hatchery. Promotion to CEO of his father's company might be no more than ten to fifteen years away. The time to develop enough management consulting experience at WM&P to handle the position would have to begin now. Grant knew it required exposure to clients a hell of a lot larger than a small fish farm in the boondocks.

Construction-snarled traffic to downtown Boston turned a thirty-minute drive into an hour's worth of bumper-to-bumper frustration. Grant's contingency allowance, based on his firm belief in Murphy's Law, enabled him to still arrive a few minutes before the scheduled meeting with his boss. He found Angus, a workaholic who crammed thirty hours of production into a twenty-four hour day, already well into his morning workload and waiting for him.

In two years Angus had converted WM&P from a stodgy old Boston financial advisory firm into one of the most prestigious management consulting firms on the East Coast. Rumor held that mothers would change their newborns' diets from milk to bourbon if Angus recommended it. Grant didn't have to be told that challenging the decision of a man who ruled with unquestioned authority could be risky.

"Come on in, Grant. Pour yourself a cup of coffee, sit down, and explain to me why I should say no to a client who represents a million and change in billings each year."

Grant figured he might need a sugar hit for this dialogue. He dumped two cubes in, pulled up a chair to face the judge, and launched his opening volley. "With all due respect for the size of CLL Capital, sir," he said, "it still doesn't make sense to send me down there just to look at one of its oddball acquisitions. Anyone here can handle that kind of engagement. This thing in Okeechobee seems like another toy Conrad Vanderslice wants to play with when he has nothing better to do." Grant shrugged and extended his arms palms up. "I thought we agreed you'd give me a shot at something more significant than this."

Angus shoved a pile of signed payroll checks into his out-box and nodded. "We did, and I will. Right now, this takes precedence. And it's significant for several reasons. One, I'm betting Conrad wants to buy the farm. Don't ask me why. Anyway, he's convinced something pretty bad's going on down there and won't make an offer until we check the place out. Two, he specifically requested you. By the way, that's quite an honor for a twenty-five-year-old with limited consulting experience, in case you didn't know it. And three, that little hatchery is apparently connected to another Florida outfit called Mayaca Corporation, which is by no means insignificant. It's in a town called Myakka on a straight line west of Okeechobee. You do a good job on the hatchery, and WM&P gets a sizable consulting contract at Mayaca. So, that may be that large assignment you've been waiting for. The trip will be good for you, Grant. Give you an opportunity to expand your experience, not to mention your social horizons. Maybe even learn something about the world beyond New England. Any problem with that?"

Grant shifted in his chair, pushed his coffee cup aside, and glanced out the window before he turned back to face his boss. He decided not to challenge the "social horizons" remark. "Okay, fine. Okeechobee is at the very bottom of my must-see list, but I get your point. Since the assignment's obviously not optional, I might as well accept cheerfully. What does Conrad mean by 'bad'? And when am I supposed to be there?"

Angus pulled a handful of mail from his in-box and leaned back in his chair. "I've known Conrad for more than ten years, and if he thinks something's bad it's probably worse. We didn't talk much about it, but he seems to think someone is stealing money from the farm, like big time. If true, it would make that little company's net worth appear smaller than it should be. I think Conrad simply wants to know. The problem is this: if Conrad acquires an entity — no matter how small — that implodes later on because of a weakness he should have spotted, he loses more than money. He loses face among his peers in the higher echelons of the New England business community. You know Conrad and his ego. Therefore, he wants the best and he wants you. Jennifer has your plane ticket on her desk. You're flying out today. Now go and make me proud."

Satisfied that the assignment was no longer subject to debate, Grant picked up his ticket and almost made it to the door before Jennifer caught him up short.

"Hey, Lonsdale, you better come back with a tan and a triumphant grin on your face. Also, a dozen oranges on my desk would be a nice incentive for me to process your reports ahead of anyone else's."

They exchanged smiles, and Grant headed for a place he wasn't sure could even be found on the map.

* * * * * *

On his way to the ATM, Grant stopped at his apartment for a change of clothes. He'd moved out of his parents' Beacon Street mansion with a wardrobe that far exceeded the size of the closet in his new digs. While he fumbled through the garment overflow piled on the table, he let his thoughts wander. The Okeechobee thing was a damned fish farm, anyway — probably located between two mud holes. No need to take a suit or anything more formal than slacks, tee shirts, and a sports jacket. The worst of it would be exchanging a weekend of recreation in Boston for a trip to no-man's land in South Florida.

His undergraduate degree in engineering at Yale, and twenty-some-odd away games as a defensive lineman, had involved plenty of travel. Fortunately, nothing had taken him south of the Mason-Dixon Line. Convinced the Okeechobee job would be an easy one he could wrap up in a couple of days, he packed light and caught the noon flight out of Logan International.

Accustomed to a better quality bourbon than the first class offering, Grant started to turn it down, then had second thoughts and grabbed two of the miniature bottles. With luck it might help him forget about Okeechobee and the last conversation with his mother. Still rankled at his Yale decision, she'd never been able to bring herself to refer to the place as anything other than "that New Haven School." At least she admitted he'd made some measure of atonement with his graduate work at Harvard, which she considered the only appropriate institution for a Lonsdale.

At the end of an uneventful flight, during most of which he slept and dreamed of bigger assignments, Grant stepped out into the heat of Orlando. The moment he inhaled the hot, humid air he felt a sense of hopelessness. He rented a car, cursed Angus in an uncensored release of his resentment, and plotted his itinerary on a map that made Florida look like a large network of rural roads.

The busy four lanes from the Orlando airport gradually narrowed to two and splintered off in various directions, bristling with dots on the map, bearing names like Holopaw, Yeehaw Junction, and his destination, Okeechobee. They all seemed, somehow, more appropriate to the far reaches of the Australian outback than to the United States. Sun-bleached flatlands, punctuated with pale green palm trees and ragged palmetto bushes, passed monotonously in stark contrast to the rolling hills, white birches, and blue-green firs of his native New England. An occasional cluster of bright pink roadside oleanders sprang up here and there as if in mute apology for its drab surroundings.

The radio in his rented Lexus introduced him to deep-down country music. He listened with mild curiosity to the mournful strains of *Only Daddy That'll Walk The Line* by Shawn Rader and the Redneck Riviera Boys. Touted by the local radio station as a country-western favorite, its twanging melody and redundant lyrics rang in Grant's ears as a cacophonous insult to Beethoven, Mozart, and all things beautiful in music. The less time spent down here the better.

Signs along the gently winding approach road into Okeechobee posted a forty-mile-an-hour limit. The mile-apart advisories left motorists free to interpret them either as thoughtful safety alerts or fair warning of a lurking patrol car. Grant had never paid much attention to speed constraints before and didn't see any need to then. Lulled by the nothingness of the flat landscape spread out ahead of him, his thoughts wandered in and out of his family's history of relentless obsession with wealth accumulation through selective marriages.

It might have been heat-induced fatigue, or maybe his focus just lost its edge. Whatever the cause, the sharp curve ahead came up so fast he didn't see the Brahman until it was too late. With the unexpected view of the animal's rump filling his windshield, he gasped, clenched the steering wheel and jerked it to the right, barely in time to miss the lumbering beast, but not the roadside stump.

Simultaneous sounds of grinding metal and an exploding tire wrenched Grant's gut, blocking out all intelligent thought except the blurred image of his Lexus catapulting forward into a partially filled drainage ditch. Moments later, after he stopped shaking, he stepped out into water up to his knees, briefcase in one hand, suitcase in the other. He slogged up the bank to the side of the road, fighting for traction on the moist soil. He bent over once or twice to squeeze out some of the water and shake mud and loose grass from his soggy trousers.

Hands on his hips, he stared down at the stricken vehicle and turned to curse the dumb animal. This day's getting worse by the minute, he thought. Why would anyone want to buy a fish farm at all, let alone in this God-forsaken place? He heaved a sigh and figured the client must have seen something he wanted. Conrad Vanderslice could smell a windfall profit a mile away, and it didn't have to be legitimate money. But why in a hell-hole like this? "Damn it." He kicked a loose stone into the ditch after he surveyed the un-Lonsdale-like nature of his situation. "Vanderslice can take this job and shove it, along with the rest of this backwater cow town."

His fuming had only partially run its course when an oversized, red pickup pulled over on the shoulder a few feet ahead. A Confederate flag hanging conspicuously in the rear window only partly blocked the hunting rifle mounted over it. A red, white, and blue sticker on the rear bumper issued a prophetic warning: *When Guns Are Outlawed Only Outlaws Will Have Guns.*

A girl climbed down from behind the wheel of the pickup, glanced first at the stranded Lexus, and then at Grant. She shook her head. "Looks like you got yourself into a real mess, mister." Her denim shirt and faded blue jeans were enough to take gorgeous out of the equation, but what was left looked like an angel in cowboy boots sent to rescue him. Tall, blonde, busty, but not overly so, she moved toward him with sensuality he didn't expect in someone who drove a truck. The snug-fitting work clothes seemed to accentuate every curve in her body.

"Yes, that cow and I just missed each other," Grant said, pointing to the Brahman munching grass across the road, "and the ditch seemed like the path of least destruction. Why the hell was a cow wandering down the middle of the road, anyway?"

"Oh, that's one of Sam Tillery's herd. It happens every now and then when one of 'em breaks through a weak spot in the fence. It's a bull, by the way, not a cow. You're not from around here, are you?"

"No. I don't suppose I could get towing service to get my car out of this muck."

"Well, you're looking at it, so just step back while I free up that pretty Lexus."

She reached into an industrial-looking metal box in the back of the pickup and pulled out a long chain. While Grant watched her effortless movements with amazement, she hooked one end onto the pickup's trailer hitch and moved toward the Lexus with the other.

Grant put his hand up. "Whoa! You can't do that by yourself. Here, let me give you a hand."

"Forget it. Your shoes are already a mess, and you'd just get the rest of that nice suit all dirty. I've done this before. My name's Luanne Gibbs. What's yours?"

"Grant. You sure you want to do this?"

"Yep. You got a last name, Grant?"

"Uh, yes. Lonsdale. Hey, why're you taking my bumper apart? Why don't you just hook that thing underneath it?"

"You don't know much about cars, do you, Grant Lonsdale? I'm taking the little panel off so I can attach the chain to the tie-down hook the Lexus Company was smart enough to install inside the bumper. So you and your briefcase just stand over there and wait while I bust this car loose."

She hopped back into the seat beside him, maneuvered the vehicle into a position closer to the ditch, put it in forward gear, and slowly accelerated. The low growl of the pickup's engine escalated into a roar of determined commitment as the chain tightened. The Lexus lurched forward and, with a loud whooshing sound, the ditch reluctantly released its prisoner.

After Luanne put the truck in neutral, she climbed out to assess the damage. She shook her head again and turned to Grant. Her sparkling blue eyes held steady on him. "Well, your car's out on dry land, but it's not going anywhere. The fender's jammed against what's left of your tire. And I mean jammed."

Grant surveyed the stranded vehicle, now trapped like a helpless insect in Okeechobee's spider web of ditches and serpentine roads. "So, isn't there a repair service in town that could tow it in and fix it?"

"Yeah, but it's after four o'clock. Lem's three sheets to the wind by now. Around here everyone knows not to ask him to do anything after about noon. Look," she said as she unhooked the chain, wrapped it into a neat coil, and heaved it into the box, "I'll drop you off at a motel, and Lem can bring your car in tomorrow morning."

Grant shook his head. "Great. A one-horse town and no car." He threw his suitcase into the back of the pickup, folded his jacket over his arm, and climbed into the passenger seat with his briefcase and a scowl that made him look as if he'd been born angry.

Luanne slid in behind the wheel, looked down at the briefcase between Grant's legs, and giggled. "Hey Grant, what are all those initials for on your briefcase?"

"My name."

"So what do they stand for? And what are those three lines at the end?"

Grant frowned at her. "They're Roman numerals. They stand for 'the third.' I'm Grant Abbot Lonsdale the Third. Look," he said, trying to ignore her giggle, "it's a family name, and I wasn't consulted when it was chosen. If I had been, I might have come up with something more resonant, like Whip Sheldon Lonsdale, or Wade Remington Lonsdale. But that didn't happen and it is what it is."

"Wow. The *third*! So they gave you the same names your ancestors had, right? I mean, every male in your family is called Grant Lonsdale, right? That's a pretty big load to drop on a little kid, isn't it?" Her mouth curved in a teasing smile while she waited for a reaction. Grant shook his head without responding.

Luanne tittered. Her hand went to her mouth. "Oh, I'm sorry. It's just that you're the first man I've ever met with three last names and a number." She giggled, her hand over her mouth again, while she accelerated around a plodding John Deere tractor pulling an empty trailer.

"It's a matter of lineage, damn it! Something I wouldn't expect you to understand."

"Oh. Well, it sounds to me more like a lack of imagination. Hey, Grant, did the other Lonsdales let you have any pets of your own when you were growing up?"

"Not that it's relevant, but yes. I had a turtle. The part of Boston where I grew up didn't lend itself very well to keeping pets."

"A turtle, oooh, that sounds exciting," she said, breaking into a wide smile that annoyed and mesmerized him at the same time.

Before the tractor had even begun to recede in the rear view mirror her eyes went wide in concert with the tightening of her lips. She swerved the pickup off the road and slammed on the brakes, pitching Grant forward hard enough that his head would have hit the dashboard had the seatbelt not restrained him.

"Holy cripes! You're *him*, aren't you?" A sharp glare replaced her smile.

"What?"

"You're the stuffed shirt they're sending down from Boston to take Daddy's company away from him, aren't you? I should have known it the minute I saw your fancy suit. Hell, I should've left you right there in the mud."

He could almost feel her scowl. He met her glare. "Look, I'm not here to take anything from anyone. I'm here simply to review a possible, although unlikely, acquisition. So can we—"

"Yeah, well we don't need any 'acquisitions' down here. Daddy and I are doing just fine thank you. So you can haul your damnyankeeass back to Boston and leave us alone!"

Still reeling from the sting he hadn't seen coming, he couldn't help but marvel at how smoothly she blended three unrelated words into a single obscenity, as though that was the way it should always be pronounced. He held up his hands in a gesture of mock surrender. "Believe me, there's nothing I'd rather do right now, but I've a job to complete. I'm going to do it quickly and then hop the next plane to Boston. Not to mention I'm stuck here until your inebriated friend can find it in his busy schedule to dry out and fix my car."

She turned away and glared out the window in silence. They sat for a few moments without speaking before Grant decided he needed to break the impasse.

"Okay, Luanne, I'll share something with you I probably shouldn't. I can't see what our Boston client could possibly be interested in down here. But based on the research I've done, I think I can safely say there's not a snowball's chance in hell anyone's going to want a little fish farm."

She turned her glare at him again for a moment. As if to translate her feelings into action, she pressed the accelerator down hard, launching the pickup forward and onto the road. His head slammed against the seat back. It might have been just his imagination, but it seemed she deliberately aimed at every pothole, tossing him forward, back again, and sideways, the seat belt doing its best to leave a diagonal bruise from his right collar bone to his left ribs.

"Okay, okay. I get the picture," he said, bracing himself against the dashboard. "How about if we just agree on a truce for a couple of days, and then I'll be out of your hair?"

Luanne said nothing, her jaw set and lips compressed.

"Would that be okay? I mean if we made a truce?"

"Fine." She made it sound more like a snort than a word. She swerved to miss the next pothole.

They rode in silence for about a mile with no further pothole encounters before Grant decided he needed more information. "Luanne, I know the name of your father's company, but—"

"My father's and *mine*."

"Right. Sorry. I wasn't given your father's first name. I know his last name is Gibbs, but I'd like to know his first so I don't sound clueless when we meet."

Half a minute passed.

"Luanne?"

"Major. Major Gibbs is his name."

"Well, okay but I meant his first name, not his rank. And I didn't know he was still in the military."

"He's not in the military," she snapped. "Major *is* his first name. It's a fairly common first name down here. Of course, that's something I wouldn't expect you to understand." With an angry gaze riveted on him, she made it clear any further conversation would be less than friendly.

"I guess I had that one coming. Well, I'd like to meet your father before I check into a motel. Are you okay with that?"

"Yeah, I'm sure he can't wait."

She ramped up the speed to sixty and held it there through the outskirts of Okeechobee.

Right after they passed a sign advertising the city as the "Speckled Perch Capital of the World" Luanne gunned the vehicle to seventy. The scenery rushed by too fast for Grant to read the narrative on the landmarks referencing the Seminole Indian Wars of the mid-nineteenth century. He couldn't resist one more attempt at some kind of friendly communication.

"Luanne, where does the name 'Okeechobee' come from?" The question prompted another, not unexpected, pause before she decided to respond.

"It's a Seminole name meaning 'Big Water.' It's a reference to Lake Okeechobee, which is the largest fresh water lake in the United States."

"Really? I thought the Great Lakes were the largest."

"No, I meant the largest lake occurring entirely in one state." She glared at him with a didn't-you-think-I-knew-that look in her eyes.

Silence again. Two or three miles later she brought the vehicle to a stop in front of a building ruggedly landscaped with hibiscus, pampas grass, sago palms, philodendron, and flowers Grant couldn't remember having seen before. The whole mixture was arranged as though specifically intended to highlight a large sign that read "South Atlantic Farms, Where the Healthiest Angel Fish in the World Are Bred and Raised." The flowers seemed to explode in brilliant colors unlike anything on Beacon Hill.

"We're here," she said, turning off the engine. "Don't forget your monogrammed briefcase."

"Yes, thanks," he replied, bending to wipe mud off his Brooks Brothers trousers.

She led him into an office that looked like it had been ransacked. His eyes scanned the room, searching for any two pieces of matching furniture. The rank odor of dry fish food assaulted his nostrils in concert with an oily, metallic smell from a few small-horsepower air pumps under repair. Surrounded by shelves stacked with unfiled old documents and jars of live brine shrimp, he felt claustrophobic and dirty. A palmetto bug scurried between his feet. He wondered what other forms of insect life he'd never seen before might come crawling out of the woodwork. The scroungy little place made no pretense to be something it wasn't. Damn Angus for this dead-end assignment.

A tall, lean, suntanned man wearing a broad smile, grass-stained blue jeans, and a beat-up baseball cap hauled himself slowly out of a fully depreciated swivel chair. He shook Grant's hand with a vise-like grip. His leathery skin made him look like he'd spent so much of his life outdoors that he and the land belonged to each other. Underarm sweat stains darkened the upper part of his denim shirt.

"I'm Major Gibbs. You must be Mr. Lonsdale. Welcome to South Atlantic Farms."

"Daddy, this is Grant. I picked him out of a mud hole near Sam's ranch where his car got stuck." She gave him a sidelong glance. "I'd introduce him by his full name, but it would take too long and I know you're busy. Do you want me to stay?"

"No, honey, I want to talk to this young man alone. You just go on and we'll all get together later for supper."

"Okay. I'll be working on that broken pump if you need me." She managed to fire one last glare at Grant before she slammed the door, a final punctuation of her contempt for him.

Major grinned. "Whew! I don't know what you two talked about on the way in here, but whatever it was it sure got her dander up." He pointed to a chair, ran his hand over it to sweep off some dried fish food flakes before Grant sat on it, and returned to his swivel. "I ain't seen Luanne so mad since her momma made her stop playing baseball with the boys and start dressing like a girl. Don't get me wrong," Major said, "Luanne's a bright young lady. Graduated top of her high school class and won herself an athletic scholarship to Florida Southern. But her momma died before she could get there an' I needed her in the business. I always felt kinda bad about that, like I cheated her out of something rightfully hers. Her momma didn't leave her much except a full-time job and a trunk full of memories."

"I'm sorry about your wife, Mr. Gibbs. I'm sure Luanne's a fine girl, although she really went into orbit when she realized I was sent here to assess South Atlantic as a prospective acquisition. Maybe you can fill me in on what's transpired between you and Conrad Vanderslice, because he didn't tell me much about it."

Major threw his hand up and shook his head. "Ahh, he's tried to buy me out a couple times before. His offer price was way too low and I'm not interested in sellin,' anyway. Those high rollers up there in the big cities just don't get it when I tell 'em this company's gonna be Luanne's future after I'm gone, so there's no way in hell I'm lettin' go of it. Sometimes I think them smart-ass big city bankers don't have enough common sense to pound sand in a rat hole. Only reason I let you take a look is that Vanderslice promised I could set the price myself after your look-see. Just between you and me, I still won't sell but I'd kinda like to know what the company's really worth."

Major leaned forward and swung his chair around to his right. "Say, I'll bet you could use a good stiff drink. Here, wait 'till you get a taste of this." He leaned over, reached into an old wooden cabinet, and pulled out an unlabeled bottle of a pale yellow liquid that looked to Grant like old-fashioned, homemade corn liquor.

Grant winced. "I'm really not all that thirsty, Mr. Gibbs, but thanks any—"

"Naw, this ain't what you northerners think. Once you've throwed this down your throat, you'll feel better'n you ever felt. I guarandamntee it."

"What is it, if I might ask?"

"We call it Okeechobee Comfort." The cork squeaked against the bottle top. Major grinned, poured a few shots into a ceramic mug stamped with a picture of an angel fish, and handed it to Grant. "You can't get this nowhere in the U.S. of A. except right here. And you can drop the 'mister' and just call me Major. And I'll call you Grant."

Grant sipped tentatively at first, as if the mug might contain a toxic chemical. The liquor tasted better than he thought it would. He touched his mug to Major's in a toast, and they downed a couple of hearty swallows. The earthy informality of it all brought to Grant's mind contrasting memories of upper echelon Boston cocktail parties, yacht races at Marblehead, and the annual beer bash at the Harvard-Yale homecoming game. It conjured up the sound of ice cubes jangling in drinks amid discussions of elegant skiing vacations in Switzerland.

After a couple more swallows, Grant decided it was time to get to the subject at hand. "Major, when I looked at your last year's financial statements, which Conrad gave me, I sensed there was something very wrong but I can't precisely identify it. I need to know, first of all, why the company's debt-to-equity ratio is so low."

Grant's question was met with a frown and a pause. Major tipped his cap back, and ran his long, bony fingers through his hair. "Son, how about running that by me again in plain English."

"Well, what I mean is you have a lot of equity on your balance sheet and not much debt. In other words, the stockholders hold most of the claim to your company's assets, and the creditors' claims are relatively small. That's a bit unusual in this day and age. I was wondering if you could tell me how that came to be."

"Ah, I guess you'd have to ask Luanne about that. She keeps the books mostly. Is that bad or good? I mean about having all that much equity."

"Well, it's good in the sense that you're virtually debt free and aren't burdened with a lot of interest and principal payments. That means you have plenty of borrowing power. But it raises the question of why you haven't used your borrowing power to expand the operation." Grant's glance around the cluttered room raised an afterthought as to whether an expansion could actually survive the man's disorganization.

"Well, hell, I can answer that." Major stood to sign for a UPS delivery and then returned to his seat. "We don't need no more expansion. We got about all me and Luanne can handle right now. We're doing just fine as it is. So is that why this Vanderslice guy has been pestering me? I mean, is it because we haven't expanded?"

Grant shrugged. "That's a good question. His company doesn't actually need your debt capacity or your cash, so I can't honestly see why he would pressure you to sell."

Major leaned back, lifted his cap a few inches again, and scratched the top of his head. "Well then, what's he looking for?"

Grant reached for his mug and took another gulp. "He wouldn't say. He simply insisted that I come down here and review the whole operation. My managing partner and I surmised it must be for a potential acquisition. Therefore, I'll need to scope out how the company works, and take a detailed look at your cash flow, financial statements, and your annual audits."

"Okay. You can get the financial statements from Tommy Rawls down at the bank, and Luanne can show you the operation. We don't get no audits."

"None at all?" Astonished, Grant cocked his head and frowned. "I can't believe your stockholders would allow that."

Major leaned forward, placed his elbows on his knees, clasped his hands together, and rested his chin on cupped fists. "We only got three stockholders, son. I own thirty-one percent, Luanne owns twenty, and the other forty-nine is owned by our biggest supplier, Aqua Star out of Bogota, Colombia. That's where our breeder fish come from. And that's why we get such a good price on all our stock and supplies — because most of our profits go back out to the stockholders in dividends. Me and Luanne do well, Aqua Star does well, and that's why I ain't sellin.' So now you see why no one's ever asked for an audit."

Major drained his mug, put it down on the desk, and rose out of his chair. "Okay, young man, over here's our conference room, right next to this office.

This is where you can set up and start your work tomorrow. Got a couple of good filing cabinets in there, too."

"Thanks. That will do fine." Grant stood and welcomed the sight of an uncluttered space.

"On the other side of it is the accounting and record storage room where Luanne and her assistant, Maria, work. They'll dig up whatever you need. Now come on, let's you, me, and Luanne go have some dinner. Essie Mae's little restaurant don't look like much, but you ain't gonna find better food anywhere."

Grant swallowed the last drop from his mug and threw a doubtful look at Major. From what he'd seen since his plane landed, good food and local restaurant dining were a contradiction in terms. He remembered what happened before he wrecked the Lexus. He'd stopped for a snack at Bubba Bobby's Family Restaurant where grits were served whether you asked for them or not, and catfish was featured as the main entrée along with a green, mushy substance the waitress identified as a grape leaves wrap. Faced with the Hobson's choice between that and a greasy-looking breakfast menu, Grant opted for the latter. Clearly insulted by Grant's selection of scrambled eggs as the lesser of the menu's culinary evils, Bubba Bobby and his waitress had seemed as happy to see him go as Grant was to get back on the road.

* * * * * *

Major had been right. Essie Mae's didn't look like much. It was a far cry from Boston's Top of The Hub or Menton's at $145 a person. The clientele looked a cut above Bubba Bobby's, though not a lot. Cowboy hats and baseball caps with logos advertising places like the local tire shop never left the heads of their wearers during the meal. Little square tables, each covered with a red and white checkered tablecloth, with a tiny flower pot of fake blue and yellow pansies in the center, made the place look like a small pizza parlor in South Boston. The buzz of conversation at the tables seemed restricted to the mundane events that defined the parameters of daily life in the local area: cattle prices, upcoming farm equipment auctions, and Edna Lou's hip replacement.

On the positive side, the dinner was everything Major said it would be. Catfish was optional and, thankfully, not the only offering. A deliciously-spiced meatloaf put an end to Grant's fear that the Okeechobee assignment had condemned him to a culinary hell of grits and grape leaves. Luanne's temper cooled down, another welcomed surprise. After the mellowing effects of a couple of beers, she managed to tease him once or twice before she launched into the operations he'd see the next day.

"Grant, you're not listening," she said. "Why are you staring at your dessert?"

"I'm trying to identify the thing. Looks like an upside-down pudding smothered in syrup. Does it have a name?"

"Yes, flan, a very popular dish. I'm sure it won't bite you. Don't they serve Hispanic food in Boston?"

He took a precautionary bite. "Not where I eat. But you're right, I like it. And I *was* listening. Now tell me about the financial statements. Your father told me your banker keeps them. I'll need the statements for each of the last five years, and I'm a bit surprised that this guy Rawls is the custodian."

"Well, don't be," she said. "Tommy Rawls has always maintained our financial records. After supper I'll call his cell and tell him to make copies for you."

While the waitress refilled their coffees, Grant caught Luanne eyeing him in a thoughtful, almost forgiving way, as though perhaps acknowledging that a more objective reassessment might be in order.

"You didn't have much of a childhood, did you?" she asked. "I mean, your life must have been pretty restricted under all that lineage and stuff."

"I grew up with a lot of freedom and probably more than my share of privileges. The restrictions came, I suppose, more in the form of with whom I could associate and with whom I couldn't."

Luanne leaned toward him on her elbows with her chin in her hands. "Like what kind of associations?"

Surprised by the intimacy of the question, Grant stalled to consider an appropriate response. How much do I want to reveal to these people? I don't know them. Not even sure I like them. Nonetheless, I'll probably have to share something if I expect to extract information from them.

He pushed his coffee aside and leaned forward toward Luanne. "Well, for example, one of my earliest recollections dates back to age seven when I brought a new-found friend home for a sleepover. He was a nice kid who needed a friend as much as I did. It seemed like a good idea until my parents explained that the boy came from a neighborhood they frowned on. That made it a forbidden relationship. Only that word was never used. It was 'inappropriate,' they said, but I knew what they meant." He decided against any further reference to the parental restrictions that had robbed him of the childhood they purported to protect.

Luanne persisted. "How about girls? Any restrictions on those?"

His lips tightened in a reflexive response to suppressed memories that surfaced again through the fragile seal Luanne had broken. He hesitated, partly because of the guilt that seemed inseparable from the memory, and partly because he'd never intended to reveal the South Boston incident to anyone. Submerged crosscurrents of remorse and quiet resignation flowed into his consciousness once again. "Ahh, I think that's a rather personal—"

"Well now," Major said, "I think we've imposed about enough on this young man's privacy, honey. It's getting kinda late and he's had a long day, so why don't we just pack it in and let him get some sleep?"

Grant smiled, grateful for the intervention.

Luanne's expression made it look like she was struggling to hold back still more penetrating questions. "Sure, Daddy, I guess you're right. I'm sorry, Grant, I didn't mean to pry. I'll pick you up early tomorrow and we can get started."

Major dropped him off at the Blue Moon Motel, handed him a bottle of Okeechobee Comfort, and parted with a grin. Grant found the minimally furnished room, with its Gideon Bible and a small writing pad bearing the logo of Lem's Towing and Repair Service, neat, clean, and comfortable. A pleasant surprise for a backwater town.

He climbed into bed and tried to force a sleep that wasn't ready to come. He tossed and turned, trying to remember exactly what managing partner, Angus MacIver, had said about Conrad's hidden agenda. Grant's disappointment at being shunted off on an insignificant project had allowed his mind to drift off to the edges of the conversation, and obscured most of Angus's orientation instructions. Except the part about there being something seriously wrong at the hatchery and Conrad needing to find out what it was.

Even on the surface it didn't smell right, and questions that refused to go away swirled around in his mind. What's Vanderslice's hidden agenda, he wondered. What's the Colombian partner covering up by avoiding audits? Why doesn't the bank object, and why is a banker handling the business transactions?

Grant opened Major's bottle and took a shot at trying to douse his suspicions. For a quick reread he opened the South Atlantic file Jennifer had given him. He concluded it didn't contain enough information for a defensible assessment of the hatchery's operations — except that they showed one hell of an impressive profit. The little battery-operated digital bedside clock showed one in the morning. Grant finally succumbed to his fatigue and fell asleep to the low-decibel hum of a chorus of cicadas performing against the background of unfamiliar nocturnal sounds in the nearby swamp.

Chapter 2

A local fisherman discovered Luis Fernando's decapitated body floating in Bogota's Cauca River. News of the gruesome finding attracted little attention in a city of eight-and-a-half million inhabitants, where more than five thousand homicides had occurred the year before. Salazar Corazon had been head of the Quevedo drug cartel long enough to assume this was a necessary *muerte*, customary when an operative makes an unforgivable mistake. Even so, he demanded an explanation from his financial group manager, Pedro Essante.

Salazar reserved a table in a secluded corner of Mijaro, a restaurant he knew wouldn't be busy at three o'clock in the afternoon. He ordered his customary *ajiaco* soup and waited for Pedro, who burst through the door ten minutes later, sweating and out of breath. "Sit down, Pedro. You're panting, like you ran all the way. Would you like some dessert?"

The rotund man dropped his two hundred seventy-five pounds ungracefully onto a little wooden chair. It squeaked softly in rhythm with each movement of his heaving chest. He ran his hand over a head of black hair that looked as though oil had made it shiny. Pedro threw a nervous glance at the black cobra tattooed along the length of Salazar's right arm. The open-jawed reptile seemed to move with a carefully controlled savagery in response to each ripple of Salazar's muscles. "No thank you, sir, I've already eaten. I came as quickly as I could because you sounded angry."

"Not angry, just surprised. I've always thought Luis was one of your most effective men. What happened, and how did you find out about it?"

"Well, sir," Pedro paused to catch his breath, "the taxi drivers on our payroll do a good job of keeping me informed about the movements of dignitaries and officials around the city, and in and out of the airports. My own security operatives keep their laptops and other electronics fired up to monitor phone calls in strategic places. Both sources got wind of what Luis was doing at the same time. I got right on it. He was under strict orders not—"

"Which cell, Pedro?" Salazar pointed to his selection on the menu, and gave it to the waiter.

Pedro shifted his bulk in the chair. "Luis was in charge of number five. I'm sorry. I should have been more explicit." Pedro paused, distracted by Salazar's gold bracelets that clinked when his arm moved. "But, as you know, we have a basic rule that operatives who handle product must not function outside of their assigned territories. This was your own rule, Salazar, and I was simply complying with it." He tapped his finger on the table.

"Relax, Pedro. I'm not asking for an apology, just an explanation. I'm assuming Luis broke the rule, yes?"

Pedro's breath came in short bursts. "Yes. To make matters worse, he broke it in your old territory — South Florida. I'm told you used to run that operation as a territory manager before you…ah…took over the business. Worse yet, he was moving marijuana at twelve hundred dollars a pound. As long as he took the risk of breaking the rule, he could at least have done it with cocaine and sold it at twenty-five thousand a kilo. He showed a lack of judgment as well as disregard for our policies. An example had to be made. I'm sure you understand."

Salazar paused to scoop up a portion of his *cuajada* as soon as the waiter delivered it. "I do, and I assume you've found an appropriate replacement."

Perdo's breathing evolved from rapid gasps to a more rhythmical sequence. He pulled out a kerchief and wiped rivulets of perspiration from his face and neck, although the thickness of both made it impossible to determine where his head ended and his neck began. "Yes, Andres Felipe — a good man. He ran a profitable *celeno* in New York. Now sir, you said you had two matters you wanted to discuss. What was the other?"

Salazar pushed the soup bowl aside to make room for his coffee, and took in another mouthful of the *cuajada*. "It's come to my attention that a prominent financial advisory firm in Boston has been engaged by one of its clients to examine our Okeechobee operation. Presumably, it's for acquisition purposes, which is not unexpected in view of the operation's profitability."

"What are you going to do?"

"Nothing right now. However, according to my sources at Mayaca Corporation, the examiner is a young Harvard MBA who just might get carried away with himself and dig a little deeper than necessary to complete his assignment. If that were to happen, and I'm not suggesting it will, but if it does, a terminal solution might become necessary."

Pedro shrugged. "Why don't you simply step in and stop the examination?"

"No. That might raise questions about issues I don't want dredged up." He fixed a firm gaze on his group manager. "I want you to monitor this new development closely for me, using our connections at Mayaca. Another…ah…incident in Okeechobee would raise suspicions, and right now I don't need that. I'll keep an eye on the overall operation myself, of course, but I'm putting the hatchery's daily observation primarily in your hands."

Salazar leaned back and stared out the window toward Avenida Cuidad de Cali without looking at anything in particular. "I'm sure you know, Pedro, our cartel no longer enjoys the unobstructed flexibility it had before the Mexicans began biting big chunks out of the Colombian trade. Changing extradition laws now make it much easier for the United States and other countries to extricate anyone for whom they can show cause."

Fully aware such a discourse was probably unnecessary, given the experience of his audience, Salazar continued anyway because he enjoyed the cathartic effects of it. "Jail time in many of these countries can no longer be reduced by buying off the right officials. And, as you've witnessed yourself, many of our old trafficking modes, like smuggling drugs in car batteries, no longer work. In view of all this, a profitable operation such as Okeechobee, that functions smoothly and free of outside interference, deserves to be well protected. And now, it seems, all of that may depend on what this young man might do up there."

Salazar took a moment to savor a few sips of his coffee, then turned back to face Pedro. "I want you to get in touch with Mayaca right away, and find out if Luis has moved any product into Okeechobee. I don't want narcotics mixed up with what I have going there. I want everything in Okeechobee to remain so quiet you can, as the Americans would say, hear a rat piss on cotton in that place. Keep me informed. Do you understand?"

"Yes, sir, it will be done." Pedro hoisted himself upright with difficulty, and the wooden chair groaned again under the punishing weight of the obese man's extraction. "Thank you for your trust in me."

Salazar watched Pedro leave, taking with him all but a faint remnant of body odor. He continued to savor the remains of his coffee while he listened to the engaging lyrics of *Noches de Cartagena,* sung by a lone guitarist tuning up at the back of the restaurant for his evening performance. For Salazar, the creative energy and sadness of the song captured the essence of Colombia's contradictory mixture of prosperity and poverty, Maseratis and mules.

He reflected on his own long road, over which he'd ridden the narcotics trade from the slums to Quevedo. He'd done everything he could to suppress the images of his youth, so that most of the life he remembered began in the middle. Now, as he grew closer to the end, he found himself on the back of a tiger waiting to devour him if he slipped.

He finished his coffee, paid the bill, and headed for an unavoidable meeting with a group of drug-funded terrorists who called themselves *Fuerzas Armadas Revolucionaries de Colombia.* Years earlier they were virtually unknown. Recently, they'd become such a household name they had their own acronym —F.A.R.C. Threats to Salazar Corazon's cartel continued to grow in number. Now they included an Ivy League bookworm.

Chapter 3

The sound of Luanne knocking on his motel door at five-thirty in the morning jarred Grant from a deep slumber — or what was left of it — and drew him, mercifully, from a dream of Sarah and what might have been. Her quiet presence in his mind persisted as a bittersweet reminder of the love they shared. Even then he knew its termination would become a requirement of his responsibilities as heir to the Lonsdale fortunes. Their banished romance, and the life it might have offered, survived only in his memory.

Grant sat up, rubbed his eyes, and felt a sense of relief from the guilt that had darkened his dream. He ran his fingers through his rumpled hair and blinked at the faint glow of light that forecast the approach of dawn. He knew its arrival would wait another few minutes to be officially announced by the sun's emergence on the horizon. He threw on a bathrobe, groped his way across the room, and opened the door to let Luanne in. A deep yawn drew into his nostrils the intoxicating scent of nearby jasmine sweetened by an early rain. A gentle breeze blew the aroma into his room, like an invitation to follow it to its source.

Luanne brought him a full tray of breakfast, a gesture that might reasonably have been interpreted as the ultimate in peace offerings were it not for the large helping of grits. They seemed as unappealing as the ones at Bubba Bobby's. Now almost fully awake, he recoiled in a gesture designed to let her know he'd already clearly expressed his distaste for that odd Southern staple, the popularity of which he still couldn't understand.

"You can eat whatever you want in Boston," she said as she placed the tray down on the table beside his bed, "but down here we eat grits. So you might as well learn to like them."

Grant glanced at the grits and winced. The little white mound looked like a glob of maggots.

Luanne ignored the reaction. "Now, enjoy your breakfast, get dressed, and I'll be back to show you around the farm. Did you bring any old clothes?"

"No, just a pair of slacks."

"Probably designer slacks, so I'll bring you some boots, one of Daddy's work shirts and a pair of blue jeans."

"Thanks. Is there a reason we're doing this at the crack of dawn instead of at a more civilized hour?"

"Yeah, we have a shipment of broodstock angels and other cichlids coming in. Their spawning habits haven't recognized Boston leisure time. We work a full day around here, Grant Lonsdale. I'll be back in half an hour with your clothes. Eat your breakfast."

After he devoured most of the ham and eggs, he showered and shaved off all but an irreversible shadow of his dark beard. He ran a brush through his dark hair, looked down at the unfinished portion of breakfast, and smiled. His parents, too, he thought, would have refused the grits. In fact, that might be one of the few points on which he and his parents could find agreement. There hadn't been many ever since he elected to do undergraduate work at Yale instead of following his ancestral path to Harvard — a decision his mother referred to as a gesture of defiance.

Luanne returned with his new wardrobe and watched with apparent fascination while Grant stared in despair at the kind of clothes in which no Lonsdale would ever be seen. She flashed a flirtatious smile, and he tried to ignore a discomforting sensation that the life he woke up to this morning might never let him return to the one he had before.

"How about turning around?" Grant asked. "Or should I go into the bathroom to dress?"

"I didn't know they were all that shy in Boston. Fine, I'll step out. Don't take too long. We have a lot to do."

Grant poured his muscular six-foot-two-inch body into clothes that didn't fit, wolfed down one more bite of the ham, and climbed into Luanne's pickup with his notepad. Although he tried to listen politely to her description of various landmarks on the way to the hatchery, his thoughts wandered back to the last time he saw Sarah. The South Boston memory, along with its guilt, stubbornly refused to go away. He wondered what it would be like to be able to retrace his steps backward far enough to change the events of that day.

Luanne pulled the truck up to the front door of the building and parked it between a blue delivery van and two boxes of angels deposited on the driveway. She hopped out and waited for Grant with a kind of I-see-you-don't-have-much-experience-getting-out-of-pickups smile on her face.

A man in a blue shirt with the Southern Delivery Service logo handed her a clipboard, and pointed to a line on the attached invoice. "If you'll just sign here, ma'am."

"I want to take a look first." Luanne turned to the field hand standing nearby and motioned to him to open the top. "You might want to take a peek, too, Grant. If you look from top down you can't see a whole lot, but these boxes are why you had to roll out of bed so early."

Grant leaned over the open box. A swarm of finny little creatures, roughly three inches long from mouth to caudal tip, moved about sluggishly in response to the first daylight exposure since they were packed for shipment two days earlier. Luanne was right, he thought — you can't tell much about fish by looking straight down at them.

He turned to Luanne. "These are the breeders?"

"Yep. They look okay, but I'm going to have them taken to the quarantine tank for a full inspection before we put them to work." After she signaled again to the field hand to pick up the boxes, Luanne signed the forms and motioned to Grant to follow her.

He looked forward to getting started on this ugly assignment — partly to get it over with and partly to free himself from the introspection borne of inactivity.

"Okay, let's start with our display room." Luanne led him through Major's office, opened a door Grant had failed to notice the day before, and turned the tank lights on.

Grant found himself unprepared for the magnificent view surrounding him when he entered. An impeccably landscaped indoor garden filled the floor space in a circular room almost large enough to house a small gymnasium. Bathtub-size fish tanks, teeming with a variety of brilliantly colored tropical fish, were built into pinewood walls lining the room. The effect of it all made him feel as though he were standing on the ocean floor looking at an eerie aquatic world. A small, arched wooden bridge over a koi pond in the center of the garden gave the scene a Japanese appearance.

Overwhelmed by the unexpected beauty of it all, Grant hardly listened as Luanne described the occupants of each tank, along with their mating habits. When she finished, she turned and smiled at him.

"Well, Grant, what do you think?"

"I think I'm speechless. This is a royal garden out in the middle of nowhere. Are all these fish bred here?"

"No, only the angels are raised here. The rest are other freshwater ornamentals and, for show, a few saltwater varieties from all over the world. This room is a combination of Daddy's idea of heaven and my version of good advertising. And by the way, we don't think of ourselves as being in the middle of nowhere. I see you're taking notes on that pad of yours. Why are you doing that?"

"In order to assess your financial statements, I need to understand the business which generates them. Not to change the subject, but I had some difficulty taking my eyes off the angels. They seem to glide effortlessly through the water rather than swim like other fish. They're kind of aristocratic in their deportment."

"Wow, *deportment.*" She came out with that teasing smile again. "I bet no one's ever talked about them like that before. Yeah, I guess they are sort of in a class by themselves. Come on, let's take a walk over to the breeding building. It's the working end of the business, where our money's made."

By the time they finished the fifty yard trek, Grant's accumulating perspiration felt the same way it did during football practice at Yale. Except it dried more quickly in New Haven. He used the back of his hand to wipe the moisture from his brow.

"Grant, you're starting to sweat already. It's still early morning. I'll get you a glass of water inside, but you'll need to get used to this climate…afternoons around here are even warmer."

"I'm fine. Don't worry about it. I'll cool down in a few minutes."

She led him into a dull gray concrete block-building completely devoid of any exterior charm. Grant found himself in another exotic aquatic world, cluttered with pumping and filtering equipment that sent a network of PVC pipelines in every direction.

Luanne pointed to a row of shelves containing ten-gallon glass tanks. "These are the breeding tanks. When the young grow large enough, we transfer them to the ponds outside where they grow to breeding size. We also bring in wild ones from the Amazon basin to supplement our breeding stock."

The Amazon reference reawakened Grant's interest in the Colombian operation. He flipped to a new page on the notepad. "Tell me, Luanne, how does this whole process go, starting with bringing fish in from South America?"

"Well, it starts with a few native fishermen catching a handful of angels in a net from their canoe. They sell them dirt cheap to a local consolidator, who adds on a little profit and ships the fish to Aqua Star in Bogota. Aqua Star adds some more profit and distributes to retailers and hatcheries like ours. Since it's better for us to raise fish domestically, most of the aquaculture process is done here, whenever possible."

She went on to explain that of every two-to-three thousand mature adults, two-to-three hundred might be good breeders. The hatchery produced twenty to thirty thousand fish a week. Keeping them healthy wasn't easy because it required special effort to ensure optimal environmental conditions in terms of water salinity, filtration, temperature, larval nutrition, and chemical balance. Otherwise, the fish got stressed and didn't breed, or just died.

"It's kind of like raising rich kids in Boston," she said. She threw another flirtatious glance at him and turned away before he could respond. She waited for Grant to scratch out more comments on the pad. "Come on, let's look at the ponds." She prodded him gently in the ribs.

By the time they made the hike over to the ponds, the sun was fully up, the humidity had skyrocketed, and Grant found himself soaking under a withering sun.

"Okay, Grant, we have forty ponds here. Each one's about thirty feet wide, by sixty feet long, by six feet deep. These all contain... Grant, you look like you're fading out. Don't tell me the heat's bothering you that much already?"

"Ah, no, I'm fine. Go on."

Luanne gave him a skeptical look. "Grant, you're trying to be a sturdy New England Yankee. Are you really okay?"

"Yes, I'm all right, really. What are those gnat-like insects hovering around our heads?"

"We call them no-see-ums. They're small biting flies that show up in late spring or early summer. Just shoo them away." Luanne reached over just in time to pull him quickly away from a small mound of fire ants before his foot could come down on their frenzy. "Watch your step. Believe me, you don't want those things crawling up your leg. Here, you need a little shade. Follow me." She led him to the protective canopy of a small stand of young oak trees.

"Anyway," she continued, sweeping her arm again in a gentle arc, "these ponds contain all our maturing angels until they're bred or harvested."

"Harvested?"

"Yeah, sold commercially."

"Oh. Why are there nets over the top of the ponds?"

"The nets keep out predators, mainly birds. Ospreys will sometimes swoop down, but mostly the nets are to keep out the wading birds, like herons. If the long-beaked herons get into a pond they could have a real feast. Not good for us."

"Not to change the subject again, Luanne, but as we were leaving the building I saw a guy emptying some boxes into a tank in the corner. What was that all about?"

"That was Enrico Diaz. Whenever we get a shipment of wild stock in from South America, Enrico puts them into a quarantine tank, where we can test them until we're sure they're not bringing in any diseases. He's kind of a jack-of-all-trades. He takes our deposits to the bank, runs errands, and he also does some maintenance, since we have about six acres here. Got any other questions?"

"Yes. How do all these fish get shipped out of here to wherever they go?"

"Enrico or Daddy take them by truck to Tampa. Bet you didn't know the two largest bulk shipments flown out of Tampa are tropical fish and cadavers."

Grant cocked his head to one side. "Cadavers?"

"Yeah. Florida's a big retirement state, and when retirees die they often want to be buried in their home state. Not a pleasant thought, but interesting. So, try not to expire here, Grant, or you'll just add to the cargo going to Boston." Luanne winked and motioned him to follow her. "Let's walk around the property. After that you can spend the rest of the day poking around in our files like you analysts love to do."

Grant tucked the clipboard under his arm and stuffed the pencil in his pocket. "I don't love sifting through your records, but you know I have to do it."

"I know." She forced a reluctant smile.

"Do you happen to keep any records showing operating statistics for other hatcheries so I can make some meaningful comparisons?"

"Yeah, we have a lot of industry data, sorted by size and type of hatchery. Daddy has a thing about keeping stuff like that. Maria in the office can help find things for you."

"What kind of work does she do?"

"She was my mother's main assistant and sort of my chaperone during my teens. Maria was a migrant worker before Daddy offered her a job and got her out of the cane fields. I've told her to get you anything you want, and you can introduce yourself. Daddy and I have to drive a shipment of fish to the airport. We won't be back until tomorrow night, so you'll be pretty much on your own. By the way, Lem's mechanic called on my cell and said your car is fixed. Well, at least enough so it'll run. He'll bring it over this afternoon. Let's take a walk before it gets really hot."

He pulled out an already damp kerchief and wiped his neck and face. "I can't imagine it getting any hotter."

"Well, it will." She walked silently with him before asking. "Are you learning a lot about our operation?"

"Yes. This whole exercise has provoked a new kind of contemplation for me."

"Contemplation about what?"

"I'm thinking about miniature underwater worlds, where thousands of tiny creatures are cultivated until they grow large enough to provide an adequate return on investment at 'harvest time' as you called it."

She grinned. "I never thought of it that way. Yeah, I guess that's the business we're in."

* * * * * *

Tired from the morning's combination of information overload and the long trek around the ponds, Grant hit the shower, changed into his own clothes, and moved into the relative comfort of Luanne's air-conditioned office. Maria Martinez, a short, stocky, dark complexioned fortyish woman with long black hair tied up in a bun, greeted him with a warm smile.

"Good afternoon, Meestair Grant. Luanne she said for me to I help you, but she didn't tell me what you want."

"I'm pleased to meet you, Maria. Luanne told me you're the one who really keeps the company going. So let's start with the legal documents. I need the ones showing the company's formation, including the stock transactions records, and all the board meeting minutes. Can you get those for me?"

"Only copies. Meestair Tommy keeps all originals. Okay?"

Grant shook his head. Tommy Rawls again. "Sure, that'll be fine. I'm going to spread my documents out on the conference table, so just put the records there, thanks."

Grant's afternoon struggle to make sense of the company's ledgers and journals turned out to be like a walk through quicksand. It confirmed his suspicions that they were prepared by someone who wanted to hide something back when the company was formed: critical transactions were only cosmetically referenced, as though they were anxious to become invisible; vague narrative where there should have been documentation; account totals without supporting entries. Secrets buried for seven years. Secrets no one apparently wanted discovered.

By the end of the day, the combination of suspicion, fatigue, and the eerie quiet of early evening drove Grant's imagination to a new level. He felt the sensation of being in some kind of paranormal place where logic drowned peacefully in a flowing tide of fantasy. In the soft, swishing sound of the pages as he turned them, he imagined their contents whispering *catch me if you can.*

"That does it." He slammed the record books closed in a frustrated refusal to be haunted by any more of their elusive secrets. "I'm out of here." He locked the documents in the cabinet, splashed some water on his face to wash away the drowsiness, and headed for Essie Mae's.

* * * * * *

An order of veal parmesan, two pieces of garlic toast, and a black coffee got his brain working again — if only to resurrect his earlier suspicions. An unaudited company with financials that didn't pass the litmus test; internal business transactions handled externally by a banker; inadequate records; overall, an environment ripe for fraud. No wonder Vanderslice wanted an in-depth look at this place.

Grant pulled his cell phone from his pocket and punched in the number. "Angus, Grant here. Sorry to bother you at home." He handed his empty plate to the waitress. "Look, I'm not sure how to tell you this, and I don't want to disturb Vanderslice with it yet either, although I agree with his suspicions. My own perception that something's wrong at this place has now become a conviction. It's almost like the company's start-up transactions were contrived. Whatever the malfeasance is, I'm afraid it's buried deep, and it'll be difficult to identify, probably increasing the likelihood it's serious."

"Well, Grant, we need something a bit more tangible than your suspicions. Keep looking, and call me when and if something turns up. If it's going to take more time than we budgeted for, better clear it with Conrad before you continue. He's the one paying the bill. I hope you both are wrong about all this, but keep me posted. By the way, aside from your growing doubts, what do you think of that little fish operation?"

"Angus, I think I've learned more about fish than I ever wanted to know. But, it's been a period of discovery. Could even be described as a reawakening. You ought to come down and see this place."

"Well, I may just do that someday. Sounds like you've found a new world." Angus laughed. "Look, I knew this trip would be about more than the hatchery assignment. I've always looked at you as a protégé with untapped promise. But I felt you needed to stretch your sphere of experience beyond the confines of New England. How do you like the folks down there?"

The question revived Grant's recollection of Angus' remark about expanding his horizons. Until now, Grant had never questioned the breadth of his own social perceptions. "Ahh...let's just say they're different, Angus."

"Different? How so?"

"Oh, I don't know. It's a strange culture down here. These are people with the likes of whom I've never had occasion to mingle. I guess I'll eventually get used to them."

After they hung up and just as Grant's thoughts had turned from what was in the documents to what was not in them, a tall, powerfully-built man wearing a cowboy hat laid a sinewy hand on his shoulder.

"Good evening, son. I'm Sam Tillery. I reckon I owed you something for thinking fast enough to avoid messing up my bull. So I arranged with the insurance company to get your car bill taken care of at Lem's." A wide grin spread across the man's leathery, sun-darkened face. He exuded a kind of warmth that belied his rugged exterior. "Mind if I join you?"

"Thank you. I'd gotten so wrapped up in my work I forgot all about the bill. Please forgive me. I'd be glad to have you join me. In fact, you'll witness my first experience with key lime pie, something that doesn't show up much on the menu where I come from."

He watched the rancher ease his lanky frame into a chair way too small for him. Sam looked like someone straight out of a Remington "Wild-West" painting. Grant surmised the man's faded denim shirt, tired blue jeans, and dusty cowboy boots had probably been through the worst of environments. A top-of-the-line Rolex watch on his muscular wrist, attached to an inexpensive old leather watchband, looked like it had married below its class.

"Well, down here you'll most likely run into a lot of things you've never seen before. And call me Sam."

After they had shared the customary small talk for awhile, Sam ran his finger along the edge of his knife-like chin and came to the point. "Major told me why you were here. He's a little worried about you."

"Why?"

"He's thinking you might be doing a lot of poking around while you're looking at all his records and things."

"Well, that's definitely my plan. But why would Major worry about it?"

Sam reached out and put his hand gently on the waitress's arm to get her attention as she walked by. The ropy muscles in his neck bulged as he turned toward her. He ordered two pieces of the key lime pie, told the waitress to put Grant's meal on his bill, and leaned back in his chair again. He studied Grant for a few moments before he responded. "Maybe it's none of my business, but let me give you some advice. And I'm saying this without knowing hardly anything about you or your capabilities. We have an old homespun rule down here. If you're gonna run with big dogs you better be able to pee in tall grass."

Grant surmised that, under all the homespun rhetoric, this rancher was a man of sober temperament, not given to idle conversation or off-the-cuff responses. "Sam, what does that mean?"

Sam paused again while the waitress placed the pies on the table, and waited for her to leave. "It means there are folks who won't be taking too kindly to you digging into that hatchery. Some of them will probably just get a little defensive about it. Others, I'm afraid, are likely to get downright angry."

"You're referring to the Colombian investors, I assume."

"Yep. I've never met 'em, but I hear they're meaner than a cornered cottonmouth."

Grant listened while Sam shared what he knew about South Atlantic Farms and its relationship with the Colombians.

The rancher polished off his pie, wiped his mouth with one of the red-and-white checkered napkins, and stood to leave. "Look, son, you gotta do what you gotta do. I'm not trying to steer you away from that. Just be careful. I'm late getting back to the ranch, so I'll be on my way. We'll talk again. Take good care of yourself, and say hello to Luanne and Major for me."

Sam pulled a wad of twenties from his pocket, peeled off a couple, and slipped them under his pie plate. He shook Grant's hand again with a vise-like grip, and disappeared through the door.

The last remnants of Grant's drowsiness finally disappeared. Sam's warning took care of that. He even found himself becoming accustomed to the little checkered tablecloths with their token artificial plant in the center.

His corner of the restaurant became, thankfully, less noisy when the mother at the next table finally caved in to her three-year-old's screams to be taken to go potty. The foul odor, which soon found its way from the child's britches to Grant's nostrils, confirmed his suspicion that her capitulation came a bit too late. He took a deep breath and exhaled in an effort to force the odor out of his lungs.

Grant took a moment to contemplate the possible downside of parenthood before he settled down to his coffee. He allowed his thoughts to wander back to where he'd left them when Sam showed up. People don't get defensive unless they've something to hide. Major didn't say much about it, and Luanne never even mentioned the Colombian investors. Odds-on bet they have something Vanderslice wanted, and no one was about to own up to it.

He could feel his mental capacity to deal with the unsolved issues of the day running out at about the same time he ran out of coffee and the key lime which tasted better than he'd thought it would. He stood, about to leave, when a woman sidled up to his table, sat down, and flashed a smile as wide as Lake Okeechobee. Unable to manage an appropriate comment, Grant smiled back at her, and returned to his chair, wondering if it was a local custom to sit down uninvited.

He guessed she was in her forties. The receding pastel colors of her tired dress seemed more a function of excessive wear than design. Deep lines in her face had replaced the smooth skin of youth, suggesting she had probably worked hard all her life. He could only imagine how the harsh economic environment of a rural Southern town might have drained her beauty, without commensurate monetary compensation for whatever work she might have found there.

He wondered if her internal marks of hardship were as permanent as the ones on the outside. Although she appeared past her prime, she looked attractive enough to not need all the makeup she wore in an obvious effort to look younger than her years. Her perfume, also applied in more abundance than necessary, gave off a pleasing lilac fragrance in contrast to the lingering odor of cigarette smoke on her clothes.

"Hi, I'm Essie Mae. I hope you're enjoying our food here. We make everything from scratch and it's all fresh. No canned stuff." Her soft, warm smile seemed to contradict the huskiness of her tobacco-hardened voice. "You're Mr. Lonsdale, aren't you?"

"Yes, and please call me Grant. Your food is everything Major said it was and more."

"Well, thanks. I hear you're looking over the hatchery. We're sure glad Major and Luanne chose our town to set up their business. They're really great folks, and everyone really likes them. I've been here all my life and I can tell you things got a lot better once they settled down here. Look, I know this is none of my business, but they're not thinking of leaving, are they?"

Grant shook his head. "Not as far as I know. Why do you ask?"

"Well, I mean when someone comes all the way from a place like Boston to do a look-see, it usually means something's going on. You know, like maybe they're selling the business or something."

"Essie Mae, based on what I know so far, I'd have to say Major and Luanne have no intention of selling. So, I think you can probably rest easily on that one. At least, that's my best guess. Tell me something. Have you ever met the people from South America where Luanne and Major get their fish and supplies?"

"You mean the Bogota boys? Yeah, they tried to buy my restaurant some time ago. I told 'em I didn't want to sell. What I didn't say was I didn't want to sell to *them*. They're not very nice people, to say the least. You want some more pie?"

Grant pushed his empty plate away and folded his napkin. "No thanks, I'm full. Why would they want to buy your restaurant?"

"You got me. They sure seemed anxious to get it, though."

Grant rubbed his chin. "They probably wanted a business where everything is on a cash basis."

Essie Mae stood and smiled again. "Yeah, maybe. Anyway, I won't bother you anymore. I just wanted to meet you."

Grant shook her hand and watched her walk away with the kind of barely noticeable shuffle typical of someone whose feet had hurt for a long time. He made an effort to suppress a twinge of sympathy, then headed back to the motel with the full intention of getting a better sleep than he'd had the night before.

During the gradual transition from being tired-but-wide awake to drowsy-and-ready-to-fall asleep, his thoughts found their own quiet journey through the events of the past few days. These were a different kind of people down here, with a friendliness not customary among his Beacon Hill and North Shore acquaintances. Their personalities seemed to reflect the openness of their surrounding flatlands.

Sam's words of caution about big dogs and defensive people set off shadowy thoughts that kept him awake longer than he'd planned. Eventually fatigue won out, and the taste of Essie Mae's pie occupied his last recollection before sleep finally overcame consciousness.

Chapter 4

Tommy Rawls ushered Grant into his office with a please sit down remark that sounded like he didn't really mean it. The balding banker curled his thin lips in a half smile, as though the gesture came at the expense of considerable pain, but he refused to offer a handshake.

Grant ignored the slight, and forced a smile of his own. The banker's impassive expression left no doubt that this would be an adversarial relationship. The slope of the man's high-bridged, pinched nose began between two beady eyes and ended with a slight hook over a narrow mustache that almost wasn't. Grant glanced around the office. For a small town bank, Rawls' domain looked majestic, with a desk large enough to intimidate anyone not sitting behind it.

While Rawls reached to pull South Atlantic's file from his desk drawer, Grant allowed his thoughts to wander again. He imagined himself in Emerald City, about to be allowed a rare interview with the Wizard of Oz. The absence of a table-top computer, or any of the customary stacks of work product, left the vanadium sheen-polished desk free of clutter. Grant could only surmise the bank's work was done by all the employees sitting at cluttered, unintimidating desks outside Tommy's office.

Without further comment, Rawls spread the South Atlantic Farms file folder out on his desk. The slender, tidy banker folded his hands in an imperious gesture, and looked at Grant with an expression of disdain that appeared to be effortless and perfectly natural.

"I'm curious, Mr. Lonsdale, as to why Major and Luanne Gibbs allowed you to review the hatchery's detailed financial statements. These are not publicly distributable documents, as I'm sure you must know." He unfolded his hands, picked up a pen, and began a tapping sequence that suggested an impatient anxiety for a comforting response.

"They allowed it because I can't conduct a review of the operation without the financials, Mr. Rawls. They agreed to have a review done so they can compare what the company's really worth to what's been offered for it by my client."

"Well, I'm sure you must also know the Gibbs have no intention of selling." Rawls' lips curved slightly in a mild gesture of self satisfaction.

Grant felt a twinge of irritation at the banker's air of open condescension. "I really don't know anything of the kind for sure, although I've inferred as much from their remarks."

"Then why is your client interested at all?" Rawls leaned back and pushed the file aside.

"As I told Major, the client wouldn't say. I'm presuming it's for acquisition purposes."

"Well, your client has approached Major several times before, and we've made it quite clear we aren't interested."

The comment, which suggested a violation of the appropriate arms length relationship between banker and customer, took Grant by surprise. Grant leaned forward. "Excuse me, Mr. Rawls, did I just hear you say *we* weren't interested?"

"Yes. We're not big city people here, Mr. Lonsdale. Our bank takes a genuine interest in its customers. I told both Luanne and Major, as their banker and financial advisor, that turning the farm over to a new owner, particularly one who has no understanding of tropical fish breeding, could wreck it. Moreover, that could happen even before the buyer had made full payment to Major and Luanne for their shares. And that's all assuming the minority stockholder, Aqua Star, would be willing to sell. I believe that's highly unlikely."

Grant shifted uneasily in his chair. There didn't seem to be a tactful way to break through Rawls' air of superiority and ask how the man managed to become so involved in the hatchery's operations. So, what the hell, he thought, just put it on the table outright and see what happens.

"You seem to have a good deal of control over their decisions, Mr. Rawls. Not to mention a surprising knowledge of the minority shareholders who, I understand, are all in Bogota. How did you happen to come by that?"

Rawls' expression hardened and his eyes turned cold. "I don't think I like your attitude, Mr. Lonsdale. And I don't mind telling you I resent your inferences. I would also remind you you're here to assess the company's financial condition, not my role as its banker. I rose from teller to president of this bank by providing the kind of personalized customer service people can count on. South Atlantic Farms began as one of my smallest customers. It's now one of the largest. All my customers know The First Regional Bank of Okeechobee would never betray a confidence by releasing the kind of information I now find myself required to share with you."

Rawls leaned toward Grant with the kind of menacing expression that usually prefaces a threat. "Let's have no misunderstanding about this, Mr. Lonsdale. I didn't like it when Luanne forced this on me, and I don't like it now. And if I should discover you're doing anything more with this information than providing your client a brief financial summary, I will recommend to South Atlantic that your access to the records be revoked immediately. I will also urge that your materials be confiscated, as Major has every right to do." Tommy's lips drew tight, his eyes now bright with anger. "Do I make myself clear?"

Grant glared back at him, then decided to heed Sam Tillery's advice about running with big dogs. "Yes. Please forgive me, I didn't mean to overstep my boundaries. It's just that I've never worked with a company which leaned so heavily on both its banker and its minority shareholders. Luanne told me she records all the business transactions. However, she turns them all over to you to determine where and how they will be shown in the financial statements. Does that include all the cash receipts?"

"Yes, of course. What you need to understand, Mr. Lonsdale, is that Luanne, unlike her mother, is not an accountant. I've been doing this for them at their request since they started the business years ago. And, I might add, it's worked well as you will see from the company's historic profitability as shown on the financial statements."

Rawls rose from his chair, unlocked a file cabinet, and pulled out South Atlantic Farm's financial statements. He rang for his secretary. Grant could hear her shoes squeak softly, even on the carpet, as she approached.

"Jolene, please make a copy of these for this man." He extended his arm toward the door, signaling Grant to leave. "I'm a busy man, Mr. Lonsdale. I have customers waiting outside to see me. My secretary will give you your copy."

"Just one more question," Grant continued. "Who does the company's tax returns?"

"That would be Clete Morris down the street. Now, if you'll excuse me, I have other business to attend to."

They parted without shaking hands. Tommy huffed his way past Grant and out the door. Grant walked out of the briefest meeting he could remember. While Jolene made copies, he waited at her desk, where she performed her primary function as Tommy's gatekeeper. She handed Grant his copy of the financials, as though she were serving him with an eviction notice — which, in a way, she was. Grant characterized her as one of those officious little snips who wear their boss's rank like an emblem on their sleeves. Her shoes squeaked even louder, like an un-oiled wheel, on the tile floor outside Tommy's office.

Grant made a point to exit via the long route past the cluttered desks in the new loans and deposit accounts area. He glanced over his shoulder and could see the disapproving stares of the clerks, as though they sensed he'd made their boss mad, and therefore they probably shouldn't trust him. He nodded politely at one or two who smiled at him on the chance that he might be a new customer.

He removed his jacket and stepped out of the air conditioned bank into a breathtaking humidity that wrapped itself around his lungs like a boa constrictor. The leaden air seemed almost too heavy to inhale. He paused to take a guess at whether "down the street" to Morris' office meant left or right. Then he saw the sign with its illustration of a cleverly reproduced IRS form 1040. On the hope that the day wouldn't become any worse, Grant headed left toward the sign.

* * * * * *

During tax season, or when he wasn't out bass fishing, Cletus P. Morris, CPA, worked out of a little red brick building almost identical to many of the other office buildings in the strip known as the "downtown annex." It wasn't tax season and, when Grant stepped into the office, he found the man at his desk, hunched over a stack of IRS rulings. Grant took it as a sign the fish weren't biting that day. Or, maybe it just happened to be one of those days when Clete felt like working. The combination of his dress shirt — unbuttoned at the top — and sports jacket, gave him an informal appearance, but not casual enough to suggest that fishing would be on his agenda that day.

"Good morning, Mr. Morris," Grant began tentatively, "I don't mean to bother you but—"

"C'mon in." Clete laid his pipe in the ashtray, stood to shake Grant's hand, and flashed a welcoming grin. "You must be Lonsdale from Boston. Can I call you Grant? Sit down, and please call me Clete. Want some coffee?"

"I'd like that." Grant pulled up a chair and scanned a floor-to-ceiling set of shelves containing Internal Revenue Service bulletins, tax rulings, and court cases. "Black, no sugar. And thanks for seeing me. I wasn't sure whether I'd be shot or thrown out, after my brief encounter with your town banker."

"Ah, well, that's Tommy. He's always been a little suspicious of outsiders and he's real possessive about his customers. Don't take offense, that's just the way he is. So let's see now, there could be only two possible reasons you came to Okeechobee. One was to run over Sam Tillery's bull, and the other to see if Major's company is worth buying. I'm betting on the second one."

Clete poured coffee for both of them and sat down. The man's natural friendliness and broad, contagious grin came as a welcome contrast to Grant's earlier experience. It provoked the first good, hard laugh Grant had enjoyed in several days.

"I guess news travels fast around here, Clete. You just won your bet. As far as Sam's bull is concerned, I'm afraid my car came out second best. Look, I didn't come down here to inject myself into other people's business. I have a job to do and, although I honestly don't think anything will come of it, I still have a lot of information to collect about South Atlantic Farms. I think I've extracted about all I'm ever going to get from Rawls. So I was really hoping you might be willing to help."

Clete leaned back in his chair. "Not a problem. What do you want to know?"

Grant savored a few sips of coffee while he organized his thoughts. "Well, first of all, I've only read the most recent financial statements provided by my client in Boston. I've not had time to look very closely at the ones Rawls just gave me, covering the last five years. Even so, Major's little company appears to be extremely profitable for a fish hatchery, in comparison with industry averages. I wondered if you've ever perceived that much profitability as a bit unusual when you were doing the tax returns."

Clete grinned and reached for his lighter. "Grant, the IRS doesn't care how much money you make, as long as you pay the right amount of taxes on it." He reached over and re-lit the gnarled old pipe he'd let go out when Grant walked in, and puffed gently to get a good burn going again. The CPA leaned back again, watching the wisps of smoke, as if to assure the delicate procedure had been done properly before he continued the dialogue.

"I have two kinds of clients. Repeat clients, like South Atlantic, who file well-documented tax returns on time, and clients who come to me to defend them because they've either cheated big time, or screwed up their past returns big time. Yes, South Atlantic Farms is highly profitable. But that's partly because it has to be."

"What do you mean *has* to be?" Grant watched Clete take a few more puffs while he paused before responding, much like Sam Tillery did before offering his prophetic advice.

"How much do you know about those South American investors, Grant?"

Grant took a moment to ingest another swallow of coffee. "Only that they own forty-nine percent of Major's business. According to Rawls, they'd not likely be willing to sell their stock even if Major and Luanne were willing to sell theirs."

"That's right, they probably wouldn't. And they wouldn't allow Major or Luanne to sell either."

Grant frowned. "What do you mean? How could they stop them?"

Clete leaned forward and lowered his voice, even though he and Grant were the only ones in the office. "Okay, what I'm about to tell you must not leave this room. I've had some difficult encounters before with those Colombian investors — or rather, their tax representative. He's a mountain of a man named Pedro Essante. There were certain tax issues on which we didn't exactly agree. I don't mind telling you I've had my own suspicions about their role in that hatchery's history. These Colombians are powerful people, headed by one really tough hombre named Salazar something-or-other. He and his company, Aqua Star, bankrolled Major's purchase of all the property and everything on it.

"Aqua Star put up most of the investment money. Then Salazar — I guess his name is Corazon, now that I think of it — gave back just enough of the stock to make Major and Luanne majority shareholders. That is, as long as they combined their shares to total fifty-one percent. It was probably more for appearance purposes. You know, to show American ownership."

"I see." Grant leaned back to finish off the last of his cup, and mull over the comment. "Well, that seems rather generous of him."

"Not really. Rumor has it Salazar became obsessed with Luanne and tried, in every way possible, to get her to marry him so he could end up with exactly what he wanted in the first place — a sexy, young trophy wife and a majority interest in South Atlantic Farms. That is, after he'd made Luanne turn her shares over to him so his forty-nine percent and her twenty would give him a controlling interest. He even gave her a new BMW for her birthday a couple of years ago. Oh, and a case of vintage wine."

Grant shook his head. "Wow! Sure beats a bouquet of flowers and a box of chocolates. So what happened?"

"She gave him the cold shoulder, traded the BMW in for that red pickup and some change, then she gave the wine to the field hands. Rumor has it Salazar blew right through furious and became apoplectic about the whole thing. He's still pursuing her, but he doesn't dare push it. South Atlantic Farms pays top dividends and represents Aqua Star's biggest fish and supplies buyer. Salazar needs Major's expertise to keep the hatchery up and running profitably. He's not about to mess up a good thing by pressing Luanne too hard."

"In other words," Grant said, "sex is fine but it can't beat big money."

"Yeah, something like that."

"Clete, what do you think about this business of Luanne turning all the transactions data over to Rawls, including all the cash? It would seem that she and Major really have no assurance that he's actually handling it all properly, if you get what I mean."

"I see where you're going. Yes, the internal controls leave a lot to be desired. But I think Tommy's a good, honest man in spite of his rather territorial approach to his customers. My guess is he's probably working in their best interests."

Grant held the unaudited financial statements up so Clete could see the first page. "How do you feel about the complete absence of any annual audits?"

"Well, I'm a tax man, Grant, not the Securities and Exchange Commission. There's a place for annual audits, of course. But a company like South Atlantic Farms pretty much slips under the SEC radar because it's relatively small. Its stock hasn't traded since the initial issuance, and the company operates exactly like a privately held entity. So South Atlantic has gotten away without filing audits. You look like you're pondering something. Still worried about no audits?"

Grant stuffed the documents back into his briefcase and helped himself to more coffee. "No, something else just occurred to me. Luanne was furious because she thought I was down here to bring about a buyout of the business. But if this guy Salazar won't let them sell, then why would she be so concerned about an acquisition?"

"Probably because Major's the only one who knows about that restriction. Luanne handles the day-to-day operations of the hatchery, and Major deals with all the financing and investor relations."

"Well, okay, then, that raises another issue. Major told me the only reason he authorized my review of the business is that he wanted to know how much it's really worth. And, strange as it may sound, he actually seemed glad I was here to appraise it. But, if he knows he can't sell, then what good would it do to know the value? And why didn't he tell me?"

Clete rested his chin on his cupped fist. "Hmmm, good questions. Maybe he wants to keep it under cover, as a potential bargaining chip in his future dealings with the Colombians. Hey, it's about lunch time. How about I take you to lunch at Essie Mae's? I hear you have an insatiable craving for grits and catfish." A sardonic grin spread across his face.

"Clete, I'll take you up on that under two conditions. One, I buy and, two, I walk out of there if grits and catfish are the only lunch options today." They laughed loudly enough to be heard out on the street, and left for Essie Mae's.

They found a quiet corner where their conversation would be less likely to be overheard. By the time they finished, Grant figured he'd learned as much as he could, for now, about South Atlantic Farms and its owners. He sensed that Clete was holding something back, but decided this might be the wrong time to press him on it. They parted with Clete's assurance he would always be available to answer any questions he could. Grant psyched himself up for another assault on the company's records that afternoon.

* * * * * *

Toward the west the scattered, wind-driven, pink clouds of morning scudded into unevenly rounded mountains turning a dirty gray. They bulged with the promise of a downpour at any moment and merged into a seamless, darkening sky. Grant could hear rolling thunder in the distance. Lightning began in the west with one sudden bolt that pierced through the charcoal skies while the sun was still shining over South Atlantic Farms.

The humidity peaked at ninety percent for the second day in a row and, once again, Grant welcomed the air conditioned office. He hadn't seen Luanne for the last twenty-four hours, and felt a mild discomfort at the sudden realization that he missed her.

Rain began steadily but gently at first, as if to offer fair warning to the unwary. The darkness deepened. Within minutes the swollen clouds burst, unleashing a torrential reprimand for all who failed to heed the warning, or simply couldn't find shelter in time. Grant remembered having been one of the unwary ones on the drive from Orlando. Forced to pull off the road under the sudden monsoon-like storm, he'd considered the possibility that Florida didn't want him there and, sensing an intruder, had sent its foulest weather to attack him. He recalled a gray wall of water rumbling toward his vehicle, and the miserable hour he spent waiting by the side of the road for the storm to subside. Now, as then, the lightning shot intense, bright, yellow/white tentacles across the angry skies. Sharp, hard, needles of rain pounded the windows of the conference room. It all made Beacon Hill seem that much further away.

Maria brought in an armful of documents and ledgers and heaved a sigh of relief the moment she laid them down on the table. The woman's strong arms and rough-looking hands confirmed Luanne's remark that her assistant hadn't always worked in an office. "Here you are, Meestair Grant. I have make for you copies of sales and cash receipts. I have also get for you copies when stock was sold. Do you want copies of checks we write?"

"No, Maria, that won't be necessary. However, I would like a copy of your check register showing all the disbursements for the most recent year. If that's not too much trouble."

"Yes, sir, I get that for you."

"When will Luanne be back? I mean Luanne and Major."

"Don't you remember, sir? They go to Tampa for a shipment. They be back tonight."

"Right. I guess I forgot."

She smiled at him in a knowing kind of way that made him feel just a little more uncomfortable.

Driven by angry gusts of wind hissing through tiny cracks in the doorframe, torrents of rain continued to slash at the windows and drum on the roof. Grant and Maria agreed that working straight through until the weather let up would be the best use of time. After she returned to a desk stacked with invoices, Grant opened the Stock Issuance Records and Board Meeting Minutes — two black binders that contained the company's certificate of birth and the story of its life thereafter.

By the time he'd made it through page four, he'd seen enough to feel the recurrence of the old sensation that something way beyond legal was going on at the little hatchery. Before he could act on his suspicions, an ear-splitting thunder clap followed a blinding flash of lightning. Grant instinctively ducked before he glanced out the window in time to watch the wind rip a once-proud tamarind tree from the ground, exposing its gnarly roots. The sudden power outage plunged the office into darkness, and rain thumped against the window so hard Grant feared the glass might break.

He thought about the fish. The "little aristocrats" would now be without the oxygen supplied by aerator pumps. Where did *that* thought come from, he wondered? He'd never cared about fish before. "Maria, what happens to those tanks in the fish room when something like this occurs?"

"Is no problem. Emergency generator comes on. They okay."

The two of them sat in the dark with flashlights while Grant grilled Maria on the history of the hatchery and the Gibbs family. Maria's recollections and the recordings of the Board meeting minutes in the black binders didn't match. Grant decided it wouldn't do any good to press her for a reconciliation.

After an hour of furious weather the power came on again, and the storm exchanged violence for three more hours of steady downpour. An hour before evening darkness the precipitation dwindled to a light drizzle, and the irascible weather offered its apology in the form of a high-arcing rainbow from one horizon to the other.

Maria left for the day, while Grant stayed to ponder his next move. He needed more evidence before he shared his convictions that South Atlantic Farms was in trouble. Friday evening had come before he was ready for it, and he hadn't even begun to untangle the mystery. Forget about wrapping this assignment up in two days, he thought. The hatchery had all the earmarks of another Mount Vesuvius about to erupt. The drizzle stopped and Grant decided he'd had enough for one day. He turned off the lights, locked the door, and walked out into an ominous dampness, even though the storm had freshened and cooled the evening air.

Chapter 5

Grant launched into Saturday with a cup of Maria's coffee and documents stacked up on the conference table like burial mounds in which dirty transactions had been interred. He pulled out his cell phone, dialed the Beacon Hill mansion, and prepared for a confrontation of a different kind. Mignon Chester Lonsdale could be counted on to request either a description of her son's whereabouts or an update on his progress toward finding a suitable wife.

"Good morning, Mother. I'm sorry I couldn't get back to you sooner. Things became a bit hectic here. How was your bridge game at the club the other day?"

"It was fine, dear, except some of the women were wondering when you'd be settling down and getting married. I'm wondering the same myself."

Grant rolled his eyes. "I'll do it when I've met someone I love, Mother, and not before."

"Grant dear, we've talked about this several times. Your father and I have introduced you to a number of the most respectable girls in Boston, any one of whom could make the perfect wife for you. Take Victoria Prentiss, for example. She's—"

"Mother, I couldn't bear the thought of spending the rest of my life with Victoria Prentiss. I thought I made that clear some time ago."

"Please listen to me, Grant. Victoria's from the Prentiss banking family. She's bright and beautiful. She knows the sacrifices necessary to help you run Concord Industries and manage our family assets. It's time you realized power doesn't come without its commensurate sacrifices."

"You mean like abandoning inappropriate relationships?" The facetious remark came out unintentionally, before rational thought could filter it.

He knew the sacrifices his mother had made to get where she was. During one of her tearful outbursts a long time ago, Mignon confessed to him his

49

father had not been her first choice for a husband, although she knew she could learn to love him. Under unwavering pressure from her parents she married him as part of a deal that made her the linchpin in the consolidation of the Chester and Lonsdale dynasties. Grant knew he should have cut her a little slack, given all she'd been through. He felt a twinge of guilt that he hadn't.

"If you're referring to that teenage romance of yours," Mignon continued, ignoring the sting, "she was common, Grant. The girl was blue collar, from an impoverished neighborhood. One of those ghettos where parents send their children to public schools and perceive high school as higher education. You two were far too young then to appreciate the responsibilities you would eventually be called on to shoulder. Your father is counting on you to succeed him as CEO of Concord Industries. You know that. It's been his dream ever since you were born. That young girl was simply not suitable, although I hope you had the decency not to tell her right out."

"I said it as delicately as I could. I'm afraid she got the message. Sometimes I wonder, Mother, where we got all this culture that seems to separate us from other people."

"Grant, my dear," Mignon drew her response out in slow measure, "we didn't *get* our culture, as you so casually put it. We *have* our culture. I assumed you knew this by now."

He shook his head. "I have to run, Mother. This review is starting to get messy. I'll call again later."

"Grant, is that review one of Angus MacIver's jobs?"

"Yes, and I'm here because it was one of Angus' clients who wanted me on it."

"Well, I hope you remember your father and Angus agreed you'd work there just long enough to gain experience in mergers and acquisitions before you came back to Concord Industries. That was part of the deal."

"What deal?"

"I thought it would have been obvious. You can't very well run Concord without some mergers and acquisitions experience. Angus hopes he can bring in Concord as a client. Everyone benefits. That's the way business is done. There are a few things that aren't in the Harvard textbooks, dear."

"Ah, I see. Well, I'm getting experience, and then some. Give Dad my love. And stop worrying about everything."

"I'm not worrying. I'm just concerned. How are you getting along with all those hillbillies down there?"

"They're not hillbillies, and I'm getting on just fine. Have to go. I'll call you later."

Grant clicked the off button and slumped back in his chair. He knew his mother felt more than concern. It was fear. Fear about management succession. Fear about erosion of family wealth. This was how it had always been with her. Mignon's fierce commitment to the preservation of the Lonsdale dynasty had become as natural to her as breathing.

The Lonsdale family tree dated back to the mid-eighteenth century. However, the real expansion of the family holdings began later. In 1857, Henry Pierpont Lonsdale, whose mother came from landed French gentry, consolidated a group of small New England manufacturers into an industrial fiefdom. He replaced the old fashioned guild style of operation with machine-based mass production methods and implemented a new set of factory management techniques. The holdings grew into an empire.

From the day of her marriage to Grant's father, a skeptical Mignon saw the overextended conglomerate as a dinosaur, helplessly sensing its own extinction. Together, she and her husband reinvented the sluggish empire through selective spin-offs and divestitures, restructuring, state-of-the-art technology development, and cost-effective outsourcing. Grant's mother never tired of telling the story.

He also remembered his mother's repeated insistence that any other strategy would be no more effective than, as she said, "looking back and asking your shadow where you're going." Mignon had made it clear that the continuation of the dynasty's prosperity depended upon her son and his descendants through appropriate marriages. Grant knew his apparent lack of commitment to that objective revived the ghosts of her worst nightmares.

He tossed the cell phone onto a chair, as if to get as far away from his mother's voice as he could. He then refocused on the stock transactions records. Whoever the preparer of those documents was had built a brick wall around them. The initial issuance seven years ago constituted the sole transaction, with no sales or other issuances since then.

Ten thousand shares of common voting stock had been authorized by the State of Florida at a par value of five dollars per share. One thousand shares were issued and currently outstanding, of which Major owned 310, Luanne 200, and the Colombian contingent the remaining 490. The unaccounted for difference between the par value and the actual issuance price of the shares caught Grant's attention with a jolt. Each of the thousand shares, recorded at five dollars par, was sold for $10,000. In total, the issuance represented a ten-million-dollar transaction. Such an outrageous spread between par and selling price left Grant so stunned he didn't see Luanne coming up behind him.

"Good morning, Mr. Busybody." She smiled and put her hand gently on his shoulder. "You look like you've seen a ghost. What are you staring at?"

It took him a moment to break out of his trance. "Luanne, are you familiar with the company's initial stock transaction?"

"Sure. More or less. Hey, don't they say good morning in Boston?"

"I'm sorry. Good morning. Please forgive me. It's just that this initial stock issuance is such a monster I'm going to need an explanation."

"Why? What's wrong with it?"

Grant turned his hands palms up and shook his head. "Well, why would anyone buy five thousand dollars' worth of shares and pay ten million for them? I mean, you would expect a selling price in excess of par, of course. And I realize the initial offering of a stock can be made at whatever price the buyer is willing to pay. But *this*? And where did you and Major get that kind of money to buy your shares?" He knew the ten million in equity funds, plus another four million in loans, had been provided by the notorious Salazar, but wanted to find out just how much she knew.

"Daddy said Salazar Corazon loaned us the money. We've already paid it back from our share of the company's profits." She shrugged her shoulders. "So, what's the problem?"

"Well, the problem is I need to follow the money trail here. What did you, Major, and this guy Corazon do with fourteen million dollars in capital funding?"

She looked at him with an air of exasperation. "Lordy me, Grant. Did you come all the way down here from Boston just to ask that?"

"No, I have a number of questions. But let's start with that one. What happened to the money?"

Luanne threw her hands in the air, exhaled a loud sigh, and glared at him. "Okay, Salazar loaned Daddy and me enough to buy our shares. Then the company deposited the money in its bank account. Does that answer your question?"

"Partly. Then what did the company do with the money after the deposit, Luanne?"

"Good grief, Grant." Luanne shook her head and scowled at him. "We used it to buy the land, put up the buildings, equip them, dig the ponds, purchase good breeding stock from Aqua Star and so on. What did you think we used it for?"

"Right. But you didn't need ten million in equity plus four million in subsequent loans from Salazar just to buy six acres of land and throw up a few buildings."

"Well, we sure as hell did!" Her chin protruded with that same blend of stubbornness and indignation he'd seen before. "Look for yourself, Grant. Our records will show the company paid all that out, and Tommy Rawls helped us determine how to set the assets up on our books item by item. And, like I said, Daddy and I paid the loans back from our share of company profits. So, what's wrong with that? Don't people pay off their loans in Boston?"

Unable to come up with a meaningful reply, he turned away, shook his head and mulled it over. How do you assess a completely bizarre scenario which, somehow, seemed to make perfect sense to everyone else? Clearly, there wasn't much point in continuing to press Luanne on a subject that would only irritate her without producing any further clarification. Grant decided to table the issue until he could discuss it with Major.

"Hey, Grant Lonsdale the Third." She suddenly dropped her indignation and smiled warmly at him. "Why don't I take you for a drive around Okeechobee County? It'll give you a break, and you can learn something about the place and how we live down here. Besides," she leaned over and whispered in his ear, "Maria said you really missed me."

"I just wondered where you'd gone, that's all." He saw that teasing smile of hers again.

"Oh, I see. But now you're blushing a little." She laughed. "So it must be true. Why, Grant Lonsdale, you really did miss me. Come on, let's take a ride. You can tell me how pretty I am while I try to figure out why a Harvard MBA would miss a high school graduate from Okeechobee."

He felt blood rushing up from his neck into his cheeks. He turned away, hoping she couldn't see.

* * * * * *

They didn't talk for the first few miles. With or without conversation, it didn't seem to make much sense to sit next to such voluptuousness without taking a look now and then. A pair of stylish sandals had replaced the cowboy boots, making her shapely legs more visible than before. She made no effort to prevent her skirt from sliding upward a few inches as she maneuvered the pickup carefully around the potholes. Her slightly open-at-the-top blouse revealed much more of her full breasts than the buttoned-up blue denim shirt had. He tried hard not to take more than one furtive glance, concluding that all this exposure might have been purely unintentional on her part, but probably wasn't.

"Okay, Grant, off to your left is the start of Lake Okeechobee. The Kissimmee River flows into it." She gave him one of her heart-melting smiles and placed her hand on his knee until she had to remove it to negotiate a sharp turn. She continued her geography lesson. "In the wet season water flows out of it southward into the Everglades. You know about them, right? I mean, even in Boston they recognize the Glades, right?"

"Yes, I've heard about them. Isn't that where those imported anacondas were dumped and now threaten to infest the place?"

"Yes and no. We're getting them under control. The bigger threat is the pythons, which seem to be spreading fast. Anyway, this sheetflow nourishes the sawgrass, giving the Glades its nickname, River of Grass. If you ever get time to visit down there you'll see gorgeous cypress swamps and mangroves running throughout the Glades. You won't find another place in the world as fresh, uncluttered, and teeming with wildlife. Now I'll show you some of the towns around here."

The tour consumed the afternoon. Luanne's docent-like lecture included everything from Okeechobee's origin to Zachary Taylor's role in the Seminole Indian Wars. Grant marveled that a girl who had never gone beyond high school had command of such historic detail. By the end of the tour he felt he could appreciate her fierce pride in the fish farm and everything around it. In the true spirit of aquaculture, Luanne Gibbs had raised millions of large, healthy angel fish as easily as though she were Mother Nature's right hand. It seemed she could listen to the breeze drifting through the rivergrass and know the secrets of a marshy land where the Seminoles once lived.

"Luanne, I think I now understand that vulnerability I saw in your eyes that day we met, and you thought I was about to take all this away from you. I'm sorry about that."

"Hey, it's okay. I was angry. But truthfully, you didn't really look like such a bad guy after...hold on a minute..." Her cell phone rang and she put it to her ear. She shook her head while she listened without responding. Grant could tell by her expression it was bad news.

"Grant, I'm going to have to drive you back and drop you off at your motel. Enrico discovered a worm disease that attacked a vat of angels. It could make the whole lot useless for breeding if we don't get at it right away."

Aside from her brief explanation of the disease and its accompanying risks, Luanne remained silent during the drive back.

The red pickup barreled along the same road that had brought Grant and the Brahman together only days before. Except Luanne knew where the bends were. The passing scenery invited a recurrence of his tendency to conjure up contrasting images of South Florida and New England. He wondered what were his peers at WM&P doing at that moment. Particularly the one assigned to fill the large-client spot he'd left vacant.

* * * * * *

Alone with his thoughts again at the Blue Moon Motel, Grant ordered a pizza and dined in the emptiness of his room. He threw himself on the bed, stared at the ceiling, and thought again about Sarah and how she, somehow, had become such a deep part of his memory. The demands of his heritage had long since banished the life they might have shared together, but never completely crowded her out of his thoughts. Still, it was the feeling lodged in his heart that troubled him.

He managed to push the regrets out of reach of his consciousness long enough to get in some work. Hunched over a desk barely large enough for postcard stamping, Grant spent the next few hours writing up his notes. He stuffed them into his briefcase and downed a glass of Okeechobee Comfort. After giving some consideration to the possibility of making an effort to reconnect with Sarah, he dismissed the idea, and dropped off to sleep to the soothing hum of the cicadas' evening chorus.

Chapter 6

During the night the temperature took a rare plunge to a low for the week — sixty-eight degrees. Grant enjoyed his first good night's sleep without the intermittent surge of the air conditioner struggling to obey a capricious thermostat. Better yet, Sunday morning came fresh with an unexpected dryness that drove the incumbent humidity into temporary exile.

He awakened invigorated by the cool air that poured into his lungs, and the pleasing fragrance of jasmine. Shower, shave, a quick omelet-and-coffee stop at Essie Mae's, and he was ready to regroup. Today he'd make another attempt to exorcise the demons barricaded deep in the hatchery's convoluted information system.

He didn't expect to see Maria in the office on a Sunday, but there she was.

"Good morning, Meestair Grant. Did you sleep well and have a good breakfast?"

"I did, Maria. Good morning. I assume those are the sales and deposits records stacked up there on the table, right?"

"Yes, sir, everything here."

"Thanks. By the way, did you ever happen to meet any of those investors from Colombia?"

She turned away without responding, and began dusting the furniture and cabinets.

"Did you, Maria?

"Yes." She turned to face him as though she'd decided that the urgency of the question outranked her reluctance to answer it. "They come every year for meeting with Major, Luanne, and Meestair Tommy."

"What kind of people are they?" Grant had been curious about that ever since his meeting with Clete Morris. Maria continued her dusting without a response.

"Maria, I know you're not comfortable with this, but I value your opinion."

"They pretty tough. They come with guns in their coats."

"Guns? Why?"

"Salazar bring his bodyguards."

"Well, how about Salazar, himself? What's he like?" He knew he was pushing her, but felt the question was becoming sufficiently relevant to justify whatever discomfort it might cause.

"He the boss. He like Luanne but she not like him. I say no more, Meestair Grant. Okay?"

"Okay, Maria. I didn't mean to press you on this. It's just that I have some concerns about him. I won't bring it up again." He poured a cup of coffee, sat down, and prepared himself to attack the documents when Major walked in.

"Hey, Major, I didn't know fish farmers worked on Sundays."

Major patted him on the shoulder. "The fish don't take Sundays off, and neither do we. I found some sick fish that need to be quarantined. I told Maria to come in special for you 'cause I figured you'd need her. Well, son, by the look of that pile of papers, I'd say you're planning to give us that missing annual audit after all." He grinned, grabbed a Styrofoam coffee cup, and filled it.

"No, sir, I'm just starting my due diligence. I do have a question, though, if you've a minute."

"Sure, fire away. But remember, I'm not an accountant."

"Well, sir, I see the initial investment in the farm was ten million dollars, plus another four million in loans. That seems like a lot of money just to buy six acres of land and put up a few buildings. In New York that might make sense, but it's pretty much off the charts in Okeechobee."

"Well, Grant, all I can tell you is we really did pay that amount to get the business started. Now, that included interest on the loans and all the consulting and soil testing fees. It all just kind of added up, I guess. It costs a lot of money to go into business."

"Yes, sir, I hear what you're saying. I wonder if Maria can pull up the old invoices that show the details of those expenditures."

"Sure, just ask her and she'll get whatever you want. I save everything. Nothing around here gets trashed unless I say so." Major tossed down the rest of his coffee, pitched the empty cup into a waste basket, and headed for the door. "I have to get back to the quarantine tank. You got any more questions before I go?"

"Only one. Luanne told me you both paid off your combined four million loan. However, the records show half of that amount was not actually paid off, but was forgiven by Salazar. It showed up as a quiet little book entry transforming two million in debt to two million in equity under the heading 'additional paid-in-capital.' I thought maybe you could tell me what that was all about. I mean, why did he do it?"

Major pushed his cap back and scratched his head. "Well, I guess no one ever knows why Mr. Corazon does half the things he does. He told me he believed in doing favors for his friends. Said he kind of owed us for all the work we done building up the business and all. I asked Tommy how that would come down in the records. He said he'd show Maria how to do it an' not to worry about it."

"Sounds to me, Major, like Tommy Rawls was the only one who understood the transaction, and the IRS doesn't care as long as South Atlantic pays its taxes."

"Yeah, well I wouldn't know about that. But me and Luanne are sure glad he did it. Took a load off us. Anything else?"

"No, sir, I guess that'll do it for today. Good luck with the sick fish."

* * * * * *

Grant yawned, pushed the sales and deposits records aside, and immersed himself into the property records like a knight in search of the Holy Grail. An hour later all he had to show for it were enough paid invoices and bank statements to confirm that Major and Luanne were right. They really had paid fourteen million dollars.

He put his head in his hands, ready to admit defeat, when it hit him. It should have been obvious. All fourteen million had been paid through Mayaca Corporation. The carrot Angus had dangled in front of him became his first break in a search that had, so far, produced nothing but frustration. Why hadn't he seen it? No company buys a hundred percent of its assets from a single vendor. The whole thing began to stink again.

"Maria, all these start-up invoices, except for the principal and interest payments, are from one vendor. What's Mayaca Corporation, and who owns it?"

"I don't know, sir."

"Okay, never mind. I'll call an old friend of mine. He'll check it out."

58

By the time he'd spent another hour sifting through the sales and deposits records, Grant found himself back in a frustration mode again. Nothing about this damned hatchery looked clean. Or conspicuously dirty. No black or white, only a fuzzy gray. He tried to follow the money trail on each of several transactions to see if he could match collections with their respective specific shipments. When that didn't seem to work, he called Maria over to his table.

"I need your help, Maria. Look at these two sets of shipments. The sales value of the first set was three thousand dollars. The second one, a week later, was five thousand. But the sales that were recorded for these two specific sets were five thousand for the first one, and seven thousand for the second. Why were these sales receipts each recorded at two thousand dollars higher than what they actually were?"

"Yes, I record the sales when Enrico make the deposit in the bank. Look, you will see for these days deposits of five thousand and seven thousand dollars."

"Okay, I can see that, but why is Enrico depositing cash for more than the sales the company made? And where is he getting it? I've seen skimming off the top where deposits are less than actual cash collections from customers. But this one's going the other way."

"I don't know, sir. I just record what Enrico's deposit receipt say."

When tears began to well up in her eyes he put his arm around her. "It's all right, Maria. You didn't do anything wrong. There's just been a difference I have to track down. You go back to what you were doing. It's all right." She managed a faint smile before she retreated to her desk-top screen of accounts receivable.

One discrepancy seemed to follow another. Under an equipment repair warranty offered by Mayaca, South Atlantic invoiced Mayaca for all repairs. South Atlantic received the money, then it paid an unidentified facility to do the work. In an effort to thwart the onset of a feeling of dull despair, Grant left another message for his classmate. He locked all the documents in a file cabinet, and acted on an impulse to get away from there.

* * * * * *

The drive to the town of Myakka, south a few miles on the northeast border of Lake Okeechobee, allowed Grant some relaxation. For the first time he could remember, he stayed, for the most part, within the posted speed limit. The sun relented a bit as evening approached, and an intermittent fresh breeze sweetened the evening air and seemed to wash away some of the humidity. He stopped by the side of the road to stare at a wide expanse of sawgrass like the kind Luanne had referred to earlier. Soft, delicate, and painted a pale yellow by the setting sun, the blades stood motionless, as though waiting patiently for the next gentle breeze to stir them.

He'd never actually seen the Everglades. Still, he felt he could almost picture them from the rivergrass-like scene in front of him. He recalled Luanne's description and tried to envision the legendary protective spirit of the primeval wetlands — dormant during the dry winter, shaken out of its lethargy by the violent thunderstorms of summer, finally, rising to take up its role again as the last guardian of ecological survival.

He turned for one last look at the sawgrass landscape that now included a Great White Heron swooping in for a landing, wings widespread to slow its descent. Luanne was right. He really hadn't seen a place as undeveloped and teeming with wildlife. There was something primitive about it that captured his imagination. The heron stood motionless for a moment before it plunged its head into the grass to stab and retrieve some hapless little creature. Grant stared in fascination at the downward moving lump in the bird's long neck as it struggled to swallow whatever the creature had been. After a few more minutes of contemplation, he put the car in gear and headed for Myakka.

He'd borrowed Major's clothes long enough. It was an imposition, and the clothes didn't fit very well, anyway. The quick two-day trip for which he'd originally packed now had all the earmarks of a much longer assignment. By the time he reached his destination he'd decided it was time for a suitable wardrobe of his own. Myakka seemed as good a place as any to meet that requirement. The "Leisurely Styles for Men" sign over the brick-front store with two white columns caught his eye. Glad to see the little shop open for business that late on a Sunday afternoon, he pulled over and walked in, not sure whether he should be looking for something "leisurely" or not.

The fresh odor of new, on-the-rack fabrics caressed his nostrils the moment he entered. An end-of-spring fifty percent off sign accounted for the ninety-five-dollar bargain sale price of the suit sported by the window mannequin. Grant hoped he could browse uninterrupted for a while but the smiling, elderly sales lady would have none of that.

"Yes, sir, may I help you?"

"Well, I'm looking for a pair of plain casual slacks," Grant replied.

"Then you've come to the right place, young man. Now, you look like about a thirty-fouah-long. Am ah right?"

"Close enough, I guess, but I need something cool."

The lady flashed an I-have-just-the-thing-for-you smile, reached for a pair of light green polyester trousers, and held them in front of him.

Grant pictured his body morphing into a giant grasshopper the moment he appeared in public wearing them. He shook his head, partly as a gesture of "no, thanks" and partly to shake off the image of an irreversible mutation. "Let's try something else," he said as politely as he could.

"Very well. You maht lahke these." She held up a pair of dark maroon slacks and turned them so he could inspect front and back. "They're very popular with the young folks 'round heah."

He shook his head again in response to an image of beets his mother used to force him to eat, and which he'd loathed ever since. "Don't you have something in gray or beige?" he asked.

She flashed a conciliatory smile. "Why, yes. I'm sorry, honey, you just didn't look like a beige type. Just a minute."

She disappeared behind a counter and emerged moments later with a pair of khaki-colored slacks marked "Durawear." They seemed to have a slight gloss, as though they had been polished.

Grant swallowed hard, resigned to the realization that nothing in Mayaca could replicate anything on Newbury Street in Boston. He stared at the offering for a moment, then forced out his statement of reluctant surrender. "I'll take two pair." He didn't like them any more than the beets but refused to leave empty handed. With painful misgivings, he paid for two complete outfits he vowed to destroy before returning to Boston. The denim shirts were a no-brainer. He'd become more or less accustomed to them by now, and wearing one that fit would be refreshing. The khaki-colored pants with the "Casual Styles By Durawear" label were another matter entirely.

In the privacy of the fitting room Grant removed his designer outfit, cursed Angus, and climbed into the denim-and-Durawear combination. It wasn't so much the un-Lonsdale like nature of the garments. He knew no one on Beacon Hill would ever see them, anyway. It was more the queasy thought of them touching his skin for the next week or so. Or, maybe it was the sheer humiliation he felt looking like one of the local farmers. Nonetheless, he had to wear something. Grant tucked under his arm the box stuffed with the other outfit and his former ensemble, forced a polite smile, and left with the hope he hadn't offended the nice lady by failing to conceal his distaste for the whole experience.

Mayaca Corporation turned out to be nothing more than a few small real estate offices, all of which were closed. Grant found a small restaurant where he secluded himself in a quiet corner. The catfish special seemed like a now-or-never opportunity, so he took a chance and washed it down with a beer while he pondered the deposits problem, along with the solitary vendor peculiarity. What the hell, he thought, maybe I can get all the bad stuff out of the way in one day. I hope Angus appreciates my giving up the weekend for a damned fish farm.

"How did you like your dinner, sir?" The waitress, clad in sandals, a tank-top, and faded blue jeans cut off above the knees, leaned over his table to remove the empty plate.

Not yet ready to offer an open admission that the catfish tasted surprisingly good, Grant smiled and gave her a thumbs-up. In retrospect, he hadn't liked lobster at first either, but in New England you either develop a taste for it or move to New Jersey.

All the way back to Okeechobee the deposits mystery haunted him. What if the solitary vendor anomaly and the deposits discrepancy were somehow related?

He pulled up in front of his motel in time to watch the sun slip below the horizon. Grant didn't mind the thought of Sunday coming to an end. He scrunched his legs under the tiny desk for another two hours writing up his notes. Tired of thinking about the whole mess, he collapsed on his bed and waited for a sleep that didn't come easily.

When unconsciousness finally swept over him, it immersed him in a paranormal environment he later attributed to his reaction to the Durawear trousers. It was the kind of chimerical dream he had once in a while as a kid after a really bad day. His mother used to tell him nightmares always came to children when they'd been naughty. He found himself lost in a cavernous tunnel winding through undiscovered catacombs beneath the streets of Rome. Ancient manuscripts harboring warnings to the Roman populace sprang up before him. Anxious to examine their contents, he opened them, only to be attacked by evil, red-eyed, prehistoric flying creatures which burst forth from the yellowed pages and tore at his flesh.

In a pool of sweat, he lurched awake from his attacking demons and lunged for a swallow of Major's elixir to drive the images away. It worked.

After he vowed to try again the next day to draw out the secrets hidden in South Atlantic's infrastructure, Grant faded off to a more peaceful sleep.

Chapter 7

Thanks to his fragmented night's sleep Grant felt more in the mood to lounge around than embrace Monday morning. Even so, equipped with a new appreciation for Major's pale yellow concoction, he decided to make it a long day and then some. Ten straight hours of painstaking review brought him to the disturbing conclusion that the hapless little hatchery was trapped between Colombian money flowing in and Mayaca Corporation's control of the cash flowing out. Chased by a fox, the rabbit could only run toward a hole where a rattlesnake waited for it.

In flagrant violation of his mother's dietary instructions, Grant's sustenance for the day consisted of two burritos, a cheeseburger, and half a dozen cinnamon doughnuts. He washed it all down with an obscene looking purple carbonated drink the locals referred to as Cajun Smash. He grinned several times at the realization that these local dietary selections all seemed perfectly consistent with his new wardrobe.

Major poked his head in once, after his daily tour of the ponds. Grant's hopes that Luanne might drop by disappeared when Major informed him she'd gone deep sea fishing off Port St. Lucie for the day. "She does that every now and then, Grant. Kind of gives her a chance to relax and forget about things. Nice lookin' outfit, by the way. Anything I can help you with?"

"No, I'm still working on the apparent discrepancy between sales and deposits."

"Well, I can't help you much there. Anyhow, I gotta run, and you look like you could use some sleep. Sometimes it don't do no good to burn the candle at both ends like you been doin.' See you tomorrow."

The evening shadows had long since surrendered to enveloping darkness by the time Grant decided to call it a day. Gradually mounting evidence that the hatchery had been turned into a conduit for something highly illegal added a measure of tension to his fatigue. Unable to think of anything better to do at the moment, he decided to take Major's relaxation advice. He pushed his work aside and wandered into the display room which he'd taken upon himself to call "the fish room."

In accordance with Major's recommended procedure, he turned on only the lights above the surrounding fish tanks, and sat down to take in the view. Bathed in a silence interrupted only by the soft, almost imperceptible, murmur of the tiny pumps providing oxygen to the tanks, he leaned back in his chair and tried to think of absolutely nothing other than his immediate environment.

Grant's gaze followed the contour of the room, pausing at the dazzling array of color in motion offered by each tank. Arranged in a complete circle around him, tiny creatures swam silently, gracefully, around the rocks and dark green plants that landscaped each tank. Beams from the tank lamps reflected bright little flashes of light off the silver angels as they turned and wiggled in the water. He allowed his mind to imagine his entire universe condensed into the space of the most comfortable room he'd ever seen.

As though he were now absolved from all demands and ancestral restrictions, Grant Abbot Lonsdale III relaxed for the first time in weeks. He stretched his legs and allowed his thoughts to wander back to Sarah. His parents referred to her more than once as "common." He'd never challenged the adjective, simply because he knew it had become little more than a descriptive term they used to launch their central theme that she was beneath his station.

He'd found it difficult, back then, to relate the responsibilities of his station to the level of sophistication they deemed necessary in a wife who would share in its responsibilities. However, once he'd managed to make the connection, he reasoned it all made sense. With painful reluctance, he'd renounced his "ill advised" relationship with the girl from the wrong side of the MTA tracks, and set his sights on the inevitable journey to the presidency of Concord Industries.

Now, in the quiet surroundings of the fish room, Grant began to reassess the basic premise underlying that renunciation. Hell, he thought, my parents would probably call everyone down here "common." Damn it, they're not. Then why did I buy into it with Sarah? Was I weak, or just naive? So now what? I don't need an emotional contradiction on top of the mess I'm already immersed in down here.

He took a few more minutes to savor the serenity of his environment before he hauled his tired frame from the comfort of the chair, turned out the tank lights, and headed for his motel. Once there, he flopped down on the bed, pulled out his cell phone, and punched in Angus' number. Grant guessed his boss would still be at the office and he was right. "Angus, its Grant. You got a minute?"

"Sure. Fire away."

"Look, I'm certain this little fish farm is laundering dirty money. What bothers me is that Vanderslice is either clueless about the scam, or he wants to buy the place *because* of it. I'm not sure how aggressively to pursue the matter if the latter case is true. I mean, we both know how money-hungry the man is. Especially where big dollars are involved. He just might have a hand in all this and wants to enlarge his share…or maybe take a shot at walking off with the whole pot."

"Grant, you'd better be careful. You're treading on mighty thin ice here. Conrad is one of our largest clients, and infuriating him is not part of my long range plan. Remember, we've talked about this before. If we're going to allege that something as serious as this is going on, we need more than circumstantial evidence to support the claim. And even if we could prove it, there's no reason to believe that Conrad is involved…unless you know something you're not telling me."

"No, I guess I don't really have any substantive proof that he's in on this. I'm damned sure the Colombians are calling the shots. So far, I haven't been able to dig up enough hard evidence about the exact nature of the money laundering either, although I'm reasonably sure it's been going on for years. I'm going to get an investigator involved and move forward as fast as I can, if I have your backing."

"Who's the investigator?"

"Chad Winslow, my good friend and college roommate. He's the kind of born-maverick who runs a successful investigating firm by throwing away the book and doing things no one else could ever dream of. If I promise not to spook Vanderslice, will you go along with that?"

Angus' delayed response conveyed a message of its own. "I will, but only because it was Conrad himself who charged you with the mandate to dig in and do a thorough job. Be careful, though. Neither you, I, nor our firm needs a front page headline about libel litigation. Are we in agreement on this?"

"Yes, sir. I'll move quietly and listen to what Chad says."

Grant put away the phone, tossed down a cup of Okeechobee Comfort, typed a few more notes into his laptop, and let a thought or two about Sarah carry him off to sleep.

Chapter 8

Tuesday began like a mirror image of the day before, another reminder of the lost weekend he'd intended to enjoy in Boston. The very presence of stacks of printouts and other documents forced him to acknowledge the ugly truth — that he'd made no significant progress ferreting out the malfeasance he knew they harbored. The accumulating documents on the table cried out for some kind of resolution.

Maria saw him staring down at the neatly stacked piles of his failure. "Meestair Grant, Major say you work all day yesterday and sleep here last night. You no sleep in your room?"

"I did sleep in my room, Maria, but not well. The outcome of yesterday's labors kept me awake. Did you know Salazar forgave half of those loans a few years ago?"

"Yes, sir. It was a birthday present to Luanne. But she still not like heem."

"Lucky girl. A few more of those birthday presents from her South American suitor and she'll be able to retire before she's twenty-five." Maria offered a weak smile.

"Well, for two million dollars and a BMW you'd think she could like him just a little bit more, don't you, Maria?"

"No, sir," she said, her face solemn again, "not heem."

Luanne burst into the office. "I heard that. And speaking of presents, I have one for you, Mr. Lonsdale. Here." She held out a ticket marked "good for one flounder at Ed's Seafood Market."

"You bought me a flounder?"

"No, silly, I *caught* you a flounder yesterday. I wasn't fishing for flounder but when it wouldn't get off my line I kept it because it reminded me of you. You know, eats junk food off the bottom, keeps a low profile, and doesn't have much of a sense of humor."

Maria burst out laughing, and Grant tried not to but couldn't help it.

67

"Anyway, your cell phone's ringing, so you better answer it." She glanced at him flirtatiously out of the corner of her eye. "Might be your mother, wondering why her little boy didn't come home for the weekend. Oh, hey, I heard you learned to like catfish."

Grant reached into the deep pocket of his Durawear trousers, ignored Luanne's giggle, and pulled out his cell phone. He waited until Luanne and Maria left the room before he answered. There was no mistaking the sharp, Midwestern accent of Chad Winslow.

"Grant, it's Chad. Say, how come you only call your old classmates when you have a problem?"

"It's good to hear your voice, Chad. I called because I know you thrive on problems, and I've a monster for you here. This one's almost as bad as your senior year project — you know, your bank caper in New Haven, when my father had to use all his influence to get you out of jail and reinstated on campus."

"That wasn't my senior project. The damned bank rejected my proposal for an improved security system. The *system* was my project."

Grant grinned just thinking about the incident. "Right. And you wiped out your savings account to pay a couple of local thugs to help you rob the bank to prove your point."

"It was worth it. And as you well know, I returned the money first thing the next morning...along with another copy of my proposal."

"You're lucky you're not still in a New Haven jail."

"The City of New Haven couldn't wait to get rid of me. The bank was so embarrassed it didn't want me around either. I don't believe in God but I pray to your father every night before I go to bed. And not just because he sprung me out of jail. I mean, because his contacts in Boston helped me get my private investigation firm started.

The two chatted for another few moments before Chad got down to business.

"Anyway, I received all your messages about Mayaca Corporation, and your description of what's going on down there at the fish farm. I've done some initial research on it. By the way, with all the big clients your firm has, how did you get stuck down in the cane fields with a jerkwater operation like that?"

Grant shook his head. "Ahh, my boss assigned me to this thing, much against my protest. According to Angus, Conrad Vanderslice specifically requested I be the one assigned to it. Then Angus threw in his own two cents by proclaiming I needed to broaden my horizons beyond New England. So here I am. My only option now is to do such an impressive job that WM&P has no choice except give me the kind of prime clients they should have assigned me in the first place."

"Grant, I'm not even going to touch that one. Except to reiterate what I told you for four years in New Haven. You Bostonians all think the South begins in New Jersey and our western frontier is Pittsburgh. One of these days you're going to find out that Boston is actually *not* the center of the universe. Enough said. Okay, tell me what you know about Vanderslice."

Grant slumped into his chair and put his feet up on the table. "Not much. He's one of our larger clients, who apparently wants to know what South Atlantic Farms is worth and whether it has any merit as another of his prospective acquisitions. This is all based on pure inference, because he still hasn't told us exactly why I'm on this mission, except that he thinks someone's stealing cash. So what information do you have?"

The momentary silence at the other end offered an inference of its own. "Grant, old buddy, you're not going to like this."

"Okay, give it to me straight. Why?"

"Well, for starters, Mayaca Corporation is basically a shell. It does some real estate transactions, but mostly it's a holding company. It operates like an umbrella over a host of other operations stacked one on top of the other, but tied together like a spider web. The hub is so hidden in the tangled organization structure I could only conclude the whole thing was set up specifically to conceal the true ownership. By the way, it took me all day to track that down. Guess who the owner is."

"I have no idea."

"It's Conrad Vanderslice. Mayaca itself is a wholly owned subsidiary of his main company, CLL Capital. Mayaca buys cheap real estate in low-value, commercially zoned areas, then hires a contractor to build on it. The company takes a nice profit on the construction and subsequent sale of the property. One of Mayaca's customers happens to be South Atlantic Farms, which I thought you'd appreciate."

Winslow paused. Grant said nothing while he let the news sink in.

"Now, here's the kicker," Chad continued. "Get this. Mayaca sells equipment to South Atlantic, and then pays South Atlantic for under-warranty repairs. South Atlantic pays the money out to an outfit called Hendry, Inc., which does the repairs. Care to guess who owns Hendry?"

"Okay, three guesses and only one counts. It's probably Mayaca."

"Right. And all proceeds to Mayaca go fifty percent into an off-shore bank account somewhere in South America, and the other half into some local bank in Okeechobee. Rumor has it Vanderslice is also tied in with some shady deals, including narcotics. I also found out — and this is no rumor — that Aqua Star, your little hatchery's main supplier, is owned by a guy named Salazar Corazon, who also heads up Colombia's second largest drug cartel. That's where the trail ends. But, Grant, if I had to guess, I'd say you've a real mess on your hands, my friend. And the question you need to ask yourself is why Vanderslice wanted your firm, and specifically *you*, to do the kind of analysis that might uncover whatever it is he might be hiding."

Grant remained silent for a moment while a plethora of thoughts raced through his mind, but none that would enable him to connect the dots on this one. He stood, poured a cup of Maria's coffee, and paced back and forth. "Chad, the evidence I've turned up so far seems to offer a pretty strong indication that South Atlantic Farms has been turned into a conduit. Large sums of money, originating in South America, are being filtered through it."

"You're talking money laundering?"

"Probably. Stated more specifically, it's an odds-on bet the company's investment loans represented drug money going in dirty, mixing with legitimate hatchery money, and coming out clean. Sweet and simple. The best kind of operation, I guess, if you're going to run a large dollar scam. But I can't be sure. Until I find sufficient proof and can explain the deposits discrepancy, I can't make any defensible accusations. Anyway, thanks for everything, Chad. Bill my firm for your time. I may need you again. I'll stay in touch."

Grant stuffed the cell phone into his pocket, dropped back into his chair, and put his feet up on the table again. Okay, he thought, let's review the bidding on this. Big money is being flushed through here. Large investments — tip of the iceberg. Property and equipment kickbacks? Maybe. Oversized deposits — where's the money coming from? How does Tommy Rawls fit in? Vanderslice — that one's starting to stink as well.

Grant knew he was tired. He knew it because the unanswered questions began to morph into the red-eyed flying creatures from his recent nightmare. The chimerical cast of characters now snuck onto the stage of his thoughts, as if he'd unwittingly invited them back for a matinee performance. With some effort he hauled himself out of his chair, stashed the mounds of defiant little documents away, and walked out. Like Scarlet O'Hara, he'd think about it tomorrow.

Chapter 9

Hans Drukker knew the financial market held him in contempt for what he'd done. He felt neither guilt nor remorse. In fact, he took pride in being known as a financial sniper, willing to take out anyone trusting enough, or dumb enough, to get caught in his crosshairs. He'd already sold out most of what few friends he had, and screwed all his business partners. By now, he'd become number one on the financial community's list of top ten scumbags. Fortunately for Hans, he was Conrad Vanderslice's kind of guy, who could count on complete protection as long as he remained loyal to Conrad, and continued to structure deals which made Conrad richer.

The only confrontations Hans disliked were the ones with his boss. However, the Okeechobee situation could no longer be swept under the rug, and Hans found himself with opinions diametrically opposed to Conrad's. Like it or not, a confrontation had become unavoidable. Hans stiffened his courage and strode into Conrad's office without knocking.

"Look, Van, you know I've never argued with you. For years I've respected your obsession with that damned fish farm without saying much. But there's a litany of things wrong with it, and we need to talk."

"Hans, I'm beginning to think you just don't like little fish. Okay, sit down and tell me what could possibly produce a whole litany about a hatchery lost out in the middle of nowhere." Conrad leaned back in his swivel chair and lit up one of his thirty-four-dollar Cohiba Esplendido cigars.

Hans settled into his chair and the patter of his toe tapping resonated, softly at first. "Well, to begin with, the very fact that it's *little* is a problem. Here's the thing. Our deals are all big dollar undertakings and we accept commensurate financial risks with them because the payoffs are big. Not so in Okeechobee. The pittance we're getting out of South Atlantic Farms is chump change, and you know it. Moreover, it has serious risks that far outweigh any likely payoffs. And I think you know what I mean."

71

Conrad blew a thick cloud of blue smoke into the air. "If you're worried about the Colombian investors, you needn't be. I know what they're doing down there, and, frankly, I don't care."

Hans threw up his hands. "Damn it, Van. What if the authorities get wind of it? They'll come after everyone who has a hand in the cookie jar." The toe taps became louder and faster.

"You're probably right. But here's the whole point, Hans. I'm not down there with my hand in the cookie jar. I'm up here, simply waiting for the jar to tip over and fall on the floor. Then I pick up the pieces."

"What pieces? The assets will be impounded, Van. They'll be worthless. And what if the authorities follow the trail back to you?" The accelerated tapping of Hans' foot reflected his mounting discomfort at the possibility that the trail might also lead to him.

Vanderslice exhaled another cloud of smoke. "I don't think there's anyone in government smart enough to trace anything back to me. And, if they do, well, I'm just another one of those poor innocent chaps who had no idea there was anything wrong with the money."

"That's not going to fly, Van. Look, you agreed to disassociate us from this thing. We sat right here in this room and committed to it. What happened to that agreement?"

Conrad gently laid his cigar on the ashtray before he rose from his chair. He stepped over to his office door and closed it, making it clear he didn't want anyone to hear the rest of the dialogue. He returned to his chair, reconnected with his Esplendido, and leaned toward Hans. "The situation has changed. A once-in-a-lifetime opportunity has presented itself, and I intend to take full advantage of it."

Hans rolled his eyes. "What opportunity? All I see is potential disaster." He pulled out a handkerchief, dragged it across his brow, and stuffed it back into his pocket.

"After almost thirty years, Hans, I finally have a chance to even the score with an old enemy. I'm going ahead with it. I've waited too long to let this pass by."

Hans cupped his hands on top of his head and closed his eyes. "Oh, for God's sake. If you're referring to your rivalry with Lonsdale and Concord Industries, I say forget it. He's beaten you on a few business deals and you've beaten him just as often. You're already even. In fact, if you hadn't screwed Lonsdale out of that merger in Ohio you wouldn't be heading up CLL Capital today. So it's even. Forget it."

"No. It won't be even until I say it's even."

Hans shook his head. "Aw, come on, Van, what else are you....whoa! Whoa! Hey, hold on here a minute. This isn't about money, is it? Damn it, this is about the one girl you couldn't have, isn't it?"

Conrad's countenance darkened. He put his cigar down and spoke slowly through clenched teeth, as if to make a clear distinction between what he was about to say and anything he'd said in the past. "Mignon Chester was the only woman I've ever loved. And she loved me. But I was damned near broke back then. I had to borrow a car to take her out on a date. We ate at cheap restaurants and we entertained ourselves at places that didn't cost much. But we had fun and she laughed all the time."

Vanderslice went silent and stared off into space. He knew he'd be able to support her in style someday, and she said it didn't matter. They had each other. Then along came Lonsdale with all his damned family money and that Ivy League crap, and scooped her up behind his back. When he confronted her about it all he got was a lot of bull about how her parents were pressuring her to marry into an appropriate family. Then she disappeared from his life forever.

He turned to Hans again. "Anyway, she called the whole thing off. Okay, so I wasn't good enough for her. Well, now it's payback time. First, I'm going to send her kid back to her in a body bag. Then, after I've extracted everything I want from that little fish joint, the two owners who've resisted my offers to buy all these years are going to jail. And that pathetic little place is going to crash and burn. And then, Hans, I'm going to buy the pieces from the Feds at ten cents on the dollar and sell them for six times that. Now, this discussion is over. Get back to work."

The spastic toe tapping would probably have become worse had Conrad not ended the meeting abruptly, and sent the perspiring Hans on his way. Conrad pulled out the Okeechobee file and buzzed his secretary.

Gertrude Mulky represented the most recent in a long line of executive secretaries, none of whom had lasted longer than three or four months. Gertrude could count on a longer tenure at CLL Capital because she was both extremely competent and incredibly unattractive. These were two qualities the personnel director made sure she possessed when he hired her. It had been necessary because everyone had grown tired of dealing with the careless procession of gorgeous airheads Conrad hired simply because he found it more convenient to have sex with his secretaries than to cruise the town looking for it. Rumor around his office held that Gertrude represented Conrad's first, and last, subordination of easy sex to operational efficiency.

"Trudy, do you have young Lonsdale on the phone for me yet?"

"Yes, Mr. Vanderslice. I'll put him through."

Conrad left his cigar to smolder itself out, and grabbed the phone. "Hello, Grant! How are you doing down there in paradise?"

"Well sir, I'm making progress, but it's become clear this assignment is going to take a lot more time than I thought it would."

Conrad pushed a stack of cost-overrun sheets aside, leaned back in his chair, and laughed. "Sounds like a slick way to tell me my bill is going to be higher."

"No, sir, it's just that I've uncovered a few discrepancies I need to resolve. I'll try to keep the billing as low as possible, but it would help if you told me exactly what you want me to find out. So far I've been going on Angus' supposition that you want to know the acquisition value of this place, and whether cash is leaking out."

"Well, Angus has it right. I need to know all the strengths and weaknesses of South Atlantic Farms, and everything in between. I selected you because Angus spoke so highly of you. Rumor mill around town says you're one of the best the B-school ever put out. That's why I stuck my neck out a mile entrusting a task this critical to such a young man. So, don't let me down. Now, what kind of discrepancies are we talking about here?"

"I would say they're more in the form of strong suspicions than actual discrepancies at this point. The investors seem to have generously overpaid for their stock, and then compounded the problem by allowing the business to purchase capital assets at prices substantially in excess of their intrinsic value."

"I wouldn't worry about it, lad. That happens a lot in Florida. Real estate and construction prices quite often reflect anticipated growth in market value as opposed to current intrinsic worth. What are your other findings?"

"I'm seeing an unaccounted-for spread, more like a huge chasm, between the cost of their fish and the selling price to the retail customers. To make matters—"

"That's called profit, son, in case they neglected to cover that one at Harvard."

"Yes, I know. But, Mr. Vanderslice, the problem is the bank deposits for their sales are even higher than the sales receipts. And, frankly, I'm still trying to identify and dig up the documentation I need in order to be able to account for it."

"Well, do the bank statements reconcile with the cash shown on the books?"

"Yes sir, they do. But you see—"

"Well then, who gives a damn about the size of the deposits? Hell, those profits are what makes this operation attractive to me. That's precisely why I had Angus send you down there. So, keep up the good work. And tell that backwoods old redneck they call Major to keep those profits coming. I have to run, but we'll talk again soon. By the way, have you been able to take his sexy little daughter to bed yet?"

Grant's response sounded like it came through clenched teeth. "No. That wasn't part of the assignment. And she's not that kind of girl."

Conrad heard the loud click of Grant's cell phone punctuating an abrupt end to the conversation.

Gertrude stuck her head through the doorway. "I think he's hung up on you, Mr. Vanderslice. Do you want me to get him back?"

"No, Trudy. Just make a note to remind me to educate that boy on the finer points of life before he grows too old to do anything about them."

"Yes, sir. Exactly what points would those be?"

"Trudy, I'm just kidding, damn it. Ring up Mike Rinelli at Mayaca. And if he's not there, leave a message it's urgent I talk to him." Conrad fired up another cigar and muttered something about the upside of risk.

"I beg your pardon, sir?"

"Nothing, Trudy, I'm just talking to myself."

He waited for Trudy to return to her desk. "Okay, do you have Rinelli yet?"

"Yes, sir. He's on the line."

Conrad had hired Mike Rinelli because he figured the man's splotchy ethics would make him a good fit at CLL Capital. A born entrepreneur, Mike didn't find an opportunity to demonstrate his skill until age nine. That's when he discovered that lost golf balls he found as a junior caddie at the local country club could be cleaned up and sold for fifty cents to a dollar. New ones that he managed to pilfer from the bags of golfers for whom he caddied sold for two to three-and-a-half, depending on the manufacturer.

Convinced fortunes could be made in South Florida, Mike plunged into his adulthood by cruising the coastline on his motorcycle from Naples to Miami. Along the way he set up one business after another with other peoples' money, selling everything from fast food to small watercraft. Trouble was, Mike had more raw ambition than good business sense, and left a wake of bankruptcies behind him. Eventually, Vanderslice discovered him floundering in a sea of lawsuits and decided that Mike, like Hans, was his kind of guy. Conrad settled all the lawsuits and set him up as the front man at Mayaca. Grateful for his oversized salary and bonus arrangement, Mike Rinelli could be counted on for loyalty to Conrad and CLL Capital.

"Mike, Van. We may have a problem at the hatchery."

"You mean South Atlantic Farms?"

"Right. Remember when we sold them all that land and then billed them for all the construction?"

"Sure. Most lucrative deal we ever made. Why?"

"Well, I sent a guy down there to find out how much the place is worth. I just talked to him, and it turns out he's taken it upon himself to turn the place upside down. Not that I really mind, because I do want an accurate assessment. But I don't need a slew of unnecessary disclosures about that real estate transaction — or a couple of others, if you know what I mean."

"Yeah, I follow. What do you want me to do?"

"Nothing, as long as he lets certain matters drop, as I told him he should. But I want you to keep an eye on him in case he exhumes things better left buried, and starts making noise about them."

"And if he does make noise?"

"Then I want you to get in touch with those Colombian boys and fill them in. Just to keep them informed, you understand."

An awkward silence followed before Mike responded. "I'll keep an eye on him, and I'll keep you fully informed, Conrad. But I'm not calling those Colombians. That's your job."

"Why not? What are you afraid of?"

"I don't want any part of what happens to your guy if the Colombians get spooked. I'm keeping my hands clean on that one. Business deals are one thing. But they don't need any more 'accidents' over at that place, and neither do we. That's all I have to say on the subject."

Conrad heaved a frustrated sigh. "Okay, just keep him on your radar. Call me if something happens."

He reached into his desk drawer and pulled out the dossier Angus had prepared for him on Grant Abbot Lonsdale III. He reached for another cigar but pulled back and aborted the effort in favor of a quick reread of the dossier. Grant's accomplishments were impressive: honor graduate of Yale

University with a degree in mechanical engineering; starting running back for three years on the varsity team, and winner of two MVP awards despite the team's three losing seasons; graduated with high honors from Harvard with an MBA in finance and accounting; record unblemished except for fourteen speeding tickets and a wrecked car; father presides as CEO of Concord Industries, a privately held conglomerate poised to go public pending completion of a transaction involving mezzanine financing; mother had managed, for the last fifteen years, the family's personal investments as well as the unrestricted portion of Concord's liquid assets.

Conrad slipped the dossier back into the drawer. He leaned forward, elbows on the desk, face in his hands, and tried to banish Mignon Lonsdale from his thoughts.

Chapter 10

Tommy Rawls agreed to meet with Grant again, only because Grant insisted on it. Both of them knew an outright refusal to meet would likely have put a serious strain on Rawls' relations with Major, and possibly set off a chain of local rumors of the kind his bank would not welcome.

Grant took his seat and peered across the oversized, uncluttered table at a sullen Rawls, who, as usual, glared disdainfully at him.

"Mr. Lonsdale, I thought you'd be long gone by now." He eyed Grant with a dangerous gleam, and motioned his secretary to come in. He interrupted the conversation to sign a few payroll checks, and turned to Grant again after the woman and her squeaky shoes left.

"I'm curious as to what there could possibly be about a little fish hatchery that would keep you here so long. I'm particularly curious as to why you thought it would be necessary to take up my time with it. I'm hoping we can keep this short. I have other things to do."

"The length of this meeting, Mr. Rawls, will depend entirely on your answers to a few questions I've accumulated. To begin, you and your bank have been involved in each of several transactions that appear to be a bit unusual. First, I discovered that—"

"Excuse me, Mr. Lonsdale. Is this going to be your *second consecutive* attack on my integrity? If it is, this meeting is already over." Rawls rose from his chair and extended his arm toward the door, palm up, in a gesture clearly intended to usher his visitor out.

"Sit down, Mr. Rawls," Grant said, "or my next meeting with you will include the Gibbs family and the banking commission." With the words barely out of his mouth, Grant found himself a bit surprised at what he'd just said, but inwardly pleased that it had the desired effect. A startled Tommy Rawls returned to his chair.

"Now, as I started to say," Grant continued, "I've found some transactions which I believe only you, as the financial advisor to South Atlantic Farms, can explain."

"And exactly what might those be?" Tommy's question came out more like a hiss between his teeth. He fired a malicious glare at Grant, who made a point not to notice.

Grant reiterated his findings: Major and Luanne's stock purchase at a price far in excess of its intrinsic value; payments for land, equipment and construction well in excess of fair market values; additional loans subsequently forgiven by Corazon for no apparent reason; bank deposits in excess of the actual customer receipts the deposits purported to represent. "Since all these rather difficult-to-explain transactions were handled by your bank, under your personal supervision as a financial advisor, I thought you would be the most appropriate one to explain them...Mr. Rawls."

Aware of the not entirely intended sarcasm that crept into his own closing sentence, Grant wished he could have retracted the statement. An awkward silence prevailed while Rawls made no effort to mask his mounting rage during the brief moments it took him to respond. His face flushed with anger, the agitated banker stood and pointed a menacing finger at Grant.

"Now listen to me carefully, you pompous Bostonian smartass. I'm going to preface my answers to your insulting questions by informing you that, if you ever threaten me again, I'll make sure you spend the rest of your life regretting you ever showed up in this town. Now, that having been said, I'll explain this to you for the last time.

"I had no say in the stock price the company set. I'm a banker, not a stock broker. I had no part in their construction transactions. If you don't like the prices they paid, then I suggest you take it up with Mayaca Corporation. As for the loans, Corazon forgave them to clean up the hatchery's balance sheet and his own. I'm not responsible for what their deposits look like. My bank's only function is to make sure their deposits are properly recorded and safely guarded. Now, your little interrogation is over, Mr. Lonsdale, and this had better be the last time I see you in my bank." Eyes bright with anger, and lips now drawn tight, Rawls returned to his chair.

Grant stood, returned the banker's malevolent glare, and walked out with visions of Tommy Rawls being devoured by the same red-eyed creatures that had populated his own nightmares. Adrift in his own thoughts, he managed a polite, if not sincere, smile as he strolled past the curious clerks who gave him the same distrusting looks they did the first time he had rattled their boss.

This, he decided, would mark the beginning of his own private war against the Colombians and that damned Rawls.

Grant returned to South Atlantic's conference room, slammed the Rawls file on the table, and scrunched down in his chair to gather his thoughts. This would be a different kind of war. A head-on attack would be futile given how firmly ensconced Tommy and Corazon were in Major and Luanne's fragile world. Nothing less than an overwhelming preponderance of evidence would be required to release South Atlantic Farms from Corazon's vise-like grip, and discredit Tommy Rawls at the same time.

* * * * * *

Angus MacIver made no effort to conceal his surprise. "Grant, we were talking about mere suspicions the last time you called. Now it seems we're talking about some real allegations. What's happened since, and where are you in this process?"

"Angus, things have changed, I'm afraid. This place seems to be a very profitable conduit for money, but I don't think it has anything to do with profit."

"What are you saying?"

Grant slipped back into his habit of pacing back and forth when he felt pressure. "I'm saying it has all the trappings of drug money being laundered. However, I still need to get some tangible proof." He related the sequence of suspicious discoveries and corresponding events with all their accompanying details, including his confrontations with Rawls and his dialogue with Vanderslice. In spite of it all, his only real apprehension was that Angus just might pull him off the assignment and order him back to Boston, leaving the Gibbs family at the center of a potential implosion and Rawls a clear winner.

"Hold on a minute, Grant. Is Vanderslice aware of all this?"

"Angus, I tried to tell him, but he's so bent on proving the place is worth a lot he just blew me off. Nonetheless, you can bet he knows more than you think he does. Did you know he owns Mayaca Corporation, the outfit that sold all the capital assets to South Atlantic Farms?"

"No, but that doesn't surprise me. What about it?"

"Well, it means he's getting a piece of all that excess money paid out over and above the real value of that property, for whatever that observation is worth."

"I wouldn't worry about it. Conrad's always been a few columns to the left of ethical. Now, have you any thoughts on how you're going to proceed with this?"

Grateful for the implied go-ahead, Grant returned to his seat and began his response with a mixture of enthusiasm and trepidation. He hoped his boss didn't notice the change in his tone.

"I've more pieces of this puzzle to put together yet, Angus. I've discovered most of South Atlantic's repair and maintenance expenses were paid for by Aqua Star, the company's supplier. That's an accounting anomaly in itself. However, I've yet to figure out how things like five thousand dollars received by South Atlantic in the form of customer checks became seven thousand by the time it was deposited in the bank. I guess I've been duly warned about the risks involved here, and I can't do much about them except be careful. I'll keep you posted. Thanks for giving me a shot at this."

"Grant, I'm allowing it with a great deal of reluctance. I'm jerking you out of there at the first sign of any trouble, understand? Make sure you let your father know about this. If he wants you out of there, I'm backing him. I want daily reports and then some. Got that?"

"Yes, sir."

Grant's feeling of relief lasted about thirty seconds. Luanne stormed into the room and stood in front of him with arms akimbo. She issued an ultimatum between clenched teeth. "Grant, please join Daddy and me in his office. Now."

Grant more or less expected a reaction to his meeting with Rawls, but had hoped it wouldn't happen. He'd learned, his first day there, that news probably traveled fast in Okeechobee. He followed Luanne and took a seat in front of Major's desk. Luanne glared at him as though he'd just contaminated the fish tanks.

"Grant," Major began slowly in a tone that smacked of imminent parental discipline, "I just got an angry call from Tommy Rawls at the bank. He says you insulted him, were rude to him, and called him a criminal and a liar. Now, I told him that didn't sound at all like anything you'd do, but that I'd take action on it after I got your side of the story. So let's have it. What happened?" The old farmer leaned forward. His eyes reflected disappointment rather than anger.

Grant shook his head and raised one hand in the air in a gesture of surprised disgust. It now seemed as if all those secrets, which had fled into the dark tunnels of South Atlantic's accounting system, had resurfaced, taken the offensive, and cleverly marshaled his allies as well as his enemies against him. He related the sequence of events during his research, as he had for Angus, this time with more emphasis on the actual exchange with the damned banker.

Luanne broke the long period of silence that followed. She slapped the palm of her hand on the desk. "Daddy, I think we owe Tommy an apology. He's done a lot for us over the years, particularly since mom died. I really feel bad about this. Grant, even though you maybe didn't actually *call* him a cheat, you certainly implied it. I just can't believe you did that."

Grant looked off to the side while he tried to frame a response. How do you tell a squirrel that the rattlesnake hasn't been guarding its nest all these years simply to protect the inhabitants? "Luanne, I simply confronted him with the facts, looking for explanations without intending to imply anything. Any inference he might have drawn was entirely his own. Look, I didn't come down here to castigate anyone. I didn't even intend to investigate anything.

"You and Major can apologize to Tommy and throw me out any time you want. However, I'm now convinced your Colombian investors are using South Atlantic Farms to launder drug money. I'd like to be given enough latitude to prove it. What bothers me is that you two don't seem to be aware of what's going on. Weren't you a bit suspicious about the injection of all that money into this company?"

He knew he'd been the harbinger of bad news, casting a dark shadow over people who had been part of the events that shaped the lives of Major and Luanne during most of the last seven years. Any thought of possible betrayal came equally matched with the realization that, without all those people, South Atlantic Farms wouldn't exist. Without their hatchery, Major and Luanne would still be working for the sugar company down in Belle Glades, supervising itinerant laborers swinging machetes in the cane fields.

Another long silence. Major and Luanne looked alternately at each other and at Grant. Major breathed a sigh of reluctant resignation and spoke first. "Son, this little company is all me an' Luanne got. Yeah, we always kind of figured the boys from Bogota were doing something that wasn't just right." He shrugged his shoulders. "But this is a good company. And we're doin' good things selling a good product that a lot of people want. I guess we just didn't want to bust that all up. Yeah, I know now we need to do something, but I'm not so sure just where to start."

"Lordy me, Grant." Luanne rolled her eyes. "This was a peaceful, quiet place, running smoothly until you showed up. You're just the biggest damned troublemaker I've ever met."

Major shook his head. "I guess I have to agree with Luanne, son. You sure made a mess. But seein' as it looks like we don't have much choice, I say go ahead and see how bad this is. You okay with that, honey?"

Luanne stood and paced back and forth. "No, I'm not, Daddy. But like you say, we don't have much choice." She stopped and spun around to face Grant. "Tell me something, Grant Lonsdale the third. Did they teach you enough up there in business school for you to get us out of this?" Her face reflected a contradictory mixture of fear and hope.

The question was logical, and one that Grant had already begun to ask himself. Now that he'd become the messenger they'd just tried to shoot, he felt forced to answer it. "No, Luanne. I can pull a few more pieces together, but I'm going to need some big time help in order to get us out of this one."

"And who's going to come up with that kind of help?" she asked.

"A very unorthodox old friend of mine named Chad Winslow. I'm putting him on this right away. You understand, this is just between us. I don't want anything that went on here to leave this room. And keep Rawls out of it. This guy is *not* your friend. Trust me."

Major came around and sat on the edge of his desk. "Son, I think you need to tell me and Luanne just who this Winslow fellow is, and exactly what he's going to be doing."

"He heads up an investigative firm," Grant said, "and he's good at what he does. I'll need him to get his arms around your company's history, including anything related to those boys down in Bogota."

"Grant, how much do you know about them?"

"Enough. Yes, I know. I've been told they're…what was the expression? 'Meaner than a cornered cottonmouth,' I believe. No matter, we have to get you and Luanne out from under all this, company or no company."

Major slid from his perch. He walked up to Grant, put his arm around him, and gently nudged him toward the door. "Okay, son. You need to relax and so do I. So we're going to take the rest of the day off. You go climb into those old clothes Luanne dug up for you before you got fancy down there at Mayaca, and meet me back here in ten minutes."

"Where are we going?"

"Well, we're going to get a bite of lunch first. Then we're going to spend the rest of the day doing something you probably won't get much of a chance to do up there in Boston."

"What's that?"

"Hunting alligators. Something you can tell your kids about someday when you're sitting around a warm fire during one of those New England winters. Now, go climb into some old clothes. You're gonna need them."

Grant felt a sense of relief coming on again. Angus hadn't fired him from the assignment and Major hadn't thrown him off the property. Hunting alligators would be his only punishment for turning everyone's world upside down.

Chapter 11

The red pickup bounced over a narrow, winding dirt road along the edge of a cypress swamp and out through the pine flatwoods. Late winter and early spring rains had left deep, mushy ruts that made the road progressively less navigable until it vanished altogether. Miniature pools of muddy water oozed up into the tire tracks. Major turned eastward until he found a drier stretch of road, and finally rolled to a stop at the gate to Kip Moffit's farm. A stocky man with a ruddy complexion and a chaw of tobacco bulging his cheek slid off the fence and greeted them, rifle in hand. He smelled like a mixture of manure, tobacco-flavored breath, and underarm sweat.

"Kip, this is Grant Lonsdale," Major said. "He ain't never hunted gators before, so I figured the education would do him some good. Grant, Kip Moffit can sniff out a gator a mile away."

Kip's wide grin exposed a set of tobacco-stained teeth in need of repair.

They shook hands, and Grant couldn't hold back a smile at the sight of them. Together, the tall, lanky Major and barrel-shaped Kip looked like a couple of weather-beaten cowpunchers out of an old Western movie. The leathery duo seemed as indigenous to the rough country surrounding them as the cypress trees that lined the edges of Okeechobee's swamps.

"Okay, then let's do it," Kip said. He turned and spat out a dark, wet glob from the chaw. "If y'all are ready, I got the boat outfitted and we're good to go."

No one spoke for the first few minutes. Major guided the muscular pickup along another well-worn cow path that suddenly disappeared into a thick patch of palmetto bushes. The vehicle barreled forward, humping and bumping its way in and around the thick undergrowth, sometimes creating its own path. Aside from the fluttering wings of startled birds, the only audible sound was the whump and thump of the brush against the undercarriage of the truck. Grant recalled his recent experience with the drainage ditch and winced. The truck rocked and bounced its way toward what appeared to be a swamp, densely populated by cypress trees draped with long, hanging shrouds of Spanish moss.

"What's the plan, guys?" Grant tried not to reveal his mounting anxiety.

Kip turned to Grant. "There's a rogue alligator been eatin' chickens, a couple of good hunting dogs, and one or two of Sam Tillery's calves that came to drink at the edge. It scared hell out of the kids who live around here. We think it's a female that's dug a nest right where Turtle Creek spills out into the swamp about a mile from here."

They pulled up beside a thick stand of palmettos, climbed out, and approached the water's edge in single file.

"This here old boat ain't pretty," Kip said, "but she gets the job done." He pointed at the flattest, most unseaworthy boat Grant had ever seen. The vessel looked like an oversized wash tub with an antiquated Evinrude protruding from its stern. A weary old barge that probably should have been retired years ago.

"It's sort of a converted bass boat, Grant," Kip explained. He turned away to ejaculate another mouthful of tobacco juice, less the thin, saliva-diluted dribble that meandered down his chin. "We're gonna stalk that old gator for awhile an' try to catch her when she ain't lookin'. Just push those gaff hooks aside and have a seat." He grinned and handed Grant a rifle. "Here, you're gonna take a shot at your first gator. Ever fired a .243 before?" His eyes twinkled and his grin widened as though he knew he was looking at a young man whose hands were clearly not those of an outdoorsman.

"No sir, afraid not. My only experience has been hunting squirrels with a .22."

"Well then, Major and me'll try to make this an exciting afternoon for you, boy." Kip pushed the boat away from its mooring and revved up the outboard. He handed Grant a broad-brimmed cowboy hat and a half empty green tube of 50-block sunscreen. "Here, you'll need these. Just smear this bug juice on your face and arms. It don't smell real good but it keeps the skin from burning up, and stinks just enough to keep the swamp angels away."

Grant frowned. "Keep the *what* away?"

"Skeeters, son. Mosquitos to you northerners. They're vampire insects, and they grow big enough out here to steal your lunch."

"Pardon me guys," Grant said, "but I hope we're not going to try to fit an alligator in this thing you call a boat."

Major chuckled. "No, son, we're going to kill it and tow it in."

Enveloped by oppressive humidity and trapped between a merciless sun and its glare off the water, Grant Abbot Lonsdale III found himself in an environment savage and yet so beautiful that it seemed to obliterate everything in his past.

Conversation included only the minimum necessary. The only sounds Grant could hear were the monotonous laboring of the outboard and the occasional hrrrump of a bullfrog. There were brief spells so quiet he could hear himself swallow. Twice, the dull silence was broken by the slapping sound of a largemouth bass re-entering the water after a successful surface-to-air strike on a dragonfly that made the mistake of hovering too close, too long. Now and then a curious snapping turtle's head pierced the surface like a shiny triangular knob, quickly disappearing again as soon as the boat came too close. A water moccasin slithered among the lily pads — a living reminder of Sam Tillery's "cornered cottonmouth" expression.

The little boat glided slowly around the perimeter of the swamp, weaving its way among the canopy of cypress trees from which large, agitated crows cawed out their raucous complaints. Grant scanned the glassy-smooth water until he spotted the animal's head some thirty feet away, almost invisible except for its eyes and the tip of its snout barely protruding above the surface.

"There!" he shouted and raised his rifle. "I see our gator."

"Nope, too small," Major said as he slid a protective hand between Grant's and the trigger. "He's only about eight feet."

"How can you tell that from here?" a somewhat deflated Grant asked, staring transfixed at the sight of his first alligator up close.

"By the distance between his eyes and his snout. Believe me, you'll know the one we're after when you see it."

"I suppose an alligator with jaws that size can crush its victim, right?" Grant hoped the question sounded more intelligent than his last one.

"Yep, he could," Kip answered, "but that ain't how gators kill. A gator will drag you under an' then do his death roll by spinning over and over until you either come apart or drown. That way the gator don't take no chance on you killin' him."

Grant remained silent while he mulled the disconcerting image over in his mind.

Another two hours went by. One by one the three men ate their way down to the last of the sandwiches. Nothing came into view except a few large white herons standing in the shallows, their long, reedy legs almost completely submerged in the dark water. Grant couldn't suppress a grin at the thought of a bird stalking fish with more success than the three men were having hunting their prey. Half a dozen brownish-black buzzards could be seen tearing at the carcass of a dead possum lying on a nearby sand bank. Aside from the mosquitoes swarming about, there were no signs of life.

Grant unintentionally dozed off for a few minutes, amid pleasant thoughts of Sarah. He woke to the explosive sound of an osprey's almost vertical dive toward the water. Grant snapped his head up and turned just in time to see the large bird struggle to rise from the surface. Its extended talons clutched a medium sized largemouth bass, heavy enough to require its captor's maximum effort to gain altitude. The determined osprey refused to release its flapping, twisting, oversized quarry. The predator bird pumped its great wings furiously, bouncing and dragging the fish along the surface for thirty feet before finally gaining altitude. Grant watched, fascinated, as the bird soared skyward, circled, and disappeared over a wall of cypress trees on the horizon.

For one foggy moment Grant's world disappeared into his reflections on what had just happened. The dark, silent swamp came to mind as an unforgiving place of abundant life and swift death, where predator becomes prey without warning. For no apparent reason images of what Salazar Corazon must look like hugged the edges of his thoughts.

Lengthening shadows of cypress trees provided a small measure of relief from the sun and signaled the approach of early evening. The five-gallon jug of orange Gatorade had long since been drained in an only partially successful effort to combat dehydration. The sandwiches were gone, sweat had soaked through most of his clothing, and Grant found himself ready to risk offending his hosts by asking how much longer their quest would continue.

Before Grant could open his mouth, Major raised his hand and, in one swift movement, grabbed his rifle, silenced the engine, and steered the boat toward a secluded inlet. While the boat's momentum continued to carry it silently toward the cove, Kip thrust the .243 into Grant's hands. He directed Grant's attention to the prehistoric beast clinging to the bank, its tail partly submerged. The reptile looked like some overpowering creature straight out of *Jurassic Park*, dangerously close and getting closer as the little boat continued to glide noiselessly toward it.

"Aim at the base of the skull," Kip whispered. He disengaged the safety on Grant's rifle for him. "Then squeeze the trigger slowly. You'll get only one shot, so make it count."

The weapon felt heavier and much more awkward in his hands than the .22 he was used to, and this was no squirrel. Grant fought to shut out visions of what might happen if he missed, or worse, simply infuriated the animal. He lined up the sights with an imaginary spot between the reptile's scaly neck and its huge, triangular head, and squeezed the trigger. The loud crack echoed across the silent swamp at precisely the same moment the beast lunged upward, exposing all sixteen scaly feet of its body.

Enraged, the monster spun around to face them. It opened its cavernous jaws, exposing a deadly array of ugly, unclean teeth designed for tearing meat or snapping the head off a calf. In confirmation of Grant's worst fears, the beast plunged into the water toward them and submerged. The wake of its thrashing tail left no doubt as to its intent to transform the hunters into the hunted.

Seconds later the creature surfaced. With one violent lunge the reptile clamped its jaws tight around the bow of the already time-weakened boat, inches from Kip's feet. At the same moment that two-and-a-half feet of the boat's side collapsed under several thousand pounds of pressure, Major grabbed the rifle from Grant and fired twice into the animal's head. The beast released its crushing grip, rolled over, and began a slow descent to the bottom.

Immobilized, fear rising in his chest, Grant watched Kip drop to his knees in water now streaming into the boat, and plunge the gaffing hook into the gator to arrest its downward progress. In what looked like a single instinctive movement, Major dropped the .243, revved the engine, and steered the sinking vessel toward the nearest shore. Seconds before the boat took on enough water to stop its forward progress entirely, Major beached it on the same bank from which the angry animal had launched its attack. Kip wrapped a nylon line around the animal's upper jaw and tied the other end to a cypress stump to keep the reptile from sliding back in.

Minutes later three soaked hunters, exhausted from dragging the alligator halfway up the bank, sat on a log between a now useless boat and the animal's carcass. Major fired off a cell phone call to a neighboring farmer for help.

Still shaking from the ordeal, Grant tried to collect his thoughts. There they were, waiting for a tiny piece of twenty-first century technology to rescue them from a primordial Darwinian swamp. The whole place seemed too buried in the past to have a future. Once again, Beacon Hill never seemed so far away. Grant thoughts drifted even further, wondering where Sarah might be and what she might be doing. Whether she ever thought of him, and if it would make any sense at all to try to reconnect with her after all these years. It was the second time that thought had crossed his mind.

"Don't look so downhearted, son," Kip wrapped an arm around Grant's slumping shoulders. "Your shot hit right where it was supposed to hit. Look here, see the hole? That ole gator just needed a couple more shots to kill her, that's all."

"Yep, he's right. You did just fine." Major patted him on the back.

Grant forced a smile. He'd come a long way from caring for a pet turtle to killing a several-thousand-pound alligator. The experience produced a strange sense of satisfaction in his realization that he had now, surely, met whatever Angus' criteria were for broadening his horizons. For reasons he couldn't entirely articulate, Grant sensed the beginnings of an unexpected kinship with these down-to-earth people, with their denim shirts and scuffed boots. All the other places on the limited itinerary of his life had been yanked into the twenty-first century's world of Internet technology. Not this place. Anchored to its moss-dripping cypress trees, pampas grass, and palmettos, the whole area seemed to cling tight to a self-made culture the rest of the country had long since given up for dead. Grant's emerging feelings only served to elevate the importance of solving the hatchery's mysteries.

By the time Elmer Bartles and Hank Riefsnyder eased their two powerboats close enough to the bank for the stranded hunters to climb aboard, the sun had almost disappeared behind a wall of cypress trees.

"Damn, Major," Hank blurted out, "looks like you guys done it!" He slapped Kip on the shoulder and turned to fix an inquisitive stare on Grant. "I'm Hank and this is Elmer, son. Don't believe we've met." He held out his hand to Grant while Major helped Elmer re-wrap the gator's jaws and secure the line to Elmer's boat.

"Name's Grant. You guys are a sight for sore eyes. We're glad someone showed up from somewhere in time to keep us from the unique experience of spending the night out here."

Hank grinned. "Well, it seems you showed up from somewhere, too, young man. Now, you wouldn't by any chance be that aristocratic college boy from way up there in Boston, would you?"

Major whirled and fired a glare at Hank. "He ain't no damned aristocrat. He's one of us. And that bullet hole in the back of that ole' gator's head is his."

Hank held up his hands in an apologetic gesture. "Okay, okay. No offense intended. I'm a believer. Welcome to Okeechobee, son. Now, how about we all move on out of here and get you guys dried off?"

With the gator in tow, they made it back to Kip's landing under the light of a pale moon, which cast an eerie glow on the glassy surface of a place where monsters live. After a few creative jokes about what happens when a gator meets a damn Yankee, they parted with a high-five or two. Major dropped Grant off at his motel. A hot shower, a slug of Okeechobee Comfort, and Grant piled into bed too tired to worry about not having had any supper.

Chapter 12

Mignon waited for her husband in the living room, where the Lonsdales held difficult conversations.

A magnificent room, said to be the favorite of Henry Pierpont Lonsdale, the clan's founding father, it dominated the mansion's ground floor. A twelve-foot-wide tapestry depicting Napoleon's victory at the battle of Austerlitz in 1805 hung on the south wall, well lighted by an imported chandelier suspended from the center of a soaring ceiling. A virile stone fireplace dominated the east wall, opposite a sweeping west wall of sturdy, floor-to-ceiling bookshelves fully stocked. On the north wall a forty-eight by forty-eight inch portrait of John Quincy Adams had hung since 1825, the year Renee Pierpont, Henry Lonsdale's mother, ordered the construction of the mansion. Opinions ever since had been evenly split as to whether the building was designed to impress or intimidate. What relationship there might have been between John Quincy and the Lonsdale line was anyone's guess. One rumor held that Renee was John Quincy's mistress prior to her marriage.

The moment her husband walked through the door Mignon handed him his favorite martini, stirred but not bruised. She took his jacket and waited for him to ease his six-foot frame onto the sofa. Patience is a strategy, she frequently remarked, not a virtue. She settled down beside him with her hand on his shoulder. "We need to talk, Grant. It's about Grant Abbot, and it's important."

Her husband leaned back against the cushions, sipped his drink, and paused to stare absently at the tapestry. "Now Mignon, if my memory serves, the living room and martini combination is usually reserved for whenever you're at your wit's end. So, what has our son done this time? Is this about that article in the paper he e-mailed to us? I mean, the one describing his role in that alligator hunt?"

"No, although I'm as upset over that as you should be. My God, a damned swamp venture when he should be preparing himself to take his place at the helm at Concord."

The senior Lonsdale tried unsuccessfully to stifle a chuckle. "True, that was an unexpected detour, but he's one hell of a hero down there. I don't know, maybe it was good training for when he takes over the company. I kind of liked that part about how a visiting Bostonian collaborated with two local hunters to end a monster's reign of terror. Didn't you?"

"No. The whole charade was disgusting. We can talk to him about it when he gets finished down there, if he ever does. He's been there almost a week, now. So much for his little two-day trip. Oh, never mind. I'm much more concerned about a bigger problem we need to deal with right away."

"I'm all ears, honey, as long as we make it quick. I missed lunch and I'm hungry. Let's have it." He yawned and turned to glance at the stone fireplace, as if to check that his favorite piece of décor on the east wall was still in place.

Mignon leaned toward her husband, eyes ablaze with a mixture of frustration and anxiety. "I'm worried that Grant Abbot still hasn't even begun to look for a suitable marriage partner. God knows we've done everything we could to introduce him to the most respectable girls in Boston. He just doesn't seem to understand the importance of a capable wife when he succeeds you."

"Honey, I think he simply isn't ready to make the commitment yet."

"It has nothing to do with commitment. I think it's that other girl. You know the one."

"No," he said, running his index finger gently around the lip of his martini glass before taking another sip. "I have no idea what you're talking about. What girl?"

Mignon bounced up and stood to face him. "I'm referring to that little mouse he met when he cut his foot that time and she patched it up for him. You know, the one whose father was a custodian or something."

He set his martini aside on the end table, and leaned toward her. "Good Lord, Mignon, that was years ago. I'm sure he's forgotten about her by now."

"As a matter of fact, he hasn't. I was in his room glancing at some of his graduate school class notes the other day, and I saw her name scribbled in the margins a couple of times. What I didn't see were any mementos of Harvard, only his wall pennant from that New Haven school. Somehow I think he knows that irritates me."

Grant frowned. "What were you doing in his old room? He's had his own apartment for several years. There's nothing in that room except some outgrown clothes."

"Actually, he stored several years' worth of his papers there. I was, ah, glancing around and I—"

"Damn it, you were spying, Mignon." Grant picked up his drink, took an angry-looking swallow, and set it down again.

She placed her hands on her hips. "Oh all right, so I was spying! It was necessary. That girl is still a threat and you know it." Mignon paced back and forth in front of her husband for a few moments, looked over toward the north wall at the portrait of John Quincy as though she were seeking some kind of authoritative confirmation, and sat down.

Grant scratched his head. "What was the girl's name?"

"Sarah."

"And her last name?"

"Oh, Grant, I don't know and I don't care. We have to do something, that's all I know." Mignon stood again, threw her hands in the air, and renewed her pacing.

"And just what would you suggest?"

She whirled to face her husband. "I suggest you make it unmistakably clear his entire inheritance and, yes, his future depends on his marriage to a respectable girl."

"Mignon, you're way out of line. I would consider that only as a last resort. The fact is he hasn't found a respectable girl yet. At least not one he likes."

"Well, it's about time he started to look, Grant. There are several I can name."

"Like who?"

"Like Victoria Prentiss, Pete Prentiss' daughter. She'd be the perfect wife for him. And Pete's banking connections wouldn't hurt, either."

Grant shook his head. "He doesn't like Victoria Prentiss. Seems I recall his being rather adamant about that the last time you tried to match them up. Look, if we make an issue out of this it'll only make him more determined to resurrect this Sarah thing." Grant glared at her while he polished off the rest of his martini. "You know how he is. Now, I've had a long day and I'm hungry. Let's eat."

"Grant dear, you are burying your head in the sand. After years of hard work we've finally positioned Concord to become a world-class corporation." Mignon kneeled in front of him, leaned forward, and placed her hands on his cheeks, her face almost touching his. "We're almost there, darling. And by the time Grant Abbot is ready to take over, we *will* be there. And he'll need a suitable wife. One who can oversee our investments when I'm too old to do it. We simply *cannot* afford to throw everything away now by condoning our son's affair with a soup kitchen girl."

Grant reached up and gently pulled her hands away from his face. "By that I assume you mean this Sarah girl is either poor or uneducated."

As if in reluctant acceptance of her husband's gesture Mignon placed her hands on his knees. "I mean she's *both*. Have you forgotten already? Good Lord she probably thinks high finance is taking out a loan to buy a used car. Grant, I want you to get our son straightened out. He won't listen to me."

After a long pause her husband let out a heavy sigh, handed her the empty glass, and hauled himself off the sofa. "Okay, I'll have a talk with him as soon as he comes back." He put his hand on her shoulder. "Stop fussing about it. Come on, I'm sure Mary has supper ready by now."

Mary O'Brien Coyne had served the Lonsdales as live-in housekeeper, cook, and surrogate mother to Grant Abbot long enough to know when to announce dinner and when to hold off until living room summit meetings were over. Probably alerted by the quiet that signaled some form of consensus had been reached, Mary ventured into the room, offered a soothing smile, and lowered her head slightly toward Mignon. "Your dinner's on the table, mum. Here, I'll be takin' your empty glass."

Grant seated his wife, reached for his napkin, and settled into his chair at the head of the table. Mignon recognized the mixed expressions of fatigue and puzzlement on his face. They confirmed her suspicion that he didn't know, any more than she did, about what to do with their son.

Chapter 13

No one ever walked unimpeded into Salazar Corazon's office on the twelfth floor of Bogota's Torre Colpatria building. The occupants of the three desks arranged in a semicircle in front of the executive suite were trained to make sure that such a lapse in security never happened. The two men at the desks flanking Salazar's office looked like nerdy white-collar clerks — except for the Smith & Wessons tucked into the shoulder holsters under their suit jackets and the AK-47's slipped under their seats. Even Salazar's soft-spoken secretary, positioned between them at the entrance to his office, had qualified as an expert on the firing range and held a black belt in karate.

Pedro Essante's well-recognized face didn't exempt him from a thorough search before the gatekeepers allowed him to enter in response to Salazar's summons. Pedro settled into one of the leather armchairs in front of his superior's Carpathian Elm oval desk, and laid his twenty-page report on it. "I've completed my investigation of the Bostonian's activity in Okeechobee, Mr. Corazon. You'll find a complete description in this report. May I speak frankly, sir?"

"Of course. You and I have always been able to communicate openly, and I would not want that to change no matter what. I could tell you're troubled, even more so than usual. Speak."

Pedro held his folded his hands in front of him. "Please forgive me for saying this, but I think you made a mistake by allowing this man access to the hatchery. My report is self- explanatory, and I suggest you read it as soon as possible."

Salazar pushed the document aside. "Thank you, Pedro. I'll digest every word in it later. I want to hear your summary first. Right to the point, do you think the young Bostonian is a problem or not?"

His investigation of Grant Lonsdale's activities now completed, Pedro breathed easier than he had in some time despite the worried expression on

96

his face. The shortness of breath produced by his obesity hadn't changed, but his lung function sounded more rhythmical. "I do, Mr. Corazon. My recommendations are in the report. I believe this is something that requires action immediately."

"What kind of action?" Salazar's experience in the narcotics trade had taught him that actions taken in defense of the cartel must be both swift and appropriate to the offense. Delayed or insufficient action conveyed a message of indecision or, worse, weakness. Too harsh an action invited either retaliation or the kind of publicity that invites government intervention.

"The decision on that is yours, sir. But I must tell you this man knows enough right now to destroy your Okeechobee operation. Maybe even you. What we don't know is whether he's transmitted any of his information to anyone else. I'm thinking now of the FBI, for example."

Salazar turned away, picked up Pedro's report, glanced at the cover, and turned the thing over several times without opening it. He put it down and turned to face his subordinate. "And exactly how did you reach that conclusion, Pedro?"

"I base it on a number of my findings, all of which point to the Bostonian's intent to bring the Federales down on you. South Atlantic's long-time employee, Enrico Diaz, has proven to be an effective spy for me. He's turned up valuable information. For example — and this is all in my report — the Bostonian has challenged your man, Tommy Rawls, in a very accusing way. He's charged Rawls with—"

"Excuse me, Pedro. I fail to understand how a field hand becomes privy to a banker's private conversations. Explain, please."

"Yes, sir. It happens the old fashioned way. Enrico sleeps with Mr. Rawls' secretary, Jolene. She despises the intruder who's been sent down here to go through South Atlantic's records. Refers to him as a damned Yankee of the worst kind. She tells Enrico everything. Told him Lonsdale is a direct descendant of General William Tecumseh Sherman. You know, the man who left a trail of—"

"I know who Sherman was. I also know Jolene's opinions are usually unencumbered by factual information of any kind."

"Well sir, Lonsdale questions Maria, the bookkeeper, and inspects the empty shipping boxes Enrico has piled up. He talks to local people about things that are none of his business. He has seen the notes Lonsdale left lying on the conference room table when he's at lunch. What has me puzzled, though, is Enrico's claims that he overhears telephone conversations between

Lonsdale and a man named Conrad Vanderslice in Boston. Wasn't Vanderslice one of your business contacts when you financed the hatchery's initial setup?"

Salazar frowned and his jaw muscles tightened. "I see," he said without answering the question. "Does your report explain the details of those conversations?"

"No, sir. That's still a mystery. But it really doesn't matter. Each time Lonsdale talks to anyone about the hatchery, or our role in it, suspicion is raised somewhere. I'm sure you don't want hostile operations finding out what's going on there anymore than you want drug enforcement agencies poking around in Okeechobee."

Salazar paused to glance out the window, then stood and smiled. "The fact is, I didn't want that young man to be allowed in there at all. But refusal to allow it would have raised suspicion. I've never been comfortable with the involvement of Mayaca Corporation either. However, we need an outlet to route the comingled funds back to the cartel. Anyway, I appreciate what you've done, Pedro. Good work. That'll be all for now. I'll be in touch if I need you after I've read your report."

He slapped Pedro on the back and walked him to the door. "Again, well done, my old friend." Salazar reclaimed his chair and leaned forward with his elbows on the desk and head in his hands. The damned egghead from Boston had now placed the Okeechobee operation in the center of a dangerous triangle consisting of the Federales, a potentially exposed Mayaca Corporation, and the Mexican operation always on the watch for weaknesses in Salazar's Quevedo cartel.

Chapter 14

Line one on Tommy's phone lit up. His secretary's deep southern drawl purred through his speaker. "I have Mr. Corazon on the line, Mr. Rawls."

"Thank you, Jolene." Tommy pressed the button and reached over the deposits summary sheets to pick up. His lips tightened. The deposits reminded him of Grant and his damned allegations. Tommy's underlying anger hadn't subsided. It had simply morphed into a state of chronic discontent, fueled by his growing realization that Grant might be a bulldog that wouldn't let go.

"Good afternoon, Mr. Corazon. Thank you for returning my call. We have an issue here I think we should discuss before our board meeting tomorrow."

"And why can't this wait until I get there?"

"It's urgent, sir."

The response that came after a long pause sounded reluctant. "I'm listening."

"Our intruder from Boston has gone beyond the scope of a normal acquisition review," Tommy continued while he tapped his pen on the table. "He's done exactly what I warned him would give us a legitimate reason to fire him. I think we need to confiscate his papers and computer files. Major and Luanne would never refuse if you insisted on it."

"What exactly has he done, Tommy?"

"He's dug up enough to challenge me personally about the investment money. He's questioned the deposits and the amount paid for the property, plant, and equipment. I don't need threats about the banking commission any more than you need suspicion cast upon your investments and property transactions here. I say this little investigation of his needs to stop. You can put an end to it at the meeting tomorrow."

Another long, ominous silence at the other end of the line reaffirmed what Tommy already knew — Salazar was not a man to allow himself to be intimidated. Tommy fidgeted and resumed his tapping while he waited.

"Firing this man accomplishes nothing, Tommy. Simply postponing the inevitable is not a solution. I'm surprised that a parliamentarian like you has overlooked that such an action would be entered into the board minutes. It would remain there as the kind of evidence which, in itself, would create more than mere suspicion."

"Well sir, then with all due respect, I would suggest, ah, perhaps a more permanent solution. I recommend that—"

"Excuse me, Mr. Rawls. You are not in a position to recommend anything. You are a banker, nothing more. Use your head. Another on-site incident would not survive federal investigation. This will be handled my way. The young man will be taken care of. But it will be done far enough away from the premises to avoid direct connection with South Atlantic Farms."

"You mean like that compu—"

"I mean, Tommy, that the board meeting must be conducted as usual. If it's Major's wish that this man attend, then so be it. I want him to feel completely safe during the few days it will take me to make the necessary arrangements. Your position in this must remain the same as always. Should there be an investigation, you are South Atlantic's banker and financial advisor, and *only* that. I'll see you tomorrow."

* * * * * *

Salazar arrived for the meeting in his customary rented black limousine, with his ape-like bodyguards gathered around him. He and his three barrel-chested companions wore dark, Giorgio Armani suits over Dolce & Garbanna shirts. Of the four, Salazar's was the only suit coat that didn't reveal the bulge of a handgun. Major and Luanne welcomed them courteously, if not enthusiastically.

Salazar hugged Luanne around her shoulders with one arm, while he slid his other hand down to caress her derriere. She jerked herself free and stepped back quickly. Salazar glared at her. His face tightened. Then, as if the incident had never happened, he turned and scanned the room before he sat down, as would one whose daily survival depended on being careful.

Ruiz and Armand pulled up seats protectively flanking Salazar. Chuzo, arms folded across his chest, leaned his thick frame against the door, completing the cordon of security. Tommy filed in behind them and took his customary seat at the head of the table in time to throw a glare at Grant, who slipped in last.

With each glance at the Colombians, Grant found his imagination conjuring up unwanted images of tiny kilo-bags of white powder marching two-by-two into the back door of South Atlantic Farms and parading out the front as neatly wrapped bundles of thousand dollar bills. He couldn't help wondering how many of the white bags it took to support the lifestyles of Corazon and his thugs. They seemed to be of a different world, a place where assassination was probably a routine business transaction, as necessary as it was impersonal. Grant felt a sudden chill.

While Maria served coffee and cookies, Major's brief introduction of Grant met with polite, but expressionless, nods from the four Colombians. As usual, Tommy filled his role as self-appointed master of ceremonies by starting the meeting in proper parliamentary fashion, with a request for approval of the prior meeting's minutes. He then launched into the business at hand, which included a brief discussion of corporate issues in the order in which they appeared on everyone's agenda. Major nodded from time to time, and Luanne took notes. Neither said anything, as though they were either afraid to or didn't feel sufficiently knowledgeable.

Before Tommy could complete his call for a motion to adjourn, Salazar raised his hand to interrupt. He turned an impassive face toward Grant. "Mr. Lonsdale, I understand you've been sent here to review this company. What is the current status of your progress?"

After he exchanged glares again with Tommy, Grant glanced over at Major, as if seeking some sign of approval or otherwise. Major nodded. Grant knew Salazar Corazon was a man of ruthless judgment. It would be unwise to refuse to answer his question. Grant surmised additional time would now be his best ally. That could be purchased only with the kind of comforting response that would provoke no immediate action by Salazar. A lie would be necessary.

"Well sir, I've completed the information-gathering phase," he said with as much confidence as he could gather. "I'm in the process of wrapping up and writing my report. I had a few issues that needed to be addressed, but they've been resolved." Grant deliberately avoided noticing Luanne's startled expression.

"Good," Salazar said with a hungry grin. "When may I look forward to receiving a copy of your report?"

Grant shifted uneasily in his chair. "As soon as my client authorizes its release."

Salazar put his elbow on the table and rested his chin on his fist. "I assume you're referring to Conrad Vanderslice."

Grant sensed a hardening of the tone, and felt on the defensive again. Still, he could think of no logical reason not to answer the question. "Yes."

Salazar's feral face tightened. He fixed his cold, dead eyes first on Major, then on Grant. "Get the authorization as soon as you can. I want to read your report."

Grant nodded. "Yes sir, I will."

Small talk followed until the coffee and cookies were depleted, after which a more relaxed Tommy Rawls wound up the business formalities and called for adjournment. He followed the Colombians out, while Luanne carefully positioned herself behind Grant to block any further attempts by Salazar to hug her. She didn't release Grant's arm until everyone disappeared from view.

He could see tears welling up in her eyes.

She released his arm, and looked up into his face with the desperate expression of someone who had just been betrayed. "Grant, why did you decide to quit on us like that? I thought you were going to help get us out of this."

"I'm not quitting. I had to say something that would convince these guys I was no longer a threat to them. If they—"

"What are you talking about?" She threw him an incredulous look.

"Never mind. I'm simply saying I'm not quitting. You can count on that."

She smiled and wiped her eyes. "Oh Grant, I didn't really think you'd leave us. And I'm sorry for all the things I said to you that day we met. And for all the bad thoughts I had about you. Forgive me?"

Grant shook his head. "Forget it. I must have looked to you like the grim reaper coming to take your future away. I guess I was looking at it as a simple, straightforward assignment, and failed to appreciate the internal dynamics of the whole thing. Look, I've bought some time today, but not much. I'm going to have to put all my findings together sooner than I originally thought."

"Why? What happened?"

"Do you remember when I told Corazon I needed my client's permission to release my findings?"

"Yeah. What about it?"

"Well, Corazon knew my client is Conrad Vanderslice. No one at South Atlantic told him that. So he could only have found out from Tommy Rawls.

Conrad owns Mayaca Corporation. I don't know why it's taken me so long to figure this out. Corazon, Rawls, Vanderslice, and Mayaca are in this together. That means I need to get the feds involved, like right away, even though I'm still missing some parts to this puzzle."

"What parts?"

"First, the real reason why Vanderslice sent me down here; second, proof about those damned deposits. Anyway, where has Major gone?"

"He went out to the quarantine tank to check on a new South American shipment that just came in. Come on, let's meet him down there."

* * * * * *

The evening shadows vanished with the last remnants of dusk. Except for Major's flashlight beam bobbing up and down, Grant and Luanne found the quarantine room completely dark.

"Luanne, why is your father working without turning on the lights?"

"Daddy prefers to peek into the tanks with a flashlight when he examines a new shipment. He says the overhead lights rouse the fish and they move around too much."

Grant scratched his head. "This may be a dumb question. Do fish actually sleep in the dark?"

"No, not really. They just remain sluggish. Where are you going?"

"Nowhere in particular. Just looking at those boxes. I'll join you two in a minute."

Luanne walked over and put her arm around her father. "Daddy, how does the new batch look?"

"Perfect, honey. Or at least as close to that as it gets. Where'd Grant go off to?"

"I think he's right outside messing around with the boxes the last shipment came in."

"Why? They're empty. Tell him to come on in. There's something I want to show him. I'll bet he's never seen coal black angel fish before."

"Grant, come here for a minute," she yelled. "Daddy wants to show you something."

It took him a few minutes to maneuver around a network of PVC pipe lines, the veins and arteries of the hatchery's life support system. Grant shook his head. "Okay, but I can tell you this place wasn't designed much for walking around in the dark. Anyway, I have a question. I noticed some of the boxes show a Miami origination, and some look like they come directly from South America. I thought you said they all came from South America."

"They do, Grant, but some are held up in Miami for inspection and repacking by one of Aqua Star's handling stations."

"Why?"

"Well, if the shipment has been delayed enroute and sat around too long there may be some damage to the fish."

"Oh. Well, what happens if one of those boxes starts to leak during shipment, or while it's waiting around in Miami? Wouldn't the whole batch of fish die?"

"The boxes won't leak. They're double layered with an inner and outer shell. The outer shell would absorb any blow to the box to prevent penetration of the inner layer. Now, come, look at these new angels."

Grant had seen black angels before, but none of breeding size like the large, discus shaped fish illuminated by Major's flashlight. Grant moved in closer to watch the probing beams sweep their way around the dark tank.

"What's Major doing?"

"He's looking for signs of disease or fungus while the fish are still sluggish."

Luanne watched her father. "What do you think, Daddy?"

"Well, looks like this one's a damned good shipment, I'll say that. I guess we're done here for tonight, but we'll watch 'em a few more days before we turn 'em loose in the ponds. C'mon, kids, let's go for a walk."

They strolled over to the edge of the nearest pond where hundreds of angels were growing to breeding size. The early moon cast an eerie light on the surface, and a gentle breeze drifted in listlessly from the southwest, carrying the scent of freshly mown grass from between the ponds. It nudged the branches of the crape myrtles lining the path to the ponds, until their loose petals drifted like snowflakes to the ground.

All three stood in silence, listening to the cicadas and the syncopated croaking of frogs. The screech of a broad winged hawk echoed from a treetop and pierced the quiet air. Grant sensed again that more than distance separated Beacon Hill from these people and this anachronistic place, where alligators and armadillos crawled about as living footprints of a prehistoric age. Still, he felt a sense of camaraderie with these people — or, at least most of them — drawn together in the presence of a carefully veiled evil.

An uninvited recollection of his mother's reference to the locals as "hillbillies" stabbed into the heart of his peaceful reminiscence. He'd begun to understand their culture and the land from which it derived its vitality in a way he felt sure his family never would. In sharp contrast, the Lonsdale version of heritage required the perpetuation of family wealth through strategic alliances with people who promised an equivalent contribution of assets. This, in turn, demanded the kind of self discipline which prohibited impulsive freedom of social tolerance.

People like the Gibbs, he'd been taught, were not the kind with whom empires could be built. Grant cursed his self-destructive obedience to parental obsession with ancestral purity.

Chapter 15

Sam Tillery offered a choice between jeep and horseback when he invited Grant to tour his ranch with him. The jeep decision seemed like a no-brainer. Wrong choice — there were no roads through the ranch.

"Horseback might have been an easier ride for you, Grant," Sam said, seconds after the jeep began its thump and bump itinerary over the rough terrain. "But I didn't want to influence you one way or the other, not knowing how familiar you were with horses."

"Not a problem, Sam. I haven't ridden anything down here yet that didn't end up way off the beaten path somewhere. Even the boats I ride in don't seem to stay afloat."

Sam slapped his thigh, threw his head back, and let out a loud belly laugh. "Yeah, I heard about your swamp adventure. I see you three guys made the front page. Nice photo of the gator. That was one big mama. Congratulations."

"Thanks, but I really wasn't much help. So tell me about your ranch and the cattle I almost ran over." He'd always thought of ranching as a sort of a monoculture unique to places like Texas or Oklahoma.

Sam flashed a broad grin. "You may not believe this, but Florida is one of the leading cattle producing states in the country. Here in Okeechobee County it outranks dairy and citrus production. The early pioneers started with imported breeds from Spain and other countries, then they gradually moved into mixed breeding involving Angus and Hereford stock. They eventually developed hybrids that could thrive in Florida's hot, humid climate."

Sam maneuvered the vehicle to avoid the cattle and a group of little white cattle egrets busy stabbing the ground between the feet of their milling food sources. He gestured with a sweep of his arm. "Now, all across here you'll see wiregrass, some of it burned. That's because, if you burn it in the winter, the flatwoods and grass offer more nutritious spring feeding for the cattle. And since cows drop their calves in the spring, it works out for the whole herd."

Grant had seen Jerseys and Holsteins before, but they didn't look anything like the creatures milling around him. Dark grayish in color and hump-shouldered, the animals' horns curved up before pointing outward. They looked almost identical to cattle he'd seen as a child when his parents took him on a tour through India. "What kind of cattle are those?" he asked, his curiosity outweighing his reluctance to ask a stupid question. "They look like the one that almost decorated my car."

"Brahmans. I have a lot of them, as do many of the ranchers in South Florida. What you're seeing now is the foreign influence of the kind you won't see up in the Northeast."

"How do you round up all those cattle?" Grant asked, hoping to chance upon an intelligent question.

"Well, sometimes we use what's known as 'catch dogs' because they're willing to jump into ponds, snake-infested swamps, and thick palmetto bushes to herd out wandering calves. But most of the time we do it like anyone else would, except that we use braided whips. Western ranchers don't have much use for 'em, but they come in handy around here. In fact, whip braiding is a craft done right here in Okeechobee County."

The more Grant sensed he was beginning to know Sam, the more he recognized in him the same ingrained pride in the land he'd observed in Luanne. He felt an unexpected surge of respect for these people, and all that they represented. He closed his eyes for a moment while his thoughts drifted into the realm of imagination. He saw Spanish explorers chopping their way through the distant palmettos and wading across shallow swamps at the edge of what was now Sam's ranch. He wondered if the land appeared as strange to them as it had to him.

The careening jeep, weaving around grazing cattle, forced him back into reality. He couldn't help smiling at the memory of Angus' challenge to expand the boundaries of his experience. Grant watched a soaring hawk make its sudden descent, talons forward, toward some hapless creature. The kill took place silently in the deep, yellow grass. A few moments later the bird rose skyward with its quarry hanging limp in its grasp.

A stand of trees seemed to appear out of nowhere, after the jeep bounced through a shallow creek bed. At first they didn't see the ugly, black, grunting animal coming out of the grove toward them. Sam reached over Grant's shoulder and pulled a rifle from behind him. The creature stopped short, as if having realized the jeep was a larger animal that couldn't be frightened away. Its beady eyes glared malevolently. It pawed the ground with its hind legs, gave out a final grunt, and trotted back into the thick brush. It turned once to throw one last agitated snort over its shoulder before it disappeared. Sam returned the rifle to its original position.

"What in the hell was that?" Grant asked, in a low, nervous tone. He tried hard not to show the same kind of fear that gripped him at the sight of the alligator a few days before.

"A wild boar." Sam turned the wheel to avoid the trees. "They're predators that sometimes kill and eat newborn calves. They also make one hell of a mess rooting around. But I guess you've gotten pretty used to predators after your meeting with that old gator."

"Sam, I don't think I'll ever get used to them. That boar looked mad enough to be dangerous."

"Yep, you wouldn't want to be walking around here by yourself without a rifle. They're ornery, and they'll charge. Their tusks can do some real damage."

"Not that I'm concerned about it, but I heard something about panthers around here. Are they native to the area?" Grant tried to conceal his anxiety under the guise of a casual remark.

"Well, the Florida Panther has a pretty wide roaming range," Sam answered, as though he either hadn't noticed, or pretended he didn't. "They wander about once in awhile down here, but you don't see them very often. They're pretty wily."

The tour lasted another hour, after which Grant's backside began to feel the effects of riding in a jeep with shock absorbers that had long since retired from active duty. Aside from a small rattlesnake scurrying into the scrubs, the only other wildlife they came across were the ubiquitous cattle egrets and a gathering of buzzards fighting over the carcass of a dead armadillo. The motley birds squabbled over each bite. Dirty, black-brown colored scavengers, they performed nature's necessary waste disposal function with remarkable efficiency. Like some of the other strange wildlife he'd seen during the past few days, the buzzards, Grant surmised, must belong to a primitive natural order of things the twenty-first century had bypassed. The ranch, the swamps, and even Major's ponds, all seemed part of an anachronistic world where humans and beasts co-existed on more or less equal terms imposed by nature, not technology.

By the time they completed the tour, their skin shone with perspiration. Sam parked the jeep next to a house guarded by a stone Spanish archway fashioned in stucco and embedded with cocina shells. Grant noted the inscription *Hacienda de Cuidad de Hierba* carved in the stone. The sprawling, one-story building looked like nothing Grant had ever seen before. Sam led him into the kitchen, reached into the fridge, and set a six-pack of cold beer on the table.

Grant stared at a painted mural that told the story of Juan Ponce de Leon and the first Europeans to set eyes on Florida in 1513. While New England's colonial history echoed throughout the world, the flatlands of South Florida could only whisper the myths of the conquistadors and the legendary fountain of youth. "Sam, I thought Boston had a lock on unusual interiors, but this place is a first. I understand your kitchen-wall mural but I'm not sure what the inscription on the outside archway means."

"The house is an old Spanish design I modified a bit. The inscription reads 'House of the City of Pasture Grass.' My own private reference to the good grazing land I have for my cattle. The mural shows Ponce de Leon and a few of his conquistadors in claiming Florida for Spain in 1513." He pulled a beer from the six-pack. "Like I told you that night at Essie Mae's, you'll see a lot of things down here you've never seen before. So grab a beer and tell me how you're coming on that survey of yours. You about got it all done?"

Grant took a gulp of his beer. "No, I haven't, although I'm glad you brought it up. I've wanted to talk with you about that… and a few other things. I'm telling you this because I trust you to keep it confidential. I told Tommy Rawls and Corazon I'd finished everything except writing up my report. I said it because I now believe that little hatchery is a bomb waiting to explode."

Grant went on to explain that Corazon and Tommy already knew what he'd dug up. But they didn't yet think he'd figured out what those discrepancies meant, or what he'd planned to do about them. "It won't be long before they do. And then they'll be coming after me. I think Major, Luanne, and Maria will be next. I'm going ahead with my review, but I don't have much more time before they figure out what I'm up to. I have a private investigator friend of mine helping me sort this all out."

"Sam, you've known the Gibbs family ever since they moved here," Grant concluded. "I was hoping you might be able to fill me in on the history of that fish farm, and what's been going on there. As far as I can tell, Major and Luanne are too scared of the Colombians to say anything. Plus, they're afraid they might lose South Atlantic Farms completely. They're caught between the proverbial rock and a hard place right now."

Sam reached for the six-pack, pulled out two more cans, and handed one to Grant. He leaned back in his chair while he took a leisurely gulp before responding. Grant had seen him pause like that before, when he was about to offer a significant observation. After a few moments he put the beer down and leaned forward toward his guest. "Grant, how much do you know about Miranda, Luanne's mother?"

"Nothing, really. Major told me she died right before Luanne finished high school."

"Did he tell you how she died?"

"No. I just assumed it was cancer or something. Why?"

Another few gulps, another pause. "She drowned. Major and Luanne were out of town picking up a shipment of fish or something. A field hand found her face down in one of those little ponds they have all over the place. Major went berserk and drained that pond. He let all the fish in it die, filled it with dirt, and never used it again. Almost like he was trying to bury the bad memory under all that dirt and punish the fish for what happened."

Grant shook his head. "I can almost picture Major doing that. I'm sorry. So, what happened then?"

"They said it was a heart attack," Sam went on to explain, "but I don't think an autopsy was ever done. Tommy Rawls acted as the family spokesman at the time because Major and Luanne were in such a state of grief. Tommy determined that neither an autopsy nor an investigation was necessary. Just between you and me, Grant, I've always thought the whole thing stinks. I questioned the medical examiner about it right afterward. He supported the heart attack theory, and I doubt anyone ever really looked into it after that."

"Which field hand discovered the body, Sam?"

"Ahhhh…I think it was the one who examines the incoming shipments. Can't remember his name."

"Enrico Diaz?"

"Yeah, that's the one. You know him?"

"No, but he's the one who takes the money to the bank, gets Tommy to review the deposit slip, then gives it to Maria who posts it to the ledger. You sound like you think Luanne's mother's death was caused by something other than a heart attack."

Sam drained the can, pulled a couple of cigars from his pocket and extended one to Grant, who put up his hand to reject the offer. "Well, talking about discrepancies," Sam continued as he lit his up, "I can tell you a few sure went down over Miranda's death. For one, it apparently happened at night, which made me wonder what Miranda was doing wandering around out there after dark. She was the bookkeeper, pretty much an indoor person, unlike Major and Luanne. She had no interest at all in the fish or their breeding, only her family and the business. So it would have to have been one hell of an event to get her out there at night by herself. She was considerably younger than Major, with no apparent health problems. In other words, I guess I've never really bought into that heart attack ruling."

"Sam, do you happen to remember the date she died?"

"No, not exactly. Let me see…it was two or three years ago, I guess. Right after that computer guy took off while he was smack in the middle of chasing down some software bug in their computer. Miranda got left holding the bag right in the middle of their year-end accounting closing. Worst possible time, but she was pretty good at solving computer problems. She fixed it by herself, I'm told."

"Do you happen to know the computer consultant's name?"

"No, but Luanne or Major could tell you. Look, Grant if you think the Colombians are a threat to you, you need to get the police involved."

"I can't."

"Why not?"

"For one thing, it's a federal matter, and the local cops probably won't want to get involved. For another, I'm not sure the local police aren't tied in, somehow, to this whole thing. I don't think this scam could have persisted so long without some kind of local protection."

"Okay, young man, I don't like your answer on that one. But like I told you before, you gotta do what you gotta do. I guess you know your business. Now, I have to get back to work. There's a lot needs doing around here before the sun goes down. You know, I always thought people up in your neck of the woods were social snobs, but you've changed my mind. You take care of yourself. Let me know what turns up. By the way, if those Colombian boys start to come too close and you need help, you call me, understand? I'm pretty good with a gun, and I can hustle over there fast."

"You have a deal. Thanks for everything. I've a feeling a showdown with the Colombians isn't far away."

Chapter 16

When Luanne knocked on his motel door, Grant was wrapped in a comfortable cocoon of solid slumber. At first, he resisted the invasive sounds by pulling the covers over his head and trying to draw himself deeper into the cocoon. The knocking grew persistently louder, accompanied by the sound of his name. Once his protective unconsciousness yielded to the sound of urgency in her voice, he felt himself being dragged into the world he thought he'd left behind.

The little bedside battery-operated digital clock's red numbers glowed five minutes after midnight. He kicked away the sheets, swung his legs over the side of the bed, wrapped a bath towel around his waist, and stumbled to the door.

"Hi," she said, standing there in nothing more than shorts, a sweatshirt with her high school logo, and a sheepish smile. "My air conditioner went out. I just got a little lonely and wanted some company. Mind if I stay here tonight? I won't bother you."

Still half asleep, he reached the fuzzy conclusion that letting her in would probably generate fewer repercussions than sending her away. Grant rubbed his eyes and motioned her in. After he'd blinked away the last remnants of sleep, he turned to smooth out the sheets on what he planned to designate as her side of the bed. By the time he finished and turned to face her Luanne had removed her clothes and stood before him completely naked.

Until now, Grant had been able to successfully suppress any visible reaction to her compelling sensuality. This had been made possible partly by the fact that she had always remained fully clothed, and partly by his simply turning away and focusing on other things. The sight of her, more voluptuous than he had ever imagined, obliterated all his defenses.

She let her long blonde hair down for the first time he could remember. She allowed it to flow loosely over her shoulders like a golden waterfall in a way that brought out the softness of her upper body and the firmness of her ample breasts. His bath towel turned out to be unequal to the task of concealing the effects of such stimulation, to which she responded with a knowing and mildly triumphant smile.

"Grant, I didn't mean to startle you," she cooed softly. "It's just that I always sleep this way. I hope you don't mind." She slid onto his bed in a movement that went beyond seductive — an almost irresistible combination of her beauty and athleticism. She smiled and motioned him to join her under the sheets.

The sudden emotional collision between his painful craving to enjoy what might easily be the best sex ever, and that damnable little voice in the back of his mind that told him this was the wrong time, the wrong place, and the wrong girl, left him standing virtually paralyzed in the middle of the room. "Luanne," he began haltingly, groping for words that would give both of them a way out with some measure of dignity, "I can't do this."

He couldn't believe what he'd just said. Luanne's eyes widened and her jaw dropped in a silent affirmation that she couldn't believe it either.

"Oh, Grant," she countered in the tone of a mother scolding her child, "We both know you want to."

At that precise moment the doors of his subconscious flew open and the demons he'd imprisoned there rushed to escape. He realized, for the first time, what he'd never been able to admit to his parents, or even to himself. His hesitance to make love to Luanne had nothing to do with moral considerations or even his personal respect for both her and Major. It was Sarah. By defending his conviction that he'd done the right thing in rejecting her, he'd spent years denying the wrong of it. His noble surrender of love in exchange for inherited obligations had, he now understood, been a hollow sacrifice.

"Luanne, it's a long story I don't care to get into right now. Please put your clothes back on. It's better that you go home before Major finds out and gets so mad he throws me off this job right on the spot." Grant stepped back, bracing himself for the expected reaction of a woman scorned. Her silent glare could mean almost anything, so he waited, his loins still aching.

She glared at him, picked up a pillow, and threw it in his face. Then, much to his surprise, she slipped back into her sweatshirt, pulled her shorts on, kissed him on the cheek, and walked out without a word.

He threw himself backward onto the bed and stared blankly at the ceiling. What had just happened was excruciatingly real. Still, the bizarre nature of it made it seem like a dream from which he had just awakened. Whether he wanted it that way or not, the event made him realize he'd only been partly alive before. The denim-clad people of this rivergrass country had forced him to recognize who he was. Luanne had exhumed the truth he'd interred nine years before, and forced his discovery of who he wasn't.

Grant felt a sickening sensation that his life had been moving in the wrong direction, and he could no longer blame it entirely on the restrictions of his ancestry. He recalled a Japanese expression: *unmei wo seisu,* which meant "I control my destiny." From this moment on his destiny, he decided, would be of his own making.

No longer in a mood for sleeping, Grant jerked himself to a sitting position and threw his legs over the side of the bed. He leaned forward with elbows on his knees and lowered his face into his hands. Thoughts raced in rapid succession through his mind while he tried to reconcile his past with visions of his future. Okay, what exactly *is* my destiny? My chances of reconnecting with Sarah are slim at best, although parental approval if I do is irrelevant. I don't give a damn whether they like her or not. If I can't marry Sarah I don't need a wife. I can run Concord without one.

Grant slammed his fist into the wall, took a long shower, and tried to recover whatever might be left of a good night's sleep.

* * * * * *

An early morning rain pounded on the conference room window for several hours before it surrendered to a bright sunshine that seemed hotter than usual for the season. Infuriated by his failure to find the secrets buried in the documents piled on the table, Grant felt like sending them flying with a sweep of his arm. No doubt about it, he thought, South Atlantic Farms had become a conduit into which drug money entered dirty and came out clean. Grant didn't have to ask what happened to the fourteen million of invested drug proceeds, or all the narcotics-funded property, plant, and equipment acquisitions. For seven years the Colombian drug lords had raped the hatchery. Genetically cleansed in its unresisting womb, the bastard funds emerged to find immediate adoption in Tommy Rawls' bank.

The whole damned dirty-to-clean transition of the money seemed neat and simple — all except for the proof, his pursuit of which had now reached the point of diminishing returns. He knew he had to establish some form of defensible documentation before he could make a case for federal intervention. He also knew the Feds would want to be sure the fourteen million represented a laundering of narcotics money rather than a perfectly legitimate business transaction.

Grant walked away from the conference table and wandered over to the fish room, brightened enough by the sun that he could watch the fish gliding about without having to turn on the tank lights. Once again, the soft hum of the aerator pumps sent waves of relaxation through his body, washing the tension away. He made a mental note that, when he returned to Boston, he would build a room like this in his own house someday and fill it with softly humming tanks and colorful little occupants to transport his mind to gentle places far away.

His graduate school instructors had been adamant about critical analysis. The student either learned to think abstractly, unchained by immediate circumstances, or that student would not remain enrolled for long. The business school's curriculum had been designed to put a premium on resourceful and holistic thought. Grant had managed to do it well when he was there. Yet there had been only a few occasions since when he'd found it necessary. Theorists called it "thinking out of the box." Grant disdained the expression because he considered it trite.

In the quiet of this underwater world he could shut out the chaos of unresolved discoveries, and free his mind to brainstorm their possible underlying causes. Grant began to examine his problems from a different perspective.

Okay, start from the beginning, he muttered to himself. Major, Luanne, and Maria are the only ones with a hands-on connection to the hatchery's information system…and they don't really understand it. Rawls set the thing up and he's hiding what he knows is in it. Corazon never demanded an audit — an egregious violation of his fiduciary responsibility. Only Luanne's mother and a computer consultant were involved with the system intimately enough to know its contents. Miranda's dead and the consultant is gone. Rawls has probably aborted any subsequent investigation.

That leaves Clete Morris as the only other savvy person, and the druggies have obviously shut him up because he's holding back something. Bottom line: all those who could possibly know anything have been silenced one way or the other. What did they know? And did it put their lives at risk? Time to reactivate Chad Winslow.

* * * * * *

After his encounter with Luanne the night before, Grant found himself reluctant to approach her until she felt ready to talk to him. Nonetheless, he needed answers that couldn't be postponed any longer. He stiffened his resolve and tracked her down in the breeding tank area.

She smiled at him, as though the events the night before had never happened. He stood back while she turned away and poured a container of small, live creatures he didn't recognize into one of the vats of angels, and watched the angels swarm to feed voraciously on the hapless little things. She put the container down and turned back to face him.

"Good morning. Grant. You look like you're lost. What brings you out here?"

"Good morning, Luanne. I guess we need to find time to resolve what happened last night, but right now I need to know why that computer consultant walked out, and where I can reach him."

"I have no idea why he quit, except he spent more time pestering my mother about something than he did trying to fix the computer. She finally got mad at him. I guess he got kind of mad, too." She bent over to pick up a box of tiny instruments. "They had a real nasty argument. He left the next day and never came back. But his name and number are still in our computer files under the corporate designation Soft Care."

"What were they arguing about?"

"Oh, I don't know. I think he criticized the way she posted transactions to the ledger or something." She paused for a moment to check the salinity in another tank. "I think she told him to mind his own business and stick to the job of fixing the hard drive. Anyway, she fixed the problem herself after he disappeared."

"Luanne, did anyone else know about the argument?"

"Good grief! How should I know? Who cares, anyway?"

"It might be important, Luanne. Try to remember. Did your mother tell anyone other than Major and you about it?"

Luanne rolled her eyes to make sure he knew she considered it a ridiculous question, and pouted while she thought about it. "Yeah, I guess I told Tommy about it because the argument had been partly about cash, and I

116

knew my mother relied on him. Tommy thought the computer guy was just being a jerk, too."

Grant shook his head. "I should have known Tommy Rawls would be involved. Okay, I'll check it out." He started to say something about what had happened the night before but thought better of it and simply walked away.

Chapter 17

Grant's walk back to the conference room didn't make him sweat this time, which suggested either a significant climate cooling had begun or he was becoming accustomed to the local temperature. He slumped down in a chair and kicked off his shoes. His thoughts of dozing off for a few minutes were interrupted by the sound of his cell phone. He clicked it on to the sound of an excited Chad Winslow.

"Grant old buddy, I have some interesting information for you. You're going to love this."

"Good. I was just about to call you. I've some information too. You go first."

"Okay, here it is. Salazar Corazon has significant investments in two other hatcheries in Florida, and a restaurant. South Atlantic Farms is his largest hatchery, according to my research. Now, get this. At two of the other places the accountant was fired and replaced by some clerk, or someone who had no accounting or bookkeeping training. At one of them the accountant apparently died in an automobile accident. The official report called it a DUI, but my sources tell me that the girl was a complete teetotaler. Kind of strange, don't you agree? Okay, you said you wanted to tell me something. What do you have?"

"Chad, I know the fourteen million paid out to set up South Atlantic Farms was drug money, but how do I prove it? I mean, I don't think I can get the Feds involved without some kind of proof. What are my options?"

"Well, based on what you've already told me, I'd say the proof is right in front of you. You said the investment was far in excess of the normal cost to acquire those assets. You also said the hatchery's dividend payouts to the investors were far in excess of normal payout ratios. So don't you have average industry statistics to support your allegations?"

Grant shifted in his chair. "Yes. But how do I prove the excesses represented drug money being comingled with legitimate money to cleanse it?"

"You don't have to. All you have to do is lay all the transaction documents in front of the Feds, along with your industry statistics and all the other facts you've uncovered. They'll trace the money through Mayaca, where you already said it went, and out to the cartel along with the dividends."

"Okay, that sounds simple enough. Let's call the Feds and do it."

"Hold on a minute, Grant. It's not quite that simple. There are two problems. One, the Feds will probably want to close down Mayaca Corporation long enough to do a fraud audit. That's going to alert the cartel, giving your druggies time to obliterate evidence. Two, your friends Major and Luanne Gibbs are going to find themselves in a heap of trouble, since they were dividend recipients along with the Colombians."

"Major and Luanne are innocent, Chad. They were clueless at first, and I have reason to believe they're too terrified to say anything now. They can't be blamed."

"Oh yes they can. Grant, my friend, I hate to tell you this, but pleading ignorance is not going to be an option for anyone who's received large sums of narcotics money over a seven year period."

"Aw, come on, Chad. Until recently they had no idea it was dirty money. They're guppies swallowed by a damned shark."

"Doesn't matter. The law isn't going to ask *did* they know. It's going to ask *should* they have known. The minute the feds get into this your friends are going down, and there's nothing you can do about it."

"Damn it, Chad, that's a bunch of garbage!"

"Sorry, old buddy. It is what it is. You're the one who asked the question. You're going to have to resign yourself to their inevitable conviction as felons. We're talking federal offense here. So what other questions do you have?"

Engrossed in his thoughts, Grant didn't respond — If Chad's right and the Gibbs are inexorably caught in the stranglehold of their own past, then the past has to be changed.

"Grant?"

"Yes. I was just trying to think of a way out of this."

"There is no way. Now, what else do you have?"

Grant took in a deep breath and paused for a moment. "Ahhh...I need you to locate a computer consultant named Carlton Feicke who was employed by an outfit called Soft Care. But their number is no longer in service. Now, I've a question which you probably can't answer. I'll ask it anyway, and maybe you can find out if you don't know. Can a medical examiner identify the exact cause of death on a body that's been exhumed after three years? And what protocol is required to have it exhumed?"

"Jeez, Grant. What kind of questions are those? Hell, I don't know. Why? Are you adding a corpse now to all the mess you've gotten yourself into down there?"

"Yes, I'm afraid I am. Check on it for me, will you? If I question any of the authorities around here I'm only messing with the good old boy network. Our lives will be even more at risk than they already are." Grant wasn't sure whether the long pause at the other end of the line indicated an affirmative response was forthcoming or an articulate Chad Winslow counterargument.

"Listen, Grant, I'm not talking to you now as an investigator. I'm talking to you as your friend and former roommate. Get out of there. That place is a death trap. You're riding on the back of a hungry lion about to decide that you're its next meal. Go home."

"Believe me, Chad, I intend to as soon as I can. But I'm not the only one at risk here right now. So just do as I ask. And call me as soon as you can, okay?"

"Okay, it's your funeral. But I'll tell you this. You're one hell of an optimist."

"Is that so? Define optimist, Chad."

"Sure, okay. It's a camper who wakes up in his tent in the middle of the night to a swarm of mosquitoes buzzing around his head and assumes they're just looking for a way out. Talk to you later. And by the way, that part about the funeral was just an expression. I didn't mean it literally."

* * * * * *

The trail had come to a dead end. Grant knew that unless Chad could come up with something conclusive, he faced a simple Hobson's choice. He could reveal what he'd found so far, with only his analysis of the transactions to back up his allegations. Or, he could face the unappealing prospect of calling in from the outside someone more capable than he was to solve the deposits problem and provide defensible proof of money laundering. A clear failure on his part to solve the problem either way, but time was running out.

He'd begun to think seriously of opting for the latter course of action when Luanne stole in quietly and sat down beside him.

"Grant, I want to apologize for last night. I had no right to presume things like I did. I hope you'll forgive me. I want you to know I was sincere about my feelings for you and they went beyond sex. I could have competed with any previous girlfriend you may have had. But I know now I can't compete with a ghost."

"What do you mean a ghost?"

"I mean Sarah. I've known about her ever since you began cluttering up our conference room with your junk."

It was the second time in twelve hours she'd rendered him almost speechless. Who could have told her? Even *he* hadn't put it all together until last night. His thoughts became words almost before he knew it.

"Who told you about Sarah?"

"You did, Grant. I saw her name scribbled in the margin of your notes after you finished all that stuff about the stock prices we paid. In fact, you doodled her name a couple of times since then. You must really love her. Who is she?"

He pondered the question while she waited. The irony of this is that I have no idea any more who she is. Only who she was. I shut her out of my life for reasons I didn't completely understand then and can't accept now. Luanne has it right again. For all intents and purposes, Sarah *is* a ghost. How could what I did to her then be explained in any rational manner now?

"Luanne," he began, in the manner of a public speaker who had just thrown away carefully prepared notes in order to speak from the heart, "you probably won't believe this, but I put family obligations above love a long time ago and abruptly ended my relationship with Sarah for all the wrong reasons. Some mistakes you can recover from after awhile. Some, as I'm now discovering, you pay for the rest of your life."

He felt a sense of hopelessness engulf him again, and he turned away. He remembered an accountant friend of his who described guilt as nothing more than an emotional debt. In a typically accountant-like way, his friend defined it as "a present feeling of obligation to make a future payment in compensation for a past transaction that should have been avoided." Grant understood, for the first time, what the expression meant.

Luanne laid a hand on his knee and shook her head. "Grant, didn't they teach you anything at school? You're a really smart guy but sometimes you act like you don't have enough common sense to come in out of the rain. Use your head. Go find Sarah. Daddy always told me if you don't face your demons, they'll haunt you forever. I had to face mine when Mom died. Now you need to face yours. I want you, Grant, but not like this. Either reconnect with Sarah or find out she's no longer available. Put an end to this once and for all."

There wasn't much he could think of to say. He wiped his eyes with the back of his hand and smiled at her. "Thanks, Luanne, for more than I know how to express."

"Don't thank me. I was being selfish. I just didn't want to spend the rest of my life kicking myself for losing out to a damned ghost. So, go find her. But get us out of this mess with Corazon first." She stood and walked out, leaving him alone to wrestle with his thoughts.

Grant closed his eyes for a moment — his first mistake of the day. The familiar shroud of guilt wrapped itself around him again. Like the ghost of Christmas past, it dragged his mind back to South Boston, to the scene he'd spent almost a decade trying to forget.

He could see Sarah sobbing uncontrollably, a pretty girl in a cheap dress — polyester, maybe, or a bargain outfit right off a consignment rack. She held her arms out to him, tears cascading down her cheeks. She pleaded with him to tell her what she'd done wrong to make him not love her anymore. The uninvited flashback vanished as quickly as it came, leaving him with the same hollow feeling he'd had when he ended their relationship nine years before.

* * * * * *

Grant's most recently encountered unknown factor in the whole money laundering mess became how much time he had left before the cartel figured out what he was up to. If that wasn't bothersome enough, the growing recognition of the horrible mistake he'd made with Sarah was.

When they were roommates, Chad had authoritatively proclaimed, more than once, that the concept of there being only one special girl for each guy was pure myth. Chad contended there were at least half a million girls with whom any man could find a suitable relationship. And, to prove his point, Chad made every effort to have sex with as many of them as he could. At the time, Grant tried to believe such things because he needed to believe them. Yet, every girl he met since had simply failed to measure up to Sarah, or at least to his painfully sequestered memory of her. Now, after last night, he could no longer live with the comfortable assumption that one of those half-million prospects would suddenly appear around the next corner.

So, he thought, it's a no-brainer. Find Sarah. Chad could find her. That's what investigators did, wasn't it? Just how he would react if she had married, Grant had no idea. He'd cross that bridge when he came to it. And on the remote possibility that she was still single, could she forgive him for making it clear that day, however politely, that she wasn't good enough for him? Only one way to find out. He pulled out his cell phone and rang up Chad again.

"Chad, I have to find someone. I mean, you have to find her."

"By the anxiety in your voice, I'm surmising the mess you're in down there has reached a new level. Am I right?"

"No. I need you to find a girl for me. Her name is, or was, Sarah Jankovic. She grew up in a predominantly ethnic section of South Boston, one of the less affluent suburbs. She lived in a trailer park near a pond...I think it's called Miller's Pond, or something. Find her right away. As soon as you can."

"For God's sake Grant, where did this come from? I mean you're up to your eyeballs in serious trouble, and the most pressing thing you can think of is finding an old girlfriend? Hell, when you were my roommate you never told me you even had a romance with anyone. Why can't this wait until we find out whether you're going to survive or not?"

"Chad, I fouled up big-time back when I believed everything my parents told me. And now I need to find her. Even if she's married and under a different name. It's important."

"Okay, okay, calm down. I've never heard you so uptight before. It makes me wonder if there's something in the drinking water down there. I'll find her for you. Just relax a little. I'll get back to you when I have something."

Grant knew how to relax. He hadn't before he came to Okeechobee, but he did now. He walked over to the fish room and sat down. No lights this time, only the aerator pumps and their soothing murmur. For a few precious moments the comforting darkness washed his mind clean of everything in his life except Sarah. He made himself a promise. He would do everything in his power to correct the mistake he'd made nine years ago. Win or lose, he'd find out once and for all whether it was possible to put years of guilt behind him.

Chapter 18

Clete Morris welcomed Grant into his office with a hand wave. No smile, hot coffee pot untouched on the burner, and the usually-jovial CPA's pipe rested in the ashtray full but unlit.

"Good morning, Clete," Grant said. "You once told me to feel free to ask if I had any questions about the hatchery. I didn't then but I do now. Do you have a minute?"

"Sure. In fact I'm glad you're here. I was getting tired of filing extensions, anyway."

Grant scanned the stacks of printouts on the desk and tried to force a smile. "Yeah, I know you're busy, and that pale, drawn look on your face tells me you might be right in the middle of an ugly tax issue. I can come later if this is a bad time."

Clete handed Grant an empty cup and pointed toward the pot. "No, I'm fine. Pour yourself some java and sit down. I was about to call you, anyway. Didn't know whether you'd heard the news or not."

Grant filled his cup, pulled up a chair, and threw a quizzical look at Clete. "What news?"

"Well, I've been fired as South Atlantic's tax accountant."

Stunned, Grant raised his eyebrows. "What!? Why? Who's authorized to fire you?"

Clete reached for his pipe, then shoved it aside. "Major called me into his office yesterday and gave me the news. Salazar Corazon terminated my services. When I asked Major the reason he kind of sidestepped the question and said the cartel didn't like my attitude. Said I wasn't aggressive enough in pushing the company's deductions through the IRS. Major didn't mention any names, but he added that the cartel found out I'd been talking to outsiders. I guess, somehow, they got wind of my meeting with you. Anyway,

I could see tears in Major's eyes, so I know it wasn't his doing. I'm sure he didn't like the idea one bit."

Grant shook his head. "God, I'm so sorry, Clete. This is my fault and I really feel bad about it. I'm sorry I ever—"

"Nah, don't think twice about it. It had to come sooner or later. Probably sooner because I was about to come up with a serious challenge to the cartel's concept of a legitimate deduction."

Grant put his hand up. "Wait a minute. Corazon is not the majority shareholder. He can't fire anyone without complete agreement from either Major or Luanne."

"Grant, we both know how powerful that cartel is. It doesn't matter worth a damn how much stock Corazon holds. He owns the Gibbs. The cartel even threatened me, albeit in a subtle, offhanded way."

"How did they do that?"

"I called Corazon's right-hand man — the one I always deal with about tax issues. A guy named Pedro Essante. When I questioned him about why I was fired he reminded me I wouldn't want to end up like Luanne's mother. I got the message."

Grant stood, walked to the window, and turned back to face the CPA. "Damn it, Clete, before I came in I felt reluctant to ask for some more information that I need from you. I don't have that feeling anymore."

He dropped into a chair and leaned toward Clete. "Look, I need you to tell me everything you haven't already told me about South Atlantic. I know drug money is being funneled through that place every day. Time is running out for me. I need to provide the Feds with some kind of credible documentation sufficient to give them cause to haul Corazon in and put him away. Please tell me what *you* think is the real reason they fired you."

Clete closed his eyes and took a deep breath. He opened them and shook his head. "Grant, I'm still bound by my oath of client confidentiality, even though South Atlantic is no longer my client. But, you know what? I don't give a damn anymore because I'm sure Corazon is getting Major and Luanne into real trouble with the IRS and God only knows what other agencies. I'm thinking the cartel's illegal activities exempt me from my oath, anyway. My concern now is that I don't want to pass on information that'll get you in trouble."

Grant raised his hands in the air. "Hell, Clete, I'm already in more trouble than you can imagine. I need your information to help get me *out* of it!"

Clete couldn't stifle a laugh. "Okay, here goes. As I'm sure you must know, my tax preparation responsibilities don't require me to audit the tax information South Atlantic provides to me each tax season. However, I have a professional obligation to at least check the information for reasonableness. I did that every year, and every year the dollar amount the company claimed as revenue-earned fell way below the amount my calculations showed must have been deposited as cash collections from customers. I never questioned it until last year. Doggone it, South Atlantic is my largest client and I didn't want to risk losing it. Even so, the last three years I really got to thinking about the legality of what I was doing. And when I remembered what you told me about the exorbitant profit the hatchery showed, I guess I figured it was time to fish or cut bait. That's when I was fixin' to call you."

Grant sat silent for a moment. "Clete, I think I can nail at least part of this thing shut with your help. Could you make me a photocopy of the company's last three years' tax returns accompanied by a complete written summary of what you just told me? I know copies of the returns are on file with the IRS, but I can't wait that long to get them."

Clete shot up from his chair, clapped his hands, and made a beeline for the file cabinet. "You're damned right I can. If I'm going to violate client confidentiality I might as well be pan-fried for a fifteen-pound bass as a minnow. Hold on, I'll pack this up for you. Then I'm taking my family out of town for awhile to keep them safe. I hope you can dredge up enough dirt on Corazon to send that bastard to prison for a long time."

"Thanks, Clete. I'll do the best I can. Good luck, and don't tell anyone where you're going."

Chapter 19

Mountains of darkening rain clouds drifted inland from the Gulf during the early morning, hours ahead of their normal afternoon arrival time. They gradually fused to form an amorphous, charcoal-smudged sky. Moments later, a deafening thunderclap shattered the stillness. A succession of lightning bolts punched holes in the sullen sky, which opened up in time to soak Grant before he could complete an early morning dash from his car to South Atlantic's front door.

He changed into his spare in-case-it-rains Durastyle-and-denim outfit, brewed a pot of coffee, and began tapping his latest findings into his laptop. Halfway through, the image that flashed in and out of his consciousness before he could interpret it brought his work to a sudden standstill. Grant pushed his chair away from the table, leaned back, and stared up at the ceiling.

First it was there, then it was gone. Little more than a blurred black and white photograph, it came without warning and vanished from his mind before he had a chance to analyze it. Like a mental flashback, the faint shadow danced before him again, and withdrew before his consciousness could make sense of it. Moments later, a recurrence of the elusive image lingered, like the dragonfly in the swamp, this time just long enough to get caught.

Enrico had brought in another three boxes of angels the day before. Through the conference room window Grant had watched him unload the pickup, and thought no more about it. The next morning he could hear Enrico giving Maria instructions for completing the bank deposit slip. Grant had no idea why a sudden recurrence of the image brought the boxes of angels and the deposit together in his mind at the same time. He'd been so close to the missing component he hadn't seen the obvious. Yet, there it was, a perfect connection of the dots. Perfect except, without proof, the connection would be no better than the blurred image.

He managed to hold his eagerness in check, and waited patiently until Enrico had left for the day. The remaining hours of the late morning and long afternoon seemed to creep by with a stubborn languor. Despite his efforts to focus on the work at hand, the slowness of the day's pace gradually turned his excitement into excruciating anxiety. He tried to relax by watching the sunset — a fiery red ball descending behind a wall of dark green cypress trees. The gathering dusk finally surrendered to a welcomed darkness. Enrico and the field hands left for the day. Grant locked his documents in the file cabinet and headed for the monolithic building where thousands of angels were propagating.

* * * * * *

Grant didn't see any need to bring cutting tools to slice open the exterior shells of the boxes. If the idea that had been spawned by the image had any merit, the cutting would already have been done. Grant swung the flashlight beam back and forth until he found the pile of empty boxes, and worked alone and in silence without turning on the lights in the breeding area. He gently poked and prodded every inch of the largest box until he found the small opening sliced in the outer shell. He figured that most of the sand in the half-inch space between the shell and the inner lining had probably been poured out and dumped somewhere else. He gently explored the six-inch slit with his thumb, which he pushed through the opening until it touched the inner lining of the box.

Able to accept its simplicity now for the first time, Grant could only admire the effectiveness and simplicity of the scheme. Inspectors might open the top of the boxes to check the contents, but no customs official would risk cutting open the bottom of a water-filled container of live fish just to test the contents for smuggled items. While trained inspection dogs might sniff out narcotics, they could never detect currency encased in sand.

Successfully passed through inspection, the narcotics money would be extracted from the outer casing. Clipped together with customer checks, it would become part of Maria's daily fish sale deposits. By virtue of these clandestine transactions, South Atlantic Farms would continue to be twenty-to-thirty percent more profitable than industry averages. Chad had been right.

The felony had been going on under his nose. No wonder the financial statements looked so good.

Grant made a painstaking effort to leave the boxes exactly as he'd found them. Unable to dampen his excitement, he reached for his cell phone and keyed in Chad's number.

"Chad, I know how they altered the deposits. The fish-shipping boxes were stuffed with drug money. I think we—"

"Where and how did they stuff the boxes?"

"Ummm…I think some were stuffed in Bogota and some in Miami, which is apparently one of their waystations. The money, hundred dollar bills probably, was sealed in an outer lining. I can prove it."

"Do they know you've discovered this?"

"No, not yet."

"Good. Now, I have some positive news. I located the computer consultant who walked off the job down there. The bad news is he didn't walk off. He was found dead somewhere up in North Carolina, causes unknown. I also found out you can do a forensic examination on a three-year-old corpse. But it's kind of iffy depending on how the person died. Look, I don't want to keep sounding like a Dutch uncle on this, but I'm going to say it one more time. Get out of there. Everyone who becomes involved in that accounting and information system down there seems to end up dead. I'll get a cell phone message about all this to my contacts at the Drug Enforcement Agency and the FBI. You go home."

"I will, I will. I have to follow up on a few things first. Thanks for everything, Chad. Please go find Sarah, now. Let me know when you find her."

* * * * * *

Within hours, another communication found its way from Salazar Corazon to the bank. "Tommy, I'm sending a couple of my men up there day after tomorrow to take care of this problem. Now here's what I want you to do. I want you to keep track of where this boy is at all times until they can get up there. I want no mistakes and, most importantly, I want to make sure my men can find him as soon as they get there. I don't want them to waste any time, or be seen around town looking for him. Do I make myself perfectly clear on this?"

"Yes, sir. But why wait until day after tomorrow?"

"My arrangements in Mayaca won't be completed until then."

"Mayaca?"

"You're forgetting, Tommy. I told you this can't be done on the hatchery's premises. It would be amateurish. You said he consistently works late at night, alone in the conference room. We'll extract the boy from there and take him to the outskirts of Mayaca in his car. It will appear perfectly reasonable for him to be travelling there as part of his research. He'll have an unfortunate accident on the way. In view of his history of speeding tickets, a fatal automobile accident will be perfectly credible. My men will go into the hatchery and take everything of value, including his computer, all of his work product, and anything else to make it look like a routine burglary."

Tommy wriggled in his chair. "Yes, sir. But the people at the hatchery will know it's more than just a burglary. What about them?"

"They'll get the message. They'll continue, very wisely, to maintain their customary silence."

"Yes, sir. Ah, what makes you so sure?"

"South Atlantic is their financial future and part of ours. They know what happens to anyone who gets in the way of that. Money and fear, Tommy. The best of human motivations. Try to remember that. Now, after it's done there will, of course, be an investigation, just as before. And, as before, your position on the matter will be that of the company's banker and financial advisor, with knowledge of nothing more. Do you understand?"

"Yes, sir."

"Very well. Then, aside from your keeping me informed as to Grant's movements, we'll consider the matter closed and your responsibilities ended. I'll rely on you only to keep track and report to me twice a day."

"Of course, sir."

Tommy could feel the familiar anxiety creeping up on him again. A third execution, no matter where it occurred, would be more than coincidental. It would prompt an even more intensive investigation. The Feds would cast a wide net. Salazar had escaped such efforts before, and would again. Tommy Rawls knew he had no such protective network insulating him, and he felt a cold chill.

He considered three possible courses of action. One, he could alert Grant. The man was an adversary, but he might, out of gratitude, ask the Feds for leniency in the matter. Still, government leniency wouldn't likely make him safer. Two, he could go straight to the Feds and plea bargain for a lighter sentence. Or maybe for no sentence at all. Either way, he'd spend the rest of his life looking over his shoulder in anticipation of the cartel's inevitable revenge. Three, he could do nothing, and simply play out the investigation as Salazar had directed.

Tommy had long been a student of probabilities. Under the third option, he figured, at best, a ten percent chance the Feds would fail to trace the money or connect the assassinations. This would allow both he and Corazon to escape indictment altogether. That left a ninety percent chance the Feds would unravel Corazon's entire scheme.

Tommy figured, within that ninety percent parameter, there would be only a five percent chance that, regardless of whether Corazon was convicted or not, Tommy would not be tied in. As soon as he worked out the math on the third option, Tommy scribbled his solution on a Rolodex card, in precise banker fashion:

Freedom through complete Federal failure =	*10.0 %*
My chances out of the 90% federal success = 0.90 x 0.05 =	*4.5%*

Overall probability of my getting out completely =	*14.5%*
	======

About one out of seven. Even as a best case scenario, it didn't look comforting. Still, it was better than a zero chance of survival under the other two options. Tommy Rawls tore up the Rolodex and decided to play along and hope. Worst case, a jail sentence was better than a death sentence carried out by the Colombians. Tommy already knew what one of those looked like.

Chapter 20

The DEA almost lost the message, and then misinterpreted Chad's wording of it. An employee mistakenly sidetracked it into a banking network as a Suspicious Activity Report under section 5311 of the Bank Secrecy Act. Worse, Chad's simultaneous transmission to the FBI wound up in a Counter-Terrorism department as the result of another misinterpretation. A full twelve hours elapsed before the document finally found its way to the office of Roy Hartman, director of the Financial Intelligence Unit in Vienna, Virginia. It took him less than five minutes to track down Gene Rettig at the FBI and put a call through to him.

"Roy, it's always a pleasure to hear from you guys at FinCen. So what's up? Do you boys have trouble or do we? At any rate, I'm pushing all my paperwork aside on the premise that there's no such thing as a casual call from you."

"Gene, I'm afraid we both have a mess on our hands if money laundering fits your definition of trouble." Roy clicked on the screen in front of him to enlarge the image. "I'm looking at a bombshell here that just came through under 'specified unlawful activities.' It's not your average run-of-the-mill SUA. This one's a clear violation of the Money Laundering Control Act. I don't know if it has any terrorism implications or not, but I think you guys at the bureau need to get into this one, like ASAP."

"Okay, let's talk about it. Any narcotics smuggling involved?"

"As far as I know it's just cash, but I'm not ruling out narcotics."

"Roy, are you sure about that? I mean, it doesn't make a whole lot of sense. Why go to all the trouble when cocaine that's worth a million on the street weighs only forty-four pounds, while a million in one-dollar bills weighs about two hundred and fifty-six pounds? I mean, if you're going to run cash instead of crack, you'd better have one hell of a system."

Roy reached over to pull a file from his in-basket. "Well, I'm afraid one hell of a system is exactly what they have. Believe it or not, it's a fish hatchery in Florida. Apparently some outfit in South America is using it to turn dirty money into clean money. Look, I don't have all the details, but it looks like some drug cartel has invested a ton of dirty money in this tropical fish farm, a lot more than would normally be needed. The farm then buys land, equipment, puts up buildings and the whole nine yards. Problem is, they pay a whole lot more than those assets really cost or are worth."

Gene paused while he waited for his computer to fire up. "Okay, I've brought up on the screen my file on drug cartels. So, now what happens to the money? Have you figured that out yet?"

"The vendors take the money, put up the buildings at a windfall profit, and reinvest the excess money here in the U.S. So at the end of the day all the dirty money comes out clean because it's comingled with legitimate money in legitimate transactions. Then the cartel lends more money to the farm's owners, who invest it in the day-to-day operation of the farm. Later, the drug lord forgives the balance due on the loan, so that, too, stays clean."

Roy put the call on the speaker phone, leaned back in his chair, and cupped his hands behind his head. "Now, Gene, you're going to love this. The drug hustlers smuggle cash hidden in the fish containers coming in from South America. Somehow, it then gets deposited in the farm's bank along with all the legitimate fish revenue money, and everything ends up clean. Pretty slick, huh?"

"Yeah, sounds like it doesn't get much sweeter. You said Florida. This fish farm wouldn't happen to be in Okeechobee, would it?"

Roy straightened up "Yeah. How did you know? Look, if you guys in the bureau have something going on down there I need you to fill me in on it. Do you?"

"In fact we do. For several years we've been after a drug ring headed up by an elusive snake named Corazon. Trouble is, we never can get quite enough evidence to drag him up here and put him on trial. So now I'm hoping you're going to tell me the message you received corresponds to the one that came through to us. Ours came from a contact named Chad Winslow. Apparently a good friend of his, by the name of Lonsdale, turned up a real can of worms while he was doing a supposedly routine consulting job at a fish hatchery called South Atlantic Farms. Right now this Lonsdale guy seems to think there may be another outfit named Mayaca Corporation involved. So, talk to me."

"Okay," Roy said, "I believe we're talking about the same fish farm. My guess is this Mayaca Corporation is another funnel, along with the fish farm, through which the investment money gets washed. It's a slick operation. I'm also surmising that Mayaca sells the land and buildings to the farm in a legitimate, but highly overpriced, transaction. So it looks like our message reads about the same as yours. I'm afraid this Lonsdale chap, as well as the owners of the business, could be in serious danger. We need to get these people the hell out of there before Corazon pulls the trigger. Agreed?"

"Under normal circumstances, yes, Roy. But we've a different problem here. The bureau wants Corazon and his drug ring, and we want him bad. Now, as I see it, this little mess down there represents the best opportunity we've had so far to get him. Unfortunately, we need more hard evidence to make a rap stick. And the only way we can get it is from this Lonsdale guy, whoever he is. That means he has to stay there long enough to both gather up and transfer every bit of evidence he can get his hands on, and then stick around long enough to help us nail Corazon. Better yet — and I know you're not going to like this — but if this Lonsdale guy should happen to volunteer to help us set a trap for Corazon or one of his henchmen, we might be able to put that scumbag and his drug-hustling maggots out of business permanently."

Roy had been there before. He'd set traps with live human bait on a number of occasions and the bait didn't always survive. He slid out of his chair, sat on the edge of his desk, and paused before he responded. "To say I don't like it would be an understatement. I think it stinks. But I agree with you. We don't have much choice when you consider what's at stake here. Okay, I'm going to send one of my agents down there tonight to contact Lonsdale. I'll make sure the Treasury Department grants him full authority to make whatever deal he can with Lonsdale. I want a couple of your guys from the bureau down there as cover, in case this whole thing goes south. Keep in mind, though, we can't force this Lonsdale guy to do all this. He has to agree, or else we're back at square one."

"Right. You get your agent down there and I'll have two of ours there by tomorrow, right after I figure out how to do it without alerting any of the local residents. Roy, this is going to be difficult given the small size of the town."

Roy Hartman slumped back in his chair for a long, drawn out moment of reflection. Structuring a sting operation on such short notice presented problems from the very beginning. No one from either the FBI or the

Financial Action Task Force on Money Laundering had ever met Grant Lonsdale, or any of the employees of South Atlantic Farms.

No one knew whether the money laundering had been part of a terrorist jihad or not. Roy suspected that someone at the local bank must be involved because smurfing, or keeping deposits under the $10,000 required reporting limit, was clearly being done. Despite the small size of the bank, there wasn't a shred of real evidence to support the suspicion.

Roy shook his head, leaned forward to peek at the screen again, and pondered for another few seconds. In a worst-case scenario, if the sting operation in Okeechobee failed, the drug ring would simply pull up stakes and find another business through which to continue operations. Even if it succeeded, the economic and social effects on the local residents would likely be serious, particularly if closure of the local bank, South Atlantic Farms, and Mayaca Corporation should become collateral damage.

He leaned back in his chair again and closed his eyes. Simply shutting down the laundering operation and nailing Corazon would not be the end of it. The DEA would still have to make deals with some of the drug traffickers to identify the distribution channels. If terrorism were discovered, then Homeland Security and half a dozen other federal agencies would have to become involved. Hartman opened his eyes and took a deep breath. Rettig had actually understated the whole thing when he called it simply a can of worms. In fact, this Lonsdale guy had just kicked open a nest of angry hornets, which looked like they were about to swarm.

Chapter 21

Ten minutes late for his appointment, agent Maxwell Tolliver stood in front of Roy Hartman's desk. "Yes sir, you wanted to see me?"

Hartman made a point to glance at his watch, glared at Tolliver, and looked down again at the stack of paperwork in front of him. "Right. Have a seat." Roy took a few seconds to finish his expense report, shoved it into his out-box, and looked up at Tolliver. "My secretary will have your plane ticket in a few minutes. I want you in Okeechobee this afternoon."

The agent slid into a chair and managed a barely perceptible frown. "Okay. Where the hell is Okeechobee? And what am I supposed to do there?"

"Florida. We have our first real break in our long series of failed efforts to nail the head of that Colombian drug cartel."

"You mean Corazon?"

"Yeah. There's a young management consultant who just blew the lid off that damned thing in a fish farm down there. An associate of his, I guess, sent us a message that this guy's gathered up enough evidence to enable us to extradite Corazon. The DEA's given us the green light to go get him. Problem is we need a bit more than just evidence. We need this consultant to hang around long enough to send us complete documentation. We'd also like to use this guy to set a trap for the hit men they seem to think will probably come up there from Bogota to take him out. But we can't force the young man to do it. So I want you to hustle your ass down there and convince him it's his patriotic duty to volunteer. His name is Grant Lonsdale. Grant Abbot Lonsdale III, actually. Boston blue-blood, I'm told."

Max took a deep breath and exhaled audibly. "What the hell's a guy like that doing in a mess like this?"

Roy shook his head. "I don't know, Max. Anyway, it doesn't matter. He's in it and we need him. Get the picture?"

"Yeah, I get it, but convincing someone to leap into a plot that's almost guaranteed to get him killed is going to require more salesmanship than I think I can muster up. I mean, don't forget Corazon's gunnies have already killed three FBI agents and one of ours. And they were pros. This Lonsdale fellow is, at best, a bumbling amateur. Hell, my guess is he's not even that."

"True, Max. Still, we have no choice. It's a long shot, I know. Good news is that Lonsdale most likely has no idea about the blood we've lost chasing these druggies, and there's no need to tell him. Just explain the risks as gently as you can and put it to him as a noble cause and a civic duty that only he can fulfill because of what he knows. Compliment him on the great job he's done already and fatten up his ego to the point where he'll feel ashamed to turn us down. Okay? This'll be a big assignment for you in terms of future promotions. Now go pick up your ticket from Janice. I've included more instructions for both you and Lonsdale in your packet. Call me when you get there and again when Lonsdale accepts. Good hunting."

* * * * * *

There hadn't been a visitor in Grant's motel room since Luanne's surprise appearance. Since he hadn't expected any, the sound of the man's voice the moment Grant entered came as a shock.

"Please close the door, Mr. Lonsdale, and don't turn on another light. Do not open the curtains."

Grant spun around to face the man in the chair. "Jeez, who the hell are you!?"

"It's all right. Please keep your voice down. I'm Agent Max Tolliver from the Financial Action Task Force. FATF as we refer to it. We got your message, and that's why I'm here. Please sit down, we need to talk."

Grant shook his head. "Damn it, you scared the hell out of me. Okay, I guess I'm glad you're here, but why the secrecy? My request was that you guys come out here and simply take charge of this whole thing, right on the premises of the hatchery. I expected you to get the Gibbs family out of there and into safekeeping." Grant pulled up the only other chair. "Why are we meeting like this?"

"I'm afraid it's not quite that simple, Mr. Lonsdale. This is highly confidential, of course, but we've been tracking this operation since Carlton Feicke's murder. He put us onto this just before he died. However, until you showed up, we didn't have enough information to assign agents to it. But now we—"

"What do you mean, not enough information?" Grant spread his arms out, palms up, in a gesture of disbelief. "I've already provided that. It's all spelled out in my message."

"Sorry, Mr. Lonsdale, I'm making assumptions I shouldn't on how much you know about this case. I meant that, based on what Feicke told us, we were pretty sure this is a money laundering scheme, big time. But we didn't know who the players were. At first we suspected the two Gibbs people. The rather unusual circumstances surrounding the death of Mrs. Gibbs caused us to back off on that one. Then we—"

"Major and Luanne are completely innocent. I'll vouch for them."

"We'll talk about that later. Now, as I was starting to say, we became reasonably certain a South American drug cartel is involved, and is probably getting some collaboration from a local party here in Okeechobee. But, until we got your message, we didn't know for sure who was doing what or how. Now we know. But here's the problem. Salazar Corazon has been number one on our suspect list for years. He's big, though, and well protected."

The agent stood and began to pace in small circles. The light from a thin moon seeped through the curtained window. Its pale, slanted, beam spilled through the glass and offered Grant his first good look at the man. His face, almost as pale as the white shirt he wore, looked even more pallid against his dark blue suit. Grant wondered how the agent, looking so conspicuously out of place, ever managed to get there without alerting half the town.

"Corazon's network has distributed billions of dollars in narcotics, and quite possibly illegal weapons, throughout the United States," Tolliver continued, his circles widening as far as the furniture would allow. "The ring of criminals and paid-off government officials around him has been impenetrable. Until now we haven't had enough solid proof to nail him. Believe me, we've tried everything. Now, here's the reason for the secrecy. We need you to help us get him, Mr. Lonsdale. I have been given complete authority to make any arrangements with you within reason. Here's what we need you to—"

"Please call me Grant. And why don't you simply meet me at the hatchery, and I'll give you all the evidence you need? I have all the documentation right there, including board meeting minutes and a fist-full of incriminating documents. Then you can escort me, Luanne and Major safely out of there and go after Corazon. That was the plan I suggested when I sent you the message."

The agent returned to his seat, placed his hands on his knees, and leaned toward Grant. "Yes, we could do that, Grant, and probably shut down the laundering operation immediately. But here's the thing. We don't give a damn about the money. We want Corazon, and we need you to help us get him. The FBI is also involved, partly because this is their investigation, and partly because we believe Corazon will probably be sending one of his thugs up here to kill you. Now, the moment that event begins to take shape, our agents, along with the FBI, will close in. That'll be enough to enable us to go down there and bring him back for trial under the 1976 bilateral extradition treaty with Colombia...or kill him."

Grant stood and glared at the agent. "Oh, that's just great. Let me see if I'm getting the picture here. We're talking about a notorious drug lord who's clever enough to elude your people for years. And now you're telling me the only way you can think of to convict him is to set me up as live bait, hoping your guys can grab his hit man just before he kills me, right?"

"Ah...well, I wouldn't put it quite so brutally, but, yeah, that's kind of what it comes down to. How about it? Are you willing to help us get this slimy kingpin, and maybe his whole cartel?"

Grant knew he didn't have enough time to sort out all the thoughts that had begun to race through his mind. This whole thing had gone so far beyond anything he'd planned to do down here that analytical thinking just didn't seem up to the task. Grant wasn't even aware he'd begun to mutter out loud.

"What did you say?" Tolliver threw him an incredulous glance.

"Nothing. Never mind."

Tolliver stood again and faced Grant. "Well, what do you think, Grant? Are you with us?"

Grant returned to his chair. "That depends." Analytical thinking, on the other hand, was still part of his DNA.

"On what?"

"On your agreeing to my conditions. All of them."

"Federal agencies, Grant, are not accustomed to conditions. But, okay, what are they?"

"First of all, Max, I want Major, Luanne, and Maria taken to safety until the risk of retribution from Corazon is removed."

"Who's Maria?"

"She's their bookkeeper, assistant to Luanne."

"Okay, no problem. What else?"

"South Atlantic Farms represents Luanne's future, and Major's retirement fund. I want federal government written assurance that the business will be allowed to continue intact without seizure of its assets. The business must be allowed to keep any cash that has already been laundered and is still in its system. Nothing is to be removed, and South Atlantic Farms is to be permitted to continue its normal, legitimate business operations under Major and Luanne's ownership as long as they want."

Tolliver shook his head. "Ahhh…that's going to be a problem."

"Why? A moment ago you said your agency wasn't interested in the money."

"It's not the money, Grant. The problem is that our agency has rules about this sort of thing. Any entity involved in an illegal transfer of funds of any kind is subject to a freeze on its bank accounts, operations, and just about everything. Probably even replacement of its management until our agency can become reasonably assured that proper internal controls are in place. The purpose is to guard against a recurrence of the illegal activity."

Grant turned away for a moment to ponder the idea. Okay, he thought, let's go abstract with this. Take it out of the present situation where it looks hopeless. Think. Think. Can this be lifted from its existing environment and moved to a new venue where these rules don't apply?

Grant leaned forward toward the agent. "Okay, Max, let's say the entire South Atlantic Farms operation could be turned over, lock, stock, and barrel, to another larger, and very legitimate corporation. There it would operate as a wholly-owned subsidiary of that corporation under the complete control of the parent corporation until your agency's requirements have been satisfied. Would your agency allow South Atlantic Farms to remain open for business under those conditions?"

Max leaned forward, resting his chin on his fist while he paused to do some pondering of his own. "Well… I suppose that would be possible, except for one problem. Since South Atlantic's bank accounts would be frozen, how could the company operate without the use of the cash it generates?"

Grant drew in a deep breath and closed his eyes, as if to shield his thoughts from any outside interference. He opened them and turned to face tolliver. "Okay, all transactions would be run through the parent company's bank accounts, which are already under controls tight enough to prevent any further fraudulent activity. Thus, no cash would be deposited or disbursed without parent company review and approval. That should satisfy your agency, shouldn't it?"

Max began with a smile that gradually became a chuckle. "Grant, I must admit your theory is unusual. I can't help admiring the sheer creative fantasy of your imagination. My answer would be, hypothetically, yes, under such conditions. But where on earth would you propose to find a company with top management willing to take on such a risk? Not to mention the horrendous administrative burden it would impose without any possible payoff."

"I know a company that will do it."

"Really? And what company might that be?" The agent's grin faded into a look of incredulous curiosity.

"My father's company, Concord Industries."

Tolliver's eyes bulged. "You're kidding. Your father owns Concord?"

"He's CEO and a controlling shareholder. Concord and its predecessors have been in our family for generations. I think I can convince him to do it. That is, providing your agency doesn't take too long to become comfortable that the problem has been cleaned up. You guarantee acceptance of that for me, Max, along with complete protection for Major, Luanne and Maria, and I'll help you get Corazon. Do we have a deal?"

Max heaved a deep sigh after a long pause. "Well… they may hang me out to dry in Washington, but we have a deal. This one's going down on the books as the screwiest shenanigan our agency has ever seen, but I'll get it approved. Now, here's—"

"There's one more condition, Max." Grant pulled his chair up directly in front of the agent and leaned toward him again. "I want federal assurance that Major, Luanne, and Maria will be completely absolved of any guilt that may be attached to their accepting any of that drug money. They were innocent, and I think you know it as well as I do. Now I want the federal government to officially acknowledge it."

Tolliver threw his hands in the air. "No way, Grant. There's no way that's going to happen. Look, I'll get them safely out of there. But they're direct participants in an international felony. My guess is those three are probably going down, and there's not a thing you or I can do about it."

"Fine." Grant stood and glared at Tolliver. "Then I'm out of here right now, and you can tell your people they can shove this whole thing where the sun doesn't shine. You either accept my condition or you guys can get Corazon by yourselves."

"Damn you, Lonsdale! You don't have any idea what you're asking." Tolliver bolted out of his chair.

"The hell I don't." Grant moved to come face-to-face with Tolliver. "I'm asking you to protect three completely innocent people."

"No, damn it! You're asking at least four government agencies, including the FBI, to turn their backs on people who enabled a drug cartel to make money in violation of I don't know how many different laws. Just who the hell do you think you are, dictating terms to the government of the United States?"

"I'll tell you who I am," Grant snarled. "I'm the only hope you have of reversing the pathetic failure of at least four government agencies that screwed up their jobs so badly they can't even touch an identified drug lord. So take it or leave it. You find a way to absolve those people or I walk. And now here's *my* guess. You guys will find yourselves right back where you started, drenched in your own shame, while you're waiting to get your butts chewed out for blowing your only chance to nail this scumbag."

This wasn't the first time Grant couldn't believe what he'd just said. He briefly considered the possibility Max might take a swing at him.

In a moment of towering rage, agent Maxwell R. Tolliver turned, grabbed the little battery-operated clock as though he were about to throw it. In apparent surrender to his better judgment, he slammed it down on the table — just hard enough to split its back. Even before the clock's "Made-in-China" components spilled out onto the table, Tolliver turned back to Grant, his face flushed with anger. "Damn it, Lonsdale. This'll get me fired."

"No, Tolliver, it'll probably get you promoted, whether you deserve it or not. Think about it. It's your name that'll be linked to the demise of a monster who managed to elude your four government agencies for ten years. By the way, there's one more thing. A man named Clete Morris is the CPA who provided the tax information on Corazon. I want him given adequate protection as soon as he comes out of hiding."

Tolliver's hands went into the air again. "Oh, terrific! Anything else you can think of while we're on the subject?"

"No, that's it. Now tell me what kind of help we'll be getting on all this."

After he paced the floor twice, a still-fuming Tolliver turned to face his adversary. "All right, Lonsdale," he grumbled, "your name just got on a few nasty lists where you don't want it, but we have a deal."

"I want the whole thing in writing, Max. By tomorrow."

"You'll have it, damn it. You don't have to tell me that. Now, here's what I want you to do. I want you to fax, to this number, every single document that relates to what you told us in your original message. We won't meet again, but here's my cell number, as well as the cell numbers of the agents who will be guarding you, starting tomorrow. You won't recognize them. In fact you won't even see them. But they'll move around you as field hands, repairmen, garbage collectors and so on."

Grant rolled his eyes. "Great. And in the meantime what am I supposed to do?"

"I know it's asking a lot, Grant, but try to keep your daily routine the same as usual. Unfortunately, in order to avoid alerting Corazon, we'll have to leave the Gibbs people right where they are until we've apprehended the guy who's coming for you. Then we'll get them out of there after we've bagged Corazon and his hit man. By the way, don't drive your car anywhere except back and forth from your motel to the hatchery. One of the FBI agents will continuously check your car for explosive devices."

"Max, this thing is sounding more restrictive every second."

"I know. It's necessary. Eat all your meals at Essie Mae's. We'll plant someone in her kitchen to check your food before it's served to you. An agent will watch your motel at night. Good luck. The next time we meet I hope it will be in court when they sentence Corazon."

Grant shook his head. "I hope so. If you guys don't get him I'll be spending the rest of my life looking over my shoulder."

"We'll get him."

Chapter 22

Not having heard from his son in almost a week, the senior Lonsdale brightened when his secretary told him Grant Abbot III was calling from Florida. The CEO leaned back in his chair and swiveled around to face the super-sized, made-to-his-specifications window overlooking the Charles River. The anxious father forgot all about the gentle scolding he'd planned to administer to his son for not calling more often.

After some paternal joking about how Grant Abbot never let his own parents know where he was as a kid, his father listened with growing anxiety as his son unleashed his frightening tale of fraud and murder in Okeechobee. By the time Grant Abbot finished, his father had the call on speaker phone so he could pace the floor around his desk while he listened.

"Son, I'm appalled that you could have turned this assignment into such a situation in the first place. I'm at a loss for words. While I applaud the skill and courage you've shown down there, I'm adamantly opposed to your putting yourself at such a risk. I'm not even going to get into how your mother will react. Look, I want you to come home. In fact, I insist you leave now. I'm sure Angus had nothing like this in mind when he sent you down there, and I certainly didn't when he told me he was sending you."

"Dad, believe me, I completely understand where you're coming from. But there are two compelling reasons why I can't come home yet. One, it further endangers the lives of the Gibbs family and all their employees. Two, I've already committed to a deal I structured with the FBI and the Financial Action Task Force. Dad, I know I have no right to impose on you like this, but I need you to do something for me. I promise I won't ever ask you for anything again. "

Grant's father listened with a gradually subsiding anxiety to his son's detailed explanation. The agreement with Max Tolliver involving Concord's temporary takeover of South Atlantic Farms had been structured to prevent

144

the freezing of the hatchery's assets by the federal government. The five-minute dissertation covered every relevant activity except Grant's role as live bait — significant in its absence.

The senior Lonsdale settled down into his chair, and swung it around toward the window. In the distance, barely visible, he could see a sculling crew pulling hard on their oars on a practice run along the Charles River. The relaxing sight provided a small measure of comfort to a father who could sense his son's reluctance to ask his family for anything. He felt a twinge of sadness that Grant Abbot had always preferred to run his requests through the housekeeper, Mary, his confidante — never comfortable enough with his parents to appeal directly to them. "Grant, if I do this you must understand that these Gibbs people will have to surrender financial and accounting control of that hatchery. One of my accounting managers will have to assume responsibility for all record keeping. If the threat down there is as imminent as you say it is, we'll have to work this out with as little contact with that hatchery as possible, in order to keep it quiet. Furthermore, if I agree to this bizarre arrangement, I want you to come back to Concord. One of your ancillary duties will be to supervise the production and marketing end of this little fish farm I'm taking on. You got that?"

"Yes, Dad. That's understood. Not a problem."

"Well, I damned sure don't like it, son. But I trust your judgment. Okay, I'll set it up at this end. The tough part is going to be trying to keep your mother from coming apart at the seams. Grant, good luck, be careful, and keep me posted."

"Thanks for helping me, Dad. I really mean it."

* * * * *

When trouble loomed, the senior Lonsdale's first call went out to his attorney, Douglas 'Deke' Traynor. Deke listened patiently all the way to the end of the exposition.

"Grant, I don't know what to say. I'm blown away by this. I guess my first question is how much danger is your son in down there?"

"Well, he said he'd only be there long enough to get some documents faxed out. He's apparently been provided FBI protection. But there's still a risk."

"So then, why in the world are you permitting him to do it?"

"Damn it, Deke, I'm just his father, not his conscience. He swears it's not only critical, but imperative, that he finish whatever this thing is. I don't like it, but I trust him and told him it was okay."

"Grant, the board's not going to like this. And I don't mean just the extra cost of taking on this hatchery. I mean you're going to have trouble attracting additional capital once our funding sources find out about this. Have you considered that?"

"To tell you the truth, Deke, this all happened so fast I haven't really had time to consider it. Yes, I know what you're saying. And I don't know just how I'll explain it to the board. But I do know this. He's my son and that comes first."

"Right. I understand. Now, the other day you mentioned that he's still in love with some woman. Who is she?"

"I think her name is Sarah something or other. Mignon's having a fit about it. You know, Deke, I think I made a mistake a long time ago. Or, rather Mignon and I made a mistake. We kind of forced him out of a relationship with this girl, Sarah, whom he was crazy about at the time. I'm not sure, but I think what he's doing now may, somehow, be a consequence of that."

"Grant, what are you saying?"

"Hell, I don't know. He was always kind of a hard kid to figure. A good kid, mind you, Deke, and extremely capable. But his mother and I never truly understood some of his views on things. To tell you the truth, I honestly believe our housekeeper knew him better than we did, as strange as that may sound."

"You mean Mary Coyne, the little Irish lady who made me that fantastic Manhattan last time I was there?"

"Yes. Anyway, let's call a board meeting for next week, and get this whole thing out on the table. Grant Abbot will be finished with whatever he's doing by then, and we can let it out of the bag. I can accept whatever the board decides. And as I said before, I have other sources of financing. They're a little more expensive, perhaps, but still feasible. Pick a date that suits the board, and I'll make it a point to be available. And thanks, Deke."

After he hung up, Grant leaned back in his chair and stared out the window at the Charles. His life had suddenly changed with one phone call. In retrospect, even if the Board didn't begin to develop some second thoughts as to his sanity, Mignon certainly would. In fact, she'd probably become downright hysterical, and he wasn't looking forward to it.

He reached for his cell phone and dialed Peter M. Prentiss, president of Citizens Financial Corporation. "Pete, Grant Lonsdale here. Do you have a minute?"

"Absolutely. For you I might even carve out three or four. How's Mignon? Or maybe I should ask how your son's doing. If I don't, my daughter will shoot me. Every time the phone rings at our house she hopes it's Grant Abbot. You know how she is."

"Mignon's fine, Pete. Fact is, it's Grant Abbot I want to talk to you about. I can't get into this in much detail because I promised him I'd keep it confidential. What I can disclose is that my son has apparently made a commitment that will require me to take over a small company and nurture it until it…ahhh, shall we say, 'matures.' I'm stretching the truth a bit here, but please bear with me. Now I—"

"What company is it, and how large, Grant?"

"My son asked me to remain silent on that, but I can tell you the assets are in the neighborhood of twenty-five to thirty-five million. Highly profitable. Concord will most likely release it after a year or two. Since you're on my board, I thought I'd feel you out to get your ball-park reaction."

"I guess I'm a bit confused, Grant. What's in this for Concord if it's just a temporary arrangement? Is there a profitable future synergy here for Concord?"

Grant paused. He knew the acquisition of a fish farm by Concord Industries made about as much financial sense as merging General Electric Corporation with Okeechobee's Dunkin' Donuts outlet. The directors could be counted on to raise the same question. "Pete, my answer to those questions is 'nothing' and 'probably not,' I'm afraid."

"Good God almighty, Grant. Then why in hell are you approving such a deal? Or more to the point, why did your son commit to it? Hell, a Harvard MBA graduate ought to know better. The directors are going to vomit all over this and you know it. Can't you tell me more about this arrangement? At least give me something to hold up in your defense."

"I know, I know. Damn it, Pete, I can't divulge anything more. Not right now, anyway. But I'm already resigned to the possibility that all my financing sources will react the same way. I'll explain to the board that Concord will most likely have to resort to more expensive financing because of the perceived risk in this little venture."

"Financing this 'little venture,' as you call it, will be the least of your worries, my friend. We're all looking forward to taking Concord Industries public in the next year or so. The transaction alone will dilute the share price, and when word of this gets out the public market for Concord's stock will dry up in a heartbeat. Have you thought of that?"

Grant struggled for a response. "I know. The only upside of it all is the temporary nature of it. I'm sure we'll be rid of the entity before we enter the public market."

The long pause at the other end of the line conveyed a meaning of its own. "Okay, Grant. I've known you long enough to feel confident you'll handle this as efficiently as possible even though I can sense your own disappointment with it. I say go ahead and we'll just have to roll with the punch. I'll help you soften the blow when we get the directors together."

"I can't thank you enough, Pete. You've always been supportive, and I value that."

"No problem. What are friends for?"

Relieved the conversation hadn't turned out any worse, Grant stood and stretched. He shook his head and wondered how long the supportive relationship would last once it became known that his son had no intention of marrying Victoria Prentiss.

Chapter 23

Sarah Jane Jankovic felt the nervous tension mounting, well beyond the level of pre-interview jitters. Promotion to department head would mean more than corporate endorsement of her past performance. It would represent the final proof of her worthiness to become Mrs. Grant Abbot Lonsdale III. Once again, she felt the same uncomfortable struggle. She felt sure she loved him but couldn't erase the memory of his unspoken declaration that she wasn't good enough for him.

She'd given Concord Industries her best effort over the last three years, and always received good reviews. Two division heads had recommended her with high praise. The interview, though, would be about more than performance. They would ask penetrating questions about her background, and that could be a problem.

The executive secretary smiled at her. "Come in, Miss Jankovic, and sit down. They'll be ready for you in a few minutes. Would you like some coffee?"

"No thank you." Sarah slid as gracefully into the chair as her tension-racked muscles would allow, and forced out the most relaxed smile she could manage. She wondered how many other apprehensive candidates had fidgeted in that same seat.

Sarah knew she'd lied during her initial interview years ago. She couldn't very well have revealed the real reason she wanted to work for Concord Industries, or they would have thrown her out right on the spot. So she simply charmed her interviewer with an articulate summary of her Google research on the industry. She said she knew Concord was well positioned in the manufacturing business, felt certain she could make a contribution, and told them why. It was easy.

That was then. Now they would ask questions about her divorce, in a subtle way that wouldn't violate EEOC regulations. Sarah could explain that.

They would likely ask about her background, and she could deal with that, too. Being the daughter of a custodian wasn't a felony. Her greatest fear was that they might probe deep enough to dredge up that terrible hurt she'd tried so hard to forget all these years. Then the tears might well up in her eyes, and that would put an end to any chance of promotion. Concord would not likely entrust an entire department to a manager who broke into tears at the first provocation. She'd held back her emotions often enough before and, if it came to that, she would do it again.

A tall woman in a tight skirt and high heels that made her appear even taller approached Sarah with a smile. She looked as though she'd become accustomed to comforting nervous candidates. "Good morning, Sarah. We've met before during your initial interviews. I'm Valerie Lincicombe, Director of Human Resources." The woman turned and gestured in the direction of a short, stern-looking bald man Sarah knew she wasn't going to like. "This is George Michaels, vice president of Finance. We've heard a lot of good things about you. Come on in and sit down. This interview is really just a formality, Sarah, so you can relax. We have only a few questions."

Sarah followed them, still not ready to believe that relaxation was an option. She smiled at Valerie, shook George's hand, and tried not to look like she didn't trust him.

"We've pretty much made up our minds," Valerie said, "that you're the right one to head up the accounting department in our New Products Division. It's a small division right now, and we think the combination of your degree in finance and your CPA status is sufficient background for the job. Now let's see, by way of summary — you graduated second in your class at Tufts University. You came to work for us and earned your CPA certificate while you were a trainee, right?"

"Yes, I finished the training program. I was working for Mr. Klein, the vice president of Plant Construction and Maintenance, when I passed the CPA exam."

Valerie nodded. "Right. Then you moved on and became research assistant to Clark Bond in Marketing. How did you like it there?"

Sarah desperately wanted to shift around to a more comfortable position in her chair. She resisted the urge in order to avoid appearing nervous. The words were beginning to catch in her dry throat, and she wanted to swallow more frequently. That, too, might be interpreted as a sign of nervousness. So she forced herself to swallow only when necessary to avoid choking.

"I thoroughly enjoyed working for Mr. Bond. I learned a lot, and the tasks he assigned helped me better understand the relationship between sales and production."

The woman continued to smile her approval after each of Sarah's responses. Sarah continued to keep her answers concise, without offering any gratuitous extras that might prompt more penetrating questions about her past. Valerie turned the questioning over to George by extending her hand in his direction, and Sarah could sense what was coming. The impeccably-dressed financial guru, with his form-fitting Brooks Brothers jacket, hadn't smiled once, and seemed to have about as much personality as an amoeba. Sarah figured he'd be the one most likely to ask the tough questions.

"Now Sarah," he began with an ominous tone, "our records show you were married and under the name Sarah Brantley while you were attending Tufts, but then divorced after graduation. So, I take it Jankovic is your birth name to which you reverted following the divorce. Is that right?"

"Yes, sir."

"I'm assuming there were no children, and you no longer have any legal restrictions or financial obligations arising out of that marriage. Am I correct?"

Sarah shifted in her chair, and tugged as unobtrusively as she could at her skirt. She could sense her interrogator treading on the edge of questions he had no legal right to ask, but refusal to respond was not an option at this point. "Yes sir. I'm single, completely on my own, and financially independent. I have a house half paid for and, as you know, a 401K plan here."

"Of course. Very good." The straight-faced executive paused to wipe his glasses. "Now Sarah, this job will require a clear understanding of the difference between the kind of information we present to our shareholders and the kind your department will need to produce internally for management purposes. How familiar are you with this difference?"

Sarah smiled, more from a sense of relief than cordiality. The question was easy. "I'm well acquainted with the unique information needs of both recipients, Mr. Michaels. My department will furnish the detailed sales, production, and budget compliance information the operating managers need to run the business on a daily basis. The company's external reports are designed to provide a more concise summary in compliance with generally accepted accounting principles."

Michaels managed his first and only smile. "Well, Sarah, as far as Valerie and I are concerned the job is yours. There is, however, one more step that has to be taken before we can officially promote you. It's not a part of our normal screening procedures. In this case, though, the company has recently encountered a rather unusual situation. It'll fall largely into your hands as a new Accounting Department manager, because this...uh...new acquisition will be assigned to the New Products Division. Therefore, our CEO, Mr. Lonsdale, wants to talk to you about it. Most likely to make sure both you and he are okay with your handling this, uh, rather unique entity. So, I've set you up with him at one o'clock this afternoon. Have you ever met him?"

"No sir, I haven't, but I'm very much looking forward to it."

"Okay. Good luck and congratulations. We're looking forward to seeing you at the next executive retreat." His affect remained as flat as when the interview began.

* * * * * *

To Sarah, the two hours until one o'clock seemed to drag on as though they were four. She tried to anticipate every possible question the senior Lonsdale might ask. She carefully rehearsed her responses. The company was so large and complex in its structure that she'd never even seen the man, let alone met him. What was he like? Did he have any idea she was the one who loved his son? The very thought of meeting him resurrected the burning memory of her last moments with his son, as vividly as if the incident had all happened the day before.

She and Grant had met by accident when he stepped on a piece of broken glass while fishing barefoot in a pond near the run-down housing project where she lived. While she cleaned and bandaged his wound, they could hardly take their eyes off each other. Oblivious to the social and economic chasm that separated the two teenagers, the boy from Beacon Hill and the girl from the projects fell in love. She'd worked hard growing up in a world made difficult by her near-poverty existence. He'd moved through his life with a careless ease, in the top echelons of Boston society, without ever giving a thought to the money he spent, or where it came from. It didn't matter. She knew she loved him. Having pledged to craft a world of their own, one that would last forever, they spent the summer lost in their dreams.

Sarah hadn't seen the apocalypse coming. In one horrific moment, the romance ended with a crushing rejection that changed her life. He tried to be diplomatic, with tears, hugs, and awkward words about the restrictions imposed by his lineage. He said it all came down to the responsibilities he would inherit. The rhetoric drowned in the unspoken message. She wasn't good enough for him. Wrong side of the tracks. A potential embarrassment to his family.

Away in her thoughts, Sarah didn't hear Mr. Lonsdale's secretary at first.

"Miss Jankovic, I said Mr. Lonsdale will see you now. Are you all right?"

"Oh, uh…yes, I'm sorry. I guess I was concentrating too much on what I would say when I talk to him. Thank you."

"Well, planning is always good." The secretary threw her a condescending smile, and escorted Sarah to the most prominent office on executive row.

"Come on in, Miss Jankovic," Lonsdale called out, "sit down and let's talk. Glad to finally meet you after all the praise I've heard about you. Would you like some coffee?"

"No thank you, sir." Sarah never liked coffee, but the refusal came out before she realized she might have offended him. She could feel her chest tighten.

"A glass of water then?"

"Yes, please."

He turned to his secretary. "Catherine, please bring me some coffee and a water for Miss Jankovic."

He smiled at her again, in a way that reminded her of her own father, and she could feel her heart skip a beat. He looked just the way she pictured his son might look at that age. This would be a pleasant interview after all. He seemed like a nice man, one who would never intentionally have hurt her if he had known her back then. Even better, he obviously had no idea about her relationship with his son. Sarah felt a wave of relaxation sweep over her. Still, she had to be careful not to become too comfortable. This was, after all, a pivotal moment in her journey, and she'd come too far to risk everything with an unguarded remark.

"Sarah, I'm delighted to have you as one of my new accounting managers. I know we'll work well together. Now, I have to warn you, yours will be truly a baptism by fire. And I'll tell you why. My son has gotten me into a rather…ah…delicate situation, which, I'm sorry to say, is going to drop right smack into your lap."

She felt a flush of nervousness, and wondered if that meant she'd be working with Grant III. "Yes, sir. And what situation is that?"

With intermittent head shakes and frowns, Grant senior explained his son's story behind the planned addition of South Atlantic Farms to the Concord infrastructure. After he'd finished, Sarah felt she knew more about raising fish and laundering money than she'd ever really wanted to know.

Sarah produced her warmest smile. "Mr. Lonsdale, I welcome the challenge of overseeing the financial and accounting transactions of the hatchery." Her response brought a look of relief from a CEO who had just conveyed the impression he had no idea how he was going to handle Concord's new stepchild.

They chatted and laughed informally, shared some chocolate mints, and Grant showed her all the sights visible through his custom-made window overlooking the Charles River. Sarah continued to endear herself to him without letting down her guard, or revealing anything about her feelings for his son. She broke her vow of restraint only once, when she brightened visibly after the CEO told her his son was still single despite his mother's ongoing crusade to change that.

As soon as the meeting ended and she was out of sight of the building, Sarah did a skip and a jump that culminated in a hand-clap to applaud her success. The interview had gone well. She paused to look back on the long road from the slums of South Boston to executive row at Concord Industries. For the first time in nine years, Sarah Jane Jankovic could imagine the unimaginable. Now she could confront the man who once made it clear his ancestral requirements would prevent her from ever becoming Mrs. Grant Abbot Lonsdale III.

Chapter 24

Luanne looked everywhere for Grant before she found him in the fish room, sitting by himself in the dark, with only the tank lights on.

"Grant, what are you doing in here? Don't you want some lights on?"

"No. I like it this way. When I have to think, I think better with the overhead lights off. Sometimes I don't have to think at all in here. It's the only place in the world like that."

She could see the look of serenity on Grant's face when he leaned back in his chair, with his hands laced behind his head and his eyes closed. She pulled up a chair beside him. She decided not to say anything for a few minutes, although she desperately wanted to know the status of his investigation. His breathing slowed, which made her wonder if he'd fallen asleep. She poked him gently in the ribs. "Grant, are you awake?"

"I was never asleep," he grumbled. He shifted in his chair and gave her a gentle frown. "I was at the beginning of a quiet excursion to the bottom of that big tank straight ahead. It's the one with the large blue fish in it. What kind of fish are they?"

"Discus fish. Very beautiful, very expensive. May I ask you a question?"

"Yes, but only if you promise to let me try to relax. What's the question?"

"How are things going? And what's Maria doing in there faxing all those documents?"

"That's two questions. She's sending them to a source that will take action on them. I'm going to remove that sword of Damocles that's been hanging over you and Major."

"Sword of *what?*"

Grant yawned and straightened up "Never mind. And I can't tell you just yet what's going on. The less you know, the safer you are. I'm sending Maria home as soon as she finishes. I'd like you and Major to get out of here also, and stay out for the next couple of days. I can't explain all this right now, so you'll have to trust me."

Luanne bit her lip. "Where will you be, Grant?"

"I'll be right here. It's where I need to be. I have to get those documents sent out quickly before Corazon's boys get here and block the transmission. Please, just go."

She stood to face him while she fought back the tears.

"Corazon's sending his thugs after you, isn't he? They killed Momma, didn't they? And they killed that computer guy, too, didn't they?" The tears began a slow descent down her cheeks.

Grant turned away. "Go. Now, please."

"I want to stay with you."

"No. I want you to go. Don't argue about it."

She bent down, gave him a hard hug, and ran out of the room, wiping her eyes.

He thought about going back to sleep, but the sharp ring of his cell phone echoed so loudly in the quiet room it seemed even the fish might have been startled by it.

"Grant, it's me, Chad. Man, have I got a couple of pieces of hot news for you! Brace yourself, old buddy."

"Okay, I'm braced. But first, have you found Sarah?"

"Have I ever! You're not going to believe this. She's working for your father at Concord."

"She's *what?*"

"Yeah, believe it or not. My sources tell me he just promoted her to manager of the accounting department. Small world, isn't it?"

"Chad, are we talking about the same Sarah?"

"Bet your bottom dollar we are, my friend. Sarah Jane Jankovic of South Boston. There's more. She got married and then divorced. Then she went on to get her bachelor's degree from Tufts. If that wasn't enough, she became a Certified Public Accountant, and went to work for Concord. Or maybe the other way around, I can't remember. But I hear she just became one of your dad's new managers. And she's single, at least for now. So, what do you think of them apples?"

Grant slapped his forehead. "Jeez, Chad. Nice work. Damn, that's great news. Hey, does Dad know about us? I mean about Sarah and me?"

"I've no idea. But here's a thought. Why don't you tell him so he can fire both of you? Then you'll be free to marry without any parental garbage, and you both can come to work for me."

Grant shook his head, but couldn't stifle a grin. "Not funny, Chad. Okay, you said you had a couple of newsworthy items. What's the other one?"

"The other one's even better. My FBI sources tell me they received all those incriminating documents you dug up for them. So, when are you leaving?"

"Soon. And thanks for getting my messages through to those guys."

"Grant, what do you mean 'soon'?"

"I mean it's going to be a few more days before I can finish. I'm not quite wrapped up here."

"Grant, you stay there any longer and you're a dead man. Those thugs will be coming after you. My guess would be any time now. What's the holdup?"

"They're coming for me tonight."

"*What?* You know this?"

"Not for certain, but the likelihood is a foregone conclusion. An FBI agent called me on my cell and said their tracking system picked up a private plane flight-clearance from Bogota to the Okeechobee County Airport. He mentioned two passengers and a rental car reservation for this evening. You do the math."

"Damn it, Grant. You struck a deal with the Feds, didn't you?"

"More or less, but it was necessary, believe me."

"Does your father know about this?"

"Well, part of it. But he doesn't need to know the rest, and I don't want you to tell him, either."

"You idiot. You insufferable idiot. Grant, there's no payoff on this. Get out of there."

"There *is* a payoff, Chad. The future of this whole hatchery is at stake on this one. Just keep quiet about it and cut me a little slack, as Major would say."

"Wow! You lost me, Grant. You don't think the same anymore. You don't even talk the same. What ever happened to that good old aloof, Ivy-League-elite, me-first guy I used to know? What the devil's gotten into you down there?"

"I don't know. Maybe it's the drinking water, like you said. But don't worry about it. I'll be okay. I have to go, Chad. I'll talk to you later."

Maria walked in and handed Grant a listing of the documents she'd faxed. He checked the printout against his list, and gave her a high-five.

"Nice work, Maria. You go home now."

"I will, but you be careful, Meestair Grant. This was a beautiful place before, but now it's a very bad place. You be careful, please."

"I will, Maria. Now go."

* * * * * *

Grant turned out the lights in Major's office, sat in Major's chair, and started to pour himself a cup of Okeechobee Comfort. Then, deciding he'd better stay as alert as possible, poured it back into the bottle. They'd come soon, he was sure of it. There wasn't much else to do except wait.

He pulled the .243 out from under the desk, checked to see it was loaded, and leaned back with the barrel across his lap. Not that it would do any good against professionals, but it gave him a warm feeling. He'd never actually seen any of the four FBI agents supposedly sent to guard him, but he had to trust someone. They had to be out there somewhere. The prearranged strategy had been specific enough about that.

A soothing silence hung over the place, accompanied by a stillness in the air, until the cicadas began tuning up for their evening performance. At that moment, Grant figured being anywhere but where he was sounded like a good idea. Maybe Beacon Hill. He let his thoughts wander again. *If I come out of this alive I'll deliver the most poetic apology I can write to Sarah. It was unforgivable, what I did. My fault, no one else's, and if she becomes a part of my life I can't very well have her resenting my whole family. Chad was right. I guess I've changed. Maybe Sarah's changed. Cross that bridge when I come to it. Right now it looks like I'm in that tall grass with those big dogs Sam talked about.*

* * * * * *

In the quiet of Major's office Grant closed his eyes…just to rest them for a moment. Fatigue turned the moment into a fifteen-minute doze that began with thoughts of Victoria Prentiss…her statuesque beauty; her sophistication; the fashion-model effect of her imported wardrobe as she took her wifely place beside him to welcome their guests at company parties; how much his parents wanted her for a daughter-in-law — and how he couldn't stand being around her.

The misty images evolved into gossamer thin visions of his mother and the sacrifices she'd made as the linchpin in the consolidation of two dynasties. The visions darkened when she began to cry on her husband's shoulder. Between sobs she asked him why God had allowed a drug kingpin to kill their only son, leaving their empire without an heir. The dream turned ugly when red-eyed creatures flew in circles above his head while a crowd of long-dead drug addicts gathered around him. Their dark, hollow eyes fixed on him, they chanted in unison that their deaths had been caused by his failure to stop the white kilo-bags from attacking them.

Grant's next awareness was of a blurred shadow entering the room. It all happened so quickly he didn't have time to raise the rifle from his lap. By the time Grant became conscious enough to react, the man had grabbed the rifle and stood glaring down at him.

"Just what the hell do you think you're doing, son?" Major bellowed. "Did you think you were going to stop those gunnies all by yourself? And what the hell good did you think a rifle was going to do in a closed room?"

Grant straightened and rubbed his eyes. "No, Major, the FBI's out there," he stammered, embarrassed to have been caught napping. "I was just giving myself a little extra insurance."

"Damnation, boy. For being the smartest young man I ever met, you sometimes sure are the dumbest. Do you know where your FBI men are right now?"

"No. I don't think I'm supposed to know. Those guys are professionals, and they know how to keep a low profile in a situation like this. I thought I told Luanne to get the two of you out. What are you doing here?"

"What I'm doing, son, is making sure you get back to Boston in one piece. I'll tell you where your men are right now. They got their dumb asses hunkered down behind all that landscaping beside our front driveway. Like they think Corazon's boys are stupid enough to drive up in their limousine and honk a couple of times before they kill you. Hell, my blind grandmother could have spotted them out there. Now, I want you to come with me. I'm going to put you in a place where they can't get at you. Then I'm going to ambush those Colombian gunnies myself and get this done the right way. You made me see I been sucking up to them drug honchos too damned long. Now, come on, we ain't got much time."

159

Grant put up his hand. "Major, I appreciate what you're doing, but you're just going to compromise this whole scheme. This really isn't just your fight."

"The hell it ain't." Major pointed his finger at Grant. "Sam's pretty sure they killed my wife. And if that don't make it my fight I don't know what does."

"Yes, I understand. Sam talked to me about that. And I'm terribly sorry about your wife. But Major, in order to nail Corazon, they have to catch him in the act, or close to it. If we spook him, it won't work."

Major paused to glare down at Grant with steady eyes that never blinked. "Well now son, would that act you're talking about come right before, or right after, they put a high magnum bullet into your skull?"

Although the question wasn't entirely unexpected, Grant realized that, with all his concentration on the logistics of the plan, he probably should have given more consideration to the possibility of getting killed.

"Ahh…yes, I see your point. Look, Major, it's not that I want to throw myself under the bus, but how else do you plan on getting Corazon for attempted murder? The FBI doesn't want to send a team down there to get him without evidence sufficient to justify an international incident like that. This is the only way to build enough of a case to extradite the man. Or, at least stop what he's doing to you and Luanne."

"Well, Grant, I kind of figured this whole thing will take care of itself by the time I get through. So, you come with me and don't worry about it. Now let's go, or do I have to drag you out by your ankles?"

Grant sprang to his feet. "Listen up, Major. I have a better idea. With all due respect, there's nothing about this whole mess that's going to take care of itself. We don't have much time. So—"

"Yeah, I know. Luanne told me. Okay, you gonna let me in on this idea of yours sometime in the next few minutes?" Major put the rifle aside and placed his hands on his hips.

"Yes, sir. You go bring that FBI agent in here. Then the two of you keep out of sight in your office. I'll dim the lights in the conference room and hunch over the table, which is exactly where they would expect to find me. Corazon knows I work late and alone. When they come in, there won't be any doubt about their intentions. We have federal backup to nail them. I'll keep low over the conference room table, maybe with that .38 Luanne told me you keep hidden in your drawer. What do you think?"

Major scratched his head and frowned. "Truth be known, I think it's about the dumbest idea I ever heard." He paused for a moment to stroke his chin.

"But it might be just dumb enough to work, so I'll go along with it. But I ain't handin' you no firearm. Hell, boy, the minute they suspect you got a gun they're going to blow you away and think about it later. If it comes to that, leave the shooting to us. Now let's get this thing started. I'll go round up one of those FBI boys staked out in the bushes and hope he knows more about shooting than he does about hiding out."

Chapter 25

Corazon's assassination instructions were the same ones he had issued for the North Carolina deaths. Salazar knew how difficult it can be to prove murder in a DUI death. Chuzo and Armand were to grab Grant, put him to sleep quickly with an ether-soaked cloth, and drive him to the outskirts of Mayaca for the 'accident'. The car would be torched to destroy any evidence that might be found in an autopsy. Enrico Diaz was directed to steal Grant's computer, his notes, and every file he could get his hands on. Fear of reprisal would prevent any subsequent disclosure by anyone at South Atlantic Farms.

The two assassins waited with Enrico in the woods at the far end of the ponds. The abduction required darkness, not only for cover but to provide assurance that all employees had left for the day. Led by Diaz, who knew every inch of the grounds, the two men moved without a sound toward the hatchery's office building. From their position, they could see a figure hunched over the conference table facing away from them.

Less-than-optimal visibility became, at that moment, the only shield to the identity of the human form engrossed in paperwork in the dimly lit room. During the fifty-yard sprint between where they were and the building, they would be exposed. The three attackers darted from the protection of the trees, throwing shadows behind them on the moonlit grass in their fifty-yard sprint from the woods to the office building. They reached the building and waited for a few moments to catch their breath outside the door. The heat and humidity of the day lingered, warming the light evening breeze, which carried the smell of freshly mown grass into their nostrils. They scanned the area again to make sure no one was entering or leaving the building. The conference room's half-opened window increased the risk of their being heard, a circumstance they hadn't anticipated. All the more need to move quickly, Armand reminded them.

Diaz stepped into the conference room first. A familiar face would be less likely to alarm Grant. Chuzo and Armand moved in behind, then around him, and descended upon Grant before he could brace himself.

The sequence of events blended into a blur of movements. Chuzo pinned Grant's arms to his side while Armand applied the ether-soaked cloth to Grant's nose and mouth. In a burst of panic, prompted more by the prospect of suffocation than anything else, Grant lashed out by kicking against the table hard enough to knock his chair and Chuzo to the floor. Arms still wrapped around Grant, Chuzo forced both of them to an upright position. Armand slapped the cloth over Grant's face again.

Major charged into the room in time to catch a roundhouse right to the jaw from Diaz. The blow knocked him down long enough to allow Diaz time to throw his weight on top of him. The field hand got in two more punches before the tough old farmer managed to throw him off. "Where the hell are the damned FBI guys?" Major shouted as he staggered to his feet.

Agent Michaels, the first of the FBI backup team to step into the room, pointed his Glock 26mm and shouted for the three intruders to step back with their hands up. Armand released his grip on Grant, dropped to his knees, and pulled out his .45.

Michaels had been ordered to take the hit men alive if possible. Armand's movement eliminated that option, and the agent acted instinctively. The Glock's deafening roar sounded like a cannon going off in the small room. Everyone's ears felt the concussion. The bullet entered Armand's forehead making a small hole and exited through a larger one at the back of his skull, taking a sizable chunk of gray matter with it.

Chuzo stepped back and, with his left arm wrapped around Grant's neck, thrust his hostage in front of him. He drew his own gun and put the barrel to Grant's temple.

"Everyone back off or I kill this boy. Lay your guns down. Do it now." The unemotional firmness of his voice matched the cold of his lifeless eyes. This was a man without fear of armed lawmen, and with nothing more to lose at that particular moment. Michaels and Major hesitated before they dropped their weapons on the floor.

Chuzo motioned to Diaz with his gun. "Pick up their firearms."

The two backup agents entered the room in time to catch a hail of fire from Diaz the moment he picked up the Glock. One agent pitched forward onto the floor, the other spun around and ducked back into the hallway before Diaz could get another shot off in his direction.

163

Major took advantage of the distraction and charged Diaz. Slowed by age, the old farmer caught the heel of Diaz's gun on the side of his head and dropped unconscious to the floor.

Still a bit fuzzy from his brief whiff of the ether, Grant managed to call upon the same recovery training he'd used on the football field following a solid hit from a defensive lineman. He blinked, shook his head, swung his elbow into Chuzo's gut, and wrenched free.

Diaz repositioned the pistol in his hand, swung his firing arm toward Grant, and leveled the muzzle at him. The movement became his last. The usually quiet little room reverberated again with the ear-splitting crack of two more shots. Diaz pitched sideways to the floor, blood spewing from his ear.

Chuzo recovered his wind, straightened, and turned toward the sound in time to catch the second bullet in his chest. The force of the impact carried him backward into a file cabinet. He died before he hit the floor.

None of the three intruders had given the half-open window another thought once they were inside. Outside the window, Luanne rested the barrel of her .243 on the ledge, and stared in shock at the carnage she'd wrought. She dropped the rifle, covered her face with her hands, and began to cry.

Grant reached her first. He threw his arms around her, hugged her tight, and let her uncontrollable sobbing continue until there were no tears left.

Major rolled over, sat up, and staggered to his feet. He wobbled across the room and bent over Diaz's body. With a tight grip on his trusted employee's hand, Major stared down at him and asked "Why?" His voice sounded more hurt than angry.

Agent Michaels checked his fallen partner's vital signs, and called for an ambulance. Then he checked in with his superiors and contacted the local police. For a few moments, the distant wail of sirens was the only audible sound.

The police went through their customary questioning, documentation, and recording protocol before they hauled the three bodies off. After a prolonged discussion about what the bureau's next official actions would be, Major, the agents, and a still shaking Grant opened Major's next-to-last bottle of Okeechobee Comfort. Her head still lowered, Luanne declined to share in the beverage. The ordeal was over, and probably deserved more celebration than simply invading Major's liquor cabinet. However, no one could think of anything better to do at that particular moment.

Grant sat down beside her and drew Luanne close to him again. No one spoke until Major broke the silence. He laid his hand gently on Grant's shoulder. "Remember me telling you she was a crack shot, son? Bet you forgot, you were so all fired up that day about our finances."

Grant looked up at him. "No, sir, I didn't forget. And I'll never forget that she saved my life. I still don't know what in hell they were planning to do with me after they knocked me out, but I'm sure it wasn't going to be pretty."

He stood up and put his arm around Major's shoulder. "Major, I can't thank you guys enough for all you've done." Grant picked up his cup and raised it in salute. He turned to the FBI agent. "So, what do you think? Do we have enough evidence to put Corazon away, even though we can't put his men on the stand to testify?"

Michaels nodded.

Major looked at him as though he wasn't sure the agent had the authority to respond to that question. He shrugged his shoulders. "Well, your FBI man says so, but Corazon ain't one to give up easy. One thing's for sure. That dirtbag and his monkeys ain't gonna show up around here no more unless they want to be food for the gators. By the way, speaking of thanks, we all owe you one hell of a lot, Grant, for bustin' up this whole scam of his."

"Thanks, but I wasn't alone in the effort. With a lot of research from Chad Winslow, you folks and Sam Tillery helped make it happen."

Major rubbed his head where Diaz's gun butt hit. He nodded and grinned. "I'll tell you something else too. I'm not the only one around here who got a whole new idea about Bostonians. We watched one of 'em shoot a gator, put himself up as a target to save our hides, and stick with us long enough to pull us out of this mess. You done real good, son."

They made idle talk for a while, most of it to calm each other. The whole affair had been a traumatic experience, and Grant knew it wouldn't really be over until the Financial Intelligence Unit known as FinCen honored the arrangement its agent had made with him.

What then? Back to Boston and see if it's possible to resurrect a life with Sarah. He'd offer no apologies to his parents. He'd absolve them of any ancestral blame. His acceptance of family responsibilities would be on his own terms. Run Concord his own way. Return the hatchery to Major and Luanne as soon as the Feds allow it. If it didn't all come together the way he wanted, then to hell with it. He'd go back to WM&P and become managing partner someday.

Grant's last official act in his assignment required his signature on a witness document before the FBI took Tommy Rawls away on a host of banking violations charges. Tommy's one-out-of-seven chance of getting off clean had gone the way of most statistical improbabilities. Grant showed no feelings one way or the other when Major told him they'd cuffed Tommy. All he could think of at the time was a large, polished desk with nothing on it and, now, no one behind it. They'd have to find a new boss for the starchy woman with the squeaky shoes.

He shook Major's hand and turned to give Luanne a good, hard hug.

"Luanne, there's no way I can tell you how much I appreciate all you've done. If it hadn't been for you, I might have been still locked into my past." He hugged her again. "Thanks for the new roadmap."

Luanne stepped back and wiped her eyes. "I'm glad you finally found her, Grant. At least, I think I am. So, I guess you'll be heading back to Boston, now, right?"

"Yes. However, we'll be in contact with each other while South Atlantic and Concord merge their activities. As soon as the Feds are satisfied, we'll cut the umbilical cord, and you and Major can run the hatchery again, free and clear. I wonder if one of your field hands could take a picture of you, Major, me and Maria before I leave."

He pulled out the small digital camera he'd used to photograph the tanks in the fish room. Major recruited Diaz's assistant. Grant gave the man instructions, and stood beside the three people he'd come to respect in a way he'd never thought possible.

Major wrapped an arm around Luanne and wiped the tears from her eyes with the other. Father and daughter faced the camera until the little green light flashed. The miniature electronic device recorded an image which would eventually occupy a prominent place on Beacon Hill. They said their goodbyes, and Grant promised to come back for a visit someday — maybe get in some fishing with Major and Kip. In his heart, he knew he never would.

✳ ✳ ✳ ✳ ✳ ✳

The drive back to Orlando gave Grant time for reflection. The radio in his Lexus had remained set on the same channel he'd turned off with no small measure of disgust on the way to Okeechobee weeks before. It seemed like months had elapsed since then. He turned the radio on again in time to catch another one of those old country/western favorites — a 1970s number entitled *For the Good Times*. He tilted the driver's seat back a notch and listened to the melancholy lyrics, which resurrected the sadness that seemed inseparable from his memories of Sarah.

Grant kept the station on until he pulled off the road at Bubba Bobby's. No one even looked up when he walked in wearing the casuals he'd bought in Mayaca. His second-ever order of catfish went down well and earned him a nod of approval from Bubba himself. Back on the road again, he made it to the Orlando Airport without exceeding the speed limit…for the most part. In a few hours he'd find out whether the dream he'd shattered could be put back together after nine years.

Chapter 26

Sarah felt a sense of excitement the moment Grant Abbot Lonsdale III walked into her office in Concord's accounting department. It was as though something locked inside her for the last nine years had been set free. She wanted to run toward him. Instead, she rose from her desk and approached him slowly, as though the wall she'd built around her heart was not ready to come down. She wondered whether he shared her feeling of intense anxiety. She even questioned how he might feel about her being there at all. Self-control was only one of the disciplines she'd acquired during her long journey.

Maybe he would want her again. Maybe he wouldn't. Were the same barriers that separated them once before still there? The next few seconds would tell. Sarah Jane Jankovic made up her mind. Even though she felt more fragile than she ever had before, she *would not cry*. Nine years of determined redemption had taught her that much. She held her emotions in check as though she feared they might burst out into words before she could screen them. She could hear the soft thudding of her heart and hoped he couldn't.

He seemed taller now, his frame a little more filled out, but still as rock-hard and athletic-looking as ever. His handsomely sculpted face hadn't changed. It had simply darkened a bit with a beard that grew after his teenage years. His brown hair appeared to be a shade lighter. Maybe it just looked that way in contrast to his Florida tan. It seemed like he wanted to smile but couldn't, as though some underlying sadness prevented it, and she wondered why. Was he disappointed in the way she looked? Or would this be a final rejection from which there would be no appeal?

Despite her efforts to suppress it, she felt a familiar weakness setting in. A sudden tightening in her stomach accompanied an unexpected dryness in her mouth, just as she was about to tell him how excited she was to see him. She tried to speak, but her throat caught, and the words remained trapped on the edge of her thoughts. Sarah had played out this scene in her mind a hundred times over the years.

At that moment a transient undercurrent of deep resentment rushed in and swept her excitement away, leaving in its wake only a quiet mistrust. He'd hurt her before. She would not let that happen again.

* * * * * *

Grant moved toward her with an uncertainty of his own, fostered by the underlying guilt he'd suppressed in the far regions of his mind over the years. He'd committed himself to ask, even beg if necessary, for Sarah's forgiveness. Fully aware he might not have forgiven her had their roles been reversed, he prepared himself for a response that could go either way. She looked just like he remembered her. Maybe an inch or two taller. The innocence and simplicity in her eyes had been replaced with a knowing, guarded look. Grant felt a twinge of regret that perhaps he had done that to her. His heart beat harder.

Her raven-black hair, once tied up in a long ponytail that bounced randomly behind her when she ran, now swirled neatly in a shorter, more business-like bun. He remembered swimming naked with her in the surf at night. With each shake of her head, Sarah's long, black hair had swung across her shoulders and showered him with a gentle spray.

Grant tried to picture her tight little shorts and midriff-revealing tank top, which had always caught his attention whenever she felt it was time to flirt. They'd been exchanged for a button-up white blouse under a well-tailored dark gray business jacket and long slacks. Her off-the-rack-dresses were things of the past. High heels replaced the worn loafers he remembered her wearing without socks no matter what the occasion, but couldn't conceal the delicate curves of her feet.

Grant broke into the wide, sly grin that used to tickle her every time. "My God, you're beautiful!" He said it softly. He hesitated as though, perhaps, he hadn't given what he was about to say enough rehearsal. "Sarah Jane Jankovic, I've come to offer myself in the hope of resurrecting that beautiful dream we once shared. The one from which I foolishly turned away. I don't even know whether you can find a way to forgive me. I know I can never repair whatever damage I must have done, but, if you'll give me another chance, I'll spend a lifetime trying to make up for it."

169

He dropped to his knees in front of her. Unprofessional in a business setting, and he knew it. What the hell, it would be his company someday anyway, so who cares? He looked up at Sarah just as one of her accounting trainees entered her office without knocking. Thoroughly embarrassed at having stumbled upon the scene, the startled young man did an about-face and made a strategic retreat.

Sarah leaned forward and placed a hand on each side of Grant's head. She hesitated before she spoke. "Grant, I can't even begin to tell you how much of the last nine years I've spent hoping to hear that you still love me. Or trying to forget how much it hurt when you ended our dream. In my mind, I understood why. In my heart, I never did."

Grant closed his eyes and lowered his head. After a few moments he looked up at her. "Sarah, I owe you an explanation for actions so unforgiveable I hardly know where to begin. I used to think that my family obligations were so paramount they outranked my feelings for the only girl I've ever loved. I know it's no comfort now, but I want you to know not a day has gone by since that I didn't regret—"

"Stop, Grant." Sarah placed her finger gently over his mouth. "I never believed it was you who wanted me out of the Lonsdale family picture. In a way, it wasn't even your parents. It was a hundred-or-more years of your ancestry that I blame for that crushing moment."

He reached up and wrapped his hands around her wrists. "I know, honey, I know. Believe me, my family history and traditions will never get in the way again. Now, listen, I'll—"

"No, Grant. *You* listen. I need time to think this through for precisely that reason. I have to make sure your parents will accept me for who I am before I can say yes to your proposal. I think we both need that comfort. I—"

Unannounced, Grant's father walked in. Instead of turning around for a tactful exit, he stood in place, arms folded, looking down on them with an expression of appalled amusement. The young couple stared back at him, looking painfully aware of how awkward the situation must appear.

Grant's father broke the ice. "Well, Miss Jankovic, I see you've met my son. Now, since neither of you seems to have any use for the chairs in this office, I'm sure you won't mind if I sit down on one of them."

Sarah's face turned crimson. "Of course, Mr. Lonsdale," she stammered. "I can explain everything. "It's not the way it looks, and I apologize for the unprofessional demeanor."

"Dad," Grant began as he rose slowly to his feet, "I think I'm the one who should explain. This is the best part of a long story that I've never told you or Mother."

"Good," his father snapped. "I like a gripping mystery. I can't wait to find out why my son is on his knees in front of my new accounting manager. I'm looking forward to hearing this one." He nodded and smiled at his son. "Grant, I'm glad to see you're home safe. I heard what happened down there, and I'm not at all pleased about the part you neglected to tell me. Then again, it's hard to chastise a guy the Department of Justice has branded a hero. So, I'll simply add my own congratulations."

The chairs in Sarah's office found gainful employment again. Sarah and Grant settled back to share the story of a romance which, for years, hung by a memory which simply wouldn't go away. Grant Senior leaned back and waited.

"Dad, this is the Sarah I told you and Mother about a long time ago. I know you both expected a different outcome, but Sarah is the girl I love. I should have stood firm about this a long time ago, and maybe we both wouldn't have gone through what we did. Anyway, I'm going to set it right. I've asked Sarah to be my wife. She's deferred her answer until she has time to clear up some interfering concerns — one of which is how you and Mother will react."

Grant's father frowned. "What do you mean you should have stood firm? Please refresh my memory. What is there to set right?"

"With all due respect to our family values, Dad, I made a terrible mistake years ago. I put our ancestral traditions ahead of my love for Sarah. I've regretted it since. I know you and Mother meant well, but now I'm in a damage-control mode. I need you and Mother to stand with me, and I hope Sarah and I have your blessing."

Sarah's lips tightened. She looked at the floor, then turned to face Grant's father with pleading eyes. "Mr. Lonsdale, I know I was wrong not to tell you about us during my interview, but I just wasn't sure your son still loved me, and I wanted the job. I'm so sorry, and I hope you'll understand. Please forgive me?"

They waited several long, anxious moments for a response. This man was more than just Grant's father. He was a corporate icon, known and respected all over the world. His opinion mattered. Like defendants waiting for the jury to return with its verdict, the two youngsters made every effort to hold their anxiety in check.

"I see," the seasoned CEO began cautiously. His frown suggested that he saw only that he'd been kept in the dark by both his son and Sarah. "Well, perhaps in retrospect this whole damned mystery could have been avoided if my wife and I had been a little more open-minded." He stood and positioned himself in front of Sarah's chair. "Okay, then. It looks like it's forgiveness of me by both of you that's in order here. You've almost forgiven each other, so perhaps we should be thinking more about getting on with our lives. Sarah, I welcomed you into your new role in our company a few days ago." His expression lightened into a wide grin. "Now, I guess it's time to welcome you into our family. Like my son, I hope you'll accept. In retrospect, I can't say I'm surprised about all this. My wife Mignon and I knew there was always a Sarah in our son's dreams. We didn't have any idea it was you. Anyway, Grant's mother has always wanted a daughter, and now it looks like maybe she'll finally have one. You have my blessing, although getting Mignon's may take some doing. By the way, Sarah, I hope you'll have more success keeping track of my son's whereabouts than I ever had."

With tears welling up in her eyes, Sarah leaped from her chair and hugged the CEO.

He patted her on the head and turned to his son. "Grant, have you told your mother anything about Sarah yet?"

Grant Abbot breathed a sigh of relief. "No sir, I'm on my way to do that right now. And I'm not looking forward to Mother's reaction."

Grant's father shook his head. "Neither am I. I think you need to clear the way on that before I bring Sarah home to meet her. Tell you what. I'll give you an hour's lead time to soften up your mother before Sarah and I bring up the rear."

Chapter 27

Mignon's anguished screams echoed through the mansion, loud enough to bring Mary Coyne running into the living room to see what had so enraged her employer. Mary's job as the Lonsdale family's live-in maid and housekeeper during the last twenty years had grown to include a number of auxiliary tasks, including restraining Mignon whenever the woman felt compelled to throw a fit.

"Good God, Grant," Mignon shouted, "have both you and your father gone crazy? How could you have *done* this to me? Jankovic? *Jankovic?* What kind of a name is that? For God's sake, it isn't even American. I won't permit it, Grant, I simply won't!"

"Mother, Sarah's a wonderful girl, as you'll soon find out. I've proposed to her, and I'm waiting for her decision. Which, I might add, will depend on how she interprets your reaction to the marriage. I hope she's going to be my wife. Now, calm down. I want—"

"No. I will *not* calm down." Mignon lunged from the sofa and glared at her son. "I haven't sacrificed all my life to turn everything over now to some cheap little Slavic nobody. How could you *do* this to me, Grant? How *could* you?"

Grant rolled his eyes. "Mother, I don't know what you're talking about. You won't have to share any of your responsibilities with Sarah for a decade or more. I want you to be reasonable about this. We need your blessing. Sarah, in particular, needs your approval."

Mignon fell back on the massive old sofa, put her face in her hands, and began what looked like an uncontrollable weeping binge. Mary rushed to her side, knelt down and wrapped her arms around the sobbing woman.

"Ah, sure an' I know how ye've wanted something else all yer life, mum," Mary said, "but things sometimes turn out God's way an' not ours. Come, now. You know you can trust yer son. He's a fine lad, and I'm sure he'd never do anything to hurt you. So, come now, you an' me together. We'll stand up tall an' just hug this little girl, an' we'll teach her everything she needs to know an' ye won't be sacrificin' anything."

Mary stood and took both of Mignon's hands in hers. "Come on now, stand up an' hug yer son an' put yer trust in the Lord. This is goin' to turn out just grand for ye, I know it will. So, come on. Let's you an' me just get on with this an' we'll show 'em all what we're made of."

A welcome silence filled the room with a healing calmness of its own for several long moments. Grant stepped back to allow Mary, and other forces greater than his, to contain his distraught mother. He knew her tearful display of self-pity demanded center-stage attention and top billing. A few anxious moments later the sobbing stopped. Mary brought Mignon to a more upright position, gave her a handkerchief, and gently massaged her back and shoulders.

Mignon wiped her eyes. Usually meticulous about personal grooming matters, she ignored them for the moment. It was too late to repair the damage torrential tears had done to her abundant mascara and eye shadow. She turned, looked up at her son with an expression of forlorn hope, and heaved a sigh of resigned defeat. Before anyone could speak, Mignon Chester Lonsdale stood erect, smoothed out her skirt, and exited through the front hall she always referred to as her foyer. Head held high, she marched up the long, curved staircase to her room without another word.

About the time Mignon mounted the top step and rounded the corner to her sanctuary, Grant's father emerged through the front door with Sarah right behind him. The atmosphere seemed to have cleared a bit, but still hung heavy with tension.

"Uh, honey," a still-in-shock Grant said, "this might not be a good time to—"

"Begorra it's the best time, and it'll get done right now, lad," Mary snapped. "Well, lass, you must be Sarah. I'm Mary Coyne, and I run this place. So give me a hug."

Sarah peered over Mary's shoulder and cast a quick glance at Grant, as if to ask who this strange little lady was. Mary whispered something in Sarah's ear, took her arm, and they started up the stairs.

Grant charged after them in pursuit. "Hold on, Mary, I'll come make the introduction."

Mary turned on him. "Ye'll be doin' nothin' of the kind, lad. Right now the last person in the world the missus wants to see is yourself. I'll show young

Sarah where the room is, and she can be goin' in alone. Otherwise it'll be *tellin'* the missus she has to accept her. Goin' in by herself it'll be more like *askin'*, don't you see. They'll be needin' some time alone now."

It suddenly occurred to Grant he'd never told Sarah much about Mary except that she'd been the family housekeeper, cook, and his live-in nanny way back when. Mary knew most of the Lonsdale family secrets and could be counted on to keep them. She also had the distinction of being the only person outside the family to have been allowed free access to anywhere in the mansion at any time.

Their faces drawn tight in painful apprehension, the two Lonsdale men stood at the foot of the stairs and watched Mary escort Sarah up to Mignon's room. There was nothing more either of them could think to do.

While he waited, Grant allowed his mind to reawaken memories. He'd loved following Mary along Charles Street when he was a kid. She'd take him for rides on the Swan Boats, and afterward pull him along while she did the weekly shopping. The pretentious sales-clerks in the shops were known to treat, with guarded contempt, anyone not obviously wealthy — such as Mary, whose appearance clearly marked her as a member of the servant class. Nonetheless, all the shop owners knew Mary came as a representative of the Lonsdales and treated her with respect, especially when they saw the little heir apparent tagging along at her heels. Grant remembered them smiling politely to her face, but sneering behind her back while they whispered phrases like "shanty Irish." When he asked Mary what they meant, she told him they were just small people behaving smaller, and he was to pay them no mind.

In retrospect, the life-changing experiences he went through in Okeechobee might have had no affect on him at all had it not been for Mary's influence during his childhood. He broke into a smile, and he could feel his tension ease.

* * * * * *

Mary knocked, opened Mignon's door slowly without waiting for a reply, and ushered Sarah in. "This is young Sarah, mum. She's been waitin' to meet you. I'll just leave the two of you alone now."

Sarah did her best to manufacture a warm smile, and stepped forward with a timidity borne of her conviction that this would be a difficult hurdle in her long journey. She found Mignon sitting on the edge of her four-poster canopied bed, holding her son's college graduation picture. The room's cream-colored walls, trimmed in a dark, carved wood, made the place appear more like a presidential suite than a bedroom.

Sarah found herself surrounded by a spacious blend of sanctuary and office impeccably decorated. A chest of drawers and a vanity table seemed almost one with a computer station, all in a matching wood which Sarah assumed must have been imported, or custom-ordered, from high-end stores. The whole ensemble presented an ornate testimony to the Lonsdale family's success. It all seemed to have an old fashioned kind of odor, like wet wood and aged cheese. Only the presence of the twenty-first century electronics prevented the old New England ambience from drawing Sarah's mind back two hundred years.

A small, completely furnished reading and sitting room off to the side offered a view of the terrace below through a curved window. Sarah couldn't remember ever having seen such an expansive, curved window before. It reminded her of the panoramic view through the senior Lonsdale's office window looking out on the Charles. This family obviously liked big windows. All in all, the arranged marriage between ancestral tradition and state-of-the-art business technology provided Sarah's first glimpse into the life of the woman who would now decide the shape of her future.

"Hello, Mrs. Lonsdale. May I please come in?" Sarah struggled to squeeze out the words.

The ensuing silence seemed to wrap a sheath of ice around Mignon's piercing glare, which lasted long enough to convince Sarah this woman might refuse to talk to her at all. Still seated on the edge of her bed, Mignon seemed to be studying Sarah with an air of impending denunciation. Lips drawn tight, eyes narrowed, the woman's countenance remained hardened.

Mignon broke the excruciating silence. "I suppose so. It's apparently too late to stop you now. You're the Jankovic girl, I presume. How did you get here?"

"Your husband brought me from the office." Sarah realized her brief response probably should have been amended with something more appealing, but couldn't think what that might be.

"I see. My son tells me you work for my husband at Concord. You're an accountant, I understand. Is that right?"

"Yes, ma'am. I received my CPA certificate after college, and went to work for Concord right away. I've looked forward to meeting you, Mrs. Lonsdale. I'm really pleased to meet you."

176

Silence again. Sarah could see the continuing look of disdain in the solemn woman's eyes, and thought to herself how superfluous, perhaps even dumb, that last comment must have sounded. Sarah shifted from one foot to the other, unsure whether to move toward the woman to offer a handshake, or wait for some form of invitation.

"You're wearing a business suit." Mignon's eyes raked Sarah from the top down. "Times have changed, I see. In my day women wore dresses. Do you own a dress?"

"Yes, I've always preferred dresses but, like you said, times have changed, and now this kind of outfit is a must if you're a department head."

Mignon placed the photograph back on the bedside table, and turned slightly toward Sarah. "How long have you worked at Concord?"

Sarah reached up to brush back a loose strand of hair. "Three years."

"Did my son know you worked there?"

"No. Not until a few days ago."

Mignon folded her hands in her lap. She paused as though she was about to raise Sarah's discomfort to a higher level. "Grant Abbot told me you two loved each other since the time you first met years ago as teenagers. Is that true?"

"Yes. Even after he told me it was all over." Sarah felt a sinking feeling that perhaps she should have defined "it," rather than allowing Grant's mother to draw her own inferences. She tugged at her jacket with one hand, while she reached down as unobtrusively as possible with the other to make a slight adjustment to her slacks.

Mignon leaned forward without releasing Sarah from her glare. "Then why did you keep your employment a secret from him?"

Sarah thought for a moment. How would this woman react to the truth? The determination that kept her going all those years had been the same force that kept her silent until she had proved herself. Sarah now felt certain this woman must have been the reason behind that awful rejection nine years ago. Now she seemed to be requiring a confession from Sarah. Cain demanding an apology from Abel!

"Mrs. Lonsdale, this may sound strange. I couldn't tell him, or even reconnect with him, until I could prove my worthiness to myself and to his family. I convinced myself that doing well at his company would be the only acceptable proof. I only hope you can understand." The painful moment of silence that followed tested Sarah's self-control again. She could feel the lump in her throat.

Mignon's facial expression remained flat, her body motionless. "I see. Well, that was very courageous of you. And when you 'reconnected', as you put it, did he tell you he has family responsibilities which will demand an enormous commitment from both him and his wife?"

"Well, ma'am, I know marriage requires a serious commitment. Believe me, Mrs. Lonsdale, I'm fully prepared to—"

"No, that's not what I meant. Let me state this in a different way. If you marry my son you will eventually become my successor in the management of our family's portfolio of assets. Do you think you've learned enough in your short lifetime to enable you to take on that task?"

Sarah knew this was not a time to bluff. "No, ma'am, but I'm certainly willing to learn over the coming years."

"Well, you'd better be. I don't intend to hand my duties over to someone who sees marriage to my son as simply a path to a life of leisure."

Sarah tried not to let the sting of the insult show. During their drive from the office, Grant's father had explained a few of his wife's characteristics. Sarah wasn't entirely unprepared for the remark. She saw it as an expression of the woman's deepest fears. She also took it to be an expression of hope that the insult might evoke, from Sarah, a response which would put those fears to rest.

Sarah began slowly, not really certain exactly what she was going to say. "Mrs. Lonsdale, I think you should know that I have not yet accepted your son's proposal of marriage. The years have not erased the hurt I felt when he discarded me. I need to think such a commitment through carefully before I make it. In any case, I can assure you there's nothing about my past, or my vision of the future, that could possibly resemble a life of leisure. I'm fully aware of what Grant's responsibilities are. In fact, it was his mistaken belief I wouldn't understand them which kept us apart all these years." Sarah fixed a stern gaze on the woman, "I can also assure you I'm fully committed to preventing whatever separated us then from ever happening again."

Mignon drew her head back. "My, you're a very candid young lady. I see you're also quite assertive. Well, those are beneficial traits. Anyway, I didn't mean to offend you. Grant never told me how lovely you are. You must have had a number of... ah... romantic episodes over the years."

Sarah couldn't be sure whether the remark was a compliment or a trap. Best to assume it was a trap. "No, Grant is the only man I've ever really loved. When I was younger, I made a terrible mistake and married a man I thought I loved, but really didn't, and it resulted in divorce."

Mignon shook her head. "My goodness, you certainly are straightforward. I'm not sure I would have divulged that were I in your place. We don't divorce in our family." Still in a sitting position, Mignon placed both of her hands on her hips, and turned to face Sarah more directly. "Well, don't just stand there, child. Come sit down." She motioned Sarah forward with one hand while she patted the seat of the re-upholstered nineteenth-century chair next to her bed with the other. Sarah sat down carefully, for fear of doing harm to a chair that looked like it might be a family heirloom.

"Now, Sarah, tell me, where are your parents living?" It was the first time the woman had addressed her by her given name.

"My mother died when I was three. My father lives in South Boston now."

"Mmmm…that's a dreadful place. So you grew up without a mother. How interesting. I never had a daughter."

"Why not?" No sooner had the words come out than Sarah wished they hadn't.

"Ah… I suppose it's now my turn to be candid. After Grant was born, I was unable to have more children. I'm sure you must miss your mother."

"Yes, I miss her terribly. Dad raised me by himself, and I always admired him for that. He worked hard for a bare subsistence income. He instilled in me a very strong value system, as he called it. He was all about honesty, integrity and loyalty. I learned a lot from him. It's kind of hard to explain, but he made a lot of sacrifices for me."

Mignon paused, and her glare returned. "Yes, I'm quite familiar with sacrifices. So, your name is Sarah Jankovic. What's your middle name?"

"Jane, after my mother — Jana. Sarah Jane Jankovic."

For the first time Mignon's expression softened, if only for a moment. "Good. I like that. My college roommate and best friend was named Jane. Much to my deep sorrow she passed away last year. Anyway, young lady, I'm tired now. It's been a rather trying day. I want you to meet me tomorrow morning in the living room at nine o'clock sharp for tea. You don't work on Saturday, do you?"

"Sometimes, but I'll plan to take the morning off and meet you."

"Good. We have much to discuss. I'm a firm believer in punctuality, so don't be late. My son will drive you home. I'll see you in the morning. Tell my husband I'll be turning in now and I'll be asleep when he comes to bed."

Sarah forced a smile, which she hoped didn't betray her mixed feeling of relief, doubt, and resentment. She walked to the head of the stairway and turned to glance at the closed door of Mignon's sanctuary. No doubt about it.

This powerful woman had definitely been the author of the edict that crushed Sarah nine years before. Would tomorrow really be about tea and cozy talk, or about a final verdict of permanent banishment?

Sarah brushed back that persistent strand of hair again, straightened her slacks, and descended the long, curved staircase to the hallway. She struggled to hold back what felt like an ocean of tears rolling in on a flood tide.

* * * * * *

Grant met her at the foot of the stairs. His anxious expression mirrored the strain of waiting to see how the meeting of the two most important women in his life had turned out. "Hey, how did it go?"

"Grant, — I'm not sure." Her eyes began to fill. "I don't think your mother is ever going to like me."

"Why do you say that? Of course she is. What happened?" Grant's father moved in closer, as if in anticipation of Sarah's need for another ally.

"Well, she didn't exactly throw me out, but she didn't welcome me, either. She wants to meet with me here in the living room tomorrow at nine sharp, as she put it. I think she intends to grill me further. I don't know whether she disapproves of my background or just me." Sarah turned away, put her hands to her face, and began to sob.

Grant wrapped an arm around her. "Honey, my mother has always been slow to accept change of any kind. She just needs some time. Look, I'll come with you tomorrow and it'll be okay."

Sarah swept the back of her hand across her eyes to wipe the tears, and whirled to face him. "No, Grant. I need to do this by myself. Your mother is either going to accept me as I am, or not at all. And what did she mean by handing over her duties? I don't want her duties. She can keep them, whatever they are."

Grant's father reached out an arm between them to move his son gently away, and placed the other on Sarah's shoulder. "Honey, I think it's time for an experienced old man to step in, if I may. I know my wife, and here's what I think is happening, which I believe you'll find out tomorrow. Mignon, bless her heart, has spent a lifetime filling a financial stewardship function she was thrown into, and pressured to consent to, many years ago. With much sacrifice on her part, she's done it well, to her everlasting credit. Now, she's reluctant to pass that function on to a young lady whose capabilities remained unproven. All this has nothing to do with whether Mignon likes you or not,

Sarah. Deep down she wants you to be Grant's wife. I know she does. Otherwise, she wouldn't be up in her room planning her meeting with you tomorrow. She'd be down here kicking *my* ass all over Beacon Hill. You want to know what's really bothering her? I'll tell you. It's a nasty little thing called management succession."

Sarah pulled away and turned to face Grant's father. "Mr. Lonsdale, I think it's a bit early for your wife to worry about my capabilities. If she's concerned about management succession she should be talking to your son. *He's* the future CEO."

"Sarah, I don't mean it exactly like you think I do," the senior Lonsdale said. "Mignon's pretty sure, but not completely sure, your future husband can handle the load at Concord Industries after I retire. However, Concord is not her pet. Our family's portfolio of other assets *is*. And the stewardship of all that is what she'll be passing on to you. So, I guess you'll have to learn to accept some of those duties sooner or later. Because of what you've already accomplished in the business world, my wife is reasonably confident you'll eventually become capable of handling those tasks…over time. Tomorrow, she probably wants to become more comfortable with you, that's all."

He smiled the same way her father used to do following one of his talks when she missed her mother the most. It brought back her warmest memories so vividly the emotional dam burst, and Sarah couldn't help pouring out all the tears she'd held back the last nine years.

Grant Abbot put a consoling arm around her and handed her his handkerchief. "Hey, now," he said, "let's mop up all those tears before I have to take out more flood insurance."

Grant's father intercepted Mary coming through the door. "Mary, how about fixing us a few drinks?" He led them into the living room where Mary mixed Manhattans from the built-in bar, another fixture the likes of which Sarah had never seen before. Grant Abbot apologized for not having brought any Okeechobee Comfort back with him. They shared stories all around, and the evening ended on a far lighter note than the one on which it began. Still, Sarah knew the next day would be the final hurdle in her long journey, which, she also knew, could end well or very badly.

Chapter 28

Gertrude Mulkey's voice came through Conrad's speaker phone an octave higher than usual. She always sounded a bit tense, but this time she'd raised the bar on apprehension. "Mr. Vanderslice, that Corazon man from South America is on the line for you. He sounds angry. Do you want me to tell him you're in a meeting or something?"

"No, I'll take it, Trudy." He aborted the process of firing up his first cigar of the day, laid the Cohiba Esplendido on the edge of the ashtray, and picked up. "Good morning, Salazar. I heard you had some difficulty at the hatchery. Has it been resolved?"

"I want him dead, Conrad. I want the *cabron* dead. Damn you for sending him down there to disrupt my hatchery operation. You've insulted me and all of my cartel. I'm going to kill him this time once and for all. By all that's holy I should kill you, too."

Conrad drew his head back. "Damn, Salazar, that's one lousy way to start my day. I haven't even had my morning coffee yet. I know you're referring to Lonsdale, but what the hell is a *cabron*?"

"In your language it's exactly what that young man is — a scumbag. He's as good as dead. Rumor has it he's back in Boston. Can you confirm that for me?"

"Yes. At least that's what I heard from his boss. He's there but hasn't yet shown up for work, according to my last conversation with Angus. I want Lonsdale dead, too, for reasons not relevant to your situation. In the interests of security, I'd like you to conduct all of that business with my man Hans Drukker from now on."

"You may count on it." The tone of Salazar's voice had turned from anger to one of cold resolve.

Conrad smiled and relit the Esplendido. "Good. Now, as long as I have you on the line, let's talk more about your cartel and our agreed-upon sharing of its profits. Since it looks like the hatchery will no longer be contributing to them, we need to revise our contract."

"I've always dealt fairly with you, Vanderslice. Your stream of annuities will continue as usual. However, they may be smaller — with or without the hatchery."

"And why is that?"

"As I believe I've told you before, the Mexican organizations are cutting deeper into our trade, and now control almost ninety percent of the cocaine entering the United States. Thus, it became necessary for me to cut a deal with Miguel Cardenas, head of the Sinaloa cartel."

Vanderslice leaned back in his chair and drew in and out on his cigar until he got a good burn going. He paused to blow a small cloud of smoke into the air. "What kind of deal?"

"The Sinaloa, like most of the others," Salazar said, "is protecting its U.S. drug business by sending it further underground to be run by bosses who are less well known by the DEA. This division of the trade into smaller, more efficient units has required a move away from customary money-laundering channels into more creative and unusual ones."

Conrad motioned to Gertrude with a wave of his hand and signaled her to bring in a cup of fresh coffee. "Okay, let me guess, Salazar. The Mexicans are now following your lead and cleaning up their drug money through places like fish hatcheries, right?"

"Right, beginning with Louisiana, Mississippi, and Alabama. The problem is that Miguel now needs an experienced hatchery manager to coordinate the expansion and provide technical assistance to the units. In other words, he needs a capable fish man."

Conrad laid the cigar down and sampled his first coffee of the day. "I have a feeling you're about to tell me something I don't want to hear."

"No. I'm about to tell you that my deal with Miguel begins with handing Major Gibbs over to him as his first — and probably best — fish farmer."

Conrad pushed the coffee aside and shook his head. "Corazon, you must be out of your mind. Either that or you've badly underestimated Major. That stubborn old redneck would surrender every asset on the farm including all his income before he'd agree to something like that."

"You're probably right," Salazar replied, "every asset except one — his lovely daughter. As soon as I clear up the Lonsdale business I will make Luanne disappear. She will agree to be my wife, and she will soon adapt to her new surroundings here with me, knowing that her father's life depends on it.

Major, on the other hand, will learn that he can guarantee his daughter's safety as long as he performs his new duties effectively. Now, as to your share of our future profits, that will depend, to a great extent, on Major's performance. This conversation is over, Conrad. We'll talk again if and when I need you."

Conrad Vanderslice rose slowly to his feet, came around his desk, and walked over to the window. He stared out while he pondered a scenario which, for only the second time in his life, he could not control.

* * * * * *

Sam Tillery's comforting arm around Major's shoulder might have been the old farmer's only source of contentment while they waited in the medical examiner's office. From the moment he granted permission to have Miranda's body exhumed, Major had lived with apprehension about the results of the autopsy, and doubts as to whether he should have allowed his wife's body to be violated in such a way at all.

Major pulled away from Sam, and paced back and forth. Tears filled his eyes. "Damn it, Sam, I can't bear the thought of what they must be doing to my Miranda in that exam room. Look at those laminated charts on the wall. Hell, if they're doing all that cutting and splitting in there I'll never be able to make it up to her."

"Major, you don't have any making up to do at all. They have to find out how she died or you, Grant, and the FBI may *never* be able to find closure on this."

"Yeah, but that's my wife we're talking about in there. Just look at those damn charts. They have them hidden in that corner so people can't see 'em real easy, but I went over there and looked. An' it ain't pretty, I can tell you that."

"Major, they're just illustrations using some cadaver no one probably ever knew. I want you to stop looking at them, and start thinking about the good you're doing. You're stopping those drug monsters from doing this to other people once and for all. Look at it this way. Miranda's about to put Corazon away for a long time. Now, either you get hold of yourself or I'm dragging you out of here."

Major put his face in his hands. "You're right. You're right. I'm okay." He sank into a chair. "By the way, who are those two guys in there? Don't think I've ever seen them around here."

Sam pulled up a chair next to him. "The forensic pathologist is from Atlanta, and the medical examiner is from Miami. Grant and I didn't trust the local coroner, but at least he let us use his facilities. Hey, here they come. Wipe your eyes."

Major and Sam stood, but no one shook hands. The pathologist stripped off his apron, shoved his mask into his pocket, and deferred to the medical examiner to relate their findings.

"Gentlemen, I'm Clarence Stratton, and this is Don Wright, the pathologist who worked with me. I'll come right to the point. I know how traumatic this must be for you. In short, there was some decay, as you might expect. Nonetheless, we're certain the death was not accidental. Our examination showed signs the decedent was forcibly held under water until she drowned. There was trauma to the neck, skull, and torso. She obviously put up a fight. I'll send a detailed report to the FBI and to your local coroner and to her physician. I'll also authorize the body to be reinterred."

Major nodded and turned to the pathologist. "I need to know. I hope you didn't have to cut—"

"Major!" Sam snapped and grabbed his arm.

Clarence smiled and shook his head in a kind of knowing way. "It's okay. No, Mr. Gibbs. Only a little. Your wife's body is ninety percent intact. Here's my card if you need to reach me. We'll be on our way."

Major reached for the card, slumped back into his chair, and wept.

Sam walked the examiners to the door, then returned and stood next to Major until the tears dried up. He put a hand on Major's shoulder. "Come on, my friend. Let's go home. It's been a long day."

Major nodded, stood, and walked over to the examination room. He opened the door, peeked in, and said goodbye to his wife for the last time.

Chapter 29

Sarah wasn't about to be late. She sat outside in her car for half an hour, nervously watching the clock. No need for a tardiness penalty on top of everything else. She went in at nine on the dot and selected a comfortable chair with a good view of the fireplace, an adornment which neither space nor economics permited in her South Boston trailer home. She wore high heels, a white blouse, a dark paisley scarf draped over her shoulders, and a skirt that matched the scarf — proof that she did, in fact, own a dressy outfit.

Mary announced Sarah's arrival, brought in a two-place setting of tea, and smiled. "Good luck to ye, lass. I know the saints'll be wi'ye." Sarah felt herself forcing another smile.

Body erect and head held high, Mignon strolled in at precisely one minute after nine. She gave Sarah a once-over glance, combined with an expression that suggested Sarah's attire had improved but remained less appropriate than expected. Mignon offered a polite-but-terse "good morning," poured each of them a cup of tea, and sat down.

Sarah shifted in her chair, partly from nervousness, but mostly to make sure she sat forward enough to avoid the ultimate faux pas of spilling the tea. She crossed her ankles the way she'd seen professional models do, and braced herself for the anticipated inquisition.

"We drink our tea English style here, my dear," Mignon announced. "No cream, no sugar. Much healthier for you. Now, getting back to our conversation, I need to follow up a bit on the background research I've done on you. So, how much—"

"Excuse me, Mrs. Lonsdale. What do you mean by 'research'?"

"I mean research, exactly that. The usual background check. However, background data can only tell one so much. Beyond that one must make direct inquiries, as I'm now about to do."

"No, ma'am, I meant what kind of research are you talking about?"

"Oh. I simply meant I called one of my contacts at Concord yesterday after you left. He faxed me your personnel file. I needed to know your college grades, your CPA exam results, performance evaluations at Concord, a little more about your personal history and so on. What did you think I meant?"

Stunned by the woman's presumptuousness, Sarah's eyes widened. What kind of a mother-in-law was this woman going to be? What kind of family would this be? Maybe it was Mignon's show of distrust. Maybe it was the insult of it all. Or it might have been the culmination of Sarah's long resentment toward the person she deemed most likely to have triggered her crushing rejection years ago.

At any rate, it was the last straw. Sarah bolted out of her chair, put her teacup down on the tray, and spun toward the startled Mignon. "How dare you? How *dare* you? Aside from the illegality of what you did, do you have any idea what an insult it was? I hope you're satisfied, because I'm not. As far as I'm concerned you can keep your damned duties. Here, you can keep your damned sugarless tea, too!" With a sweep of her hand, Sarah sent the untouched cup flying toward the Battle of Austerlitz tapestry hanging on the south wall. She stormed out of the house, jumped into her car, and cried. Not about the insult, nor about the anger. Not even about the hurt. She cried about the nine-year journey she'd just trashed.

* * * * * *

Father and son descended upon Mignon moments after Mary sounded the alarm. Grant Abbot threw his hands in the air. "Damn it, Mother, what have you done?"

"For heaven's sake dear, I have no idea," Mignon said, eyes wide with astonishment. "I simply brought out the faxed data and started to tell her about the results of the research I'd done on her. She blew up for some reason. She's a very unstable girl, I suppose."

Her son put his hands to the sides of his head, spun around full circle, and glared at her. "I don't believe this. Where the hell's your common sense? Sarah's my future wife, Mother, not some damned criminal."

Grant raised his fist in the air and shook it in his mother's face for the first time ever. "All right, here's the agenda, Mother. I'm going to go after Sarah, find her and bring her back. You're going to apologize profusely for what you did. You're going to welcome her into this family, and treat her with the respect accorded the woman I love. Then I'm going to find the moron who

187

faxed you that information he had no right to access, and fire his damned ass."

Enraged, Grant flew out the door, leaving his father and Mary to tend a now-shaking Mignon. The thought that Grant actually had no authority yet to fire anyone at Concord never crossed his mind.

Mignon watched him tear out of the room and threw her hands in the air. "Oh, Mary, damn it, now I've ruined everything. What the hell am I going to do with this girl? You know I never meant it to come out that way."

"It'll be all right, mum. When yer son brings the lass back, ye can tell her ye were only tryin' to get her ready to become the keeper of the money. Y'know deep in yer heart ye'll come to love her, so just tell her. I know it's always been hard for ye to tell people y'love 'em. But just do it."

Mignon stood up and took a deep breath just in time to face her husband, who came charging toward her looking like the second wave of an all-out attack.

"Mignon, have you lost your mind? What the hell happened, and who is this culprit you conned into releasing information that should never have been removed from our files?"

Mignon wrapped her arms around her husband and laid her head on his shoulder. The stream of tears came down again. "Oh, Grant, I really messed things up. It was all my fault. I was only trying to protect things. I just don't know what to do with this girl."

Her husband unwrapped her arms and stepped back. "What do you mean *do with her*? By God, she's going to be our daughter-in-law!"

Mignon's hands found her hips and she threw an angry look at him. "Oh, hell! You know damned well what I mean. She comes from a ghetto, for heaven's sake. Okay, so she scraped up some kind of an education. So what? Can you just picture that naive little creature trying to manage a multi-million-dollar portfolio? Can you even imagine a Jankovic-from-South Boston squeezing herself into our social circles? I shudder to think how my bridge group is going to react when that uncomfortable-looking girl shows up at the club in her black business suit, and confesses that Old Maid is the only card game she knows."

The senior Lonsdale looked down on his wife with the fierce expression of an executive about to upbraid a subordinate for an unspeakable failure. "Mignon, I'm going to say this only once, and if I ever have to repeat it all hell is going to break loose. First, Sarah doesn't have to worry about our social circles, only hers and her husband's. Second, she's only twenty-three or something and she's already proven her competence in my company. There's plenty of time for her to learn about the management of our family assets. I expect you to damn well teach her. Third, I don't give a rat's ass what your bridge cronies think about her. Now, you'll need to make this up to both Sarah and our son. And doing your best isn't enough. Sarah needs your love, and you'll have to learn to *trust* her as well. Okay, I hear them coming, so Mary and I'll bug out. You know what to do. Damn it, I want it done right this time."

* * * * * *

Mignon could see the rage still trapped in her son's eyes when he returned with Sarah. It resurrected her fear that the uneasy relationship they shared over the years might never come together after this. It seemed as though the fragile bridge between them had now been washed away in the flood of Sarah's tears.

Arms outstretched toward Grant, Mignon stepped forward to plead her case before a jury which she feared had already found her guilty. "Now, dear, I know how angry you are, and you have every right to be. But, please let me apologize properly to my future daughter-in-law before you tell me again how badly I've misbehaved. Please leave Sarah and me alone for awhile."

Grant's face remained expressionless. "I think I'd better stay."

"No dear, please go. I won't do anything wrong again. I don't know if I can ever really love her, but I promise I won't hurt her. Please go and give me another chance."

Grant obliged, and Mignon found herself alone with Sarah, not exactly sure just how best to repair the damage.

"Sarah, please forgive me at least long enough to sit down and listen. Can you do that?"

Sarah took a deep breath and tried to fashion an agreeable expression that wouldn't come. "I really resent what you did, Mrs. Lonsdale. Forgiveness might take some time. Even so, I guess I was hoping we could start over. I apologize about the tea. I didn't even think about the tapestry."

"Never mind about the tapestry, dear. The tea cup fell short, anyway. Now, please sit down. This is difficult for me to explain. I don't really know where to begin. So, perhaps it's best if I start at the beginning. For years I've been...how do I say this...the trustee, I suppose, of the Lonsdale wealth. It's

189

been kind of like a second child to me. When I heard about your engagement to my son, I reacted badly."

Mignon lowered her head and put her face in her hands. "I pictured myself surrendering both my son and my 'second child' at the same time. Since the transfer itself was beyond my control, I figured the least I could do was to make sure my two main reasons for being were ending up in good hands." She raised her head and forced herself to look directly at Sarah. "That was the reason for the research, which I now realize was unnecessary, and offensive to you. Can you ever forgive me?"

"I…don't know, Mrs. Lonsdale. Maybe, as we work together, my hurt will dissolve a bit. I know I have a lot to learn, and I know you were starting to tell me something when I blew up…which I shouldn't have done. What were you starting to tell me?"

"Sarah, I need to know how much you really know about family wealth and how to manage it."

Sarah paused, as though to be sure before she responded. "Well…ah…I know Concord Industries runs a significant profit every year, and that's the stepping stone to the accumulation of wealth."

Mignon forced a half-smile. "Partly true, but what do you know about building on that wealth, and the subsequent management of it?"

"Ummm…not much, I guess."

"I didn't think so. All right, it's time for your first lesson. Who do you think earns the most money at Concord?"

The surprised look on Sarah's face confirmed Mignon's suspicion that it might have been too soon to interrogate the girl on such a subject. Still, it was necessary.

"Well…, I'd have to conclude your husband does, since he's the CEO."

Mignon managed a genuine smile this time. "A reasonable conclusion, dear. However, in this case, it's incorrect. A man named Arnold Berghoff is paid more each year than my husband. His only function is the management, under my supervision, of both Concord's accumulated retained earnings and the Lonsdale family money. He gets paid a percentage of the annual growth of our net assets every year. You look surprised."

"Yes ma'am, I guess I am a little. I never thought a woman could…I mean…well, such a huge amount of money. I mean, I'm not implying you couldn't, but…well, I'm surprised that—"

"That a woman could be so influential? Let me tell you something, Sarah. The men in our family ancestry have earned the money in their various professions. But it's the women who have seen to it that the resulting business profits are managed properly. As Grant's wife, you will succeed me in the management of these. I hope you don't have to push young Grant as I've had to push his father. In any case, you must learn certain things and, with Mr. Berghoff's assistance, I shall teach you. Anyway there's plenty of time, dear. I won't be stepping down for at least another ten years or so, God willing."

Sarah paused. "I see. So, this is the Lonsdale dynasty?"

"Yes. I hope you can see now why I've been so determined to protect it."

"Protect it from what, Mrs. Lonsdale? Did you really mean keep it from falling into the hands of a girl from the wrong side of town?"

Caught off guard by the remark, Mignon hesitated. Then she smiled a satisfied smile. Sarah had seized the first opportunity she'd had to become the interrogator. A good sign.

"Well, I didn't quite mean it that way." Mignon pulled herself up straight. "Still, I had it coming, and you're absolutely right, I'm afraid. To tell you the truth, I'm glad it came out. Let's both consider the air cleared. We have to plan for this wedding. I mean, assuming you'll accept my son's proposal."

"I already have, Mrs. Lonsdale."

Mignon beamed. "I'm delighted. And I'd like you to call me mother. I mean, since you don't have one of your own. Tell you what. Let's meet here tomorrow morning to work on it, and perhaps your father could come. After all, he should have a say in all this."

"That's nice of you. I'm sure he'd have some good ideas. But he doesn't really have any money, so he can't pay for much, I'm afraid. However, I have some savings I can apply toward covering the expenses."

Mignon shook her head. "Don't you worry about the expenses. I'll take care of all that." She smiled at the look of relief in Sarah's eyes.

"Thank you, Mrs. Lonsdale. I'll have my father here tomorrow by nine o'clock, and we can get started."

* * * * * *

Lukasz Jankovic had never even seen a place like the Lonsdale mansion, let alone been in one. He looked at his daughter as though he couldn't believe she'd become a part of something so grand. "Sarah, honey, what do these people do to live in such a house?"

"Remember, Dad, I told you they own a large company."

Lukasz pulled his gnarled, muscular, hand from the pocket of his trousers, and scratched his head. "One company pays them enough to do this?"

Sarah led him over to a chair facing the fireplace. "Dad, it's a very large company. And they already have family money from way back, anyway. Look, why don't you—"

"Well now," Mary Coyne interrupted, as she slipped in and set a tray of tea and French pastries on the table, "you must be Mr. Jankovic." Mary shook his hand, threw a sly grin at Sarah, and glanced at the tapestry. "I'm Mary Coyne, and one of me jobs as housekeeper here is cleanin' up after certain people throw stuff at that rug hangin' on the wall over there."

Lukasz thought he saw a slight blush spreading on his daughter's face. He started to say something but Sarah intervened. "Dad, here comes Mrs. Lonsdale. She likes to get right down to business, so we can get started. Please watch your language while you're here."

Mignon entered the room in the manner of a queen prepared to address her subjects. She made her way straight to Lukasz, and managed a smile. "I'm so pleased to finally meet you, Mr. Jankovic. Sarah's told me what a wonderful father you've been. I can't tell you how excited we are to welcome Sarah into our family."

Mignon ignored Sarah's look of surprise and sat down. "So, if you'll both help yourselves to refreshments we can get on about planning a wedding. Now, Mr. Jankovic, I've—"

"Please call me Lukasz, ma'am. And would it be okay for me to call you by your first name?"

Mignon drew her head back as though startled by the question. "Why…yes, of course. You may call me Mignon, Lukasz. Now, as I told your daughter, my husband and I insist on paying for this wedding, and, if it's alright with you, we'd like to hold it in our church."

Lukasz picked up an intricate pastry and paused before he put it to his mouth, as though he didn't want to destroy it. "That would be fine," he said. He turned the pastry over for one more glance before biting off a small piece.

"Good," Mignon exclaimed, with a look of relief at having encountered no opposition so far, "it's settled, then." She poured a cup of tea for herself, and one for Sarah. "Please have some, Lukasz. Your daughter has established a unique relationship with my tea," — she gave Sarah an uncharacteristic grin — "and I'm sure you'll like it, too." Lukasz thought he could see his daughter start to blush again, but pretended not to notice.

"Now we come to the matter of guests to be invited," Mignon continued. "I'm afraid our side of the family will have a fairly large number, Lukasz. How about your side?"

Lukasz paused to smile at Sarah, then turned back to face Mignon. "Well, Mignon," he said, "I think you're looking at everyone from our side. Sarah and I are about the only ones left. I guess we won't be taking up much room."

Mignon lowered her eyes. "Of course. Well, anyhow, the reception will be at our club. So, Sarah, let's you and I take a look at both the church and the club this afternoon, and plan from there. We can all three have lunch at the club. Then you can work with us if you like, Lukasz."

"Thanks, but I have to get back to work this afternoon. You two go on, and I'll leave it in your good hands."

An hour later, the refreshments depleted and the small talk dwindling, Sarah and Mignon left for the club, and Lukasz headed back to his custodial duties. He climbed into his Ford pickup and glanced at the odometer, which had rounded the two-hundred-and-fifty-thousand-mile mark. He shook his head and thought about all that had happened. His daughter had entered a new world from which he felt sure there was no return. *It's good, though. It's what her mama would have wanted.*

* * * * * *

Their afternoon at the club had been productive in more ways than simply the successful completion of the wedding plans. Mignon saw Sarah's efficiency as a ray of hope that perhaps her prospective daughter-in-law might turn out to be more capable than she'd anticipated. Mignon hoped that this feeling of respect that hadn't surfaced before might be mutual. She took it upon herself to make the first move toward reconciliation. On their way out to the parking lot she put her hand on Sarah's shoulder. "Sarah, I would like you to stop and give me a hug."

"What?" Sarah looked as though she hadn't heard it right.

"I mean I'd be honored if you'd give a nasty old woman a hug."

Sarah beamed in a way that conveyed a sense of relief, and hugged her future mother-in-law. "Thank you, Mrs. Lonsdale. I was afraid I'd never be accepted into your family after I lost my temper the other day. I can't begin to tell you how happy—"

193

"Please call me mother, Sarah. Oh, enough of that for now. What's your favorite dinner food?"

The look of surprise on Sarah's face suggested she wasn't ready for the sudden change of subject. "Well, I really prefer corned beef and cabbage with boiled potatoes. It was Dad's favorite and he liked to cook it."

"And your favorite dessert?"

"Chocolate pudding, hands down."

Mignon smiled and pulled out her cell phone. "Good. I'll call Mary and have her start preparing the meal. It'll take a while but we're in no hurry."

During the drive back they talked about everything from family history to Grant's exploits in Okeechobee. They laughed, as the intimacy of their dialogue grew with each shared secret. Before they reached the mansion the full realization of how much they had to offer each other swept in like a fresh breeze, blowing away long-standing clouds of doubt and resentment. For Sarah, it marked the last step in her long journey of redemption.

The moment they walked through the door of the Lonsdale mansion, Mignon pushed the button on the wall to ring for her housekeeper. "Mary, where are Grant and my husband?"

"They just come back from work, mum. They're down in the recreation room shootin' pool. I'll bring 'em up. Dinner's cookin' but it isn't ready yet."

The lower court had ruled in Mignon's favor. Now, with the entrance of the two Lonsdale men, Mignon could only hope the higher court would not reverse the decision. She knew a convincing summary statement might be necessary.

"I want you all to meet my new daughter. I'll call her Sarah Jane," Mignon announced. "Let's all sit down here in the living room, and I'll serve some wine. We have much to discuss."

Patience still an integral part of her repertoire, Mignon waited until everyone was seated with drink in hand. She sat erect in her favorite chair, head held high, and reached to smooth her skirt — as though what she was about to say required a proper launch. "To begin with," she said, "I wish to apologize for...well, unwittingly offending in my...ahhh, overzealous effort to protect our family's wealth." She didn't see a need to specify who she had offended since all indications were that she had alienated everyone except her loyal Mary Coyne.

"My daughter and I have reconciled any differences we might have had. Now we need to move forward. Sarah, her father, and I have begun work on the wedding plans and that's coming along well. I've made arrangements for

Sarah and Arnold Berghoff to meet. He'll counsel her on her future duties in the handling of our portfolio. Of course, she'll have years to learn about it, and I'll work with her as well." Mignon paused to size up her husband and her son, not certain whether their relaxed expressions were attributable to the wine or her summary.

"Now Sarah," she continued with as motherly a look as she could manage, "I'll introduce you to my bridge ladies, eventually. I'm sure they'll be anxious to meet you. Now Sarah, dear, I know they'll ask if you play bridge." Mignon's furtive glance toward her husband invited a be-careful-how-you-say-this glare from him. "Of course, it's perfectly all right if you don't, dear, so—"

"I do, Mrs. Lons — I mean mother. We played a lot after classes at Tufts."

"Hah!" The senior Lonsdale's triumphant laugh burst out like a shot which stunned everyone except Mignon. She returned the volley with a clenched-teeth expression which no one else understood either.

"Well, that's marvelous, dear. We'll have some great fun. I don't suppose you play golf."

"No, ma'am, but I'm willing to give it a try."

Mignon couldn't resist casting a satisfied smile in her husband's direction. "Good. I'll arrange for your lessons."

Mary Coyne's dinner announcement preempted any further conversation. Convinced she'd been exonerated, Mignon heaved a deep sigh.

Chapter 30

Department of Justice agent Zack Wilson hadn't anticipated that his interrogation of Mike Rinelli would take so long. Obviously tired, thirsty, and soaked in sweat, Rinelli had tripped over the inconsistency of his alibis often enough that Zack now figured it was time to force a confession. Zack slid his chair in close, directly facing his captive. "Rinelli, your answers so far leak like the hull of the Titanic. Now, I've removed all physical restraints so you'd be comfortable. I'll give you one more chance. You give me a straight answer to this last question and I'll make sure the court treats you as an innocent dupe in Vanderslice's scheme. If not, you're going to jail for a long time as a deliberate accomplice to murder. I want the names of all the people involved in the death of Miranda Gibbs and her computer consultant."

Rinelli unfastened another button on his shirt and squirmed in his seat. "I don't know anything about that. My job was administrative. Look, you've badgered me long enough. I know my rights. I want out of here." He pulled out a handkerchief and wiped his brow. "I don't know a damned thing, and you trying to trick me into saying I do ain't gonna work. You got no right to hold me."

Zack leaned forward and glared. "Listen, you brainless chump. You're about to get nailed with a rap you don't need to take. And for a crook who doesn't care whether you rot in prison or not. Vanderslice has already written you off as the fall guy. You're protecting a kingpin who's going to get even richer while you become some tough pervert's little sex kitten in the penitentiary. Wake up and use your head. You left a trail of illegal business deals from Miami to Naples. Your record stinks. In a court room, you're guilty the minute the judge enters the chamber."

"Yeah, well, my boss cleaned up all those deals." Rinelli stuffed the kerchief back into his pocket and sneered. "You have nothing on me, so get off my back."

Zack raised his eyebrows. "Really? How about money laundering? Racketeering? Acting as the go-between for Salazar Corazon and Vanderslice in at least two murders?"

"I don't know what you're talking about."

"I'm talking about Mayaca Corporation, Rinelli. You know, the shell game you administer. Drug money scammed through South Atlantic Farms and dumped into an offshore bank account for which you record all the transactions. Dirty money all cleaned up for Corazon and Vanderslice. They split the take while you're stuck with muddy hands that *won't* clean up, my friend. Think about it."

Rinelli's lips tightened and his eyes moistened. "Yeah, well, they did the work, I just served as sort of a desk jockey...like I said. I was only doing what I was told to do. You should be talking to them, not me."

Zack reached out and placed a gentle hand on Rinelli's shoulder. He'd induced enough confessions to know that stretching the truth a bit usually produced the fastest results. "We would, Mike. But here's the problem. Corazon's out of reach without your confession. Vanderslice will stand up with his nice, conservative, dark blue business suit, a clean record, and tell the judge he had no idea you were doing all those naughty things down there at Mayaca Corporation. With a record like yours, Rinelli, it's a slam dunk. Game's over, you lose. Both of those dirtbags walk away free and, even if you survive your prison term, the rest of your life is a shambles. I think you know what I mean. Now, talk to me."

Rinelli lowered his head into his hands and began to sob. A few moments later he looked up, tears streaming down his face. "So what happens to me if I speak out? I wasn't responsible for that stuff, and you know it."

The agent nodded and gave out his first smile. "Of course I know. Look, we don't want you. We want Corazon and Vanderslice. At worst, you'll probably end up being an unknowing accomplice. Here's how it works. You and I make a deal. You tell me everything — including the location of all the records that were missing when we searched the premises. I tell the court how much help you were, and I'll do everything I can to minimize your sentence. It's as simple as that."

In between remorseful tears and a sandwich-and-coffee reward from Zack, Mike Rinelli spilled the details of an arrangement between Vanderslice and Corazon to silence a woman who knew too much and a computer consultant who discovered too much. The confession recorded, the Department of

Justice placed Mike Rinelli in protective custody, and began the process of extradition of one criminal and the arrest of another.

* * * * * *

"Maria, you go home," Luanne said. "You don't need to stay late just for me." Luanne glanced around at the piles of new invoices and old ledger printouts spread out on the conference room table. She shook her head. "I can do this...I think. I'm going to have to know what's going on, anyway, when we transfer all the files to Grant's company. Go on before this drizzle turns to rain."

Maria slipped into her rain jacket and stuck a collapsible umbrella into the pocket. "Okay, you go home pretty soon, too. It's not good to stay here after dark. Okay?"

"Yep. Don't worry. Another hour of this is about all I can take. I'll never know how you and my mother could stand doing this kind of work all year long. See you tomorrow, Maria."

Frustrated and confused by all the numbers, Luanne cut the hour to twenty minutes. She didn't see Maria's purse lying on a chair until she reached to turn out the light in Maria's office. "Oh, hell," Luanne blurted out loud, "she's driving without her license and identification." Luanne hadn't finished punching-in Maria's cell number when she sensed the movement behind her. She jumped at the sound of the woman's sharp command.

"Put it down. Now."

Luanne recognized the voice. She whirled around to see Tommy Rawls' secretary pointing a gun at her. "Jolene, what in the hell are you doing?"

Eyes narrowed and legs spread in a shooting stance, Jolene raised the pistol to the level of Luanne's chin and spoke in a low, firm tone. "I said, put the cell phone down and turn out the light. Leave the conference room light on and dump your damned ass into Maria's chair. And don't move."

Luanne's eyes widened. "For God's sake, Jolene, have you lost your mind?"

Jolene lowered the firearm to keep it level with Luanne's chin as Luanne settled into the chair. "I'll tell you what I've lost, you sultry little bitch. You took my man away from me. Then you killed him. Your uppity Yankee friend made my job disappear and ruined my reputation. Everything I ever wanted is gone. That's what I've lost."

Luanne put up her hand. "Oh, Jolene, please! I had to shoot Enrico Diaz. He was about to kill Grant and my father. He left me no ch—"

"That's not what I'm talking about, and you know it. I'm glad he's dead. He deserved to die after he dumped me for a slut like you. And now, sexy little girl, you're going to join him in hell."

Luanne screamed. "Jolene! For heaven's sake. There was never anything between me and Enrico. I swear it."

"Oh, really? Then I suppose all those photographs of you naked that I found under his bed didn't mean anything."

Luanne shook her head. "Jolene, please! I would never have allowed anyone to photograph me like that. What photos are you talking about, anyway?"

"Damn you," Jolene snarled. "I'm talking about the ones he took of you wading into the fish pond that evening, without a stitch on, thrusting out your big boobs and swinging your derriere. And the ones he took through your bedroom window when you were undressing at night. Did you think I was stupid or something? For some time I figured his mind wasn't on me, and a few days ago I discovered why. He couldn't wait to get a piece of your curvy ass."

Luanne threw her hands in the air, then winced at the realization that the sudden movement might cause Jolene to shoot. "Good God, Jolene. I waded into the pool naked so my clothes wouldn't get wet while I scooped out a few dead angel fish floating on the surface. And I had no idea he was shooting pictures through my window. *Please* believe that. I never meant any harm to come to you. I always thought we were friends."

Jolene inched to one side to allow the light from the conference room behind her to more clearly illuminate her intended victim. "Friends? Hell, I've hated you ever since the first day you sashayed into our bank with your tight little white shorts and your superior attitude. But you know when I hated you most of all? It was when you strolled into Mr. Rawls' office and made him hand over your father's financial information to that filthy northerner who had no business here in the first place. Well, that's all past. Now it's get-even time, honey." Jolene steadied the muzzle toward the center of Luanne's forehead.

"Jolene, don't do this," Luanne pleaded. Her mouth turned down and tears welled up in her eyes.

Neither of them heard the soft whooshing sound of Maria's *machete de suelo* slicing through the air until it buried with a thud in Jolene's back between her shoulder blades. As she pitched forward, Jolene's involuntary trigger-squeeze sent a bullet whizzing inches from Luanne's head.

Maria rushed in, retrieved the cane knife, and stood over Jolene as though poised to use it again if necessary. Luanne picked up the firearm and held it pointed at the crumpled, bleeding form on the floor.

Maria tossed the eighteen-inch blade aside, and knelt to stuff her kerchief into the wound while Luanne called for her father, an ambulance, and the police.

A grueling half-hour of police questioning began as soon as the medic announced that Jolene's wound was not fatal. After the medics loaded Jolene into the ambulance, the police spent another half hour questioning Maria and Luanne.

The ordeal over, Major cradled a sobbing Maria in his arms while he tried to calm his daughter. Then he popped open a bottle of Okeechobee Comfort and poured three cups full. This time, he announced, the beverage was medicinal, and the women's acceptance of the offering was not optional.

Luanne tossed down a swallow or two and turned to Maria. "Where did you get that thing, Maria? And how did you ever learn to throw it like that?"

Major grinned. "I know where you got it, Maria. But, like Luanne, I'd sure like to know who taught you to use it for something other than cutting sugar cane."

Maria finished her cup and held it out for Major to refill before she responded. "It's from the old days in the cane fields," Maria said, addressing Luanne. "It was my father's. Before he died he taught me to use it in many different ways. After your father found me and took me in, I keep it hidden behind the file cabinet in the conference room. Sometimes a field hand he comes in drunk and wants sex with me, or his paycheck before payday. I have to be ready. This time I'm glad I had to come back for my purse. *Dios me perdone porque he pecado.*"

"What does that mean?' Luanne asked. "Somehow, that's one phrase I guess I never learned from the field hands."

Major smiled in a fatherly way and turned to his daughter. "It means God forgive me for my sin. Honey, you never knew this, but I brought Maria in to be more than your nanny when you were growing up and your mother was too busy. I asked her to protect you. She's done both tasks well. Maria, I will be forever grateful to you for saving my Luanne's life. And there's no sin in it. You know, with all that's happened around here it seems like a hundred years since we raised our first batch of angels. Do you remember, Maria?"

Maria nodded. "Yes, sir. We were all younger then — including Miss Luanne."

Chapter 31

Jennifer Lentz never openly admitted Grant was her favorite among all the young business school hires Angus MacIver had brought in during her six years as Mac's executive secretary. But anyone could tell that by the way she spent extra time polishing up Grant's reports before they hit Mac's desk for final review. Or by all the unsolicited advice she offered whenever she felt he needed a surrogate mother.

"Mr. MacIver, Grant just came in," Jenny announced over his intercom, "and I know you wanted to see him." She waved at Grant as he came through the door, and frantically pointed toward MacIver's office to let him know Mac wanted to see him right away.

"But don't forget," she yelled after him, "I get you right after Mr. Mac does. By the way, thanks for the oranges."

Angus stepped out of his office, winked at Jenny, grabbed Grant by the arm, and whisked him in before he could open his mouth. "Welcome back, Grant!" his boss barked, shaking Grant's hand with his customary vise-like grip while he flashed his client-schmoozing smile.

Grant handed Mac a preliminary draft of his Okeechobee report entitled *Conduit For A Felony*.

Angus glanced at it and laid it on his desk. "Grant, the next time I send you to do a financial review I'm going to send an armed guard along with you. Talk about rocking the boat. You just about stirred up an international incident." Angus grinned again.

Grant frowned. "I'm afraid you lost me, Angus. What are you talking about?"

"You mean you haven't heard? A South American drug lord has just been indicted, along with a guy named Rinelli and some banker."

Grant nodded. "That must have been Tommy Rawls. Did you find out what happened to Tommy after they took him away?"

"I did. He'll be doing some jail time for the next ten to twenty years."

"Twenty years? I didn't know fraud carried a sentence that long."

Jenny brought in Mac's mail and his monogrammed coffee jug. She poured two cups, picked up his outgoing correspondence, and smiled her apologies for the interruption.

Mac settled back in his chair, glanced at the mail without opening any of it, and paused to test the coffee. "It normally doesn't. But fraud combined with attempted murder does. In case you didn't know it, Corazon took all his little soldiers down with him in the attempted murder charge. That included Rawls, who was also implicated in the murder of Mrs. Gibbs and a few others."

Grant stood, walked over to the credenza to grab some sugar for the coffee, and rolled his eyes. "Mr. Mac, please tell me you have some clients who won't get me involved with the FBI."

"I do, Grant. In fact I'd planned on you working with one of them starting tomorrow. Unfortunately that's not going to happen."

"Yes, I know. I had to promise Dad I'd come back right away to Concord. It was part of the deal, not because I was in any hurry to start."

"Right. Well, it seems your dad's madder than a wet hen at me for getting you into that mess down there. True, he understands I had absolutely no idea it was going to be a war zone, but he's still pretty angry at me. We go back a long way, your dad and I, and I'm not about to do anything to jeopardize that friendship. I'm going to send you back to Concord today. I don't like it, because you're doing a top-notch job here, and I need you. But, so does your dad, and that's it, I'm afraid. I'll miss you. If you ever get tired of running Concord you've a job waiting for you here."

They talked about small things, laughed for awhile, and then MacIver's expression grew somber. He closed the door, sat down again, and leaned forward to put his face closer to Grant's.

"Now, Grant, there's something I need to bring to your attention. I received a call from a man named Roy Hartman, who was looking for you."

"Yes, I know. He found me. He was on the line with a couple of FBI agents by the time he reached me."

"Did he tell you the feds didn't quite get all of Corazon's special hit men?"

"Yes. The two guys who came for me that night are dead, of course, and a few others are now locked up for good. But Hartman said the third one's out there. He's a guy called Ruiz. I met him at a South Atlantic Farms board meeting. He's a nasty-looking character who'd probably assassinate his mother if the price were right. Hartman said he's most likely hiding out so deep in the Amazon jungle he'll probably never surface again. He said there may not be any cause to worry. I don't believe him. Damn it, how incompetent can these people be? How can they leave one-third of Corazon's hit men out there wandering around loose? I can't believe my survival is now in the hands of idiots."

Mac shook his head. "I'm sorry, Grant. I'm afraid he didn't specify exactly how careful you should be. I asked him if it was possible to put some kind of surveillance guard on you until this gets resolved one way or the other. He doesn't have the manpower to do it, and the FBI said they didn't either when he asked them about it. Just between you and me, being careful probably means simply not going anywhere near South America for awhile. Now, go see Jenny. I promised her she could monopolize your time after I got through with you. And please keep me posted on this."

* * * * * *

Jenny made sure they commandeered a quiet little table in the corner of the cafeteria before she launched into her inquisition. She stuck a dollar in the vending machine, pulled out a Diet Coke, and waited while Grant carefully inspected each row of the machine's offerings.

"Well, I didn't think this machine had anything comparable, but I thought I'd try," he said, still scanning the shelves.

"Comparable to what?"

"Comparable to Cajun Smash."

Jenny frowned. "What in the devil is that?"

"It's a delightful mixture of pleasure and pure junk, but I think you'd love it."

"Grant, I think I'll pass, thanks. I suggest you try something more civilized…like maybe a Sprite." Grant put his money in and decided to take Jenny's advice.

"Okay, Alligator Hunter," she began with her usual rapturous smile, "tell me what really happened down there. I mean romantically speaking. I already know about the rest of it."

Grant popped the top and tossed down a mouthfull. "Okeechobee's a long story, Jenny. The short version is that a girl down there — a very special girl — made me finally realize I've always loved Sarah. I thought time had erased the possibility of reconnecting, but Luanne rekindled my hopes in a way I couldn't ignore. It's as simple as that, and the truth is I'm lucky Sarah didn't write me off altogether."

Jenny grinned. "Well, Mr. Lonsdale, I think I'd prefer to hear the long version. So when's the big day?"

"We'll get married as soon as Sarah gets back. She's in Okeechobee looking over the hatchery's accounting system."

Jenny looked surprised. "Why would she want to do that?"

"She has to find out how difficult it will be to merge it with our systems here at Concord. Why the concerned look?"

"Okay, I'm going to be discreet and not ask you how this Luanne got to be such a 'special' girl. But have you thought about what happens when your number-one girl meets up face to face with this special girl?"

Grant stared blankly at her. He'd focused so intently on the logistics of the whole thing that he'd never considered the interpersonal dynamics of it. "Jenny, I guess I never thought about it. I've had so much on my mind that—"

"Well, you better start thinking about it, chum, or your marriage just might be over before it even gets started."

Grant stretched his arms out, palms up. "Come on, Jenny, I can't believe they'd actually go back and compare notes. Sarah's there on company business and Luanne's not going to do much more than show her the record-keeping system."

"Believe it, young man, believe it. You'd better get on your cell phone and catch Sarah before she talks to you know who and draws her own conclusions."

"Too late. Sarah's probably already met Luanne."

"Well, then normally I'd suggest prayer. But something tells me the Almighty's not going to want to touch this one. Maybe now's the time to give me the long version."

"Nothing happened, Jenny, I swear it. Luanne's beautiful and we got, uh... close, sort of. But I backed off because of Sarah. And that's when Luanne saw where I was coming from and fired up my dream about Sarah. After that it was a matter of my tracking Sarah down and proposing."

"Okay, I guess there's not much you can do now except wait. The good news is you've finally got the right girl. I was worried about that for a long time, but it was none of my business so I didn't say anything. I'm really happy for you, Grant. I can't wait to meet her."

"You'll meet her at the wedding if not before. The invitations will be going out tomorrow or the next day. Hey, Jenny, tell me something. Did I come back with a smile on my face and a good tan like I promised, or not?"

"You sure did, kid, and a lot more. I wasn't going to say this, and don't take it the wrong way, but I think you've grown into a first-class guy who no longer thinks the world stops at the far end of Beacon Street. Anyway, you better hope for the best when those two girls meet."

Chapter 32

Sarah hadn't planned to get wrapped up in government red tape. She felt like she'd inadvertently stuck her hand into the tar baby. Everything she touched seemed to require the filling out of another document...line by excruciating line. Her first morning, and part of the afternoon, in Okeechobee were spent signing government forms, complete with attached documentation from Concord Industries. By mid-afternoon her writing hand ached for some relief, her eyes strained to decipher the fine print, and she was ready to call it a day.

After she convinced the federal agent he could rely on her to supervise South Atlantic Farms, he left her with a signed confirmation the company could continue operations as before. This meant, among other stipulations, not freezing the company's bank accounts.

Tired of reading page after page of government legaleese, Sarah heaved a sigh of relief that the review was over. Hot, frustrated, and with her hair hanging down in her face, Sarah found herself one cool shower and an hour at the hotel hot tub short of feeling ready to meet this woman to whom her betrothed had 'drawn close.' She collapsed into a chair, leaned back, and let her arms dangle. Half in a daze, she looked up to see Luanne standing over her with a perplexed look in her eyes, as though conveying a disbelief that Grant could have turned her down for such a bedraggled creature.

Sarah drew a deep breath and rose from her chair to face Luanne. For a few moments the two women sized each other up as would a pair of prizefighters at the opening bell. Different as night and day, both knew it right away. In one swift movement Sarah brushed the hair out of her face and reached out to shake the hand of the most sensuous-looking female she could ever remember having seen. Luanne, in anticipation of meeting Sarah, had replaced the blue denims and cowboy boots with high heels, a moderately low cut blouse, and a tight-fitting skirt. All in all, it came as close to being a designer outfit as Luanne could manage. Sarah blinked. Grant had referred to Luanne as pretty, but he hadn't said anything about seductive.

"Hello, Luanne, I'm Sarah Jankovic. I'm so glad to meet you. You're every bit as lovely as Grant said you were. I want to thank you for all the work you did to make this transfer possible. I've finally convinced the agent to free up South Atlantic Farms for continued operation. So," she continued, still brushing strands of loose hair back into place, "I thought we could get started right away discussing how we'll need to work together on this."

Arms akimbo, Luanne maintained an impassive expression while she continued to inspect Sarah. The ensuing moments of uncomfortable silence made Sarah feel the same way she did at her first encounter with Mignon.

Finally, Luanne extended her hand, just as Major came into the room. "So you're the Sarah of Grant's dreams," she said with a noncommittal smile that left Sarah unsure as to how to interpret the greeting. "I'm glad to meet you, too. I'd like you to meet my father, Major Gibbs. We both owe Grant an awful lot."

Major grinned. "Welcome to South Atlantic Farms, Sarah." He bypassed the customary handshake, scooped up the startled girl, and hugged her hard. "You're sure a sight for sore eyes after those dadgum Feds that've been pestering us for the last few days. Say, you look like you could use a good, stiff—"

"No, Daddy! Not Okeechobee Comfort." Luanne moved quickly to take a defensive position between her father and the liquor cabinet. "Sarah's a high-class lady from Boston, and I don't think she drinks that kind of stuff."

Sarah's outburst of laughter lightened the tension. She put her hand to her mouth. "I didn't mean to laugh," she said, "but if you only knew. First of all, Grant told me I hadn't lived until I drank a cup of your famous Okeechobee Comfort. So I'd love to have some. Second, if you could have seen the scruffy section of town I came from you'd never in a million years think of me as a high-class lady. Although I truly appreciate the compliment, Luanne."

"Well then, it's done, ladies, happy hour just now started." Major slapped his thigh and reached for an unlabeled bottle of the pale yellow liquid Grant had proclaimed went down smoother than a dry martini.

After her exasperating morning with the agent, Sarah welcomed the soothing combination of the pale yellow elixir and Major's low-key country manner. Like Grant, she found herself in a world far removed from New England. Unlike Grant, she felt right at home.

Although Major could have drained the bottle, one cup turned out to be enough for Luanne and Sarah, by mutual consent. After some small talk and a few belly laughs prompted by Major's dramatizations of Grant's exploits with Tommy and the .243, Luanne ushered Sarah into the conference room.

"Sarah, these aren't all the records." Luanne waved her hand over them as though she was administering last rites. "But they're the ones Grant used. I pulled them out of the cabinet where he left them locked up. I understand you're a CPA, so I'm sure you'll be comfortable with them. I'll get you whatever else you want. Why don't you take some time to look at them and then, whenever you're ready, we can talk about how we can work together?"

"That would be fine, Luanne. I can get through the critical stuff in about an hour, and then let's all have dinner. We can talk about how South Atlantic Farms and Concord Industries can interface their accounting systems most effectively. You and I can get a fresh start on bringing them together tomorrow morning."

Luanne nodded. "Okay. See you later. Good luck with that ocean of numbers."

A twinge of jealousy tugged at Sarah as she watched Luanne walk out, looking less like a fish farmer, and more like what Sarah imagined a stripper must look like fully clothed. She found herself wondering how Grant could possibly have resisted the temptation.

Alone in the room where she could almost sense the presence of the ghosts Grant had chased, Sarah sifted through the piles of paper with the efficiency of a trained CPA. Documents that had harbored seven years of fraud now lay dormant and harmless, their demons having been painfully exorcised. Grant hadn't said much about his experience, and Sarah could never have known the full extent of the damage caused by the contents of these records.

* * * * * *

Major still hadn't finished the bottle when Luanne walked in, closed the door behind her, put her head on his shoulder, and began to cry softly.

"Honey, what's the matter? Hey, there's no need for tears anymore." He wrapped an arm around her and patted the back of her head like he had when she was a child. "They're not going to take the company away from us now. Grant made sure of that. C'mon, smile."

"Oh, it's not that, Daddy." She tried to wipe away the tears, but they kept coming. "It's a lot of things, I guess."

"Well, honey, what things?"

The question only made the tears flow faster. "Oh, it's just that, now the ghost has been found, she's no longer a figment of Grant's imagination. She's real. And, damn it, she's pretty." Sobs shook Luanne's body. "And she really *is* a high class lady, not an uneducated fish farmer like me."

By the time Major could conjure up an appropriate response, the cascading tears had reached the saturation point on the shoulder of his denim shirt. "Aw, honey, come on. You're the sweetest little lady in this whole damned world." It wasn't the first time he'd regretted not having sent her to college. This time the feeling of guilt began to engulf him as it never had before. "Look, tell you what. Let's you and me put in a call to that college that wanted you a few years ago an' just see if they'll take you now. How about we do that?"

"Oh, Daddy, that's sweet. But we both know I'm needed here." She straightened up, took a deeper breath, hugged him, and walked toward the door, still wiping away the gradually slowing flow of tears. "I'll be okay. I just needed to get it out of my system. Thanks for being the best daddy in the whole world. I think I'll go change my clothes and check on the net that tore on pond fourteen. I'm fine now. You go back to work, and we'll all get together for dinner in about an hour."

She forced a smile on her way out, and the old farmer felt the onset of the same, deep sadness which gripped him several years before when his wife died.

* * * * * *

The three of them shared an evening meal in an atmosphere of subdued lightheartedness. Both Sam and Essie Mae came over to their table to introduce themselves and share a few anecdotes about confrontations between alligators and Bostonians. After they left, the trio plowed into the evening meal. To everyone's surprise, Sarah enjoyed the grits and catfish enough to ask for seconds.

During the round of drinks that followed the evening meal, Major waited for the right moment — which seemed to come after Sarah reached the halfway mark on her first beer. He folded his checkered napkin and turned to Sarah. "What's going to happen to our hatchery now, Sarah?"

"Well, Major, most of the transfer paperwork is done, and the bank accounts have been set up for direct transfer of receipts and disbursements to Concord's bank in Boston. I'll need Luanne to transfer the computer files and customer and vendor lists as soon as she can. The other data can be transferred a bit later."

"Our main vendor is Aqua Star," Luanne said, "and I don't think they'll be providing product to us anymore. But I think I can strike up a direct relationship with another South American consolidator Corazon used. If he's afraid to offend the cartel, I can always find another supplier."

Sarah nodded. "Okay, we'll work with that and—"

"After we transfer records to Boston," Major broke in, "can we continue to operate like before and deposit into our bank now that Tommy Rawls is no longer there?" The look on his face signaled a lingering doubt about the whole procedure.

"Sure, Major." Sarah wrapped her confident smile in a soothing tone. "Of course you can. Now, please answer a question that's been bothering me ever since Grant came back. How did he manage to get the Feds and the DEA to agree to this whole arrangement? The guy I dealt with this morning said it was the wildest deal he'd ever seen."

Major and Luanne looked at each other without responding, as though they were waiting for some form of divine intervention.

Sarah's soft smile gave way to a stern look which she directed at Major. "Major?"

He chased a deep breath with another gulp of beer. "Well, honey, I'll just pass on these words that came from the FBI guy, not me. He pretty much hit the nail on the head when he said this whole mess would never have been fixed if Grant hadn't figured out where the bus was headed and threw himself in front of it."

Sarah's eyes widened. "Just how do you mean that, Major? Please help me understand, because neither Grant's family nor I have been able to get the whole story out of him."

Major hesitated, and Luanne turned toward him. "Daddy, Sarah has a right to know."

He nodded. "Okay, I guess she does. But I sure as hell feel I'm tellin' tales out of school." He polished off the rest of his beer and leaned back in his chair. "Sarah, the truth is Grant volunteered to be a kind of bait...you know, like what you'd call a guinea pig. He hunkered down in that ole chair in our conference room and waited for two of them gunnies from the cartel to come kill him. He'd figured out they'd be comin'. An' they damned near did kill him. They would have dragged him off to some damn killing place they had in mind if Luanne here hadn't taken them out with a couple of clean shots from that .243. That FBI man witnessed the whole thing. That and the evidence Grant sent in sealed the case. Way I heard it, the Feds yanked Corazon out of Bogota a few days ago and stuck him in a Texas jail until the thing comes to trial. Like Luanne said, we owe Grant a lot."

For a few awkward moments, it seemed like the whole restaurant went silent. Were the other tables all waiting to hear Sarah's response? Sarah pushed her unfinished drink aside and drew a deep breath before she looked straight at Major again. "And you let him do this? You stood by while he risked his life?"

Major raised his hands. "Sarah, honey, we didn't have no say in it. This was all done in private between Grant and the Feds. Just so you know, though, I didn't stand there and watch. After I gave up trying to talk him out of it, I pitched in and helped bust up the attempt to kill him. I sure hope you ain't thinkin' we let him do this all alone."

Sarah forced a weak smile. "No, Major, I didn't mean it that way. I'm just a little shocked that Grant would take a risk like that and keep it from us. Now I wonder if he *ever* intended to share it."

Major reached up and scratched the back of his head. "I can't help you on that one, honey. He kept a lot from us, too, right up until he had no choice but to spill it. Guess he's one of those quiet guys, but don't let that cause you to think less of him. You done got yourself one fine young fellow there."

Luanne nodded, pulled out a kerchief, and turned away to wipe the corner of her eye.

Major seemed to sense the mood. He paid the bill and ushered them out. He hugged Sarah again and whispered how much closer Boston seemed to Okeechobee now that she and Grant had shared a part of their lives with him and Luanne.

Chapter 33

Grant's new office at Concord looked exactly like the office of any other department head. Not an inch larger, not one stick of furniture more. Like other department managers, he shared administrative and secretarial services with two other executives, no favoritism shown. His father had been adamant about avoiding the appearance of nepotism. Everyone knew Grant Abbot Lonsdale III was on his way to the top sooner or later, barring any major catastrophes, so it was mostly for show. But the people around him seemed to feel better about it, and that was the objective.

In her new role of manager of accounting in the New Products Division, Sarah came under the same guidelines. Her office would have been identical in appearance to Grant's, had she been able to resist the temptation to show him up a little. She added a corner table to her décor and adorned it with a small tank containing two angel fish. The little twist gave everyone at Concord's headquarters a laugh, and probably did as much as anything to lessen any feelings about Grant and Sarah being Concord's heirs apparent.

Grant's first day on the job as merger and acquisitions manager began with a desk as full of documents as the conference table at South Atlantic. Continuous interruption by his mother about plans for his forthcoming wedding didn't help much.

"Mother, I don't know why some of these problems can't be handled by Sarah. Isn't the bride-to-be supposed to work with you on some of these?"

"Yes, dear, but right after she set up that little fish tank she went down there to visit that awful place in Florida. I didn't want to bother her."

"Well, I'm working too, in case you weren't aware of it. And right now my nice, efficient secretary is motioning to me that I've someone waiting outside. So, I'll talk to you later. I have to go, so just hold up on all that for awhile."

The secretary waved her hand to get Grant's attention. "Mr. Lonsdale, these two gentlemen are from the FBI to see you."

A tall man in a dark, tailored suit that seemed to hug his torso in all the right places reached to shake Grant's hand. "Good morning, Mr. Lonsdale. You're a hard man to track down. I'm agent Kent Andrews, this is agent Bob Tucker. We're from the bureau's Boston field office. Look, I'm going to cut through all the introductory formalities and come right to the point. Has Mr. Hartman talked to you about Corazon's third man running around loose?"

"Yes, he gave me the bad news. Have you guys found him yet?"

"No, we haven't. In fact, that's why we're here. I'm afraid the bad news just got worse. Our sources in Boston just informed us the Colombian cartel has apparently flown a guy up here. It was a private plane, only one passenger, no narcotics, all the papers were forged. We impounded the plane and have the pilot in jail, but he's not talking. The passenger got away and we're almost certain he's the man Corazon ordered to go after you."

Grant rolled his eyes. "Great, damn it. That's just great." He threw one hand in the air, motioned the assistant out of hearing range with the other, and cursed under his breath. "So what would you suggest I do now?"

"Well, for starters, we suggest you postpone your wedding. The reason is—"

"What? You have to be kidding."

"No, I'm not kidding. Look, from what I'm hearing, the Boston news media have broadcast your wedding all over New England. I even saw a blurb about it in the society section at my office in Virginia. The whole damn world probably knows about it by now. I guess that's the price for being rich and famous. At any rate, it's my professional opinion this guy will try to make the hit, either at the wedding ceremony or at the reception.

"So I think you and your bride-to-be should lay low for awhile. Agent Tucker and I are here to find this guy and lock him up. Our Boston office will make additional agents available as needed. Hopefully, we'll get this guy. In case we don't, I want you and your bride to postpone the ceremony. Then, after we get him, you can go ahead and invite Prince Andrew and his entourage to your shindig if you want."

Grant glared at the man. "Mr. Andrews, there's no way in hell I'm going to postpone this wedding. First of all, my mother and father had to exercise all the influence they had to virtually force the church to squeeze this wedding into its crowded schedule. Otherwise, it would have been a year before we could hold it. Second, your highly touted agents already let two gunnies through down in Florida, and almost got me killed. No disrespect intended, but I'm not all that confident about your ability to prevent one more from slipping through your hands. Do you even know what this guy looks like?"

"No, and, admittedly, that's going to make the job harder. That's one of the reasons I wanted you to postpone the wedding. We understand that you and the two Gibbs people do know what he looks like. We need you to help our forensics artist develop a picture of him to make it easier for us to identify him. We've already asked the two Gibbs folks to help, but we need your input. Anyway, our people are pros and they'll get him."

Grant shook his head. "Sorry, I'm not convinced."

"Look, Grant, you were very effective bait before in Florida, but I'm not putting you through that again. Plus, we're talking about a large crowd of people this time. You hold that wedding on schedule and someone's going to get killed. And you may not be the only one. Am I getting through to you on this?"

"Yes, I hear you. But even after I describe the man to you your men might not recognize him. So, like it or not, that makes me *numero uno* on your little team. Now, I want to coordinate this whole thing with you. And we're going to do it right this time."

Grant wasn't sure whether the long pause signaled some understandable indecision, or preparation for a new line of resistance. After a long silence Tucker responded. "We're going to do this my way, Lonsdale. That means you shut down this wedding until we take the shooter out. Now here's what—"

"To hell with you and your damned protocol," Grant snapped, "I'm the one he's after and I know exactly what he looks like. This is my risk and I'm willing to take it."

Andrews cursed under his breath. "Wrong, Lonsdale, you're putting at risk every guest who shows up. Okay, these are your people, not mine. Are you sure you want to set them up as random targets?"

Grant shook his finger at the agent. "There won't be any random targets. From what I know about Salazar Corazon, he'll send a guy named Ruiz to finish the job. There'll be three of us who can recognize Ruiz the second he pops his head into view. So let's sit down and plan this out in a way we can both agree on."

Andrews frowned. "With all the gunnies Salazar must have around him, what makes you so sure this Ruiz fellow will be the one?"

"Because he's Corazon's most trusted shooter. Corazon knows Ruiz hates me enough to do the job right in spite of the risk. Trust me, it'll be Ruiz."

Andrews threw up his hands. "Fine, it's your funeral…and I mean that literally. Now, if you interfere in any way with our ability to perform our functions, you'll be placing a lot of people at risk. And by the way, if this whole thing blows up and people get killed, you're going to have a ton of guilt on your conscience."

Chapter 34

Sarah's training began earlier than she had expected. Mignon turned out to be as good as her word. She and the highly-paid Arnold Berghoff stationed themselves in Sarah's office, ready to begin her first lesson.

Mignon flashed the kind of comforting smile that usually precedes a wholesome serving of motherly advice. "Good morning, dear," she began. "How was your trip to that fish place?"

"Ah… it was very productive… ah… Mother. What are you doing here this early? And who is this gentleman?"

"This is Arnold Berghoff, dear, the one I was telling you about. It's not unusual for me to be wandering around the company premises early in the morning. I spotted Arnold, and thought this would be a good time to begin your lessons in money management. There's so much you need to learn in such a short time. I wanted to get you started as soon as possible. Arnold, this is Sarah Jane, my soon-to-be daughter-in-law."

Arnold fashioned a partial bow, and smiled. "Good to meet you, Sarah Jane. Mrs. Lonsdale told me a lot about you, and I must say I'm impressed."

The short, balding man extended a chubby hand to greet her, loosely grasping only the ends of her fingers. She forced a smile, recalling her father's warning about never trusting a man who doesn't shove his hand all the way in to form a firm handshake.

"Well, I'm pleased to meet you, Mr. Berghoff. I look forward to working with you, but I hope you'll understand I'm new at this game."

"Of course, that's why I've brought in that pile of records you see on your desk. You may think of it as your library. They're all the guidelines I've written covering the procedures for managing the family's assets. Please call me Arnold, and I thought we'd go about this training by spending one hour each day for the next two weeks covering the procedures I use. I'll show you some of the little-known nuances involved in the nurture of large investments in liquid and fixed assets."

Mignon smiled. "First thing in the morning is always the best time, dear, don't you agree? I mean, because it's the point of highest mental receptivity, that is. I see you're pausing to consider our plan. That's good because I want to make sure we're all three on the same wavelength on this."

Sarah decided to hold her tongue while she thought about it. *If this guy thinks I have nothing else to do until ten o'clock, maybe I should tell him the previous day's accounting problems end up on my desk at seven in the morning. Oh, what the hell, she's my mother-in-law, and he's my mentor, so make the best of it.*

"That would be fine, Arnold. We might get a few interruptions as various accounting problems find their way in here from time to time. How would you like to begin?"

Before anyone could say anything, Mignon stood up, smiled, and politely excused herself. "I'm going to leave you two alone, so be nice to her, Arnold. I'm not going to live forever. Sarah Jane will be my replacement some day. And dear, on my way out I'm going to have your disbursements people cut me a check for five thousand. I'm heading up a rather expensive fundraising dinner next week, and the front-end cash outlay turned out to be a little more than I anticipated. It's fully tax deductible to the company. We do this a lot. You two have a good day."

Arnold looked eager to start, while Sarah was still trying to adjust to the casual ease with which a five thousand dollar check could be written for a non-business event.

He flashed a satisfied smile. "Now, Sarah, the first thing I want to do is show you how I manage the family's investments in equities. Have you ever spent any time trading in stocks?"

Sarah shook her head. "No. I have my 401K, but I don't have any responsibility for managing it."

"Very well, then listen carefully to how I do this. Volume, diversification, and timing are of the utmost importance, so we need to be on top of them at all times. As you can see, the Lonsdales have substantial investments in thirty stocks, as well as a portfolio of bonds of varying maturities. Now here's—"

"Arnold, how long is this going to take?"

"Oh, only a short while, my dear." He spread out half a dozen multi-colored charts on the table. "Now I want you to follow me on these graphs as I go along, and you'll be able to see the quantitative impact of what I'm telling

218

you." He hoisted his rotund frame to a sitting position on Sarah's desk beside the colorful display, and motioned his pupil to stand closer.

Arnold's hour-and-a-half discourse covered everything from adapting to new technologies to growth curve monitoring. By the time he'd launched into hedge funds management, Sarah's capacity for embracing new concepts had been saturated. She felt a headache coming on.

"Arnold, could we continue this some other—"

"We're almost finished, dear. Now, this next part is really exciting." He rubbed his hands together with the kind of enthusiasm Sarah thought might have accompanied the inheritance of a yacht. With a broad grin, he swung into the subject of municipal bonds.

After another half hour Sarah couldn't take it any longer. "Arnold, let's get excited about this tomorrow. I really have to get back to work."

"Of course, dear, of course." He slid from the desk with all the grace of a duck tumbling off a fence. "I'll leave some brochures with you and you can read them when you get home."

She ushered Arnold to the door, inch by agonizing inch — slow enough that he still had time to squeeze in a brief summary of franchise management. Sarah shook her head and took a moment to reflect on the lesson before she motioned in her waiting accounts receivable manager. *Anyone who can find hedge funds exciting has to be rewarded for his dedication,* she thought. *No wonder this droll little guy is paid the big bucks. Guess I've a lot to learn. This whole thing is starting to look like a pre-nuptial agreement of a different kind.*

Amy Finch laid the list of delinquent accounts receivable on Sarah's desk, smiled and wiped her glasses. "Miss Jankovic, these are all sixty days or more past due. I need your permission to send out another letter."

Sarah scanned the list and tried not to become distracted by Amy's shifting from one foot to the other. "Send it out, Amy. A couple of these are past 120 days. If they're not collected by the end of the month, let's contact our collection agency. By the way, thanks for the flower arrangement you sent me. It was a nice welcome gift."

Amy nodded and took a few steps toward the door. She stopped and turned to Sarah. The nervous foot-shifting became more pronounced. The girl looked down at the floor and then at the window before she made eye contact with Sarah. "Miss Jankovic, is it true that we're taking on a fish farm as part of Concord?"

"We are, Amy. However, it's basically a cash business, so your accounts receivable staff shouldn't be concerned. The fact is that I'm the one who'll have most of the accounting responsibility for it. You seem a bit on edge. Is something wrong?"

The girl tugged at her blouse and closed the door. "Miss Jankovic, I—"

"Please sit down, Amy, and call me Sarah. Now tell me what's bothering you. Is it the acquisition of that hatchery?"

Amy pulled up a chair and threw an apprehensive glance at Sarah's fish tank. She replaced her shuffling with an equally nervous toe-tapping. "No, Ma'am. Well, maybe in a way it is. I mean, we all know you're new here in this department, and some of us were wondering...I mean, well, accounting is a pretty big department even without that fish business. We all know about your upcoming marriage to Mr. Lonsdale. I guess what I'm trying to say — and I'm only saying this because I've sort of become your right-hand assistant — well, we're all a little worried that you might have been forced into a managerial position that's uncomfortable for you."

Sarah didn't know whether to be thankful or resentful about the warning. Her competence had never before been questioned. Still, it had taken considerable courage for this girl to speak up. A convincing-yet-truthful response would be necessary, not only for Amy but for Sarah's entire department. "Amy, I appreciate your sharing this with me. I—"

"Oh, thank you." Amy let out a huge sigh. "I was afraid you'd be mad at me."

"Well, I know it was difficult for you to ask if I'm in over my head. Truth is, we'll have to wait and see. But here's some facts you and the others need to know — especially if there are lingering suspicions that I got this job because of my relationship with my future husband.

"First, I'm a CPA with three years prior experience with Concord in a variety of capacities. So, I'm not new to the company. I was promoted into this job based upon recommendations from all the executives for whom I worked. Second, the promotion came before anyone in the company became aware that Grant Lonsdale and I even knew each other. My future husband himself didn't know I worked for this company because we hadn't reconnected for nine years until right after the promotion. I hope this sets your concerns to rest, and you may share it with the rest of the staff. By the way, the fish tank is a gift from me to me...it's easier to care for than a dog. Okay?"

Amy's smile returned and her toe-tapping stopped. "Yes, Miss...ah, Sarah. Thanks for being so honest with me." She stood and shook Sarah's hand.

Sarah watched her subordinate leave, and wondered if she had been too quick to dismiss the notion that people might think she owed her position to nepotism rather than competence. She fed the fish and settled down to the preparation of her part of Concord's budget for the coming year.

Chapter 35

"Trudy, get in here! Where the hell are you?" Conrad's face turned white and his hand that held the letter shook.

Gertrude Mulkey rounded the corner on a dead run. Her flat heels clicked on the tile floor almost loud enough to drown out the rustling of her bulky skirt. "I'm right here, Mr. Vanderslice." Eyes wide, she gasped for breath. "What's wrong? You look pale as a ghost. What happened?"

"Where did this come from?" He waved the one-page, hand-written document in his secretary's face. "Who put it on my desk?"

"I did, sir. A messenger brought the envelope in, unsealed with your name on it. So, I put it on your desk. The return address was on the envelope but not the sender's name. It looks like a woman's handwriting, though. Is there a problem?"

Vanderslice stuffed the letter into his pocket and slumped in his chair. "You're damned right there is. Get Hans in here now." He lowered his face into his hands for a moment and didn't straighten up until Hans Drukker huffed and puffed his way into his office.

"What is it, Van? My God, you look like the world just caved in. What's up?"

"Your conversation with Salazar Corazon the other day," Conrad said without answering the question. "What did he say?"

"He said he was going to jail. The Feds came down on him about that money laundering scheme of his. Caught up with him, I guess. I've told you all that."

Conrad shook his head and scowled. "No, no. Not that. The other thing. You said he'd completed the arrangements to have Lonsdale killed. I have to know when and where." He began an uneven tapping rhythm on the desk with his pen.

Hans shrugged. "Van, I told you all that the other day. I kind of thought you weren't listening. Anyway, Corazon's putting that nosey damn kid away permanently, just like you wanted. Hell, Van, you even pulled your head out of your paperwork long enough to smile when I mentioned it. You made some sarcastic remark that the druggies should have done it right the first time. Don't you remember?"

"Yes, yes. But when? How? Where? I need to know. Right away, Hans. I need to know."

"Okay, Van. Relax. Let me think a minute." Hans turned away and paused, finger to forehead, while Conrad's pen continued its awkward dance. Hans turned back to face him. "Okay, Van, I think Salazar said the assassination was supposed to take place at Lonsdale's wedding or something. He sent one of his shooters up there to take the kid out. I think. Some kind of wedding, huh?" Hans broke out into one of his rare grins. "Puts a real kicker into the expression 'til death do us part,' don't you think?"

Conrad glared at him. "Get the hell out of here. And bring me a copy of the society page of that paper announcing the wedding. Right away. Now, damn it."

Hans beat a quick retreat and turned to Gertrude. "You heard what he said, Trudy. Get him the issue that announced the Lonsdale shindig. What the hell's he so strung out about this time?"

Gertrude shook her head, waved one hand in the air, and put in a call to the *Boston Globe*.

* * * * * *

Mike Rinelli recognized the voice on the other end of the line. "Yeah, Van, what's up?"

"Mike, I need you to round up the two guys we used as bodyguards the last time we did business with those cocaine peddlers in New York. I have a job I want them to do now. And I mean now."

"Okay, I'll get on it. I'll have one of them call you as soon as I can locate them."

"Good. Get it done as fast as you can. In the next few minutes, if possible. Call me back on my private line." Conrad closed the door and signaled to Trudy no calls, no visitors. While he waited he stood, paced, and sat in a repetitive sequence interrupted only by Trudy's delivery of last week's society pages, and his rereading of the letter. He couldn't believe Mignon had never told him. How could she have kept something so significant from him? He had a right to know, damn it. Only a day-and-a-half until the wedding. Barely enough time to get his own two shooters up there and familiarized with the layout of the church and the reception location.

* * * * * *

The fifteen-minute phone conversation didn't leave Conrad much time to issue his detailed instructions, but the two toughies seemed to have understood the job. Vanderslice leaned back in the swivel chair and relaxed for the first time since he'd received the letter. Now, he hoped, it would be all taken care of. With a little luck the assassination would be blocked, and weeks of his own handiwork could be undone.

Before he could reflect further, Trudy burst into his office, looking terrified behind the two large men ahead of her. "Mr. Vanderslice," she said, in between gasps, "these men are from the FBI and they just charged past my desk. I'm sorry. They charged past me and I couldn't stop them."

"Conrad Vanderslice," the dark-haired man said, "I'm Federal Agent Dombrovski and this is agent Kendall. We have a warrant for your arrest." They flashed their badges and proceeded to read Conrad his rights. After the reading, Conrad nodded as though the arrest had come as no surprise.

While a small gathering of office employees watched in awkward silence, the agents cuffed Conrad and escorted him out. A shaken Hans Drukker hunkered down over his paperwork and never looked up.

Chapter 36

Grant Lonsdale Senior had never before faced a less-than-friendly board of directors. Concord's history of slow-but-steady growth in revenue and bottom-line profitability for the past ten years had prompted smiling faces at every quarterly meeting. This time the eight directors filed into Concord's board room looking more like pall bearers at a funeral. Deke Traynor seemed to be the only exception.

Grant's executive secretary outfitted the long mahogany table as she always did, with two pots of coffee, a pitcher of ice water, a tray of sandwiches, and a plate of chocolate-chip cookies. She furnished each position with its usual pad, pen, and a current copy of Concord's quarterly financial statements.

Grant poured a glass of water, forced a smile, and glanced around the table at a circle of somber faces. "Good morning, gentlemen and lady. I can see by your drawn expressions that you've heard about Concord's recent deviation from its regular line of businesses. I understand your concerns. However, let me assure you that this little fish hatchery we've temporarily taken on represents less than one-tenth of one percent of Concord's corporate revenue and expenses. It barely amounts to a footnote in the financials we've placed in front of you. That having been said, I'll open the floor to comments about it before we get into the regularly scheduled topics of the day. I want the air cleared on this before we do anything else, and I'm open to questions."

Pete Prentiss didn't get his hand up to speak fast enough, and, before he could open his mouth, Carla Davis interjected. "Grant, before we get into the details of the hatchery, I think we need to discuss its background. We've learned that it has been used to launder drug money. Frankly, we're all in a state of shock about it. What's this about a Colombian drug cartel? Any truth to that?"

Grant drew a deep breath. "Carla, that's true. However, thanks to my son's rather heroic efforts, the cartel is out of there and running for the hills with our federal government chasing it. That hatchery is a good, profitable business in its own right. But the only way the government would allow its operations to continue is if Concord sheltered it for a year or so until the Feds collared the thugs from the cartel. The drug connection is history now, and my job will be to minimize the hatchery's impact on Concord."

Carla put up her hand. "Okay. I don't think anyone here is particularly concerned about the financial impact of this on the company's operations. At least I'm not. What concerns me the most — and I'm assuming all of us on the board share this concern — is the market's likely reaction to it."

Heads nodded. Carla's reputation for turning fat, sluggish companies into lean, mean, profit-makers had brought her and Davis Co. LLC into prominence in the New England business community. "I mean, here we are," she continued, "about to go looking for an investment banking firm to prepare the company for a large public offering of its stock. And now we'll have to try to explain this crazy, completely unrelated sojourn into tropical fish. What on earth were you thinking when you did this? And why didn't you consult us before you consummated this deal…or whatever it was?"

Before Grant could respond, Jeff Wright, President of Wright Wholesale Industries, spoke up. "Grant, this is going to drive the offering price of Concord's stock down, and you know it. Hell, the underwriters are guaranteed to throw up all over this."

Grant lowered his head for a moment. He raised it again, ignored Jeff's remark, and looked straight at the woman who had historically been his most vocal director. "Carla, the only answer I can give you is that, at the time, my son had struck a bargain with the FBI to end a large money laundering scheme involving this tropical fish place. The bargain required Concord's temporary acquisition of the hatchery. Based upon my faith in my son's assurance that the deal had world-wide significance, I felt I had no choice. Since secrecy was imperative, I couldn't consult anyone about it until the Colombian drug cartel had been charged with this and a host of other infractions of the law."

Bunky Morkofsky, president of Morkofsky Hauling, Inc., shook his head. "Damn it, Grant, to hell with your reasons. The thing is you couldn't have picked a worse time to adopt a white elephant orphan. Until now, Concord's been a jewel in the business community's crown. The stock market has been drooling in anticipation of getting a piece of it. But this thing is gonna raise hell all over the place."

Pete Prentiss put his hand in the air to preempt any immediate response from the other directors. "Grant, I think what we're saying is that we assume the market isn't naive enough to get hung up on the *size* of your little aberration. What's going to freak out prospective investors is the fact that you did it at all. They're looking to you as a corporate Moses who'll lead them and their investment money out of the wilderness of a bear market. To them, Concord is an undervalued entity waiting to blossom forth like the orchid in a financial weed garden. Then you show them a screwy move like this, and all of a sudden, a million would-be investors start wondering whether you're likely to do it again in some wacky venture that really *will* destroy their stock values."

"Another problem," said a quiet Ted Wiebel at the far end of the conference table, "is the rumor I hear about your promotion of a young girl to a responsible accounting position, and the offer you made to her custodian-father to come into Concord in some manufacturing capacity. Is all that scuttlebutt true?"

Grant glared at the director and banged his fist on the table. Given Ted's human resources background, Grant found nothing surprising about the nature of the question. Still, the personal accusations implied in it hurt. "Damn it, Ted, my hiring decisions are none of your business. That 'young girl,' as you put it, is a valued middle-manager who has proven her competence for several years in my company. And as to her father, he happens to be a skilled machinist who took employment as a custodian when most manufacturing jobs dried up in New England years ago. For whatever it's worth, he declined my offer — more out of pride than anything else, I guess."

"Grant, we've all known you for a long time," Pete Prentiss said, "and no one questions your competence or your leadership." He paused to pass the coffee pot along. "You removed any doubts about those the moment we came aboard as directors. Our reservations here have to do with how the stock market is likely to react. You know how skittish New England investors are. They run for cover whenever the Red Sox lose. We're simply trying to find out how best to respond to what we know will be investor concerns when we introduce the initial stock issuance. The investment bankers who market the stock will also have to deal with questions like these. You know that."

His emotions softened a bit by Pete's comforting tone, Grant took time out to pour another cup of water and start the cookie dish in the opposite direction around the table. "Okay, my apologies for the outbreak. Look, I appreciate all your opinions, as I always have. Yes, we will have to deal with this and any other chinks in Concord's armor. I'm fully aware of the risks involved in a public stock offering. If the stock is underpriced, we shareholders lose out big time. If it's priced too high, the underwriters have to eat the difference and that gets ugly. Either way, someone gets screwed, so full disclosure of everything has to be made in order to set the offering price right the first time. I get it. The good news is I have a solution in the form of an incredibly competent businessman who has found us a capable investment banker. I've invited him to speak to us. He's waiting outside."

"And who might this be?" Pete Prentiss asked.

Grant flashed his first genuine smile of the morning and moved toward the door. The directors stopped their consumption of refreshments while Grant ushered Angus MacIver into the room. "Folks, I think most of you know my long-time friend, Angus MacIver, managing partner of Warren, MacIver & Patterson. He's identified an underwriter who will work with us, and I'd like him to tell you about it." Grant extended an arm in MacIver's direction. "You're on, Mr. Speaker."

Angus poured a cup of coffee and gave Carla a handful of brochures to pass around. "Thank you all for allowing me to be here. Grant Lonsdale has been a friend and advisor of mine for longer than I care to admit. I owe him a hell of a lot more than I can ever repay. We've discussed the issues facing Concord, including the hatchery. The brochure will give you a brief, but accurate, summary of the underwriting firm I believe can best deal with those issues. Please take a minute or two to look it over and then we can discuss it." Angus grabbed a handful of cookies, grinned at Grant, and leaned back in his chair while the board members poured over their pamphlets.

After three minutes of silence Pete Prentiss reasserted his authority as chairman of the Board and motioned to Angus. "Let's hear your plan, Mr. MacIver. We're open to any feasible option."

"Very well." Angus nodded, pushed his coffee aside, and distributed a two-page summary of Concord's individual business holdings. "This handout provides a bird's eye view of the various lines of business which comprise Concord's operations. The profitability of each is highlighted in green for net profit exceeding twenty percent, black for profit running from breakeven to twenty percent, and red for loss. As you can see, sixteen of the twenty-six units are green, six are black, and four — including my forecast of the hatchery's operations — are red."

"Yes, that's another concern we have," said Wiebel. "How do you suggest we handle that?"

Angus scanned the audience before he responded. "I believe we can provide some comfort to prospective stock buyers by spinning off the four red units into one wholly owned subsidiary, separate and distinct from Concord's core businesses. We can then footnote both the financial statements and the stock offering prospectus with a statement that the spinoff was done to give the new subsidiary time to focus on its financial recovery under separate management specializing in those markets. Any of the four units that fails to achieve profitability within two years will be sold off, with resulting loss-on-disposal taken as a tax deduction."

Wiebel grinned. "Yeah, maybe we can sell off that hatchery at a profit and recover some of our carrying costs."

The remark brought a round of laughter that seemed to ease the tension.

Angus acknowledged the group response with a smile. "Well, the footnote will provide full disclosure and enough assurance to allow the investment banker to maximize the offering price of the stock. It will also put to rest any doubts as to management's competence, or fears that the hatchery thing might happen again. Any questions?"

That Carla raised her hand first came as no surprise to Grant. "My name is Carla Davis and I like the idea, Mr. MacIver, but there remain a couple of issues it doesn't address. First, it's my understanding that this damned hatchery is not for sale. I mean, I thought it was highly profitable and was to be returned to those farmers — or whoever they are — who owned it before down there in...what's the name of that place?"

"Okeechobee," Grant replied.

"Right. One of Florida's remote outbacks. Well anyway," Carla continued, "disposal of the thing on the open market doesn't seem to be an option. Second, I support Grant's decision to finally put a woman in a responsible managerial position." She turned to face Grant. "However, this Sarah girl, who met your son when they were teenagers, is only twenty-three or something, and she's going to be married into the Lonsdale family. I'm seeing stockholders being haunted by the twin ghosts of inexperience and nepotism here."

Grant started to speak but Angus cut him off. "You raise valid concerns, Carla. I'll try to address them one at a time. I think I'm a bit more objective about this than Grant or any of you board members can be. You're right, the fish farm turned a significant profit. However, it was largely drug money infused into the deposits. Even so, there were profits, but all accrued net worth is to be returned to the owners along with the entity as soon as the federal authorities are satisfied that it's no longer being used for illegal transactions. For Concord, there are only the expenses of carrying the business for a year or so under its protection…and no profit. However the prospectus will refer to the four-unit subsidiary as a whole. The market doesn't need to know that one of the units will be disposed of in a non-sale transaction. Nor does the market really care, for that matter."

Pete raised his hand. "True, as long as we make it clear that the farm will not be part of Concord for long."

"Right. Now, as to Sarah, perhaps this will satisfy everyone's concerns. She's been an employee for three years, and her competence stood on its own after having been thoroughly tested. She's also a CPA, who I personally interviewed in anticipation of this meeting. I can vouch for her, and I believe her resume will speak for itself in the prospectus, marital relations notwithstanding."

Morkofsky clapped his hands and grinned at Carla. "Good enough for me, Carla. Now let's raise a cheer for the women's lib I know you crave, and move on." Everyone in the room except Pete Prentiss laughed.

Pete stood and again assumed his role as board chairman. "Mr. MacIver, I'll propose that we accept your offer. However, we'd like to convene a special board meeting to interview the investment banker you've recommended before we make a go-ahead decision." He turned to Grant. "Grant, please set the date, and we'll arrange our schedules accordingly. I move to close the meeting. All in favor say aye."

The ayes resounded, and the members filed out after a few minutes of small talk. Grant approached Pete as soon as the room emptied and placed a hand on his shoulder. "Pete, I want you to know how much I appreciated your support. I figure you already knew about my son and Sarah. I know you and I always kind of assumed he and your daughter would eventually marry." Grant forced a difficult smile. "I guess our kids have a way of doing their own thing, with or without consulting us. Given how you must feel, your support meant even more to me. Thanks."

"Not a problem, Grant. Love is love, and business is business. You and I can control only one of those. Yeah, I'm disappointed, but I'm old enough to know that what is, is, and what wasn't meant to be stays that way. Let's move ahead and get Concord publicly financed so it can fully realize its potential. See you at the next meeting."

They shook hands and Grant felt a twinge of sadness after his friend left. Nothing stays the same, he reminisced — and most of the changes he'd witnessed had been as uncontrollable as his son's marital decision.

Chapter 37

Mignon made no secret of her preference for a large wedding in the old stone church which had accommodated four generations of Lonsdale unions. Everyone else opted for a smaller one. After all compromise efforts failed, the capacity of the church decided the size of the invitation list. Two hundred guests filed through the open red doors, which seemed to flaunt their color in defiance of the building's austere grayish architecture. Each entrant received a program bulletin and a welcoming smile from an usher. Grant, who could recognize Ruiz, stood next to the usher to provide visual screening. Four men in dark blue suits adorned with white corsages served as part of a contingent of six ushers, clearly trying not to look like federal agents while they maintained a vigil around the premises.

The gentle strain of Mozart's "March of the Priests" accompanied the procession of groomsmen and bridesmaids to the altar prior to the bride's entrance. Lukasz Jankovic, wearing the suit his daughter had bought for him for the occasion, walked Sarah down the aisle. He'd never been inside a structure so grand, nor mixed with such elegant people. With a look of deference and pride, Lukasz gave his daughter away at the pastor's prompt, and took his seat next to Grant's father. Tears welled up in the old custodian's eyes. He bowed his head and whispered a wish that his beloved Jana could have been by his side to witness the beginning of her daughter's new life.

Chad Winslow served as best man, together with a supporting cast of five of Grant's Harvard classmates. Accompanied by her maid of honor from South Boston and five bridesmaids from Tufts, Sarah Jane Jankovic joined Grant Abbott Lonsdale III in marriage. Major and Luanne sat close to the front with Deke Traynor, Angus MacIver, Mary Coyne, and a small group of Mignon's bridge disciples from the club. Relatives and various cliques of Boston's upper echelons filled the remaining pews.

The ceremony lasted almost an hour, too long for everyone except Mignon, whose design for a longer one was unanimously voted down by her family. Grant and Sarah repeated wedding vows they'd authored together. The shared narrative reflected the strength and endurance of a romance that had already survived the effects of time and fierce opposition. Adorned in Mignon's wedding gown — a gesture based more on politics than fashion preference — Sarah looked more like an eighteenth-century queen than a contemporary accountant.

The couple exchanged rings, and the culminating embrace of Mr. and Mrs. Grant Abbot Lonsdale III put all the anxieties and guilt of a nine-year separation behind them. For reasons he hadn't shared with Sarah, Grant broke from the traditional post-ceremonial hand-in-hand stroll back down the aisle with her. Instead, he walked up to her father, took him by the hand and insisted that Lukasz take the exit walk with them.

Astonished, Sarah whispered in his ear. "Grant, what on earth are you *doing?*"

Grant grinned. "I'm making sure he comes to the reception and feels at ease there."

"Grant, honey, what are you talking about? What's going on?"

"What's going on," Grant whispered back at her, "is that your father told me this morning he didn't feel comfortable trying to make conversation with all these rich people at the reception. He said he was going home to avoid embarrassing you. I'm not going to let that happen. We're either going to make him feel welcome here, or you and I are going home with him."

"Oh, Grant." Sarah glared, and then smiled at him. "That's so sweet." She turned to her father. "Dad, come on, you could never embarrass me. Wait 'til you talk for awhile with Chad, Major, and Luanne. You'll feel as comfortable with them as I do." She took his other hand, and a smiling Lukasz Jankovic walked out of the church between them.

* * * * *

Mignon had long been a dominating influence on the activities of the Charles River Country Club. She had less say than she wanted as to the structure of the wedding ceremony, but managed to rule everything about the reception that followed. The reception participants stretched the capacity of the club, the facilities of which Mignon made sure were at their disposal. The only procedure Mignon didn't control was the cumbersome visual recognition process that had to be repeated for each incoming guest.

She found herself a surprised recipient of additional FBI attention from one of the men in dark blue suits. He ushered her into a corner, handed her a sealed envelope, and told her to destroy its contents after she'd read them. He disappeared into the crowd before she could open it.

A buffet dinner followed cocktails and hors d'oeuvres. Two of the blue-suited men inspected all food and beverage items to assure they were safe for consumption. Dancing and a host of other post-nuptial ceremonies followed the dinner and launched the rest of the evening's festive activities. Although they circulated as inconspicuously as possible, the agents' constant surveillance raised a few embarrassing questions, which required some awkwardly contrived answers from the Lonsdales.

To no one's surprise, Luanne became the center of attention among Grant's unmarried classmates — and a few married ones. Chad gave her a few minutes to size them up before he moved in. "Hello, you must be Luanne. Grant's told me so much about you I feel I know you already. I'm Chad Winslow."

"Hi. So you're the guy who robbed the bank. I'm glad to meet you." She flashed her engaging smile. Even Chad, who'd often proclaimed there was no such thing as only one special girl for each man, looked like he'd fallen under her spell.

"Well, true," he said with a wide grin, "but I think I'd rather be remembered as the one who fished Grant out of shark-infested waters." They both laughed and looked at each other as though they were alone in the place.

Major approached them and broke their shared moment of enchantment. He'd replaced his weather-worn Okeechobee attire with the only suit he owned, and wore it without much regard to how well it fit.

"Chad, I'd like you to meet my father, Major Gibbs."

"Hello, son. I been lookin' forward to meeting this investigator guy. Grant's been callin' you his sidekick in this doggone thing with them Colombians."

Chad greeted the old farmer with a smile. "Good to meet you, sir. Speaking of the Colombians, Grant says you and Luanne are the only other ones who know the identity of the hit man who's allegedly up here after him."

"Yep. I hope this whole thing's nothing more than a wild-ass rumor. Man's name is Ruiz, and I ain't seen him yet. I been talkin' to Grant's dad, some. Good down-to-earth fella. His mother's a little hard to get to know, though."

Chad smiled. "Yeah, Mignon can be stand-offish, but a nice lady once you get to know her. Here she comes now, looking like she's ready to give you another chance to do just that."

Major leaned over and whispered to Luanne. "I ain't never seen a dress that swished like that woman's or come so close to draggin' on the floor. You'd think with all their money she could buy one that fits."

"It's an evening gown, Daddy, not a dress. It's supposed to be like that."

Mignon smiled as though she'd known Major for years. Major nodded, but his frown conveyed an apparent feeling that he still wasn't sure just what to make of her.

"Mr. Gibbs," Mignon said, "I'd like you, your daughter, and Chad to meet Sebastian Darnier. He's head of staff here at the club, and a long-time friend of our family."

"Pleased to meet you, Mr. Darnier," Chad said, and turned to Mignon. "I don't mean to cloud our introduction with a security matter, Mrs. Lonsdale, but I assume all members of Mr. Darnier's staff have been checked out."

"They've all been loyal to our club for years," Mignon responded. "Have they not, Sebastian?"

"Yes, ma'am. For the most part, they have. And they've all been checked out by your agents. Well, all except Oliver Stemp who retired a few months ago, and the new man we were fortunate to hire as his kitchen replacement."

Mignon's matronly smile conveyed an air of satisfaction. "So there, Chad, you have nothing to worry—"

"Excuse me, Mr. Darnier," Chad interrupted, "did you say *kitchen?*"

Chad and Major didn't wait for an answer. They spun around and bolted toward Grant and Sarah on the dance floor. Mignon whirled around with a facial expression that suggested a sudden suspicion that something horrible was about to happen. She dashed after the two men as fast as her evening gown would permit.

They saw the waiter coming from the other direction, carrying a tray of drinks. It all happened suddenly. At first, no one saw it, although the slight bulge in his jacket should have been noticed by someone. At least his failure to remove the kitchen apron should have given him away. The man pulled out the gun with his right hand and threw the tray aside, freeing his left so he could grip the gun with both hands. Corazon's last directive to the obedient Ruiz had been simple: kill them both, Grant first, and then his bride. If further opportunity should present itself, kill at random, and get out before the police arrive.

Only one of the men in dark blue happened to be close enough, but he reacted quickly. His lunge grazed the shooter's arm just as Ruiz squeezed the trigger. The bullet went through Grant's thigh, missing the artery by an inch. Grant, the man, and Ruiz went down at the same time. Ruiz rolled out from under them and swung his firearm around toward Sarah.

With all the athletic ability she could muster, Mignon threw herself protectively between her daughter-in-law and the shooter. Ruiz fired again. The bullet shattered Mignon's hip before exiting on a deflected angle through her buttocks.

Another of the blue-suited men pounced on Ruiz and disarmed him before he could do any further damage. They surrendered Ruiz to Agent Rybeck and his partner, Agent Collins. Then they slipped away into the gathering crowd of horrified onlookers. Rybeck cuffed the shooter and dragged him out, making sure they took him alive in order to seal the pending case in federal court against Salazar Corazon.

Flashing blue and red lights and wailing sirens brought to a close the fifth generation of Lonsdale weddings.

* * * * * *

"I'm not sure I understand the question, Mr. Rybeck," Grant's father said. "I assumed all four of you were federal agents. I'm particularly grateful for the one who acted quickly enough to deflect the killer's arm, and also his associate who jumped in to disarm that thug. Look, I really don't have any time to discuss the matter. I have to get to the hospital and be with my wife and son. Could we do this some other time?"

"I understand sir, but we need to ask you again before you go. We're thankful, too, that the shooter is headed for jail. However, the two men who subdued him were not federal agents. We have no idea who they are, or where they came from. They took off before I could question them. The Bureau sent two of us, but no one else. Believe me, I'm sorry we weren't standing close enough to take effective action, but glad those other two were. We thought maybe you might have hired them and could identify them for us."

Grant senior shook his head. "Like I said before, I'm afraid I can't. I have no clue who they were."

The agent gave a reluctant nod. "Okay, well, thanks anyway, Mr. Lonsdale. Looks like we'll have to sort this one out on our own. We'll be on our way, but we may need you to come in for some follow-up questions. We'll let you know. We're sorry about your wife and son. I hope they'll be okay."

Rybeck turned to his subordinate, Agent Collins. "Mike, you must have some idea who those two guys were. Hell, you know more of the agents in the Boston office than I do."

"Sorry, sir, they told me they were here from our Washington office at the request of the groom's father. I guessed he had some pull with headquarters. I'll have to say, though, they didn't look much like what I'd expect our D.C. office to send up here. But it wasn't my place to question them."

Rybeck slammed his right fist into his left palm. "Damn it, the chief 's going to fly into orbit when he hears this. Okay, I want you to fingerprint the shooter's firearm, just on the remote possibility we can make a positive identification. And anything else they might have touched. This damned thing isn't going to go away until we come up with some answers."

Chapter 38

After all the well-wishing visitors had finally departed, Massachusetts General Hospital's room 414 became Mignon's quiet sanctuary. After the second day her pain suppressants had been winnowed down enough to enable her to emerge from her fog.

Grant sat on the edge of her bed and leaned toward her. "Mother, I want to say this now, before the nurse comes in again to check on you. We haven't really had a chance to talk like this since I can't remember when, and they're releasing me this afternoon. You'll be here for a few more days. I want to tell you how terribly sorry I am to have involved you in this mess at all. It's entirely my fault. I could have prevented it by simply postponing the wedding."

Mignon reached up, stroked her son's face, and smiled. "Yes, dear, that would have been a good idea."

Grant touched Mignon's shoulder. "At the same time I want you to know I…we… can't thank you enough for saving Sarah's life. Dad called what I did in Okeechobee heroic. But it doesn't hold a candle to what you did. Look, I know we've had a rather difficult past, you and I. But—"

"Grant, dear, you don't need to explain, or apologize for, anything. Chad told me you did what you did because you didn't want to alarm everyone only to postpone the inevitable. I do, however, think postponing it a month or two might have given the federal agents a chance to do their work. Then again, I know you were never one to wait for things. Fortunately, you inherited the best of my traits and your father's. Unfortunately, my patience was not one of them." Mignon broke into a smile as wide as her pain would allow.

Grant laughed before he noticed his mother's slight wince. "How bad is the pain, Mother?"

"Oh, it's really not as bad as I expected, considering I'm now the proud owner of a new hip. They've muffled my pain pretty well. How about you, dear?"

"I think I'm in pretty good shape, all things considered. Mother, I'm going to ask you the question I've wanted to ask ever since you so accepted Sarah into our family. I know how difficult that was for you. But I promise you'll never regret it. She's on her way here now, so I wanted to get this settled before she comes. Are you okay with the prospect of Sarah eventually assuming your role in the family businesses?"

Before Mignon could reply, a stocky nurse, who looked like she could have been a drill sergeant, burst in with a tray of clinical-looking instruments and a blood pressure cuff.

"Good morning, Mrs. Lonsdale. I'll have to interrupt for a minute to adjust this bed a little and check your vitals. How are you feeling today?"

"I'd feel better if you people would stop poking me," Mignon snapped.

Grant tried to suppress a chuckle. Two minutes later, when the broad-shouldered woman seemed satisfied that the cuff and the little electronic monitor mounted behind Mignon showed favorable readings, she marched out the door.

Mignon drew a deep breath, shifted her weight a bit, and asked Grant to stuff another pillow behind her back so she could sit up straighter to face him. "Grant, every era must eventually come to an end. And there must be a so-called changing of the guard, as your father used to say. I remember the difficulty your grandmother had with your father and me. I can tell you it was hell. I vowed I wouldn't repeat her behavior. And I apparently almost did, but that won't happen again. Sarah Jane's a very special young lady, her unfortunate background notwithstanding. I'm sure she'll grow into the job. Anyway, I'm not dead yet, so let's change the subject. It looked like Chad and Luanne were getting off to a good start before that vile man started shooting. Did you notice them?"

"Yes, Mother, I did. In fact, I told them a little about each other before they met. I did it mainly to make sure Chad didn't treat Luanne like another one of his conquests."

"My goodness, that was presumptuous. How did you manage to deliver a message like that delicately?"

"Easy. I told him if he ever hurt her I'd kill him."

"I see. Well, I hope you're still friends. I'm feeling a bit tired, now, dear, so I'm just going to rest a bit until Sarah and your father get here. You can read or something." Mignon smiled and placed her hand over Grant's. "You're a fine young man, Grant, and a wonderful son. Your father and I are both terribly proud of you. And we love Sarah. Please know that. Wake me as soon as they come in."

* * * * * *

Sarah's eyes moistened even before she reached over the bed rail to take Mignon's hand in her own. "Mother Lonsdale, I've tried to think of a way to properly thank you for saving my life. I just couldn't come up with an adequate one." Sarah leaned over and kissed Mignon's hand.

"Now, now, child. No need to thank me. You're not just my daughter. You're much more than that. You're part of the future of the Lonsdale enterprises. So, let's have no more tears. I want everyone to listen up. My husband has something to share with all of us. We've put this off until after the wedding, and now is as good a time as any."

Grant Sr. pulled up the last available chair and set his sights on Sarah and his son together. "Kids, how'd you like to spend your honeymoon in Washington, D.C.?"

The two of them looked at each other questioningly for a moment before Grant turned back to his father. "Well, Dad, we really had something more along the line of Hawaii in mind. Why? What do you have going in D.C.?"

His father gave out with one of his triumphant smiles. "Well, Grant, you know how often I've talked about how our staggering economy can be restored only through a cooperative triumvirate between government, business, and the big banks...I mean, something like Japan did right after World War Two. As it turns out, Congress wants to hear what I have to say. Maybe it's just to stop all those letters I've been writing. I'm scheduled to make a presentation to a joint sub-committee of Congress next week. I'd like you to be there with me. That is, if you and Sarah wouldn't mind spending a small portion of your wedded bliss in our nation's capitol."

Grant hesitated. "Dad, that's really great, but I don't think—"

"We'd love to, Mr. Lonsdale," Sarah broke in. "Grant can join you while I see all the sights my father used to tell me about. We're really proud of you." She turned to face her husband. "Grant, honey, it'll be fun. And it'll be an experience that'll give you added stature when it's time for you to become CEO at Concord. Let's do it."

Mignon broke into a smile as wide as Essie Mae's. She reached over and jabbed her son in the ribs.

He half glared, half smiled at her. "All right, Mother, I know exactly what you're thinking. I can just hear your applause ringing out: 'Now, that's the kind of daughter-in-law I had in mind, putting Concord first, all else second.' I get the message. Okay, Dad, you have yourself two traveling companions. But right after that, Sarah and I *are* flying to Hawaii."

They laughed and talked for awhile until Mignon's nurse returned, dragging a full array of electronic medical measurement devices behind her.

"All right, folks, I hate to break this up, but you can come back during visiting hours tonight. Right now I need to examine our wounded hero, and then I want her to rest for an hour or two." She looked down at Mignon. "We'll be discharging your son this afternoon, Mrs. Lonsdale, but we'll need to keep you here for a few days."

Sarah blew them both a kiss on her way out, while the well-muscled nurse continued to poke Mignon. "You're doing well, Mrs. Lonsdale," the woman said.

Mignon glared at her. "I've learned to steel myself against your incessant probing. When you're through, I'd like you to reach into the drawer of the table beside my bed and hand me my purse."

The nurse forced a condescending smile, complied with Mignon's request a few minutes later, and marched out with the medical paraphernalia trailing behind her like an army platoon.

Grant slumped into a chair and welcomed the warm glow of the afternoon sun in his face. Mignon turned away, reached into her purse, and pulled out a letter the agent had given her at the wedding reception. A quick glance to make sure her son was still facing the other way, and she read the letter for the third time.

My Dearest Mignon,

I can only hope with all my being that my two men get there in time to prevent Corazon's shooter from finishing what I'm afraid was my fault from the beginning.

Until I received your letter I had no earthly idea Grant Abbot was my son. Mignon, I didn't even know you were pregnant when we parted twenty-six years ago. Yes, of course I'll keep the secret. If Grant should ever find out you may be assured it didn't come from me. I wish you'd told me. Our lives could have been so different.

As I'm sure you must know by now, I'll be doing some time in prison — probably a long time. My only consolation will be a bizarre satisfaction that the son I never knew I had was the only one with enough brains to put me there. Please write to me now and then. You and Grant Abbot are, it seems, the only family I have anymore.

All my love,
Conrad Vanderslice

Mignon wiped her eyes, folded the letter in half, and tore it quietly into confetti-size pieces. Unable to reach the waste basket until the nurse could move it closer to her bed, she dumped the shreds into her purse and went to sleep.

Grant leaned back to savor the relaxing warmth of the fading afternoon sun. The same sun which, at that precise moment, he knew must be throwing cypress tree shadows across the placid surface of an Okeechobee swamp. It seemed, somehow, as though a lifetime had passed since he'd slogged his way out of a drainage ditch. For the first time, he felt a sense that the world of his past had been washed clean of all its ancestral encumbrances.

About the Author

A former auditor and partner in an international CPA firm, John is an instructor in the field of forensic and investigative accounting. His experience includes a specialty in fraud, embezzlement, and money laundering. He has written and published technical articles in various professional journals, and his fiction novels are based upon his extensive corporate and professional experience.

Made in the USA
Charleston, SC
23 October 2015